WELCOME TO THE
GAME

WELCOME TO THE
GAME

A NOVEL

CRAIG
HENDERSON

Atlantic Monthly Press
New York

For Craig E.
The best of friends, left for dead in Florida.

Fast, fast, FAST! Last night I cut the light off in my bedroom, hit the switch, was in the bed before the room was dark.

—Muhammad Ali

The Roman historian Arrian wrote of a mountaintop city in what is now southern Turkey. Termessos was the only city that Alexander the Great could not capture. Mysteriously and suddenly abandoned thousands of years ago, the place was almost forgotten.

1

Spencer

Spencer winced as his potential buyer made a rough shift. He tried to think of something else to say about the car. He had a feeling the guy wasn't for real but hadn't figured out what his deal was. Did he *want* a more unusual choice of car, or was he just flirting so he could tell the guys at work he tried all options before doing what everyone did these days: go German or prancing pony.

Spencer watched him in his expensively distressed jeans and tightly fitted T-shirt, wondering how long girlfriends had to wait before learning the meaning of the Chinese character tattoos adorning his forearms. He fancied himself a real Detroiter but said he lived downtown in Riverfront Towers, and that was luxury living for the hipsters moving in.

"So, what brought you to America?" the guy asked. The question had long been irksome.

"My wife's from Detroit, born and raised." He couldn't resist dropping the insinuation.

They turned back toward Woodward. The guy had obviously decided he'd gotten the measure of the car.

"This is what confused me when I was trying to find you. You said you were in Oakland."

"Well, we're on the *edge* of Oakland so it's easier just to say—"

"Dude, I get it," the guy cut in. "I'm a Michigan man. You want to say you're in the classy part of town, where the money is. I get that. Guy like you, with your accent, probably works better playing it like that. I mean, let's face it, you're selling expensive cars no one's heard of."

For a moment, Spencer had nothing, because it was true. When he'd set up Winchester Auto Specialists, he couldn't afford Oakland. But the north edge of Detroit on Winchester, just on the wrong side of 8 Mile, that had been right for the budget. And Winchester had an English ring to it. Anyway, everything had been right then. He and Marielle were happy, and Abby, their seven-year-old daughter, had made the adjustment from European to US schooling without too many tears over left friends. America had seemed new and exciting.

"The cars I sell are for people who like to drive but don't feel the need to follow the herd. Anyone can go out and buy a Porsche or a Beamer, but a TVR or a GT-R or this Lotus, they're different."

"That's why I came to you. I checked you out. You used to race, yeah?"

"I was a rally driver."

"Right, rally. That's racing against the clock, right?"

"Racing against other drivers, against their times, but on narrow roads or forest tracks so you go one at a time. You have to drive to the max because you don't know whether you're ahead of the pace or behind. You can't just ease up when you've got a lead like in Indy or F1."

"Yeah, I knew that. People have told me I have the mind for it."

"The mind for what?"

"I could race cars. I just need to talk to people with experience."

You are a time-wasting motherfucker, and I want to kill you.

"So, look, man," he continued, "we're coming up on 9 Mile. What would you be thinking if you were in, like, race mode?"

Ask him what he does when people take two hours out of his working day.

You need this sale.

No shit, but he's not going to buy.

He might.

They pulled up at the intersection. Spencer nodded at the light.

"I know the light on Woodward coming up to 9 Mile will stay yellow for exactly three point four seconds. The average before someone gets moving on 9 Mile will be one point five seconds. That's the average. If it's a truck nearer two, but if it's a guy in a hurry then point seven. Worst-case scenario is a guy in a fast car who's put himself so he can see my light start to change. He could be moving before my yellow has gone, but he'll be watching harder for people like me. Power band in this Lotus in third gear at sixty goes from four thousand. That's where it happens: you'll get an extra fifty miles per hour in two seconds, fifty yards in one second."

Michigan Man, hesitant, looked at Spencer. "So, I should go for it if I've worked all that out?"

"If you have to work all that out, you should never go for it."

The Lotus turned the sharp, almost hairpin turn from Conant onto Winchester and then into the Winchester Auto Specialists lot. Spencer made one more last-ditch effort.

"You feel that? Legendary cornering ability. Their suspension won Lotus the Grand Prix right here in Detroit in eighty-six. Only cars that could cope with the bumpy roads."

"No shit? They've been bad that long?"

They parked up next to Michigan Man's SUV, shook hands over the roof, and he was gone.

Spencer scanned the lot. It was triangular, wedged into the shape created by the diagonal intersection on which it stood. There were a dozen cars. They needed to be spread out a little, so that it wasn't so obvious stock was low. He needed a run of closing, maybe three or four in a week. Then the bank might be more forthcoming again with credit and he could restock. He felt a tiredness suddenly envelop him and, in cahoots with that, a car at the far end of the lot caught his eye.

He'd taken a deposit on that TVR. The guy was supposed to have come for it with the balance that morning. The TVR stared back at him, its gunport-like headlights glinting insolently in the sun.

The heat made just thinking arduous. He glanced around, checking he didn't have an audience, before getting back in the passenger side of the Lotus. There was some residual coolness inside but it would be baking in another five minutes.

He opened the glove compartment, found a wrap, and tipped out a line on the owner's manual. He rummaged around. There'd been a straw in there somewhere. He found Abby's school report and rolled it tightly.

On the far side of Conant, three men in a silver Merc SUV with smoked windows watched.

2

Dominic McGrath

Johnny Boy sat at the wheel of the SUV, noting the reaction of the man sitting next to him. Not many people could wear a beautifully tailored suit every day without looking like they were trying too hard, but he'd known a few in his time in the Chicago law offices in which he'd spent the first thirty years of his working life, and Dominic McGrath rocked it as well as the best of them.

Neither Johnny Boy nor McGrath were men who felt the need to fill a silence. McGrath had employed Johnny Boy for moments just like these: a transaction of skills and time. McGrath would come to Johnny Boy with a problem or requirement. Johnny Boy would ponder and research. He'd speculate as to what exactly his employer wanted and then—and this is what put Johnny Boy in his own league—he would speculate what his employer might not even realize he wanted.

The guy in the back wasn't as cool with silences. His foot began to drum lightly on the floor. Soon his head and hand fell in time, nodding and tapping to some imaginary beat. The movement caught Johnny Boy's eye in the rearview. It irritated him. People who brought nothing special to the table always irritated him, jittery people even more so. The guy in the back saw Johnny Boy's look in the mirror but misread it. He thought Johnny Boy was as bored as he was—a kindred spirit. He leaned forward.

"Yo bro, mind if I smoke in here?"

"I don't mind if you smoke on the sidewalk, Zeb."

Zeb flopped back with a sniffy huff.

McGrath sat with his elbow on the car's windowsill, thumb under chin and forefinger lightly against his temple, watching—watching Spencer. He knew that if he was here looking at this man, in this place, then there was a very good chance it was because he needed to be.

"How'd you find him?" he asked Johnny Boy.

"Maintains his listing with the Auto Sport Association."

"He still race?"

"Nope. Lets him say they're buying from a real race driver."

McGrath nodded. He scanned the lot, seeing the gaps where sold cars hadn't been restocked.

"Foreign, you say?"

"Yep."

"That was good thinking."

And that was another thing Johnny Boy liked about McGrath. A man secure enough to praise—, but only when it was due.

McGrath looked around. Not the worst of Detroit but . . .

"So why didn't he move somewhere better?"

"Other issues demand his attention."

McGrath nodded again. "Heard from the Yo-Yo?"

"No. But I expect to anytime." Johnny Boy glanced at the car's clock. "Imminently, in fact."

"You sure he's up to it?"

"When has he not been?"

"I know he's got no problem with the technical requirements of his job. It's just, he ain't no Robert Redford."

"I made him practice the hell out of two sentences. Even a man of as few words as the Yo-Yo can manage that."

"And Rosso?" McGrath asked the question quietly. Zeb wasn't bright, but the last thing they needed was for him to figure out why he'd really been brought along.

"Rosso is coming here. So you need to go make the call on this guy," said Johnny Boy, pointing across the road at Spencer, who was now heading, at sprightly pace, toward the doors of Winchester Auto Specialists.

Angela looked up from the reception desk as Spencer bounced in with a clap of his hands.

"Angela, I thought that TVR was supposed to have been gone by the time I got back?"

She knew attitude nostrils when she saw them, and she saw them often enough with Spencer these days. She'd decided only the previous night she wasn't going to stand for them anymore. When he'd interviewed her, Spencer had spoken a bit like that British romantic comedy actor but with less stuttering. He'd said business was on the up after the downturn and he'd seemed really charming. Now, ten months later, she realized those last two selling points should have been considered under advisement.

"I'm not sure if you meant to say that like it's my fault? The guy hasn't called yet. But the . . ."

She trailed off as he walked straight past and into his office. He was doing that sort of thing more and more, too, these days, like his mind couldn't stay focused on one thing for any length of time. No mystery as to why that might be, of course. She heard his seat thump against the filing cabinet after he yanked it out from under the desk.

While debating what to do, she looked around the Winchester Auto Specialists showroom. Floor-to-ceiling glass, a bunch of potted palms, four cars. Angela wasn't that into cars, but the old Jaguar was beautiful in a feminine kind of way. The way its body flared out and over its wheel arches reminded her of a woman's hips. It was dark green, officially British racing green. In her time there, she'd picked up stuff like that. Spencer hadn't insisted on it, hadn't even asked if she had any interest in cars when he interviewed her, but as his presence had become less dependable of late, she'd found herself talking to potential customers more often. In fact, the last few sales closed at Winchester Auto Specialists were more her doing than his, and no wonder: he went from hot to cold like the weather on Lake Erie.

Last night her husband had said her newfound salesmanship skills should at least have translated into a bonus. She'd laughed. Bonus? What a joke. Her paycheck was nearly two weeks overdue. When she let that slip, her husband had gone ballistic. As she watched him stomping around the room on her behalf, she found herself agreeing with his sentiment. She was being taken for a goddamn sucker.

As she heard the carafe bash back into the coffee machine in Spencer's office, she realized she'd become scared of giving him bad news, and bad news had been coming in more and more of late. She'd been fending calls off. Not just from the bank, but from people whose cars Spencer was supposed to be selling and even a few debt collectors. Sometimes, when she was on her own at the showroom, because Spencer was God knows where, it felt like being the lone pioneer left behind to guard the campfire. And the lone pioneer left behind to guard the campfire always bought it in the movies. When she tried to tell him, it was as if the bad news were her fault. Angela hadn't made a stand over anything in her life, but if she didn't make a stand today, her husband was going to come down here. Her mouth was dry. She rose from her seat.

3

In the Circle of Wagons

Angela stood in the doorway of Spencer's office, watching him as he watched the showroom through the office's internal window. Trophies and pictures from his rallying days filled the wall behind him. Well, they didn't fill as such—judiciously spaced around the Kentia palm they gave pretty good coverage. But they were dusty and unimpressive to her now. Most of them were from amateur events. No big cash payouts there—just promise. And the sponsors had long moved on in their quest for younger potential.

Angela had never run a business before so she didn't know what people needed to do when the shit hit the fan. But as she looked at Spencer with his feet up on the desk it occurred to her that surely he should be doing something. Phoning? Tweeting? The needle on her sympathy tank bounced on empty, and more selfish reasoning colored her thoughts. She wasn't ever going to get a bonus. In fact, something about the calls she'd been fielding that morning told her she should consider herself lucky if she got paid that month.

"As I was saying, Mister TVR Buyer hasn't called yet. I've put one call in. You said not to put more than one reminder call in so we didn't seem desperate. Ever."

She saw Spencer give an almost imperceptible eye roll.

"In addition, Ron-at-the-Bank's called. Twice. He's not happy. He didn't go into specifics because he said you'd know. I did get the impression he was pissed. He's expecting a call today. That was today by the way, did I mention that already?"

Spencer leaned back in his chair and looked at Angela like he was waiting for her to finish so he could go back to doing whatever it was that was so much more important. It was the final straw.

"Good," she said. "I'm glad you've obviously taken all that in stride. Don't let me keep you from firing up your master plan for the business any longer. I'm outta here."

And with that, she turned and left. Confused, Spencer checked his watch.

In the showroom, Angela had already picked up her bag and was heading for the exit.

"Where're you going?" he shouted.

"Home, Spencer," she yelled back, without even slowing up. "Husband? Kids? I don't get paid for being there either, but at least it's got cable."

She barely acknowledged the well-dressed man with whom she nearly collided as she left.

Back in his office, Spencer reflected on the day's progress. It had started with promise. The TVR was supposed to have gone and a test drive had been booked with a guy who Angela said had been just peachy on the phone. Both had been duds. And Ron-at-the-Bank seemed to have gone from being a staunch ally of Winchester Auto Specialists to a major-league pain in the ass.

Spencer supposed Ron had reason to take things personally. In their first-ever meeting, he knew within five minutes the guy was just loving Spencer's play: the British charm, the racing stories, the pretty American wife with her genuine Detroit grit. The farthest Ron had traveled had been over the border to see Niagara. Ron had fought for credit for Winchester and taken genuine satisfaction in its first encouraging figures. But that was then. Now he was just one of the many Spencer had to keep sweet until the luck changed.

He stared at the door out of which Angela had just flounced. She'd calm down when she got paid. His mind began to churn. What the hell should he be doing? Was there a master plan?

Of course there is.

Run it by me.

Borrow more money, until the sales start coming in again.

What if they don't?

Out of the corner of his eye, Spencer sensed movement in the showroom. He saw a tall guy in a sharp-as-hell suit. Short, tightly curled, mostly gray hair. He was looking at the Jaguar D-Type, the Jaguar D-Type with a ninety-five-grand tag, twenty-five of which would go straight in Spencer's pocket.

Hah! As I was saying . . .

Well, don't fuck it up by thinking all that negative shit.

Spencer pulled out the wrap and opened it under his desk without taking his eyes off the suit in the showroom. He dug his car key in the glistening white powder, bent over, felt the cold metal of the key against his open nostril and *blam*.

* * *

"See anything you like?"

McGrath turned from the Jag to see a slim guy in his mid- to late-thirties looking at him. Slim but not necessarily fit-looking. Good-looking—maybe, maybe a little ragged. Warm smile but a salesman's warm smile; he could have lost his entire family in a plane crash and he'd still manage that smile.

"Spencer Burnham?"

"Yes, that's me. Mister . . . ?"

"McGrath. Dominic McGrath." McGrath leaned in slightly, offering his hand. Spencer shook it. Both gripped firmly.

The two men looked at each other, only one of them aware they had different agendas. Spencer sensed something about this potential buyer though. It was as if McGrath's eyes just happened to have been resting on the Jag as he waited for Spencer. And now those eyes were on him—alert, mischievous, and all the while pulling in information. And if the smile was genuine, as it appeared to be, it wasn't diverting one iota of dataflow from those eyes. There was a nonclassic type of handsomeness and a ka-ching of the charisma that often goes with it.

"Beautiful car," said McGrath.

Spencer was about to launch into his spiel.

"What do you drive, Spencer?"

"Uh, at the moment, the Lotus."

McGrath nodded. His smile both discomforted Spencer and yet welcomed him into something *wayward*. It was the smile a teenager got from a teacher who knew what had gone down but was going to make it seem like he didn't—because he'd done worse.

"Then how about you show me what a Lotus can do?"

Moments later, McGrath was sitting in the passenger seat of the Lotus, engine running and air blasting. As Spencer locked up the doors of the dealership, McGrath opened the car's glove compartment and rummaged through. He'd seen everything he needed to—school report, hip flask, antidepressants—and closed it before Spencer joined him.

"My receptionist had to go to the dentist," lied Spencer as he put the bunch of showroom keys in the side pocket of the car door. "You sure you don't want to drive?"

"I'll learn more from watching you."

4

Lessons in Spanish

On the west side, the Yo-Yo was discovering that hooking up with an old flame could be quite the hot thrill. He hadn't ridden a motorbike for at least twenty years, but whatever had kept him alive back then, he sure as hell hadn't lost it. That bike had been a stolen one, just as this one was. Flicking the red beast from side to side, he weaved through some slow traffic on Warren. Power. Speed translated into distance almost instantly—Ducati power. A twist of the wrist and *zip* he was somewhere else. It made him smirk, which was pretty amazing even for him, considering what he was on his way to do.

He eased a right onto Junction Street. The road was already shimmering in the building heat of the morning. It was going to be another hot one, in more ways than one. Ahead, the lights on two intersections turned green. The road was clear. He could really open this baby up, just for a couple of seconds. It was tempting, but the Yo-Yo was following orders from the only guy he'd ever paid mind to, and that meant not drawing any attention—for the time being anyway.

He turned off Junction into the backstreets between Michigan Avenue and Grand Boulevard: Latin King territory, or so they claimed, seeing as of late some Black City Disciples had been mooching on down from Tireman Avenue and selling here. They didn't come alone though, which was fine as far as the Yo-Yo was concerned, because he was looking for more than one of them.

Pulling up at a stop sign on Lovett, the Yo-Yo noticed a gray Impala curbside down the block. There was something about it. He carried on across the intersection but stopped behind a semi in an overgrown parking lot. He inched forward so he could watch between the rig and its trailer.

The Impala had its back to where Lovett dead-ended onto Michigan Avenue. There were three Black guys inside. One would be for dealing, two for lookout. But he had to be certain, so he waited. In case he was being watched, he took out his phone and made it look as if he were checking something. But his phone was off because phones logged movements.

He glanced up when an old Ford pickup clattered past him and made a right onto Lovett. It pulled up next to the Impala, driver's side next to driver's side. An arm came out of its cab. The guy in the front of the Impala reached out and took its offering. Deal done. Deal done and, for the Yo-Yo, target acquired. Next, he needed witnesses. As he waited, he took out a small piece of paper with a line of neat handwriting. He started mumbling to himself, mantra-like, as he practiced the words on the paper.

"Hijos . . . No, *hee*jos. Yeah, that was it. Heejos. *Heejos* a Tireman . . ."

He heard voices from behind and glanced in his mirror. A heat-wilted Black woman with her two kids, a boy and a girl, were going to pass him by. The boy was about thirteen. Perfect. The Yo-Yo placed the phone against his ear, engrossed in an imaginary voice mail, hiding his face as he waited for them to pass—hiding his Caucasian face.

They'd be at the stop sign in twenty yards, and the Yo-Yo figured that would give them a swell view of what was about to happen. He did a quick 360 for any cops, took out the Ruger from his jacket pocket, flicked its safety off, and tucked it behind his back in the waistband of his pants. He pulled his visor nearly all the way down and hit the engine start. Time to go to work.

He made it to the stop just as the family was about to cross. They had to wait as he turned onto Lovett. As he approached the Impala, he saw three pairs of eyes zero in on him. Three guys who were trusted and experienced enough to be sent to claim territory from the enemy.

The Yo-Yo gave a small nod to the driver, who ignored it. They watched him warily as he pulled up. He killed the engine and made a two-finger sign—two G. Then he resisted the temptation to watch them in the car, sensing the tiny movements of hands cosseting guns, fingers caressing triggers. Instead, he made as if he were nervously checking around for cops—just a local Joe looking to score, the scariest moment in his day. Behind them, a refinery train clanked over the concrete bridge spanning Michigan Avenue.

When he looked back, a hand was out of the Impala, hanging loosely. One of them at least had decided he was legit.

"Two ten."

The Yo-Yo nodded and reached absentmindedly behind him. Suddenly the driver found himself staring down the barrel of the Yo-Yo's gun. Its noise was dulled by the train. The driver's head snapped back without time to register surprise. Guns on laps were guns that were too far away to be of use. The Ruger moved instantly to the front passenger and fired. The Yo-Yo didn't even see pieces of skull and brain spraying out the opposite window. His aim was jumping onto the backseat dealer whose gun arm was nearly up. But the Yo-Yo's Ruger was already covering his face and in that split second he knew he'd won, as he'd done many times in his nearly forty years. This favorite microsecond would replay in his mind. Victory, jungle law, whatever. It was pretty much the only thing worth getting emotional about, that and the next Lions game.

Orders.

The word penetrated the haze of adrenaline, not even as a thought—rather, the essence of a thought—and the Yo-Yo adjusted his aim to the man's shoulder before firing, twice. The gun fell from the dealer's hand as invisible fingers of fire nailed him to his seat, robbing him of his power to think. Two more rounds slamming into the upholstery by his head gave him back some wits and he half fell, half threw himself down across the back seat. More rounds thudded into his dead friends.

The Yo-Yo watched for a moment to see if this last one had any fight left in him. He knew where the gun had fallen—out of reach of where the guy now lay, playing dead, hoping for a miracle. Well, he was about to get one.

The train passed, disappearing with a mournful blast on its horns. In the distance, a railroad crossing bell jangled before silence descended. Then the Yo-Yo started shouting in Spanish, at the car, at the street, at the guy cowering and bleeding on the back seat of the Impala.

"Regresense a Tireman, hijos de la chingada! Regresense a Tireman!"

Go back to Tireman, motherfuckers!

He yelled it again and again. People would be listening. Eyes would be peeping through curtains. They'd hear, they'd talk, word would get around. Job done. He started the bike, U-turned, and roared back up the street. At the stop, the family had crossed the road but were frozen on the sidewalk. He stopped right by them. The mother shielded her kids with her arms, wide-eyed with terror. The Yo-Yo pointed back at the Impala.

"Regresense a Tireman, hijos de la chingada!"

What the fuck, he was actually starting to enjoy this. He'd been a little nervous about the Spanish thing, but now? Well hell, it was kinda fun, kinda like a character in a Wild West movie! He moved the bike right into the middle of the intersection. Drivers who were waiting to cross ducked behind steering wheels when they saw the motorcyclist stand astride his machine and pull out a handgun.

Bellowing in Spanish, the Yo-Yo emptied the mag in the air. Then, with a manic laugh, he roared off so hard the Ducati's front wheel didn't touch the tarmac for twenty yards.

For the next five minutes, he lit up the streets in the neighborhood, carving turns as lean angle, approach speed, and braking made their visceral transactions. When the enjoyment of speed and elation at completing the hit dropped off, he wanted to head back to the depot. Michigan Avenue had been right there behind the Impala. He could have gone east straight back to Detroit. Could have been back in time to catch the game. Then, as the Lions sent the Packers to shitland, he'd relive his own moment of triumph. And back in the day, he would have done just that. He would have turned and burned, straight back to the D, his direction noted by witnesses, his bike recorded by CCTVs. And they'd have caught him.

A while back, the Yo-Yo had been looking at twenty-five without parole at Carson City Correctional. He'd done three years and those were enough for him to realize he wasn't that clever, but at least he was clever enough to realize it. So when Lady Luck sent him a visitor, he'd been more than ready to pay attention. That visitor had taken the form of a portly guy with glasses and a beard who looked like an undertaker—Johnny Boy. Johnny Boy had been a lawyer for the Chicago mob until he was disbarred. It didn't stop him advising someone else though. New boss, new city. And Johnny Boy's boss wanted someone just like the Yo-Yo, someone who could kill in all manner of ways with neither qualm nor hesitation, who was already staring into the abyss, someone who'd be loyal and attentive in exchange for a break.

Johnny Boy had brought it to the Yo-Yo's attention that some evidence used in his trial had been garnered by inadmissible means. His state-funded defense should hang their heads in shame. Correctly handled, an appeal against his conviction would have a near-certain chance of success. Did the Yo-Yo wish Johnny Boy's employer to go ahead with the organization and financing of his appeal? And if so, would he be prepared to work solely for, and obey unquestioningly, the same employer?

Six weeks later he'd walked free. A week after that, the unfortunate death of one of the prosecution's key witnesses had made the chances of a retrial unlikely. Said key witness had inexplicably fallen twenty-eight floors from the west-side tower in which he lived. His apartment had been on the fourth floor.

So, this time, although the Yo-Yo had wanted to head back straight away, he was following orders. After blasting triumphantly around disputed turf, he dropped off the power and started working his way quietly north and then west through backstreets and vacant lots. His choices weren't random. Every so often he would pull up and take out a piece of paper covered with directions. Soon he'd turn south, for the Rouge River. Probably only one other man had followed the exact same route. That had been Johnny Boy, a careful man with an eye for detail. CCTV, after all, was everywhere these days.

5

Rosso and Cal

Rosso was also heading for Rouge River. He drove a car the same way Johnny Boy researched things—carefully. Not carefully as in always observing the speed limit, although he did, or wearing his seat belt, which he also did. Rather, he followed certain procedures when he drove: constantly checking for tails, leaving then rejoining the same expressway, double backs, no GPS.

He did this while running the errands of his job, which was moving money. Picking up dirty cash from dealers and hangouts in west and southwest Detroit and exchanging it for laundered money from all sorts of business establishments in Midtown, Downtown, and the suburbs, wherever Detroit was starting to pick itself up. No electronic transfers, just good old A to B. And the stuff he couldn't do, his employer, one and the same as Johnny Boy's employer, had a courier company infiltrated too. It was kind of funny they were called AtoB.

Five or six of AtoB's guys were on "extra pay." They'd go into a Lebanese restaurant in Dearborn with an empty package, and as the owner was signing the paperwork, they'd be exchanging money underneath it. Real magician sleight-of-hand shit that would confound any Feds who might be monitoring things. Not that the Feds monitored much, or anything, in Detroit these days. That was about the level of excitement Rosso wanted. Leave the real hot shit to the likes of the Yo-Yo.

Rosso had other things going for him. His complete inability to make a visual impact wherever he went was right up there. He was a wiry guy in his fifties from Italian stock with thinning gray hair and a face people forgot as soon as they looked at it. He drove a nondescript Japanese sedan in old-man tan. Being another guy who'd done just enough time in the joint not to look a gift horse in the mouth, Rosso was also good at doing what he was told. He was clearing three times as much as he would if he worked six nights a week as a cabdriver.

He pulled up at a light on McGraw, opened his window, and dropped out his phone, barely a week old. He watched as the truck pulling up next to him squelched it into the hot tarmac.

Rosso's car bumped down a potholed road underneath the concrete supports of the Rouge River Bridge and into the empty lot of a derelict warehouse. He stopped in the far corner, by the water's edge.

He took out a new phone and downloaded the messenger app Johnny Boy insisted on. He then sent his new number to the people who needed it.

He did it carefully. Because he didn't want to screw up. He'd been feeling tense these last couple of months. A few times he'd been stopped by the cops for bullshit reasons. Seeing as spotting and avoiding the cops was part of his job, he should have given more thought to how they managed just to come out of nowhere. On both occasions, he nearly had his employer in the car. It was an oversight not to put the two things together. Especially when it happened a third time.

The next mistake he made was not telling Johnny Boy. Sure, he could have waited a little while, maybe until the next time the Bears beat the Lions, which would put a Chicago man in a more forgiving mood, but not much longer. Everyone knew word always got back to Johnny Boy.

Rosso heard the noise of a motorcycle. He watched as the Ducati picked its way round the concrete debris and grassy lumps strewn across the old lot. The Yo-Yo sure looked comfortable on a mode of transport he'd claimed to be out of practice on. He bulged powerfully in his jacket. And he was at least 6'3"—a regular enforcer type. Yep, thought Rosso, leave the work with the high pucker factor to the likes of him. Live a quiet life. Another five or six years and he'd buy a nice house up in Anchorville. Johnny Boy would help him do it without the IRS asking where the hell he got the money. Besides, all this time sitting on his ass wasn't helping his hemorrhoids.

The Ducati pulled up by Rosso's car. The Yo-Yo killed the engine, dismounted, and walked toward the concrete-edged river. He took off his helmet and threw it in the water. Next, he dismantled his gun and threw the pieces in too.

"All good?" asked Rosso, getting out of his car.

"Help me with the bike," said the Yo-Yo, ignoring the question

This kind of thing wasn't helping Rosso's state of mind. It just seemed like he wasn't especially popular these days, like he'd said something really bad without knowing it. Well, fuck them. They should try driving dirty money all over the goddamn place without ever getting stopped. Anyway, the Yo-Yo had always been a man of few words. Everyone knew it. He only ever said hello when he was going to waste someone and even that wasn't guaranteed.

They started pushing the Ducati toward the edge. The sound of an approaching car caused them to hesitate. Rosso tensed.

"Cops?"

"Relax, Rosso."

Rosso felt the burn of humiliation. Was that it? Did everyone think he spooked easy?

As they watched the far end of the lot, a gleaming white sports car appeared. It stopped for a moment, seeming to hesitate before venturing onto the lot's broken surface—modern automotive technology in all its beauty scared shitless by the vicious ruins of the Motor City. It took the plunge and began to pick its way across the lot. Every so often it would back up and try a different route.

Rosso's heart sank a little. If the Yo-Yo could be intimidating, Cal could be a real pain in the ass. Nothing pleased the guy. He ran the books and signed the checks. Running the books meant making sure there weren't any but that people got paid. Cal was a tough guy who'd boxed for a while before he put on a suit and decided to use his head for numbers. "Cal the Calculator." Unlike the Yo-Yo, everyone had to *know* Cal was tough. It was like anger simmered underneath his apelike face with its buzz-cut helmet. Even when he dished out the dough at the end of what everyone knew had been a great time for business, it was like he resented folks for taking it. And sweet Jesus, they'd all had to say something kiss-ass about his new Porsche, even though everyone knew a Boxster was the chicks' Porsche.

Cal didn't bother saying hello either.

"How'd it go down?" he said to the Yo-Yo.

The Yo-Yo nodded.

"You left one of 'em?"

"If he checked out, he had time to talk."

For just a second Rosso thought Cal might say well done. The Yo-Yo's report had obviously put him in a good mood, because he started speaking in a fake newscaster's voice as Rosso and the Yo-Yo wheeled the Ducati to the water's edge.

"Did you know seven out of ten murders in Detroit go unsolved?"

"Nooooo, really?" called the Yo-Yo over his shoulder.

"Oh yeah. So if you wanna kill somebody . . ."

Rosso and the Yo-Yo had built up to a run and, laughing as they sent the bike into the Rouge River, replied in unison: "Come to Detroit!"

Rare of late, the shared jackassing relaxed Rosso.

Cal opened the trunk of Rosso's car and clocked a black sports bag. He unzipped it. The bag was full of cash. He closed the bag, shut the trunk, and banged it with his hand, like he was sending out a rodeo rider.

"Rosso, head up to one block south of 9 Mile. East Winchester and Conant. Pick up Dom. He's goin' with you for this one."

"Sure," said Rosso as he got in his car.

"And Rosso, you got a phone?"

Rosso patted his pocket, started up, and took off slowly across the lot. If he'd seen the way Cal and the Yo-Yo watched him go, he'd have felt even more stressed than he already did.

Rosso slowed up as he approached the Conant and East Winchester intersection, but saw no sign of Dom or his car. When he spotted Johnny Boy's SUV, he parked up behind and got out to get the lowdown.

Johnny Boy dropped his window. "How much did Cal give you?"

Rosso leaned against the car. "Twenty-nine seven hundred."

"OK, take it west: the parking structure near Telegraph and Jeffries. You know the one. AtoB will meet you there. This load's for around Livonia way. Zeb here's coming with you. Make sure you're clear of anything before you hit the changeover."

Rosso was taken aback. *Make sure you're clear?* What the fuck did that all mean? As if he didn't know the AtoB handovers were a big deal. He hesitated, not sure how to play it. All of a sudden he felt awkward, stiff.

"I thought Dom was comin'?" he said.

"He's busy." Johnny Boy nodded over at Winchester Auto Specialists, where Spencer's Lotus was waiting to pull out of the lot. "You got a problem with it not being Dom?"

Rosso wasn't sure whether it was the question itself or the tone in which it was asked that rattled him. Did Johnny Boy know there was something Rosso wasn't telling him? He debated whether to bring it up now and clear the air.

"No," said Rosso. "I just—"

"And ditch your phone," cut in Johnny Boy.

"This one's pretty clean, man."

"I don't give a damn. Matter of fact, give it to me. Zeb here's got one. Get going, both of you."

6

The Interview

The Lotus pulled onto Conant. McGrath nodded at Johnny Boy as they passed by. Johnny Boy followed, keeping his distance.

Spencer headed east then north into Macomb. He was going to take McGrath up Sterling Heights way, maybe around Palmer Woods, to find some curves to show off the car's cornering abilities.

McGrath watched him drive. Fluid, expert—and hungover. He'd known that from his breath back in the showroom, when he'd leaned in close to shake hands.

"Long way from home, Spencer." It took Spencer a moment to note that it hadn't annoyed him.

"American wife?" continued McGrath. Spencer glanced round at him, and McGrath nodded at Spencer's wedding ring.

"She wanted to come back here because her mum was ill."

"You married a Detroit girl? Good for you. What does she do?"

There was something about the way he asked that almost made Spencer inclined to be totally honest.

"She raises money for museums. Looks for sponsorship by tying up events with companies."

Spencer's mind flashed back to the first time he met Marielle. It was at a car museum in Beaulieu, a sleepy village in England. The museum was hosting some joint show with the Henry Ford Museum in Detroit and a couple of the rally drivers had had to show up to keep the sponsors happy. Spencer was one of them. Marielle had stood in line to be driven on a muddy little circuit set up in the grounds of the manor house. Most of the time the car had been sideways and Marielle had nearly died laughing. Spencer was smitten with her laugh. He'd taken her around three times, pissing off all the other people waiting in line, just so he could hear it some more.

"So how'd your cars keep selling while the Motor City's finest went under?" asked McGrath.

"Because we have corners where I come from?"

McGrath laughed. "I'll tell you why." A Buick drove by in the opposite direction, followed by a Caddy. "You see that? And that? Twelve hundred bucks of every one of them went to the unions. Handout, handout. Killing this country's chances."

McGrath spoke like a man from the streets, but one who'd traveled, climbed, and refined himself—just not so much that his roots weren't evident. But if he allowed them to show, he did so by choice, when it suited or amused him. Spencer suspected McGrath could move in the best and worst of circles yet would take shit in neither.

McGrath leaned forward and picked a small straw off the floor. "Amazing what people leave in their cars these days."

Spencer feigned bemusement. "Don't worry, all cars are fully valeted before going to new homes. So, uh, what line of work are you in, Dominic?"

"Dom, please. I run a . . . a profitable niche business you might say. Currency movement, that kinda thing."

Zeb looked at the bag of money now on the seat beside him. He was tense. He had no idea why he was supposed to come on this one or why Johnny Boy had told him to keep an eye on Rosso. Rosso was a bore. Slick driver but a bore.

Rosso turned into a parking structure and headed down the ramps. Most of the lights were out below ground. AtoB liked it that way.

At the bottom level, they slowed and looked for the distinctive green-and-white AtoB livery. They saw it on a little truck tucked away at the far end. As they headed over, its cab door opened and a man got out.

They pulled up a few car lengths back. Zeb grabbed the bag, got out, and walked to meet the AtoB guy. As soon as the bag changed hands, their dark and quiet environment detonated. Lights, sirens, revving engines. A dark sedan, red light flashing on its dash, lurched out from the parked cars and barred Rosso's way. Up ahead, a blue-and-white plunged down the up ramp and raced toward the courier truck, stopping with a little screech, bull bars touching the truck's radiator grill, hemming it in.

Zeb knew what this was. This was a ten-to-fifteen stretch for him. He was carrying dirty money and a buddy's unlicensed weapon, which could be linked to God only knew what, all with two months of parole still to run. But most of all, Zeb knew this was a setup. And as far as he was concerned, the guy at the wheel was responsible, because even though Zeb had just dived back in the car, Rosso was just sitting there, doing nothing—a man hired for his ass-kicking driving hots. The blue-and-white's bullhorn echoed around the gloom, battling the sirens.

"You in the car. Switch off your engine and put your hands outta the window! Now! Do it now!"

Rosso froze, weighing the stakes, the house in Anchorville, until he felt Zeb's gun poke him hard in the side.

"Go, Rosso! Go, you motherfucker!"

Rosso glanced in the rearview. Zeb was serious, alright. And he was right. Rosso was in enough trouble with Johnny Boy as it was. The glance in the rearview told him their back was still clear. Good old DPD with its shitty little budgets. He threw it in reverse, put his hand on the back of the passenger seat and they took off. Fast and smooth. Oh, Rosso was good. No panic in his driving, however hard his heart was beating, however much he was thinking about Zeb sticking a gun in him. They went backward up the down ramp without even skimming the curb.

Going too fast to turn and with no space to do it anyway, they raced backward along the next level up. They turned onto the up ramp so fast Zeb had to scrabble with a handful of gun against Rosso's seat to stay upright.

Rosso had found his flow. They hit the next level. The sound of the police sirens had fallen away. One more turn, one more ramp, and then they were flying out into the blinding sunlight, wheels barely touching the ground.

Straight into the police tow truck waiting at the exit.

Rosso had seen it at the last instant but too late to do anything except brace against the wheel. But as Zeb's head went through the side window and hit the doorsill, his gun fired, through Rosso's seat. Blood sprayed the windshield.

Across the street a guy in a little green-and-white truck watched it all. He made a call.

7

Buckle Up

"So how is rally so different from Nascar or Indy?" asked McGrath.

"Nascar, Indy, they go round in circles, always on tarmac. Same with Formula One. In rallying, we had to use production models. We could upgrade and modify, but we have to use cars the man on the street can buy. And we have to be good on gravel, snow, mud."

"Why rallying?"

"I'm a farmer's son. Lived miles from anywhere. Dad said if I stopped sliding cars around the farm, he'd take me karting. I had talent. Qualified for the senior British team when I was still a junior."

"So why'd you stop? Why come here and sell cars?"

"I got married, had a kid. When you're sliding upside down on your roof with a split gas tank pouring fifty gallons over you with no fire and rescue nearby . . . it's not a family-friendly job."

He knew he had to try and take more control of the situation, to ask McGrath about himself, to make the customer feel special. "You always been in the same line of work?"

Stick with the old faithfuls.

Dominic McGrath watched the gates of the Detroit Arsenal go by on 11 Mile. It made him pause before answering. He was at an age when a man reflects on the choices he's made. Whenever he saw an army base or convoy on the freeway, it took his mind back to the only time he'd ever worked for someone else, if Uncle Sam could be called someone.

He'd signed up when his criminal activities were catching up on him in Detroit. Vendettas were closing in. But he'd joined just in time for the first Gulf War. That was some badass frying-pan-fire luck. And yet he'd excelled and still maintained his illegal sidelines. Black market ops. Staff Sergeant "BeeMO" McGrath: drugs, guns, import, export.

A war on, you say? I've always been at war, you stupid little farm-boy hobos. Now put those Berettas in that coffin and worry about spending the money we're making before you're in one too.

By the time he'd made it back to Detroit, things had changed. All the people who'd had it in for him were either dead or in the pen. And the cops had even less money than they had before. And when he thought how pitiful an army pension was, he knew he'd made the right decision to get the hell out.

It was the thought of a pension that had brought him to Winchester Auto Specialists and the man driving, north now, into the comfortable golf clubs and picket fences of the suburbs.

McGrath became aware of Spencer looking at him, clearly wondering if he'd heard the question, wanting to get the conversation skipping along. The question, after all, had been one of the salesman's throwaways.

"Yep. Always," McGrath replied.

Spencer drove faster than average. And it was obviously his normal thing to do so, slipping in and out of gaps, changing lanes. It was as if he couldn't help himself but make progress, like he was in a car for a different reason than all the other knuckleheads clogging up the highway. And yet it didn't feel rushed or flashy. No one was honking at being cut up. Nor did it feel like McGrath was getting some kind of a show. Spencer just seemed to drive fast—but not get noticed. He didn't know it yet, but his passenger had a list of very specific requirements and moving fast without getting noticed was right at the top.

McGrath glanced in the side-view mirror and saw Johnny Boy's SUV several cars back. He smirked to himself, knowing the Chicago man would be working hard to keep up.

Johnny Boy was having more trouble than McGrath knew. He was taking a call. And he wasn't on speakerphone because he didn't like his calls piping through loud and clear for any recording devices, although he accepted he was possibly being a little overcautious on that score. Chicago PD might be able to afford that kind of shit, but Detroit PD spent their time racing from one 911 to the next. That's why basing an outfit in Detroit but milking the suburbs made so much sense.

Right now, though, as he tried to converse and change lanes at eighty, not being on speaker wasn't hanging together all that well. And to say the caller was severely bent out of shape would be an understatement. Johnny Boy was having to hold the phone some distance from his ear.

"I know, we're on this," he said when the other guy paused for breath. "No, we *are*. I just didn't think they'd wait and get your guy too. Sonsabitches. Your guy got any previous? Will he talk? . . . OK, then just keep him tight. I'll get to him. I'll make him happy."

Johnny Boy finished the call and then took his life in his hands by sending a text.

Up ahead, the phone in McGrath's jacket vibrated. He took it out and read Johnny Boy's message: "Hunch proved. Messy & expensive. Job vacancy."

McGrath sighed and put away his phone, disappointed for a moment, then back *in* the moment. He glanced in the side-view mirror. About five cars back, there was a DPD car with no light bar on its roof.

"Show me," he said suddenly.

"Huh?"

"Get me to the MGM Grand in fifteen minutes, and I will give you four thousand bucks. Take it as a down payment on this faggy European car."

"What're you . . . Why?"

"I have a boring life? I'm an American. Straight roads and Nascar? Enfuckinglighten me."

He put a wad of bills down by the gearshift.

Spencer looked at the money and thought about Ron-at-the-Bank, the rent he owed, Angela's pay, a few grams of coke. He thought about the thirty minutes the drive to the MGM Grand Detroit Casino would normally take from where they were.

Four grand. The Grand. Fifteen minutes. Three fifty brake horses. Zero to sixty in four point nine seconds. Ron, rent, Angela, the Grand, fifteen minutes.

"Alright."

He checked his mirror.

"Hadn't you better get going?" asked McGrath.

"Yeah, I will as soon as that cop without the roof lights disappears, the one you clocked before you put that money down."

"Those are a pain in the ass, aren't they?"

And without knowing it, Spencer had just ticked another box.

They watched the cop car turn off. Spencer downshifted. The revs jumped, but the speed of the car stayed the same. He turned to McGrath.

"You sure about this?"

"Are you sure about this?" replied McGrath, with that whatever-you-did-that-was-naughty-I've-done-before-but-worse smile. Spencer found himself liking Dominic McGrath, but he suspected that was akin to liking a dangerous animal; you wanted to befriend it, but it might well take a limb in return.

McGrath took out his phone, clicked the stopwatch, and ostentatiously put it in the cupholder.

Behind them, Johnny Boy had finally caught up. But suddenly Spencer's car was just gone, like in the old *Star Trek* episodes when Chekov engaged warp speed. Just . . . gone.

"Whoa."

8

Welcome to the Edge

And suddenly I realized that I was no longer driving the car consciously. I was driving it by a kind of instinct, only I was in a different dimension.

—Ayrton Senna

Detective Sergeant Evan Batiste and Detective Don Scott approached the steaming wreck of Rosso's car. One of the troopers asked them if they wanted an ambulance summoned seeing as the guy in the front still had a pulse. They didn't answer—neither of them cared about the guy in the front.

Zeb's head rested on the doorsill that had terminated its brain function. Batiste grasped the blood-matted hair, turned the head round, sighed—and let go. Zeb's head dropped back on the jagged glass with a crunch.

"What the hell is he doing here?" asked Scott.

Batiste thought about it, then nodded at Rosso. "They must have suspected Rosso, so they sent him with this loser, the sacrificial lamb."

Scott looked at Rosso. "So if this guy Rosso here makes it, he might cut a deal. He probably hasn't got long though."

Sometimes Batiste, a narcotics man, wondered if there was just less of a sense of urgency for a homicide guy like Scott. His clientele couldn't get any more dead after all. Still, their new partnership worked well enough even if, on paper, they were apples and oranges: Scott was white, middle class, and middle America. Batiste was Black, local—born and bred. What they shared was the challenge of working for a gravely underfunded police department in a city that had crapped on all its creditors.

As Batiste yelled at the troopers to get an ambulance, Scott spotted Zeb's bag, now in the car's footwell. He slipped on a pair of latex gloves and looked inside.

"There's got to be at least twenty grand in there, maybe thirty," he said. "The guy downstairs—the courier, he's got nearly forty."

"I wonder what Mister McGrath had to do," said Batiste, "that was so much more important than being here."

McGrath laughed. It wasn't often he was exhilarated, but this was certainly doing it. Over a hundred and they'd just swooped around four lanes of traffic when it had seemed like a truck was going to box them in.

"Nice, but that was your right of way."

"'That was my right of way' sounds like an epitaph." Spencer's tone had changed as their speed had increased, becoming more monotone, detached, as if the part of his brain operating the machine in which they were darting among all the other machines on the ninety-four was placing greater demands on it, leaving less capacity for social niceties like conversation. His eyes flicked from road to mirror to blind spots and back to the road. His right hand danced between steering wheel and gearshift in a controlled blur.

No one honked at them. No one had time to honk at them.

McGrath had a fast mind. He'd driven cars fast too. When he was nineteen, he'd fired a gun at a dealer on Warren Street from a car moving at seventy and hit the guy in the arm. But this was speed of thought and events on another level. It had been a while since he'd felt his adrenal glands so productive.

"All this seem slower to you?" he asked.

"I wish. We just calculate more things at once than other drivers. Like some people can count cards, I guess. Gaps closing, relative speeds, power bands, minimizing TEDs."

"TEDs?"

Spencer moved onto the hard shoulder to make an undertake.

"Time exposed to danger."

A Hellcat closed a gap to their side, but Spencer had seen it coming and gone to another farther ahead. "There are certain cars chosen by people who'll be less inclined to yield."

The traffic started to clog ominously due to an accident or construction work ahead. Spencer didn't wait to find out which and cut through several lanes in order to catch an exit. In spite of himself, McGrath gripped the sides of his seat as they hurtled toward the off-ramp's looming date with the surface streets. Spencer raced down through the gears, engine whining, braking hard, the car sliding slightly, and then they were off again, the back of the car flicking to the side before getting back in shape.

On the freeway it had felt like driving damn fast in a fast car with a really capable driver. On the surface streets, with corners and intersections thrown into the mix, McGrath felt like he was in a car that was on the edge: the edge of its performance, the edge of its grip, the edge of its driver's ability to take in information. All were greater than he'd experienced. He was glad Spencer couldn't see his expression. McGrath was a man who normally found it easy to keep a cool demeanor.

"You keep the revs high," he managed.

"Yeah, so the engine slows the car for turns, with less brake, which keeps it stable, ready to accelerate out of them." The back of the car flicked out on a corner again. "Oh, and don't worry. This car does come with all the usual safety gizmos: ABS, emergency brake assist, you know . . ."

My Holy Lord, thought McGrath, he's actually still trying to sell me this goddamn car.

"It's just I've switched them off."

"OK. Care to share why?"

"Switch off any electronic stability programs so it slides how and when you want it to. Not when a computer thinks it should."

"What, by feel?"

"Yeah. Tires feel different on the edge. And when they go, I don't need a big orange warning light telling me."

Gratiot Avenue was empty, allowing them to slash southwest toward Downtown.

McGrath's phone had spun around sometime during the drive. Spencer estimated he had only about three minutes by the time they hit Woodward. The Downtown traffic was sticky, as if people drove the same way as they walked in the heat.

He'd switched off the air so it wouldn't drag power from the engine. Now, as their speed was down it started to get hot again. Sweat trickled down the inside of Spencer's shirt. But the area around the MGM Grand Detroit Casino wasn't unfamiliar territory. He enjoyed the surprise he knew McGrath, a Detroit man, was getting when he ducked into a tight alley off Clifford. Let the guy think Spencer had just seen it and was taking a gamble. Let him sweat a little flying down this high-walled funnel like a bobsled.

"What you're really aiming for," he said as their speed went past eighty, "whether you're racing on the track or on the streets, is to be somewhere else."

Fire escapes flew by overhead. Yesterday's news, dragged up from the ground, billowed out behind. Tiny gaps between wall and dumpster loomed and passed like a sped-up film demo on perspective. McGrath found himself pushing his head back against the car's headrest. He was going to be mightily pissed at Johnny Boy if this English sonofabitch killed him.

"Somewhere else?"

"Subconsciously competent, not thinking, on the limit of human and mechanical ability. But not going over it."

He risked glancing around at McGrath, just to give more pizzazz to that final pearl of wisdom. When he turned back, things went wrong in a way they always did at high speed—quickly. Ahead, a pile of trash stirred and a bearded face appeared, freshly awake and wondering what that incredible wailing noise in its normally quiet alleyway was all about.

Spencer jerked the wheel and for a tiny instant, one of those nanoseconds the human brain seems able to create for itself while the rest of the world hurtles onward, they weren't sure if they might hit the wall or the guy's feet. A grumbling scrape informed them it would be the former. Spencer flinched, concentrated harder, and countered the humiliation with a joke.

"It's a rare moment."

*   *   *

The Lotus pulled up in the entrance portico of the MGM Grand. Spencer killed the engine. For a moment both men were quiet, assimilating the fact that they were now in Downtown, having been up in Macomb a short, short time before.

McGrath smiled, shaking his head as if to say that was quite a ride. He reached for his phone, looked at the screen, and then showed it to Spencer.

"So close, but people lose medals for less than that. Would have got a lot of attention if you'd hit that tramp." He took back the cash.

Watching McGrath pocket the money he'd already spent in his head made Spencer a little resentful. Thirty-three seconds out. He'd got to thinking the guy might have been a little more flexible, that what was more important was the experience rather than contractual fulfillment to the letter.

"But I didn't."

McGrath nodded. "Detroit man through and through, and I never knew about that alley off Clifford."

And Spencer never knew that that alley had ticked yet another of McGrath's boxes. McGrath waved away the valet as he got out. He nodded toward the front.

"I feel bad about the fender."

"It happens. Anything else you wanted to know about the car?"

McGrath looked hard at Spencer again, longer than the moment called for, eyes assessing again, belying the smile. He dropped the money on the seat.

"Take it." He said it with neither scorn nor bad feeling. "Spencer, there's no future in selling cars like these round here. The moment's gone."

Spencer watched him cross over Third and turn into Beech. He looked down at the money—and then up at the MGM Grand.

Johnny Boy's SUV pulled up on Beech. McGrath got in.

"Sonofabitch! Don't be saying I told you so about Rosso," he said.

Johnny Boy shrugged. Not part of his job spec.

"How were you so sure?" asked McGrath.

"Busted on two of his drops in the last month. Didn't tell me about either of them. I heard from AtoB on the first one and I've had the Yo-Yo on his ass since. When I checked back through all our shit with Sheila, you were supposed to be with him on both but something came up last minute."

"Cops might be wise to the car. Looking to take a little dirty money off the street."

"They didn't take the money."

"What do you mean?"

"I mean they didn't take the money. It was dirty as hell and a big-assed hunk of it. No explanation for it being in the trunk of his car. They didn't bother. Why would that be if it isn't because they wanted your ass?"

McGrath was silent for a moment. "Rosso's been with us for a while. Never been any issue. Delivered a lot and picked up a lot."

"And now he's getting old. Cal says he's been going on about getting a house in Anchorville. Quiet life. Maybe he's gotten a little pension conscious."

Haven't we all, thought McGrath. "We need to be sure."

"We are sure, Dom. When he left River Rouge this morning, Cal told him he'd be taking you on this next drop-off. Made sure he had a phone. Then, when I told him Zeb was going with him instead, he seemed rattled. And I took his phone off him, so he couldn't send any messages, couldn't stop the ball he must've started rolling when he left River Rouge."

McGrath sighed. "He dead too?"

"Nope. Bullet straight through his chest. Might need a colostomy bag if he gets out."

"He'll need more than that."

They watched Spencer get out of the car and head into the casino.

"No way he isn't for real," commented McGrath.

"Does that matter anymore? Rosso was our snitch. We could look in-house for his replacement?"

"Rosso was good. Spencer could be better. I need the best."

"All to make this Max Petrovsky thing work?"

McGrath turned to Johnny Boy. It wasn't the first time they'd had this conversation.

"'This Max Petrovsky thing'? You think I want to branch out? Black City Disciples on the west side, Latin Kings pushing in from the other? The only reason we're still here is 'cause they can't run a cleaning op on the lowdown. That mess just now up on Telegraph? Lowdown?"

"Well, thanks to the Yo-Yo's Spanish lessons they should be a little too preoccupied to think about handling their own laundry."

"For a while. Sooner or later one of them's going to come who can clean like us and stay out of trouble. And look at that."

McGrath pointed at a bank of new CCTVs lining the MGM Grand. "That's what's going to get us, and these." He pulled out his phone. "You know that better than I do. One big job, Johnny Boy. I don't want to be working at your age. Max Petrovsky? He's going to see to it that I don't have to."

9

A Man Worth Knowing

Spencer sat in Chris's old sofa. In, because too many springs had given up the ghost for it to perform a fully supportive function. That's why it now resided on the fire escape. The fire escape stoop was large enough to stand in as a porch for Chris's second-floor apartment. On a hot-as-hell evening it was the only place to be. There was even an old fridge—for beer and Abby's Kool-Aid. If it was stolen, the beer would be more of a loss than the fridge. And Spencer could smoke out here. When Abby went to bed he'd switch to weed.

The small three-story block that housed Chris Wilcox's apartment was the last on McLean as it dead-ended onto Brush Street. Scattered spruce and hawthorn trees threw patches of shade over the grassy area that separated the two roads. Chris had somehow made the place feel like it had been home for a long time even though it hadn't. It was where he'd landed after his life flight got rerouted by corporate downsizing and divorce. The latter left him with just enough to buy the apartment outright. Chris was Marielle's uncle on her father's side.

The sounds of industrious activity wafted out the open window behind Spencer's head. Abby had gone mad for the Romans of late and everything that took her fancy had to be printed off.

Chris's cursor hovered over the Print icon. It had been there a while. He watched Abby take pages from the printer one after another and wondered whether it would be the ink or the paper that would run out first. He was only mildly exasperated, though, because he adored her. He loved having her curiosity and laughter around his home. His ex-wife hadn't wanted kids. She'd convinced him they would be happy just enjoying the lifestyle Chris's corporate success allowed them. Believing her was his biggest regret. Abby left him in no doubt of that. This was fortuitous, as affection had become an alien concept for Spencer since Marielle's death.

It was way too hot to be in the living room that doubled as his office, but if he went out on the fire escape, Spencer would expect him to start drinking.

Chris loved a drink and knew he was much more fun after several, so he'd gotten on well with Spencer in the past. They'd been the black sheep at family gatherings, and it had seemed natural he should be the one to keep an eye on him when the hurricane hit, especially seeing as he himself was now a self-employed divorcé. But Chris was getting too old to party. The look on his physician's face when his last body mass indices pinged up had confirmed that. He was entering a new stage in life. He felt it was time for Spencer to take his next steps too. They needed to make the best of things, especially for Abby. But Spencer grieved like a soldier still on tour.

Chris peeked out the window to see if Spencer had noticed the envelope left strategically on the couch. He hadn't.

In the past, and for sure on a super-hot evening like this, a neighbor would have appeared. Everyone loved the fire escape couch and cooler setup. But neighbor relations weren't so great these days. There hadn't been a falling out as such, but no one dropped by like they used to.

Most of the other residents had jobs or were retired and worrying whether the good old city of Detroit was about to plunder their pensions. At the most, they'd be drinking three nights of the week. Initially, a few had dropped by to say hello and share a few beers with the British guy and his little girl. But Spencer wasn't an overly happy drinker and smoking dope almost every night was another level yet. Word gets around.

"Leave me some ink, Abby. I've got to print a ton of invoices tomorrow."

"Why don't all your customers just go to the gym if they don't want to be fat?" she asked.

"I sell them an easier way. And don't go asking crazy questions like that. Their fat pays the bills."

Amen to that. Silent selling, way to go, thought Spencer.

Chris was a pretty fat guy himself, which wasn't surprising, as he sat at his screen all day doctoring his website, answering queries, and blogging about how wonderful his health products were, especially Thermo Booster Burn pills—destroyers of fat for all the other folks who spent the day on their asses. Things were slowly taking off. Orders could be placed anytime. Chris was making money as he slept. The concept still amazed Spencer. McGrath's parting words echoed inside his head. Chris would be sixty this year. Budgets were pretty tight right now, but at the rate he was going he might well be a tycoon by retirement age.

Spencer knew he shouldn't encourage him to drink but they'd made a deal: Chris would drink with him if Spencer promised not to go out and get wasted in the bars of nearby Highland Park.

Spencer took a long swig. Eight o'clock in the evening and still hotter than a three-balled tomcat. He picked up the open envelope next to him. Cheap government stationery. Child Protective Services.

Chris appeared on the stoop, cleaning his glasses on his white T-shirt.

"Sorry, I just saw the address and so I opened it."

"Don't worry about it." He dropped the letter back on the sofa. Later.

"They want to see you tomorrow, no excuses."

"Chris, don't panic."

"It sounded serious."

Spencer opened a beer for him. Chris took it but didn't drink. "Why do they keep asking to see you?" he persisted.

Irritation flared in Spencer as it did more readily these days. He suppressed it though. He owed Chris. Big-time. The couch in the living room was his bed and had been for the last six weeks—since Spencer decided to hold on to stock rather than rent and wages.

"Chris, we've been through this. They opened an investigation on Abby and me. It lasts thirty days."

"Yeah, but you've never seemed bothered by why they opened it. And I'm pretty sure it's been going on longer than thirty days now."

"Like I said, Abby was late to school a couple times and I was late picking her up. One of her teachers is a hard-ass. Probably made a call. Every time I go in it's the same thing: they see Abby's fine. This situation's so under control you'd think I was seeing them for the fun of it."

Spencer hung in the doorway of Abby's room, watching her sleep. Her blonde hair had started to darken. But it wouldn't end up black, like Spencer's. There were other things too, patterns of behavior, that felt like echoes from his past. She already had her mother's stubborn quest for answers.

A glint from the framed photograph by her bed caught his eye. He went over and picked it up. Three faces smiled back. His own, his wife's, and Abby's. They were sitting in a ruined and overgrown amphitheater. Marielle had been organizing a joint project with Cranbrook House in Detroit and an Istanbul museum, so she and Spencer had decided to piggyback a family vacation on it. She'd insisted they see this lost city in the mountains—Termessos. They'd even had to get Abby her first passport. It had been an adventure from the get-go: their first and, as it turned out, only foreign vacation together.

Four years separated that moment from now. A lot could happen in four years. Recently, Abby had started asking about going back there. He replaced the picture. He had a business to save before they could think about expensive vacations.

Spencer was of the mind that alcohol was just amazing. It never ceased to impress him how everything bad could just melt away in its embrace. Old dreams got a fresh lick of paint and as for the bad things that hung around him like a heavy cloak, intricately embroidered with all his failings, it was like some well-trained maître d' just stepped up behind and coaxed it off. *Allow me, sir.*

Another few big drinks. The temperature had finally dropped off a little. The sofa felt like it was made of warm mud. Its soft, heavy cushions enveloped Spencer. It wouldn't be the first time he'd woken up there. His eyes started to close. His glass tilted and some of its contents tipped onto his leg. Liquid coolness stirred him.

Spencer feared sleep and the dreams it brought. He had his routine down to a fine art: coke to get through work, drink to get through the evening, weed to wind down. A couple of sleeping pills as a chaser.

Sometimes, though, he misjudged things—like tonight. He'd gotten home mightily pissed at himself. After the crazy episode with that suit and his bet, he could have come back with four grand. *Four grand.* Once he'd had the fender fixed—fifteen hundred bucks tops, more like nine hundred using his contacts—he could have still put a little dent in the runaway train that was Winchester Auto's expenditure. But after a bruising encounter with the tables of the MGM Grand, he barely had enough to repair the fender—at buddy rates. Besides that, there was something else niggling him. Something he'd forgotten to do, something to do with money.

Ron! You were supposed to call Ron-at-the-fucking-Bank! Fuck!

He lurched out of the seat, stood unsteadily, and fished around in his pockets for his phone. Then he saw it jammed between the cushions of the sofa. He bent over to grab it but too quickly. As he scrolled through the numbers, his circulation couldn't quite fuel his brain. He keeled over.

Chris heard the crash and knew what it would be. He went out onto the fire escape. Sure enough, there was Spencer facedown on the metal floor, phone in hand, out cold. Chris thought about dragging him inside, but the last time he'd done that he'd put his back out. He stomped back into the apartment.

Moments later he was back with some chalk. He set to work drawing a white outline around Spencer, inadvertently nudging him while doing so. Spencer stirred slightly. His finger gave a last twitch and pressed the call button. Chris, engrossed in his work, didn't notice.

Spencer moaned. "Ronaduhbank."

The phone screen said the call was being answered—either by Ron or his voice mail.

"Ronaduhbank? What the hell is ronaduhbank?" said Chris. "Screw ronaduhbank. I'm tired of being gentle with you. I'll give you something to remember in the morning."

"So you're quite sure nothing's changed?" asked Lonnie.

"Hundred percent. Why?"

Lonnie Estevez looked doubtfully at the slightly disheveled man sitting opposite. He was turning a cigarette pack round in his hand on the chair arm. She sighed her indecision, looked out of the window and then down at her desk. Spencer felt his irritation rise. Why did she want to make something more complex than it needed to be? His phone was going crazy on vibrate—all missed calls from Angela. He'd messaged her to text not call, as he couldn't speak. She'd instantly messaged him back, saying: "Call me," which was kind of annoying.

His head felt like it was stuffed full of cotton wool, and he was sweating. He needed to call Ron-at-the-Bank, too, but had yet to think of a plausible reason for not doing it the previous day.

"You've been attending at Common Ground, right?"

"You know I have."

He quite liked Lonnie. He'd made her laugh during his first session and had known from then on he'd have no trouble managing the CPS situation.

"Lonnie, why don't you just tell me what's on your mind, so I can address it?"

She played with the chain of her necklace, causing the small gold crucifix to dance in her cleavage. It was a fine cleavage, too, Spencer had always conceded. He preferred it when she wore her hair down, but obviously she was in full-on work mode today. Either that or she hadn't had time to wash it after her spin class. But down suited what was an attractive Hispanic face. Half-Hispanic, half-Navajo to be precise.

"It's your face, Spencer."

"My?" he said with a frown. Then he remembered. "Oh this," he said, pointing at the fire escape floor's pattern of elongated diamonds still imprinted on the side of his cheek. He laughed and thought fast, took grains of truth to concoct an untruth. "Scored a big sale yesterday. He wanted to celebrate with me. Those city dudes, they know how to drink, that's all I can say. And I'm out of practice these days, thanks to you."

"You know I'm supposed to sign you off today?"

"Yeah. You'll be pleased to see the back of me, I'm sure."

Spencer said it with a laugh. His laugh always seemed genuine, but she knew he was a salesman, as her father had been. He'd been able to go into a towering rage, reducing her mother to tears of fear, and then laugh through a work call like he was the most Garfunkel guy in Dayton. And Spencer was foreign to boot with that English thing going on, which was well-known to cloud an

American woman's judgment. He sounded a little like that actor who did all those romantic comedy movies. She loved those movies.

She looked up as he suddenly rose, walked round her desk, and stood behind her. He put his hands on her shoulders and gently squeezed as he nuzzled her neck. She thought she could smell alcohol behind mint.

"Just because it's my last appointment doesn't mean we can't see each other."

She pulled away from him. "Spencer, we still have to do assessment forms."

"Yeah, we have to do them at the end of every session. Let's just do what we normally do. I'll sign them before I leave and, later, you can just tick whichever boxes you think should be ticked. I trust you, Lonnie." He pulled her gently back to him, massaged her shoulders and lightly stroked her neck. "That's twenty minutes that could be better spent doing . . . other things."

Lonnie hated her body sometimes. She was a woman with an appetite. And her appetite for sex seemed higher now at thirty-six than it was when she was eighteen. She felt there was nothing wrong with having a high sex drive. What she hated was that it could so easily override what her brain was telling her about this arrangement. She actually liked this guy. But he'd been in her office a half dozen times, had been fucking her from the second appointment, and had fobbed off all her hints about getting together outside of the CPS building on Curtis Street. She was a little tired of being single, of being the only person on Tinder who was looking for love, and a little tired of having to change the date of her birthday on Facebook so her linked dating profiles still read "30."

He kissed her neck softly, one hand cradling the side of her face as the other gently cupped one of her breasts.

"Spencer, we can't . . ." Her nipple rose at the behest of Spencer's gently skimming fingertip. Why did he have to be so damned good?

"No one can hear us through these walls, Lonnie, you know that."

His assurance turned her on too. She felt the wetness between her legs. Soon she'd be soaking. He'd lift her up, hold her tightly against him while they kissed passionately, which she loved, before turning her round and taking her from behind, over the desk. They always ended up in that position, which she also loved, but she did think it might be kind of nice to see his face when he came, just for a change.

Johnny Boy's SUV was parked on Winchester. Inside, air on full, public radio chattering away, Johnny Boy was thanking whatever god of good timing had sent him to Winchester Auto Specialist's that particular morning. He heard the sound of a high-powered engine dropping down through its gears. He didn't bother craning his neck—no need.

Spencer's Lotus flashed by and turned into the Winchester Auto Specialists gateway. The tires gave a tiny squeak on the sidewalk as the car lurched to a stop. The gates were chained shut. A sign had been attached to them with cable ties. Spencer got out and walked up to it. Johnny Boy already knew what it said.

BY ORDER OF FIRST INDUSTRIAL BANK OF DETROIT. WINCHESTER AUTO SPECIALISTS HAS CEASED TRADING. INQUIRIES (INCLUDING CREDITORS) CALL 313-989-2900.

Johnny Boy watched Spencer start making calls. He turned down the radio, took out his own phone, and called McGrath.

"If it's 'yes,' the time's now, Dom."

Spencer was looking around as if checking whether the coast was clear. Suddenly he climbed over the Winchester Auto Specialists fence. Johnny Boy laughed.

"You kind of have to be here. I'm not sure whether he's got balls or he's just a total whack job."

Spencer hit the ground, stood up quickly, tucked his shirt back in, and walked across the yard. Only half a dozen cars remained. Angela's phone was going straight to voice mail and Ron-at-the-Bank's secretary was adamant Ron was away on business even though Ron never went away on business.

The locks on the front doors had been replaced. The showroom windows were virtually unbreakable. He walked around the back of the building. The small bathroom window was normally open but not now. A brick went through that window just fine though.

Spencer looked around the empty showroom. He'd part owned the Jag. The others had belonged to private owners hoping to sell high thanks to Spencer's reputation. They'd been paying him a forecourt fee. They were going to have a time of it, trying to get their property back before Ron disposed of it.

As he walked back to his office, his steps echoed in the emptiness. He dug around in his desk for any coke. He wondered about his habit, about who was in charge. He reckoned he'd stuck to half a gram a day for the last year: no more than four lines. Of late, though, the lines had been getting fatter and by the second day he'd only had enough left for three. And he'd had a nosebleed out of the blue last week. Abby had been jealous. She said that whenever someone at school had a nosebleed they were superstar heroes, at least until lunch break. Spencer wasn't feeling particularly like a superstar or heroic—just lost.

Johnny Boy watched a flatbed truck pass slowly by. Two guys in coveralls were rubbernecking, scoping the scene. The truck continued down Winchester to the stop, turned, and came back at a pace. It stopped and reversed up to the Lotus, raising its bed as it did so, until its edge scraped on the sidewalk. Leaving the engine running the two guys leapt out. One of them went under the Lotus and clipped a hook straight on its chassis. The other guy flipped a switch on the winch motor and the Lotus was dragged backward. Its rear wheels, locked by the parking brake, juddered as the car slid up onto the flatbed. It was slick and fast.

They'd lowered the bed and were securing the wheels of the Lotus when they heard a yell. Spencer had appeared from around the corner of the building carrying a trash bag. He dropped the bag, ran for the fence, and started to climb.

The two recovery guys finished lashing the wheels, leapt into the cab, revved the engine, and took off just as Spencer landed on the sidewalk. He ran into the street after them, just managing to touch the back of the truck before it left him behind.

Spencer went apoplectic, swearing and kicking the hell out of the gates. Johnny Boy waited. If there was one thing he had down, it was when to put an idea in someone's head. That wasn't when a client was madder than a rat in a tin shithouse. It was after but not so long after that they'd flopped in a sorry-assed little heap. Johnny

Boy liked to think of it as the moment in a western when the cavalry appeared. He was the cavalry.

Spencer was just about to hit Chris's number when a silver Merc SUV swung into the entrance and stopped abruptly, as if surprised to find its way barred. A guy who looked like a cross between a lawyer and a Czech music professor got out. The guy stared at the closed gates and then around him as if checking he'd come to the right place.

"Hey," he said to Spencer. "Know anything about this?"

"Who are you?" asked Spencer.

"Oh, sorry. Johnny. Well, people call me Johnny Boy. I work for a guy who came and looked at a car here. I was supposed to come down and put a deposit on it."

"Dominic McGrath? The Lotus?"

"That's right, but he wanted a Jag," said Johnny Boy.

Spencer sighed.

Johnny Boy looked at the sign again. "Guess that isn't going to be possible now."

"They'll auction it. He'll get it cheaper."

"Now is that right? I'll be sure to pass that on." Johnny Boy started back to his car but stopped. "Say, you need a ride somewhere?"

"Not unless you're going anywhere south of Highland Park."

"You're in luck."

As they drove, Spencer found himself being drawn into a conversation that spawned ideas. One of those ideas was that Dominic McGrath was a guy he needed to know. He didn't realize he was getting these ideas because the man driving wanted him to. A clever, careful man. And when they pulled over on McLean, Johnny Boy did a great job of acting surprised, but agreeable, when Spencer asked for his card.

10

The New Guy from Nebraska

Spencer held off telling Chris the dealership had bought the farm. Chris had a low stress tolerance these days. Spencer could hear him in the kitchen, asking Abby about her day. He felt guilty for not doing the same. He would, he promised himself, just as soon as he got things going again. And with that in mind, he paced the fire escape porch late into the night.

Chris was about to switch off his bedside light when Spencer's head appeared in his doorway.

"Chris, I need to borrow Penny tomorrow."

Chris was one of those guys to whom a car was strictly a means of transportation. What it said about him was of no consequence. He'd even allowed Abby to name his Prius.

"Did you say yes?" said Abby.

"Yes to what?" said Chris.

"Yes to Dad taking Penny this morning."

"Sure, why?"

"You shouldn't have."

"Why? I'll walk you to the bus."

"It's not that, Chris. Didn't you see what he was doing last night? He was making a plan. And it'll be a bad one."

"Abby, you're eleven. You were in bed. He's just borrowing the car."

"Dad's a car dealer, Chris. He has lots of cars and he hates Penny."

Chris thought about it for a moment. She had a point. "So what makes you think this plan, if that's what it is, is a bad one?"

Chris was conscious that he, a man of nearly sixty years, was in a genuine two-way discussion with a child, one in which views were exchanged and things learned, by him in this instance and not for the first time. When Chris had been growing up, kids were treated as kids. But Marielle had always talked to Abby as if she were an adult. Spencer had sometimes followed her line but it had been Marielle's "thing." Chris marveled at the results.

Abby gathered her things and headed for the front door. "All Dad's plans are bad right now. Mom helped him get successful. Women do that a lot, but they can't let men know."

Chris called after her. "OK, so why didn't you stop me?"

"I'm eleven."

The door slammed.

Penny pulled up on Winchester and Conant early. Spencer got out and walked up to the Winchester Auto Specialists gates. He checked that the street was clear before climbing over. He was going to need his tools.

Out in the yard he set to work on the remaining cars. He loosened HT leads and manifold bolts, broke the distinctive rear wing on a Subaru WRX, smashed a few windows, replaced sport rims with small emergency spares, and threw the rims over the fence into the back alley. He mixed dirt with polish and smeared paintwork.

On Conant, a big man sat astride a powerful motorcycle, legitimately purchased this time. The Yo-Yo took out his phone, zoomed in, and filmed Spencer at work.

Officer Hess, only a scrawny twenty-two but already with three years in the DPD behind him, was having a hell of a time deciding which was the better view. He could look out the third-floor window across Midtown, where he should be out patrolling, sweating his ass off, busting scum, or he could watch Nurse Abraham's tight, tight ass as she leaned over to check her patient's vitals. She was pretty well racked up front too. Probably smelled great as well. So the guy in the bed was getting an even more amazing show than Hess. Pity he was in no condition to appreciate it. Or maybe he was appreciating it because the guy sure was breathing heavy. Oh, no, wait, he couldn't breathe by himself. The ventilator was doing the breathing. Heat wave outside, miniature heat wave going on in room 478 of the trauma center for perps shot through the chest.

Hess shivered as he kicked back in his seat. The skin on his bare forearms was all goose bumps. The air-conditioning was actually a little too fierce, but he wasn't going to move anytime soon, because soon Nurse Abraham was going to turn round and answer a burning question: Would a pair of erect nipples show through the white uniform of a Detroit Receiving Hospital nurse?

He sipped his latte. Anytime Batiste asked him to do a little surveilling, and that's all the guy ever seemed to ask for, he was going to be right there. He checked his watch. Another hour and Batiste should rock up with his questions. Another hour of thinking about nurse Abraham riding him. Another hour of *bleep hiss, bleep hiss*. He'd have her on top first, facing away, so he could watch that ass. He was starting to get a hard-on.

Nurse Abraham checked Rosso's trach tube. His mouth and jaw had taken such a hit—no safety belt apparently—the ERs had had to run his air through a hole in his neck. At least he could talk and for that he'd be grateful, because he was going to be at the DRH for a while.

The door opened suddenly. Hess barely had time to register a big guy in a white coat and a guy in a lumber shirt and longshoreman's beanie, both wearing shades, before taking a fist from the big guy right in the throat. Instantly the fight was out of him. He dropped to his knees and didn't even feel the hit to the back of his neck that put his lights out.

Nurse Abraham saw it all though. She saw the big guy close the door and drag Hess's limp body across to barricade it. She saw the way he did this—calmly, efficiently. Abraham didn't make a sound. She wanted to live. She'd known the cop had been there for a reason. She hadn't asked him any questions, but he'd made her feel safe enough just by being there, even if the guy was a horndog. That had all changed in a moment and right now she was focused solely on the gun aimed at her face by the guy in the lumber shirt. She was too shocked to even raise her hands.

There was a strange tranquility in the room—just that *bleep hiss*. Abraham became conscious of the big guy standing at her side.

She didn't want to move, to twitch even. Didn't want to give that gun the slightest excuse to blow her face inside out. But she knew the big guy was watching her. Was he going to cut her throat? When she pictured herself being found, white uniform drenched in blood, she couldn't help herself; her eyes strained to the left. Lumber shirt man didn't eighty-six her for the eyeball move so, *very* slowly, she turned and looked up into the big guy's eyes. He gave a small nod as if to say he'd been waiting for her to do just that. Then he smiled, a tight smile that said, *I'm going to enjoy this. I'm not so sure about you.* And with that he swung his fist so hard into the side of her head her skull fractured. She flew across the room like a rag doll fired from a circus cannon, crashed into the metal bedside table, and landed in a heap. Again, stillness.

Bleep hiss.

Eddie removed his sunglasses, revealing that blank, off-the-wall stare of his. Eddie the new guy—wiry and lively, eager to prove, keen to learn.

"Nice. Cracked but not whacked," he observed. He'd just witnessed a specialty in the Yo-Yo's repertoire: a punch to the head hard enough to fracture but not kill. He was kind of renowned for it, actually. At seafood restaurants, whoever ordered lobster, they'd just pass it down the table to the Yo-Yo. He'd line up the pieces and *thump, thump, thump.* Hard enough to crack but not to splat.

"Did you kill the cop?" Eddie asked the Yo-Yo.

"No. Watch him. If he comes round, slug him. Don't waste him."

Eddie was flattered that the Yo-Yo thought he might kill a cop. A definite compliment. At the same time, if he were to waste the cop, he knew the trouble they'd both be in with Dom would be way too real. He should demonstrate his appreciation of that.

"I'm not stupid. Jeez." He crouched down beside Hess, checked his pulse, and then flipped him into the recovery position. He knelt and put his gun to the back of the cop's head.

The Yo-Yo turned to Rosso. When he did, Eddie turned away. For although it wasn't meant to be a day of killing, it was to be a day of pain for some, and Eddie didn't want to watch the Yo-Yo work. If he could have blotted out the noise he would have, but he, too, needed to know what Rosso might say, because he had his position to think of. Eddie was the new guy, and gaps in an outfit like McGrath's—tight, careful, old-school Detroit—didn't open up too often, especially for a loner from Nebraska.

The Yo-Yo asked his questions quietly and calmly. It occurred to Eddie that everything about the Yo-Yo revolved around the need for violence in their business. What he said and the way he said it was either leading to violence or calculating when violence might come into play. The guy watched football, drank sometimes, fucked whores but never dated. For the most part, he just waited to work.

The fear in Rosso leaked and seeped out everywhere. In his tremulous voice, made scratchy by the breathing tube, in his heart rate monitor, bleeping ever faster, and in his sweat, glistening in this chilly room.

"I'm good at this, Rosso. You know that, so you know you're going to tell me what you've told them."

"Uh-uh."

"Sure you are."

"Nothin'. Told them nothin'."

"Rosso, you told them about drop-offs Dom was gonna be on."

Rosso's tubes and pipes rattled as he shook his head.

"Rosso, don't fuck with me. Bad start. Johnny Boy's been watching you. I've been watching you. How else would the cops know Dom was supposed to be with you?"

Rosso said nothing.

"Rosso, Dom wants you to know that what's been has been. You tried to fuck us, but you can be out. That pad in Anchorville? All quiet, do some fishing? Don't you want that?"

Eddie heard the pipes and tubes rattle again.

"OK then," continued the Yo-Yo. "I'm gonna ask you one question. Tell me the truth. Don't make me do bad things to you, Rosso. Understand?"

Eddie was reminded of that game show, when some smartass decides to gamble all their winnings on getting the last question right.

"Tell me what you've told the cops about the other stuff. About Max."

"Nothing!" It was a whispered scream. Whining, grating. Vocal chords fighting with plastic tubing, pain and terror.

"That was the wrong answer, Rosso."

And the Yo-Yo went to work.

11

New Friends

Spencer slowed up on a service drive of the Lodge Freeway, took a left onto Martin Luther King, and headed west. It was good to be out. Chris had guessed something was up with the dealership and Spencer had had to fess up. But when Spencer told him not to worry, that he had a plan, and a darn clever one at that, he was taken aback by Chris's utter lack of enthusiasm. It was as if he'd been primed to be negative.

Spencer drove alongside a chain-link fence, its top crowned with coiled razor wire. Behind the fence, across an empty broken lot, stood a nondescript medium-size, two-story concrete office-cum-warehouse. The area was typical for southwest Detroit: lots of light industry and office buildings, many of them empty but not yet dilapidated.

The fence turned south along Gibson and then into Noble. Spencer counted down the numbers. He slowed as he passed a gateway, set back from the road between two warehouses. Through the gateway, across a small lot, Spencer could see the other side of the building he'd clocked from Martin Luther. Much of the ground story was given over to loading bays with steel roller shutters. A small truck was backing into one and Spencer just had time to discern cars parked inside the others.

He continued for a short distance and then pulled over. He kept the air on as it was so humid outside. Clouds were rolling in from Lake Erie, but it seemed too much to hope that the weather might break. His hands drummed the steering wheel, and he was conscious of his heart thudding. He rolled up his shirtsleeves. It was like having race nerves.

Well, it's not a race, which means all options are on the table.

Rummaging in the glove compartment, he found Penny's logbook and user manual, still pristine in their folder. He fished a wrap out from his pants and tipped a line on the plastic cover.

Moments later, he flipped a U and then turned into the gateway. He dropped the window and pressed the intercom. After a moment an unfriendly voice crackled.

"Yeah?"

"Spencer Burnham to see Dominic McGrath."

Silence for a moment. "Who'd you say you are?"

"Spencer. Spencer Burnham. Johnny Boy told me to come."

Silence but longer this time. Spencer wasn't fazed.

Ready for anything, dickwads.

He drummed the wheel, more rhythmically now.

The gate suddenly swung up. He drove through and across to the depot, pulling up in front of the far loading bay. He caught his own reflection in the rearview.

Do this, Spencer. Make it work, buddy.

*   *   *

Cal leaned against the railing that ran along the raised walkway at the back of the loading bays while he waited for Denny to report back who the visitor was. At the depot, whoever was closest to the gate intercom was the one to answer and push the button that lifted the barrier. The rule was unwritten, but observed by all, McGrath and Johnny Boy included, but not Cal. Even if Cal was closer than someone he considered further down the ladder, he'd make a point of walking away from it when it buzzed.

Every outfit has a Denny—a guy who's not especially capable but not useless, trusted but not a member of the inner cabal, only occasionally funny but always ready to laugh at the jokes of others. Sometimes, if everyone else's schedules meant the depot would be empty, it would fall to Denny, in an unspoken, informal kind of way, to stay there, so cars could be left unlocked in the shade with their windows down. Denny had never had any doubt about his place in McGrath's outfit. While that didn't burn him up like it would a lot of folks, he did have his dreams, just like everyone, and one day he might well be taken seriously.

He rejoined Cal and they watched the Prius pull up in front of the loading bays. "Sounded like he was English or something."

Spencer got out and tucked in his shirt, damp from sweat. He took off his shades, tossed them on the dash, and slammed the door—almost in one movement—and strode into the loading bays.

It took a few moments for his eyes to adjust. He made out half a dozen cars, mostly new, and a Ducati. It seemed the loading bays were used more for keeping their cars cool than for loading trucks.

He saw Cal and Denny looking at him. Cal, the big crew cut in his suit, looked unfriendly.

I don't care.

Denny, tall and lanky with a mop of dark, curly hair, had shoulders that seemed as if they'd been put on back to front. Either that or he'd left the hanger in his tough-guy denim jacket.

"Afternoon, guys."

Neither responded.

I don't care.

Spencer walked toward them.

"Here to see Dom?" He gave a slight emphasis to the shortened name.

"He don't normally use Uber," said Denny.

"Who wants him?" asked Cal.

Oh OK, so we've got the village idiot and a regular gangster.

Spencer kept on walking right to the back of the bay, just below the walkway on which Cal and Denny stood. He looked up at Cal.

"Spencer, Burnham. Here to see Dom. He and Johnny Boy asked me to come down."

Cal stared at him but said nothing. Denny nodded at a staircase behind him. Spencer realized he'd have to walk back down several bays to get the steps up to their level, so he reached up, grasped the bottom railing and climbed up and over, completing the move with a little vault.

"Thank you, guys." As he tucked his shirt in again, he nodded back toward the entrance doors. "What do you reckon? Rain?"

They didn't reply. "Hmm. OK then," he said as he walked toward the stairs.

Spencer didn't realize that driving wasn't the only thing he could do fast. He'd acquired a knack for making enemies. He could do it in a New York minute and didn't even need a fully structured sentence. Talent.

He climbed a double flight of stairs and went down a short corridor to a solid white door with a pneumatic closer. He pulled it open and his face was cooled by a blast of chilled air. He entered a sizeable reception room with two low black leather couches and a glass coffee table. The slat blinds were open just enough to let in some light.

A woman in her forties with dyed blonde hair and reading glasses sat at a desk in front of an open office door. She spoke quietly on a cell phone while reading from the screen of another. On her desk lay another four. She glanced up as Spencer entered.

Spencer heard voices in the office. He recognized Johnny Boy's, although he sounded different than when he was giving Spencer a ride home. Then he'd been avuncular and jovial, in a good old homeboy sort of way. Now he sounded serious and determined, with an eye for detail and refusal to accept that a problem might be insurmountable. Spencer could only make out the occasional phrase. There was something about whether it was possible to turn off the CCTV in a truck's cab. It wasn't interesting enough to stop Spencer from feeling fidgety. He felt the woman's eyes on him as he walked to the coffee table to get a magazine. This also allowed him a glimpse inside McGrath's office.

A guy in his sixties with silver hair swept back from a high brow sat in front of a big desk. He wore the blue-collar uniform of faded denim shirt and work pants. He was hunched over the edge of his seat, feet twitching, hands loosely clasped in his lap—like he was watching a nail-biter of a game.

The couch squeaked when Spencer dropped into it. The sound made the man turn. On seeing Spencer, he recoiled, visibly upset. His reaction silenced the conversation. Johnny Boy's head appeared in the doorway. He clocked Spencer—and closed the door. No smiles, no wave hello.

Spencer cared little. He was thinking about something he'd seen once in a bar in Highland Park. He'd been drinking with two suits. At the end of the evening, one had said his goodbyes and stepped straight into a chauffeur-driven Phantom. The remaining suit had laughed at Spencer's expression and then talked about how the other guy had been a high-level exec one minute, then jobless, divorced, and broke the next, with a kid from a previous marriage to support. Things were desperate. On hearing about a senior position going, he'd just gone to the office instead of applying, with his kid. They'd sat in the reception area and waited to see the chairman. They'd waited all day, because the chairman had forgotten his assistant had told him someone was there. The chairman eventually came out to go home and found this one guy waiting. The guy said he wanted that job. The chairman saw something in him—desperation, sure, but the sort that breeds determination. And now Spencer felt he was that guy. This was his moment.

After twenty minutes, McGrath's door opened and Johnny Boy escorted the twitchy guy out and through reception. Spencer nodded at them both. The guy ignored him, couldn't wait to get away.

Spencer had just had his second look at Max Petrovsky. One day, his life would depend on him getting a third. But he had no way of knowing that then.

"An unexpected pleasure, Spencer."

Spencer turned in his seat. McGrath stood before him offering his hand. He wore a crisp white shirt, dark tie and cufflinks, expensive, subtle cologne, and that smile with its welcome to wealth and wickedness. Spencer stood and returned the handshake and the smile without even being aware of doing so, heedless of the spell he was falling under, again.

"Come on in and let's catch up."

As McGrath passed the woman, he stopped and put his hand on her desk where she'd see it in the periphery of her vision. He waited to allow her to choose her own moment when she'd be able to handle two phones and give her boss some attention. A few more quiet words into the phone at her ear and then she looked inquiringly up at McGrath.

"Tell Cal to wait, Sheila."

Sheila nodded.

Even in his own hyperfocused state, it occurred to Spencer that McGrath wasn't playing the big, slick businessman. He really operated with a powerful but even-paced control. Spencer suspected a lot of women liked Dominic McGrath. For a moment, it awed him, and then he rallied, the artificial fuel additive pulsing through his system, inspiriting him to welcome the coming challenge.

So . . . great, I've come to the right guy.

McGrath waved Spencer to a seat and then sat back at his desk. Much of the wall behind him was devoted to a map of Detroit and its suburbs. The map was stuck on an enormous whiteboard and covered with an irregular, hand-drawn grid. Seemingly random pairs of letters connected the top and bottom of the vertical lines. Numbers on the sides of the board marked the horizontals.

Spencer surmised the whiteboard arrangement allowed the letters and numbers to be changed.

"How's things, Spencer?"

"Eventful, Dom, eventful."

"Eventful can be good or . . ." McGrath shrugged, left it hanging, waited. He sensed the man in front of him was locked, loaded, and good to go.

"Well, initially I thought bad. But now, I've come to realize the situation could offer opportunity." Spencer had gotten to launch sooner than anticipated. He'd kind of expected, hoped for, some small talk, to reestablish the connection they'd shared breaking the sound barrier on Gratiot Avenue. But McGrath seemed to be listening intently, so Spencer figured he may as well cut right to it.

"Johnny Boy came by the dealership the other day, just after I wound it up. Literally, just after. Ended up giving me a ride home."

"No shit, really? You closed down?"

"Yeah, yeah, don't ask. Turns out my silent partner's a gambling addict. I closed a ton of sales, didn't wait for the payments to come through before I brought in new stock. Just wanted to keep the wave going, you know? It's the best way to keep the closing happening."

Spencer was so far into the zone, he read McGrath's smile as one of understanding. McGrath sat back, put his feet on the desk, and steepled his hands under his chin. This was going to be entertaining.

"Anyhow, great guy Johnny Boy. Liked him."

"Yeah, he's . . . he brings a broad skill set to my operation."

Spencer nodded. "I can imagine. Anyway, he had a lot of good stuff to say about you too."

"He did?"

"Absolutely. That you were great at seizing opportunities, the whole carpe diem thing."

McGrath nodded. "I'm guessing you've got one for me?"

Spencer enjoyed the feeling of being on the same page. "Well, Dom, I think it's a definite yes on that. Best opportunity and idea to go along with it I've had for a long time."

"Lay it on me."

And Spencer did. He let him have the whole shebang. How he'd let his remaining stock get repossessed by his creditors, how they'd auction them, and how auctions meant rock-bottom prices, except—and this was the clever part—he'd damaged the stock, so it would go for even less than trade price, because appearance was everything at car auctions. But the damage had been only superficial. All it needed was for some guy with a little capital and an eye on the main chance to step in and buy all the stock right back at fire-sale prices. Spencer could fix it back up, find a place in Oakland or Livonia, and *bang* they'd hit the ground running. Huge margins. Not only that but McGrath would get his Jag—and he'd get it cheaper than a Kwame Kilpatrick credit note. And it could be put against the business.

"Really?"

"Welcome to the perks of being a car dealer. They talk about win-wins in the corporate world, right?"

"They do."

"So this would be a win-win-win."

Spencer sat back and waited, comfortable with the silence, damned comfortable. Win-win-win—that was fucking genius. He'd thought of that on the hoof.

McGrath allowed the silence to run for the minimum amount of time necessary so as not to sound dismissive.

"I don't want the Jag, Spencer."

"You don't want . . . Hell, that's fine. You don't have to have the Jag. You could have any one of those cars and it—"

McGrath cut him off. "Look, I'm going to pour us a coffee. While I'm doing it, I want to ask you a question. But I want you to know, before you answer it, that I don't want any of those cars. And I don't intend to get into car dealing."

"You don't?"

"No. I can most assuredly say I'm not interested in your proposition at all."

He laughed at Spencer's expression—a mix of crestfallen and confused. But the laugh was affectionate rather than scornful.

"So, as I was saying, this question I'm going to ask . . . Bear in mind that I may have an alternative proposition for you, one without overheads and no need to close sales but with high earning potential. How do you take it?"

"Sorry?"

"Your coffee? How do you take it?"

"Uh, black. Black with sugar."

"Spencer, did you actually like selling cars?"

Something in McGrath's voice stopped Spencer trying to think of a new angle. McGrath wasn't going to change his mind, wasn't even going to waver. And Spencer knew that McGrath already knew the answer to the question anyway.

"I guess you could say it had lost some of its shine."

McGrath handed him a coffee and sat on the edge of his

desk. "These things happen. You gotta look at the doors that open when they do."

Spencer knew he was shit out of doors. But Chris's door was going to be knocked on by some guy with a handful of court orders any day now.

"I've always been able to make deals, Spencer. Started from nothing, right here in this part of town. I been other places of course, been in the army. But you know what? I took my skill everywhere. Never stopped making my own deals. I'd have been stupid to stop. You've got a skill, Spencer. I've seen it. And you're hardly using it."

"Driving."

"Correctamundo. You've got something we can't get here. You guys get brought up driving roads that are unpredictable. Corners, narrow roads, overtakes, that kind of shit. You drive cars that are, well, they're responsive, like a rodeo horse: fast, powerful, but they'll put you on your ass if you don't know what you're doin'. Our whole car heritage is different: big V-8s, soft shocks for our long, straight trips across the desert."

He crossed to the window, cracked the blinds with his finger, looked out and then back at Spencer. A shaft of sunlight pierced the gap. Dust motes eddied. The beam lit McGrath's blue-gray eyes, focused and serious now, no twinkle, just evaluating.

"I want you to drive for me. For my operation, I mean. Drive here like they drive in London or Rome. See, I know you know what I mean by that, but faster and without being seen."

An unexpected calmness had laid hold of Spencer, the calmness born of inevitability. He looked again at the map with its changeable grid reference system, something that would be digitized in a normal office. He thought of Sheila quietly working a half dozen cell phones on a desk with no landline and of Max Petrovsky, the nervous blue-collar guy who absolutely didn't want to be seen there. He couldn't work out exactly when he'd known he was in a place where things were hidden. It had just kind of crept up on him.

"It's not quite legal, is it, Dom, what you do here?"

McGrath let go of the blinds, cutting off the sun, and sat back down.

"It used to be illegal to drink in this country. Use the wrong light bulb and you're breaking some law. There's laws and there's laws, Spencer. We aren't raping or killing here. Just working a system that plenty of other folks are working. We just do it better, with less fuss, guns, or bumping heads." McGrath leaned back. "It has its advantages for you right now: I pay cash. I don't wanna pay your creditors any more than you do."

He opened a drawer in his desk, rummaged around, and found a phone. He put it in front of Spencer.

"If you don't use your phone, then the IRS would have a difficult job proving you worked for me. Cal could take you to get some money for a car right now."

McGrath waited, watching.

Spencer reached forward and took the phone.

McGrath stood. "Four doors. Some grunt but not flashy." He walked around his desk, grasped Spencer's shoulder, and offered him his hand. Spencer rose as he took it. "Follow me."

They went down the stairs. "Don't worry if the boys seem a little cold with you," he said over his shoulder, and then he laughed. "I mean I wouldn't want to meet some of 'em in a dark alley, and my wife fucking hates the Yo-Yo but—"

"The Yo-Yo?"

"Oh yeah. Just Dwight's handle. Useful guy if people ever want to play rough. We like to avoid getting into any beefing on the streets though. Our customers do that among themselves. We leave 'em to it. We're pretty tight here, so it takes a little while to fit in. Just got to prove yourself to them, Spencer."

In the loading bay, Denny was throwing boxes out of the small truck and paying no regard to where or how heavily they landed. The boxes had pictures of high-end kettles and juicers on them.

"Need a juicer, Spencer?"

Spencer thought about the paucity of his contributions to the Wilcox household of late, since he got there in fact.

"Sure, why not?"

McGrath waved him to take one. He called into the truck. "Denny, where's Cal?"

"He's here."

Spencer and McGrath looked round to see Cal coming down the walkway toward them with Johnny Boy and two other guys. Spencer found himself wishing he wasn't holding his new, for-the-really-health-conscious kitchen appliance.

"Cal," said McGrath. "This is Spencer. He's gonna take up the driving slack."

Cal didn't have to say anything. His face said it all. McGrath turned back to Spencer. "Cal here'll take you to get some money. Like I said, fast, four doors, not too flashy."

McGrath walked through the group, slapping Cal jovially on the back as he went.

"Come on, guys. Let's send him on his way before the Yo-Yo gets back and he changes his mind."

No one laughed. As Spencer followed McGrath along the walkway and down the stairs, he felt eyes burning into him.

I don't care.

Maybe I do, a little. Or maybe it's this fucking juicer.

McGrath held open the passenger door of a sparkling white Porsche Boxster. Spencer got in. Cal intercepted McGrath the moment the door closed. "You've got to be kidding, Dom!"

"'Cause he's not from around here?"

"That's one of many reasons."

Neither realized that the driver's-side window was open. Spencer leaned over to hear better. As he did, he noticed the car's key card had been left in its slot.

"Dom, the guy is a schmuck. You're wastin' your money, our bonus."

"The guy drives at least as well as Rosso does, *did*."

"The guy don't know shit from Shinola. Eddie's a good driver. He already works for you, and you're already paying him so—"

The rest of his sentence became a yell of shock as the Porsche suddenly wheel spinned out of the loading bay, leaving them in a cloud of tire smoke. New-tire smoke.

12

Making the Right Impression

You've got to be closer to the edge than ever to win. That means some-times you go over the edge, and I don't mean driving, either.

—Dale Earnhardt

The Porsche laid two thick glossy strips of smoking rubber right out of the bay. With engine whining and sunlight glinting off rims and roof, it raced over to the far corner of the lot, seemingly going too fast to do anything other than crash into the right angle formed by the depot fence and the wall of the neighboring warehouse. At the last moment, the car whipped around, white smoke belching from screeching, juddering tires. The gears coughed downward, the revs climbed, and the back end of the Porsche slid around as if on ice. Tires fought for traction. Stones and gravel crackled off the fence and nearby dumpsters.

Back end still slewing, the car picked up speed again. No one in the loading bay spoke as they watched Cal's car heading straight toward a light pole. Must've been doing at least eighty they figured. Some of them had decided the English guy had just gone plain nuts, was still rolling only by virtue of sheer luck, and right about now was just choosing his moment to end things in a snazzy German fireball.

Inside the car, Spencer waited until the light pole was filling his windshield before jabbing the brake and flicking the wheel to the right. Then he floored the gas.

Cal's face turned to stone as he watched his car sliding around and around, front bumper inches from the light pole, the car disappearing and then reappearing among clouds of smoke like a sleek white genie. He looked back at McGrath.

"Six months old that car. Those tires are two grand a set. I'm gonna kill your new boy, Dom." He said it with righteous conviction.

Johnny Boy liked watching McGrath in moments like these. They worked with men who didn't scare easily and who weren't the rule-abiding type.

"You're the numbers man, Cal, so why can't you do the math?" said McGrath. "Both drops Rosso made in the last month were intercepted. Straight after, so they pulled in the couriers too. AtoB's guys are goin' nuts: two of them caught with dirty cash. Two guys who might talk. So you tell me, why might I want a guy who's not from around here?"

The Boxster finally stopped orbiting the light pole and headed back to the loading bays, its tail end smoking and swishing around like a snowboarder riding powder.

"I mean it, Cal. Don't think I'm just telling you to try and behave. I've got more skin in this than all Dearborn's payin' and time's a'rollin'."

The two of them faced each other. Cal snorted. "It's your call."

"That's right, Cal. And if it turns out it was a bad one, I'm sure you'll let me know. Now take him to the plaza drop. Give him what he needs. It doesn't matter if it's dirty cash. He won't be using no dealership."

The Porsche pulled up, and Spencer killed the engine. The loading bay filled with the acrid smell of burning brakes and rubber. Spencer got out and slammed the door.

"Can't beat midengine for spinnability, Cal, but you know this is the girls' Porsche, right? Underpowered. Nine eleven's a better choice for a guy. Nice interior though."

The assessment caused everyone except Cal to smirk. Talent.

Suddenly, the barrier went up and a sedan drove across the lot toward them. As it slowed, Spencer found himself locking eyes with the passenger. It was something to do with the "who the fuck are you and what the hell are you doing here" look he was getting.

Eddie watched Spencer and Cal get in the Boxster, Cal in the driver's seat this time.

Seeing Eddie and the Yo-Yo arrive seemed to give McGrath a thought. He leaned into Cal's window and spoke quietly.

"And while you're there, tell them we've located our problem. Dealt with it. So they can stop worrying."

Cal, still seething, barely managed a nod before driving off. McGrath watched them go before walking over to where Eddie and the Yo-Yo were leaning against their car.

"Nothing," said the Yo-Yo.

"What, you mean he's been moved?" asked McGrath.

"I mean he gave us nothing."

McGrath chewed it over for a moment. "Tougher sonofabitch than I gave him credit for."

The Yo-Yo shrugged.

"What?"

"I don't think he knew anything."

"You sure?"

Eddie jumped in. "Fuck that. He just knew we'd whack him if he fessed up."

McGrath thought about it. It kind of made sense. When the Yo-Yo came calling, it could take more than just the truth to save you.

Not long after, Eddie went looking for the Yo-Yo. He found him saddling up on his Ducati.

"Yo-Yo, you headin' home?"

"Bar."

Eddie nodded, deliberating. "What was the 'other stuff' you was askin' Rosso about? About whether he told the cops?"

The Yo-Yo fastened his chin strap. "Dom's got an opportunity. Something big."

"Like what? Doing what he's doing right now?"

"Nah. Different."

"Who's Max?"

"Only me and the guy drivin' need to know."

He took off without a goodbye, but Eddie had learned not to care about that.

Batiste and Scott watched Rosso's body bag glide by on a gurney.

"Expert work," said Scott. "All around. The nurse and Hess will make good recoveries. Rosso—he probably wanted to die halfway through. Made him wait."

"To see if he'd talked. McGrath's diversifying and he's show-ing real discipline about who he lets in. Rosso must've known something."

"Well, he took it with him. The captain isn't happy. Says it's already hit the internet; a patient here was tortured to death right in front of a police guard."

"At least it didn't say the cop watched it happen."

"No, there's that, I guess. But he's had a call from the mayor's office. I mean he really isn't happy, Evan."

"He'd be even less happy if he knew McGrath's started bypassing his own talent pool."

If the afternoon heat outside Cal's car was inhospitable, inside was barely survivable. They headed northwest then north. Spencer had come down from his high but hadn't regained full perspective on matters.

"Cal, if you really care about this car, you should slow up before you cross McNichols."

Cal ignored him, his fingers fidgeting on the wheel. Two of his fingers hurt. They'd been stung by the Porsche's sassy little rear spoiler when Spencer had taken off.

Just before the intersection, the car hit a vicious dip in the road and bottomed out with a grinding clunk.

Cal's jaw clenched and he breathed through his nose. Ahead, some kids laughed at them from the back of a school bus. Cal flipped them the bird as he accelerated past.

After another fifteen minutes of silence, Cal pulled into a disabled space in front of a mall. He turned to Spencer.

"How much will this car be?"

"Dom said I could have ten thousand."

"You're fucking kidding me? He said you deal in cars, so you get 'em cheap."

"That's right. That price is the trade price for what I think would be good."

"Oh, well, new news. I'm the guy who decides how much is good."

He opened the door and got out. Spencer took another shot at entente cordiale.

"Hey man, I'm sorry for what I said about your car. I was just busting your balls. I actually like—"

"Stay here." The door slammed.

"Boxsters."

After two minutes with no air he was feeling the heat. He opened the door wide.

"You gonna move this?"

Shielding his eyes from the sun, Spencer looked up to see the silhouette of a parking officer.

To try and stave off the ticket, Spencer jogged into the mall, which turned out to be a mixture of offices and shops. He searched for five minutes and was heading back to the car when he glimpsed Cal in the busy reception area of an office. Cal was talking to a skinny Black guy in a courier's uniform of green pants and a shirt with white pocket flaps and short sleeves with stripes.

It didn't seem like a normal conversation between a guy and a courier. For one thing, the courier seemed mightily pissed. But Cal seemed to be reading the guy the riot act right back. Then the courier handed Cal a digital signature box. Cal made as if to use the plastic stylus, but didn't, although he did take something from underneath the box before handing it back. He slipped whatever it was smoothly into his jacket pocket and turned to the exit, catching sight of Spencer as he did so.

Cal was barely through the revolving doors before: "Which part of 'wait in the car' didn't you get?"

"You were about to get a ticket."

"So you left the car unlocked? In Detroit?"

Back at the car, Cal pocketed the ticket with zero concern, checked his phone, and sent messages. They took off again, this time heading back south. Over the next hour they made two more stops in the projects of Brush Park. Cal would pull over and disappear down an alley or into a building. By midafternoon they were back at the depot. Throughout the whole time, neither man spoke. Cal pulled up in one of the bays and took out a thick wad of bills from his jacket. He counted some out and offered them to Spencer but kept hold when Spencer went to take them.

"Know this. I handle the accounts here. So I write off any assets that don't turn out to be so valuable."

Afterward, waiting for the barrier to rise, Spencer felt pretty good. He'd gotten a totally different result from what he'd been aiming for that morning, but it felt like a goddamn win nonetheless. He'd walked into McGrath's with nothing but a plan and a prayer and he'd walked out with a peachy job, just like that guy in Highland Park. And a juicer. Winning.

Detective Batiste watched the Prius turn onto Noble and head east. He started the Dodge Charger and followed.

They headed north on the Lodge Freeway.

Batiste found himself getting dragged away from his own surveillance work more and more these days. The previous week, he and Scott had spent six hours dealing with a domestic abuse. Not what a narcotics detective sergeant should be doing but that was how things were since the chief of police broke up the narcotics headquarter units and sent all the narco detectives back to the precincts to try and do their jobs. The precincts struggled to hit a drug target house once every two weeks, let alone pursue a long-term conspiratorial case.

He needed to get out: to the bureau or the state police. The bureau had already turned him down once. Didn't like his record: too gung ho, closed cases too early, got the guy low down and not the guy pulling the strings. He wouldn't make that mistake again. McGrath was just the sort of investigation that could impress. And right now was the golden opportunity to bring it in because Batiste's superior officer, Captain Schaeffer, was uncharacteristically playing ball. But that wouldn't last long.

Six months ago, Captain Schaeffer's teenage daughter had been fender meat. She'd been sexting her tutor at the time. There was an unspoken departmental wager as to which would happen first—the captain's breakdown or early retirement. This little ticking clock prevented Batiste from tackling this case by the book: long-term surveillance and data mining, lots of workup, lots of leaning on contacts he'd made in other agencies for more tech to build up a full picture of McGrath's op. Instead he had to follow his gut, cut corners, and hope for some sweeping spectacular.

And yet the crazy thing was that it was possible. It was possible because he had a secret up his sleeve. And no one except his partner and Schaeffer knew about it. But right now, Batiste's gut was feeling very uneasy about the guy he was following, a guy who seemed to have come from nowhere, like McGrath had suddenly thrown a curveball. This guy didn't match the face the DMV had as the car's owner. He drove differently too. Batiste had never considered a Prius to be at all speedy but this one, well, it just seemed to slip through the traffic like it'd been oiled up on the outside.

Both cars turned east onto Glendale. Batiste struggled to stay back but keep the Prius in sight. The Prius pulled off the road into a lot. Batiste slowed, U-turned, and parked up.

Spencer got out and walked to the communal front door of Chris's apartment block. Batiste took out his phone, zoomed the camera, and took a picture. A little grainy but with the address it was good enough to start making inquiries.

13

Rookie

Spencer decided to hit the car auctions. It took nerve and knowledge to buy that way but if you knew your stuff, you could get more bang for your buck. A couple of days later, amid a sudden and long-overdue downpour, he pulled into the loading bays with his new wheels.

Eddie had been leaning against the wall of the bay watching the rain lash the lot. He was chewing gum like a cow munched cud. He stood aside for Spencer's car.

"What is it?" asked Johnny Boy.

"Infiniti G35."

The deluge stopped almost as suddenly as it had come on, and sunlight broke through the dark clouds.

Eddie spat his gum out noisily. "Mileage?"

"One forty," said Spencer.

"High."

"It's got three hundred brake horsepower, and these are for fat business guys so it won't have been ragged. Reckon it's got plenty of life in it."

"Why didn't you get a four-wheel drive?" said Eddie. He whacked the hood of Johnny Boy's Mercedes SUV. If Cal had said it, Spencer would have known he was being criticized. But it was difficult to gauge Eddie.

"SUVs are top-heavy. They roll easily if you brake during a quick lane change."

"Better in the rain," said Eddie, nodding at the wet concrete lot now steaming in the sun.

"Eddie, they call SUVs four-wheel drive, but the power's only going to two wheels at any one time. And those wheels can be any two of four. If I really wanted control in the wet, I'd go for an all-wheel drive car. Then the power's going to all four wheels, all of the time. Your moneyman kept my leash too tight is all."

Having eavesdropped Cal on his first day at the depot, Spencer had sussed Eddie out as the competition before they even met. And yet he didn't seem to outright hate Spencer. He had a weird off-the-wall stare. Spencer couldn't figure out whether it was because he could suddenly go batshit mad over some little thing or whether something was missing up top. At least with Cal you knew where you stood. And it was little wonder McGrath had no trouble when money was owed with someone like the Yo-Yo knocking on doors. He'd probably been the kid who wasn't allowed to take the school pet home for vacation due to the danger of torture.

Johnny Boy, a careful man, quietly took this all in, not because he was especially interested in cars but because he appreciated an eye for detail. And he liked seeing evidence that his research was on point.

Before they put him to work, Spencer had a man-to-man with McGrath.

"You're going to fit in here. Everyone's still laughing at the bitch-slapping you gave Cal's Porsche. But I want you to be aware of something." He nodded at the map behind him. "Where we are, our operations, it's a different world than what you're used to, if you don't mind me saying."

Spencer didn't mind, because he wanted a piece of whatever McGrath fed from. It couldn't be worse, morally, than a day at the office for one of those bankers, just like Ron-at-the-Bank.

"Some things we're going to ask you to do might seem strange, even pointless. Remember, though, I may like you, but you work for me now. I say run, you run. I say make sure of something, then you make goddamn sure. You make a little mistake, pick something up and give it to the wrong guy, or you miss some punk or cop on your tail, then you're gonna cost me. Most times you aren't even gonna be doing anything much wrong: carrying money the IRS is wanting a chunk of, say, but you're a business-man. I don't have to tell you how hard they can come down on the ass of a working man."

He didn't.

"I know you got an agenda, Spencer. Debts, you like a drink, maybe more?" He laughed then at Spencer. "What? You think the guys who work here are angels? Come on!"

Spencer relaxed, felt less judged.

"Say, do people call you Spence?"

"Sometimes."

The almost constant hint of a smile suddenly vanished. "In the army, Spence, we had a lot of horseplay, did some naughty shit. But my guys still did their job. When you're at war, and there's one weak link in a squad, he gets the whole squad killed. You follow me?"

And not for one moment did Spencer suspect that being a weak link was what had brought him there.

Spencer returned to the loading bays to find Denny half-inside the trunk of his car. He'd already pulled out one of the speaker units, leaving its casement empty, and was in flagrante on the second.

Spencer yanked him back by the shoulder. "Hey, what the fuck are you doing?"

"Whoa, cowboy, easy!" said Denny.

"This isn't your car to get all bent out of shape about."

Spencer spun round to see Johnny Boy. "Denny'll seal up the boxes so they look nice, but I'm afraid if you want music you're going to have to make do with the front speakers."

Denny went back to work.

"Your work phone?" said Johnny Boy.

Spencer fished it out and handed it over.

Johnny Boy downloaded a messenger app. "Only use this app for calls and messages. No WhatsApp, no email, no Facebook, no OnlyFans." He handed Spencer a list of names and numbers. "Put those in. But not the names. They're our names. Think of a way to remember who everyone is."

"You can put me in as M," came Denny's muffled voice. "That's M for mechanic not the guy in James Bond."

He and Eddie just about died laughing. Spencer thought Eddie seemed to take longer to get the joke. Either that or he was being careful about choosing what to find funny.

Spencer went to put the list in his pocket.

"Do it now."

Johnny Boy watched as Spencer put the info in his phone. "Who's W?"

"Sheila," said Spencer.

"W is for woman?"

"Yep."

"Why am I LT?"

"Lawyer type."

"Think of something else."

When Johnny Boy was satisfied, he took back the list. "These numbers change." He looked at Spencer's gray Infiniti. "Good color."

Spencer followed him up to reception, where he asked Sheila, "What have we got?"

Sheila spun one of the phones on her desk. Johnny Boy checked, then waved Spencer over.

"See that?"

"B7?"

Sheila sighed and shook her head.

"We don't say it. We remember it," said Johnny Boy. "Where to, Sheila?"

Sheila spun another three phones around. More letter-number pairs. Johnny Boy jotted them down on a piece of paper. "And there's a moving drop," said Sheila, adding two cross streets to Johnny Boy's list. "Message me when you're twenty minutes away, and I'll let him know."

"Got it," said Johnny Boy.

Spencer followed him through the open door of McGrath's office. McGrath was finishing a call. He looked up and smiled like a friendly colonel. "Taking the new boy out, Johnny Boy?"

"Best start making some of the money back he just blew on those wheels."

Johnny Boy stood in front of the map. "Come over here."

McGrath handed Spencer a pen and paper as he went by.

The letter-number pairs Sheila had given corresponded to addresses on the map. Beside each, two words were written.

"First word is the name of the company; the second is our contact there. Normally that intel doesn't leave here unless it's in your head, but we'll go easy on you today. Write them down. Look at the map. Plan an indirect route to them. Don't set it in stone though. OK, you see where that is?" Johnny Boy pointed to the initial letter-number pair Sheila had given: B7.

Spencer checked it on the map. Nately Place apartment complex. He recognized the name. The last of the Brewster Projects' folks had been relocated there when their homes were demolished.

"Rough part of town, right, Spencer? Sometimes you'll be picking up from a place like that, sometimes dropping off. OK, let's go."

Five minutes later they were heading east on Martin Luther. They could have hit Trumbull Avenue and headed north, a short trip, but Johnny Boy insisted Spencer take a roundabout route.

He made Spencer pull up to check if they were being tailed. He made him flip a U, drive onto the Lodge Freeway and then straight off again, made him keep the pedal down—for most of the time.

"Long probation period in this, Spencer. Know what that means?"

"Sure, means you can fire me."

"Means we can watch you. We will watch you. We know where you're going, and we can pick you up at any one of your drops. If we do, we don't want to be able to tail you. You follow?"

"Sure." Spencer didn't much care for the tone. He'd just been starting to relax a little, thinking the cloak-and-dagger bullshit was just something to put up with. And he was fine with that. He'd known he'd be breaking some laws even before he left the loading bay with Cal. He'd never done anything illegal before, unless he counted his drug habit (which he didn't) or breaking the speed limit, and he didn't think too highly of getting busted. So he was quite happy to follow the rules. He'd already decided this was a finite job, until he had a healthy stash. Then he'd move on to something respectable. But right now, the aroma of fast money hung in the air.

"So the stopping, the driving fast without being noticed, the checking, all that shit?" said Johnny Boy. "That is what you do. And when you're done, you delete messages. Always. These are the rules. Following them is what keeps us ahead in this game. The last guy? He didn't follow them so well. Got sloppy, greedy, whatever. I had him whacked."

Spencer did a double take at Johnny Boy.

"Yeah, that's right. I had him killed."

They nearly ran a light.

14

The Game

The two men looked at each other. Neither spoke. Spencer heard neither cross traffic nor engine throb. Johnny Boy's face was challenging in its blankness, his eyes deep pools of blackness. No longer the favorite uncle.

Johnny Boy stared back saying nothing, his muteness confirmation in itself. Horns sounded.

"Light's changed, Spencer."

After one more incredulous look at Johnny Boy, Spencer pulled away.

Five minutes later, Johnny Boy suddenly erupted into laughter, slapping his hand on the dash as he doubled up in great belly-aching fits. He put his other hand on Spencer's shoulder and tried to speak but couldn't—he was laughing so hard. Spencer, nonplussed, tried to concentrate on the road.

"Your face!" Johnny Boy eventually managed. "Oh my guiltless

God, if you could have seen your face, boy! Like, who was the guy, Yosemite Sam? I say, I say, I say *what?*"

Johnny Boy kept on laughing. Eventually Spencer started chuckling too.

"Jesus, Johnny Boy! What the fuck!"

"'Had him killed.' Ha ha. I was going to say I had him tortured first, but I would have lost it."

He got himself under control. "No, Spencer, I fired his ass. I'm just telling you: Don't get bored. Stick to my rules or I'll fire your ass in a heartbeat. Got it? Now pull up next to that alley, the one running into this apartment block."

Johnny Boy peered down the alley, checked his phone, then checked the alley again.

"Keep your wits about you in these areas, Spencer, at least until they know who you are. Then you should be fine. We do these people a favor."

Spencer saw junkies and pushers working their pitches, clear as day. He didn't associate his coke with this kind of scene. Vincent, his most reliable dealer, seemed like a regular guy. Creative musician type, hardly dangerous. Vincent was always on the verge of moving to LA. He'd leave a wrap in the tailpipe of Spencer's car or even meet up for a coffee. None of this rot-to-the-fabric-of-society bullshit. But the stuff going down here was crack. Kids Abby's age were being used as lookouts and runners.

Only for a while. Make some cash.

He and Johnny Boy were the only white faces he could see.

"How come Dom doesn't have any Black people working for him, anyways?"

"All Dom's people go way back together."

A rangy Black guy in a puffer jacket and red headscarf emerged from the shadows of the alley, flanked by two compadres.

"These gentlemen here? They're clients."

The lanky guy got straight in the back while his two bodyguards leaned up against the wall.

"Hey, Pucky," said Johnny Boy.

"JB."

"What's it been since I last saw you, Pucky? Like, two months?"

"Fuck knows. Probs."

"I thought you guys were going to do your own thing."

"We was."

"What happened?"

"Where you bitches been, man? There's a fuckin' war on y'all. Fuckin' *war*."

"Yeah I heard a little something happened over on the west side. They got three of your guys?"

"Yep. One of them was Sweepstakes."

"No way. Your little brother?"

Pucky nodded. "Fucking little taco niggers. Anyway, they got it comin' good."

He took a bag out from his coat and almost tossed it at Johnny Boy.

"No doubt," said Johnny Boy. "Something showy right?"

"You know it. Whole world's gonna know not to mess with these niggers. Black City Disciples are claiming those bitches' turf."

Johnny Boy nodded thoughtfully. "It's the only way. They've got to have no doubt." He held up the bag. "Well, I guess we'll just keep handling this side of things for you guys while you handle business. What have we got here?"

"Thirty-nine eight. That's everything from here over to Clark Park."

"Clark Park? That's way west for you guys, that's—"

"That's right. Decided those Vernor niggers ain't so bad. We workin' with them now. Pullin' resource, man. An' they think we payin' yo asses way high."

"Is that so?" said Johnny Boy. "Drive us around the block, Spencer." Johnny Boy took out a pair of surgical gloves from his pocket and put them on. Pucky laughed.

"Always careful, Pucky. That's us. That's why you pay us." He started counting the money into smaller plastic bags.

Pucky eye locked Spencer in the rearview. "You the new man, huh?"

Spencer nodded. There were times when he felt his English accent wouldn't serve him well. This was one of them.

"Yes, this is Spencer, Pucky," said Johnny Boy without looking up. "Spencer took over from Rosso."

After a few circuits they pulled up back at the alley. Pucky went to get out. Johnny Boy had noticed one of his bodyguards sweet-talking some girls. He was a good-looking guy as far as Johnny Boy could tell. "Hey, Pucky, that guy of yours, he's got a way with the ladies, doesn't he?"

Pucky laughed. "Scoop? Oh yeah, he just scoops them up. Don't care what color they is neither. I gotta tour, bitches." The door slammed and he was back on the street.

Johnny Boy stayed in the back. "Drive, Spencer. Head west. Livonia. Impress me by not going right there on the freeway."

As they went, Johnny Boy folded down the split rear seat. He reached into the trunk, popped open the speaker cases, and stuffed the bags inside.

Spencer was thoughtful as he drove. Johnny Boy, back in the front seat, watched the wheels turning.

"So those guys back there, Pucky and his crew, we're working for them?"

"I wouldn't say we work for them."

"With them, then?"

"We provide a service for them, because, well, how can I put it? They don't have a particularly long-term view on things."

"No kidding. Let me get this straight. They just lost three of their people. They know the guys who did it, so they're going to go kill those guys, but they're going to do it in as obvious a fashion as possible?"

"That's probably an accurate summation, yeah. Seems just plain stupid, doesn't it?"

"Just a little."

"You've been spending too much of your time up in Oakland. This is what happens here in the D. When there's no new sales territory, people have got to fight to keep what's theirs. Now you got the Latino gangs moving up from the West Coast, hitting Chicago, expanding out this way. So when the Latin Kings go waste a bunch of Pucky's guys, then Pucky's got to send some guys to go waste some Latin Kings, and they've got to do it in a way that tells the world who did it."

"So that means they're either going to get killed by the next in line or go to jail."

"Spencer, don't you know, these folks are in the Game?"

At first Spencer thought it was his imagination, but as Johnny Boy spoke, his gestures, mannerisms, and soon his whole demeanor changed, becoming more . . . youthful, more potentially aggressive.

"The Game?"

"What is the Game? The Game is about honor. Honor demands that if you front me off, in front of my peers or the public, in my universe, I have to do something about it. So when I do a drive-by in the middle of the day and let everybody see it, I'm trying to get my honor back."

"What's the point of having your honor if you're dead or in jail?"

It was more shapeshifting than mimicry, as if Pucky were back in the car, using this suited white guy who had to be nearly sixty as a mouthpiece.

"Spencer, if I'm in the Game, then I don't care. 'Cause I'd rather die like a G than live like a punk."

"A G?"

"A gangster. And yeah, you're right; if you die like a G, it's a lose-lose situation. Number one you lose because you're dead, and number two the person who shot you, if they get caught, they go to prison. So it's a lose-lose proposition. However, this is the world they'd rather live in. Because if you're Pucky and you let it go, then you gotta live like a punk, and everywhere you go you gonna be treated like a punk. You can't go down to the liquor store and demand respect. Why? 'Cause you've been punked out and everybody knows it. Take a left here."

Spencer knew then that Johnny Boy observed people more closely than was normal. Like many before him, he failed to appreciate the power to manipulate such a trait bestows.

"It's the same the world over, Spencer. Wherever they've got the same toxic value system. Pucky and co, they might talk about having a beef, the Latinos they talk about machismo, in the Middle East it's called *thar* I believe. Even you English had your pistols at dawn. The Albanians call it *lekë*, and they goddamn wrote the book on killing for honor."

"So where do we fit into this?"

"Can't you guess? While these guys are so busy beefing, they can't handle their business. And if they do, they do it sloppily so when they get big, they get taken down real quick by wiretaps and the Feds' money-laundering guys. Or they get taken down for a murder rap. It's a shame because they're making money. So we handle their business. We clean their money and take a cut. A big cut. And we stay out of trouble."

"Sounded like they think our cut's too big for them, like they want to take your, I mean our, service in-house."

Johnny Boy chuckled, waving Spencer into an alley behind a row of stores. "Yeah, well that wasn't the first time I've heard that kind of sentiment. Funny thing is, though, something always comes along to distract them."

What Johnny Boy neglected to mention was that he, McGrath, Cal, and the Yo-Yo would be bossing it at Algernon's seafood restaurant over on Grosse Pointe that Friday. Hearing what Pucky had to say was too good not to celebrate. They'd be asking the Yo-Yo to treat the table to his Spanish as he performed his bare-hand party trick on everybody's lobster claws. Or maybe they'd invite everyone: Denny, new boy Eddie, maybe even Spencer for the laugh of hearing him speak. But if they did that, then they'd keep quieter about what they were celebrating. Careful was how Dom liked to roll, and Johnny Boy was down with that. Finding out Rosso had been a snitch had shaken the hell out of everyone. Needless risks were for their clients in the Game.

For the next few hours, Spencer and Johnny Boy visited three respectable-looking businesses in Livonia: a bakery, an Italian restaurant, and a barber. The money they'd picked up from Nately Place was handed over slickly with a handshake. School photographs were shown off by the manager while a bag of clean money was handed back in a food hamper. Business was roaring in the suburbs.

And while Spencer drove in that special way of his, he assimilated the additional precautions that Johnny Boy had insisted on. He did it willingly, intuitively. There was something exciting about the job. Maybe it was seeing just how much money was flying around.

"You only hand money to the name written next to that company on the board in Dom's office, Spencer. If he isn't there looking out for you as you pull up, you can put your head around the door, but think of a reason why. Other than leaving him some money. He might have some for you. If he does, you check it, message me the amount, and I message you what to do with it. Maybe come back to the depot for some new drop-off locations."

Johnny Boy removed the last bag from the speaker case before they hit the road again.

"See this, Spencer? Bigger, right? That's because we've got a moving drop. If it's a moving drop, then that gets a third to a half of whatever you pick up."

"Why?"

"You'll see," said Johnny Boy, not looking up as he read a message on his phone. "Head up Farmington and take a left on Lyndon."

Five minutes later they were waiting in the Eddie Edgar Ice Arena lot but at the back, under some tree branches that needed cutting. Johnny Boy was intently working his phone, looking up whenever he heard a vehicle.

Spencer glanced at Johnny Boy's phone as Johnny Boy flipped from Facebook to Instagram. It seemed as if Johnny Boy worked social media like Abby worked her Spotify.

"I thought you said no Facebook or anything?"

He didn't look up. "It's not my Facebook, Spencer. Keep your eye on the entrance over there. You're looking for a green-and-white delivery truck. Name on the side is AtoB. These guys are couriers, so if we give them some money to process, they're going to divide it up on their rounds. So they can handle more. It means more people taking their little cuts, but it's safer. They're doing the same kind of thing as you. We work together."

"He's here," said Spencer.

The truck drove slowly into the lot. When the driver looked their way, Johnny Boy gave a discreet wave. The truck headed over and parked beside them. Real close.

"Window down, Spencer."

The courier driver did the same. Spencer recognized the uniform of green pants and shirt with its white pocket flaps and sleeve stripes. The courier was a fat, unfriendly-looking Hispanic guy with a regular Freddie Mercury moustache, its thickness probably encouraged to cover acne scarring.

Johnny Boy passed Spencer the last bag of money and motioned him to throw it to the courier. The courier threw a bag back at them. "There's thirteen seven in there. How much in this?" the courier asked.

Johnny Boy leaned forward so he could see the face of the courier through Spencer's window. "Six nine."

The courier nodded. He had a quick look inside the bag before stuffing it into a gym bag behind his seat. He nodded at Spencer. "Who's this?"

"Rosso's replacement."

The guy looked long and hard at Spencer. "He find you?"

Johnny Boy seemed to be expecting a question along these lines because he fired his answer back without hesitation. "I found him. Random. Not from around here."

"Hey," said the courier to Spencer. "Where you from?"

Spencer hesitated before answering. "Britain."

The courier looked at Johnny Boy, then back at Spencer. His big swarthy moon of a face cracked into a smile. He shook his head as he started his truck. "Hey, Johnny Boy, McGrath? He don't pay you enough."

They watched him drive off. "Why'd you hesitate, Spencer?"

"That question, it just kind of irritates me."

"Well, get over it. You hesitate on a question like that with these people, any of these people we met today, they get nervous. You don't want that. OK, day's over. Back to the depot."

He was about to hit his phone again but then: "And Spencer? Cal and I check all these numbers. Cal especially. You probably don't need telling that you made an enemy of him. That doesn't take much, but you took it to the Super Bowl. I know you got . . . shall we call them personal expenses? Keep them and what we pay you separate from the cash you're dealing with. We pay generously, but you fuck with us, well, Cal, he's the type of guy who takes it personal. You get me?"

He went back to his phone.

* * *

In the cyberworld, folks can be whatever they want. A forty-year-old guy can be a schoolgirl in the sixth grade looking for playmates. A 250-pound menopausal preacher's wife in South Dakota can be a lonely model in Louisiana looking for love. As Spencer drove them back to the depot, following a roundabout route of course, Johnny Boy was a hot little nineteen-year-old Black girl working as a retail assistant in Midtown. Over the last month, she'd made friends with a bunch of guys who bounced around Nately Place and a bunch of girls who hung with the guys around Clark Park and the Vernor Highway. And boy did those girls like to talk about the hot guys. And boy did those Vernor guys not like it when they got a little taste of how chicks really talked about men. Why, they could get downright jealous and insecure. Especially when they got blown out on a date by some hot chick who seemed peachy keen until she'd met a guy called Scoop who said all the guys around Vernor were little-dicked faggots, especially so-and-so and so-and-so. And hell, no one likes to be called a faggot in the hood. It was the kind of thing that would fracture a blossoming little alliance and make things flare up hotter than hell's waiting room. Making war could be a part-time job and it could be darned fun too.

"Where are you guys headed?"

Abby and Chris looked around to see Spencer standing by the car with two bags of groceries and looking mightily pleased about it.

Chris hesitated. "You're back earlier than you said. I was just running Abby over to Amy's."

"Chris, I got this. You've been like the school bus driver. I've got a car again."

"Hey, no, we're ready to go. And you got the groceries there."

"Can we just go, Chris, Amy's messaging?" said Abby suddenly.

Spencer looked over and saw she wasn't holding her phone. Chris noticed too. There was a moment's silence.

"What's up, guys?" said Spencer.

"Nothing's up," said Abby, a little flustered. "I just want Chris to take me today. He's been working and, and he might get that thing that kills people who don't move their legs enough."

"A DVT? Well, Chris can just go for a walk?"

"Dad, can we talk about this later?" She paused, then spoke in a rush. "Amy's parents think you're weird, OK? They say one second you're grumpy then you're like, super happy. I, uh, said you aren't, OK?"

Chris inhaled through his nose and looked straight ahead.

Abby turned on Chris's radio and started flicking through the stations.

Chris signaled Spencer to lean in. "She's Marielle's daughter. Marielle used to run rings around your ass."

And with that, he drove out of the lot.

Spencer watched the Prius trundle up McLean, the heat haze distorting its outline by the time it reached the light. He kept watching as it disappeared into the flow of traffic, watching but not really seeing.

15

Red Mist

If you're not a race driver, stay the hell home. Don't come here and grumble about going too fast. Get the hell out of the race car if you've got feathers on your butt. Put a kerosene rag around your ankles so the ants won't climb up and eat that candy ass.

—Dale Earnhardt

Spencer was getting worked pretty hard but there was something about the driving that McGrath and Johnny Boy wanted from him that came naturally. It was different from racing and yet just as demanding. But it was also somewhat enjoyable. Spencer had stopped enjoying racing. He couldn't remember exactly when. It had probably been a slow burn. The thing about racing was that the pressure was immense. If you raced, you raced to win. Second place was first loser. It had gotten to Spencer after a while. Everyone had race nerves, but Spencer's pre-race nerves got to be so bad, they fucked his performance sometimes, causing him to make the mistakes he feared making.

But this, this driving for McGrath, there wasn't the same pressure. There wasn't winning or losing. There was just moving. Moving like mercury through traffic driven by different, slower beings. And then the checking, the tricking: it was like a game, a game within the Game of which Johnny Boy spoke and along the edges of which Spencer now danced, like a dragonfly skimming over a lake—flying, hovering, occasionally touching to take but not tussling with the birds or fish, yet feeding plentifully all the same.

Night or day, wet or dry. Spencer powered through the dark and broken parts of town doing his rounds and then crisscrossed the suburbs that seemed to flourish from Detroit's pain. But just as in nature there are careless creatures that follow the same path or drink from the same watering hole, Spencer didn't realize predators were everywhere in this way of life. They watched from alleys and street corners, the human equivalent of a trapdoor spider waiting in its hole for some hapless creature to make the mistake its mother warned it never to make. Forgetfulness, laziness, pre-occupation: Darwinian sins that can be just as momentous for a modern man.

Biggy Freak watched the light down on Gallagher and Davison. The traffic stacked up here, after coming off the freeway—where it was safe enough to have a window down seeing as no wiseass was gonna jack your car at seventy.

Biggy Freak had a few places he liked to watch, but this was his favorite. He'd loaf around in the shadow of the underpass behind a line of dumpsters, watching through the gaps at the victims lining up, getting all sacrificial-like. He could work his magic (he called it freakin' them with the Biggy Freak) and then choose one of three escape routes, none of which anyone in their right mind would follow him down. And he was one big mother to boot: 6'4" in his Converse with a long-assed Chuck Norris of a blade hangin' in his pants, so it was no matter that his gun didn't work. Ain't no chicken hoe gonna take that chance, especially some whitey business guy who'd forgotten to put his window back up as he smoked a cig in his fully loaded Infiniti like he hadn't a care in the world.

The first Spencer knew of his carelessness was when his head was forced back by the barrel of a gun shoved hard into his chin.

"What up, G, in your G35?"

Spencer nearly swallowed his cigarette. It tipped to the side, spilling hot ash down his cheek. He yelled and instinctively tried to jerk his head to the side. Biggy Freak kept a firm hold. He'd seen it coming. He liked shocking these dumbass suckers. Grit on them fast and hard, don't give 'em time to get their shit together.

"Unload that Michigan bankroll, friend."

Spencer attempted to get a bead on the situation. All he could see was a huge black face shaded by a Tigers cap pulled low. He couldn't even see for sure that it was the barrel of a gun at his throat, but he certainly didn't want to take the chance. His head had been forced so far back it had slipped between the headrest and the door pillar, so he couldn't reach the wheel even though the car was in Drive. If he simply took off, he'd hit the car in front.

"Get the fuck on with it, motherfucker, or I'm gonna unload this bitch through your sorry-assed skull." Biggy Freak loved his work, loved the easy money, loved being able to impress his girl with the lines he'd used during the day. Shanique had sure gotten wet for that one.

"OK," grunted Spencer. "Let me reach for the glove compartment. I'll give you my cash, no worries." He stretched out his right arm and waggled his fingers. He gave a silent prayer of gratitude for having followed Johnny Boy's advice thirty minutes before. He'd been collecting all day and had two rolling drops coming up that night. There had to be forty thousand stuffed in the car's speaker casements.

"Yeah, you reach, bitch." Biggy Freak pushed Spencer over toward the glove compartment, keeping the barrel of the pistol up tight in his flesh. This guy would have something to remember Biggy Freak by next time he shaved.

Spencer opened the glove compartment and pulled out his wallet. He went to open it, but Biggy Freak snatched the whole thing off him.

"Now gimme the phone."

"You don't want my phone, man, it's—"

"I'll tell you what the fuck I want, bitch, and if I say I—"

"Mate, it's thumbprint. It won't work for you." Spencer knew he was taking a risk, but he was gambling that the guy would be happy he got the ready cash and would want to split.

"Fine, give me that watch."

Spencer looked at his watch with its brushed-steel case that would catch the sun sometimes as he turned the wheel. It was the watch Marielle had given him on their fifth wedding anniversary, bought secretly on finance, paid off less than a year before she died.

"Come on, man, it's not worth much." Spencer prayed desperately for the douchebag up front to just get the hell out of his way so he could floor the gas and save this little bit of Marielle's love that he still carried.

"Give me that watch, you sorry-assed cocksucker, or I'm gonna fuck you the hell up." Biggy Freak wasn't looking for lines to arouse Shanique now.

Spencer felt sick. He thought about the forty thousand cash in the trunk. Two casements. Twenty thousand in each. He could give this guy one load. Twenty thou, not as bad as losing everything. "Dude, let me give you more money. I've got a lot more in the back. If you let me—"

The barrel of Biggy Freak's harmless pistol felt as if it would punch through the soft flesh between Spencer's Adam's apple and his jaw. He was in instant agony, lifting off the seat to try and lessen the pressure.

Biggy Freak showered him with spit as he shouted in his ear. "Last chance, motherfucker!"

Spencer scrabbled his watch off. Biggy Freak snatched it out of his hand and was gone before Spencer could catch his breath. Up ahead, the light changed and the guy in front pulled away. Spencer watched him go. He felt sick.

Spencer had hours to kill before meeting the AtoB guys. He couldn't settle. He wanted to do something about what had happened but couldn't think of anything viable. Anger and frustration grew as he aimlessly cruised the streets. When a guy in a Lexus cut him off at a red light on Van Dyke, Spencer went vector compound. He drove right up the guy's ass while revving his engine and yelling insults. Lexus guy ignored it. Spencer, out of control and ready to rumble, opened his door. Lexus guy took off before the light changed, unnerved by how insanely pissed this guy was over a minor beef.

In the small streets south of McNichols and just north of Hamtramck, Spencer coasted past empty houses with smoke-blackened window frames and small, dilapidated apartment blocks with sagging realtor signs. Up ahead, cop cars and a crowd of bystanders blocked the road.

Shouting, radio squawk, and the smell of the hot, sweaty crowd filled his car. A woman cried, cops held shotguns. Over their heads he could see the top of a house in which all things bad had probably happened.

The car shielded him from the reality that was going down but didn't exonerate him; he'd done pickups not far from there. He turned, punched the gas, and headed east to nowhere in particular.

After a while he found himself in an abandoned industrial area. It was strangely peaceful. A light wind moaned amid the desolation. Dust devils danced.

A plane flew low overhead, across the falling sun.

Spencer cruised slowly through the Detroit that was: the arsenal of democracy that fueled the American war machine, helped to bring down the Japs and the Krauts, then filled the country with cars and the music the workers listened to while building them. And now he was viewing these skeletal behemoths in a Japanese car. He drove on, killing time.

His work phone pinged. He ignored it.

Another plane flew very low overhead: freight, not passenger.

He turned into the art deco entranceway of a derelict factory. Immediately he had to slam on his brakes. Some of the concrete floor had collapsed, forming a trench, its edge hidden by shadow.

He got out, walked around the trench and into the cavernous loading bay. Sunlight spilled through a doorway at the far end. The doorway led to a stairwell. Looking out, he saw that he was now several stories up. The front of the building was on one level, but behind it the ground dropped steeply away to some old railway sidings and a highway storage area with great piles of gravel.

Spencer looked at his bare wrist. He felt an actual pain in his chest at the thought of his watch. Gone forever, probably already pawned, lost, like his love for this place. Spencer had taken on his wife's loyalty to Michigan's broken heart, that love felt all the keener by Detroiters, knowing as they did the rest of the country's fretful disdain and hating.

Another plane flew over, so low the cracked window glass rattled.

Christ, he needed a drink.

16

Shooting the Shit

"With absolute respect, Cap, I disagree," said Batiste.

Captain Schaeffer took a deep breath. "Evan, listen to me. I'm trying to help you. If I put your Dominic McGrath into the Drug Trafficking Areas database, there's no one else working him or his outfit. No one's interested in him. He hasn't been tied to any murders, narcotics-related or otherwise, and he doesn't control any narcotics sales in any part of the city. You've been working him for months and all we've got is two low-level bodies, a nurse with a caved-in skull and a cop who won't be able to speak for weeks. No one's looking good right now."

Batiste said nothing.

Scott was intrigued. The last time he'd been in their superior's office, Captain Schaeffer had seemed a little beat. But this was more like the ass-kicking name-taker the guy used to be, the guy who'd earned the Medal of Valor on the wall behind him, in a good old hostage situation no less.

"You guys know who killed Rosso?" asked Schaeffer.

"We do," said Batiste.

"Bring him in, take the credit. Draw a line under this whole thing. This isn't a request."

Batiste hesitated, then decided to risk all. "Cap, have you ever wondered why McGrath still exists if he's small fry? Why doesn't he get swallowed up or whacked by the bigger guys? It's because they can't stop fighting each other and McGrath's not like them. That's how he stays off our radar. But he gives a service second to none and only his scumbag lawyer and accountant know how big it is," said Batiste.

"No, Evan, it's just you who knows. McGrath *is* small fry."

"No one's analyzing stats in DPD, Cap. We're all too busy rushing from one 911 to the next. I did some pondering. The mayor and his buddies are saying narcotics activity is going down, because less money is getting recovered from drug trafficking. And in a way, they're right. But really, it can't be right, because if you look at almost all the High Intensity Drug Trafficking Areas in this city, the number of drug-related busts has stayed pretty much the same over the last four years. Same in Livonia, Dearborn, Fraser, Redford, a bunch of suburbs basically."

"You checked Metro Detroit too?"

Scott noted Schaeffer was surprised and a little impressed, just as he himself had been.

"Sure. Loads of those white boys have money for drugs, so the trade grew in the suburbs. It just doesn't look so gritty. But busts are still being made there too. Yet, in spite of the number of busts going on, there's been a fifty to seventy-five percent drop in dirty money being recovered. So this means less of the busts lead to a successful prosecution, so hey, everyone's happy because it seems we're winning this war."

"And you're saying McGrath's handling all of that fifty to seventy-five percent?"

"Why else would I be putting us all through this? All of us—and you know what I mean by that."

Scott's phone vibrated, drawing everyone's attention in the silence. He apologized, took it out, and glanced at the screen. His wife. Would he be able to get away early? He'd promised. Their youngest had a lead role in the school play. He switched it to silent and put it back in his pocket.

Captain Schaeffer sat back in his seat, eyeing them both. And suddenly, Scott thought he looked old again. His uniform seemed to hang off his sagging shoulders.

Scott also felt a little uneasy about what his partner had given up. Correct protocol would be to involve other law enforcement agencies in something big. He knew Batiste wanted to use this case as his ticket out. That wouldn't happen if Schaeffer made them play by the book. Scott didn't care so much. He was secretly toying with the idea of transferring to the coast guard. He had a buddy there who made less money yet seemed to have a better quality of life—and marriage.

Schaeffer spoke as if thinking aloud. "The mayor said I should be calling in the FBI for this homicide. What do I tell him?"

"The FBI isn't interested in small time," said Batiste. "They want the people up the chain: politicians, maybe the odd mayor. Tell him that from the detective in charge of this case."

Neither of them expected Schaeffer to do anything of the kind.

* * *

Milt Blake was happy to shoot the shit all night long. What was the alternative? Watching the bugs going mad for the lights over the pumps? The TV? The TV that had to play promo crap round and round on a loop. That would surely drive him Old Man Jenkins.

Milt always worked the graveyard shift at the gas station store. Didn't care much for the daytime rush. People just flying through, barely having time for a howdy doody. This time of night, he could meet some mighty interesting folk, like the guy he was talking to right now. British guy. The way they spoke was awful sophisticated-sounding. The guy paid cash for his gas. Old school. He seemed like he'd had a hog wild day and just needed to catch his breath.

"Damn right the AC in here is topflight," Milt was agreeing. "Whenever the D's havin' a hotter-than-hell spell, I like seeing the relief on folks' shiny faces."

Spencer wasn't paying much attention, but the good ole boy working the till was helping time pass.

"And if you don't mind my sayin', I saw you taking a few pulls on that flask of yours, sir, and I just about came right out and said you may as well come into the cool and drink 'cause I seen you anyhow."

Milt laughed at the other man's discomfiture. "What you really gotta ask is if you taking a swig is hurtin' anyone. It'd be a sin if your drinking brought a blight to a good person's life. That's a lesson I learned too late."

"How so?"

"Ruined my marriage. I never went with another lady as long as I said 'I do,' but the bottle was a mistress the whole time we was together."

Spencer said nothing. The silence wasn't uncomfortable, but it let itself be heard nonetheless.

"If you don't mind my sayin' also," said Milt after a while, "you seem like you have a whole heap of shit on your mind."

Spencer didn't mind for some reason. The man had an easygoing, nonjudgmental affability and a worldliness to him. Spencer felt like telling him about his loss that day, how tired he felt most times.

Milt took off his blue company baseball cap and pushed back his mop of longish white-and-gray hair. He had a thick moustache and eyes that crinkled right up at the corners, giving him the air of a Badlands sheriff. He pointed at his name badge. "Milt, by the way."

"Spencer."

"Good to meet you, Spencer. You live here?"

"Yeah."

"You seem at home . . . just not at peace."

A Chevy Suburban pulled up by a pump. The store door opened with a friendly *ding-a-ling* and an obese guy in khaki shorts and a Hawaiian shirt waddled in, paid, and waddled back out to start pumping forty-five gallons.

"What happened with your wife, Milt?"

"Long gone, son, lonnng gone. Along with my daughter. She's grown up now. Ain't seen either of them for nigh on twenty. They upped stakes to Florida when she was in the sixth grade. You married?"

"Was."

"She's passed, ain't she?"

Spencer nodded.

"What was her name?"

"Marielle."

"Sure is a beautiful name. What took your beautiful Marielle from this earth then?"

"She was driving her mother up on I-75. Tire blew out. Car went under a semi. She was dead before they stopped moving. Her mother took another three days to join her."

Milt nodded. They watched the Chevy chug out of the station.

"How come you never moved on? Most folks, after suffering somethin' traumatizing, they move on elsewhere."

"I don't know. Our daughter's schooling I guess."

"She must really like it here?"

"You'd have to ask her."

Milt smiled and gave a small shake of his head. Spencer caught it. "What?"

"Well, son, it's just a strange thing to say. If there's anyone on the Lord's earth who should ask a daughter shit like that, it's her father."

Spencer looked out at the small pool of brightness that was the gas station forecourt. A bastion of light hard-pressed on all sides by the gloom of the hot night: frontier land.

"It goes real quick, Spencer. The time we're given with people. My wife and daughter, they're most likely still alive. Couldn't say where. We're as good as dead to each other. Your girl? That's what you still have from your beautiful Marielle. I'm tellin' you though, they grow up fast these days, and if you ain't worth missing, then they'll be gone quicker than you might be expecting."

Bang! The shop door crashed open so hard it sent soda cans tumbling from shelves.

"What up, mofos!" yelled a guy as he strutted down the aisle toward them. He had his hood up and drawstring tight so most of his face was hidden. From what little they could see he was white and no older than twenty. He held a pistol on its side in that exaggerated, way-of-the-street manner. Behind him two more kids bounced in, hoods up, drawstrings tight. They were smaller, Black, no older than fourteen, possibly younger.

The guy with the gun aimed at Spencer's face. "What the fuck you lookin' at, faggot!"

You have got to be shitting me—twice in one day?

"Hey, calm down, buddy," attempted Milt soothingly. "It's all c—"

"You calm the fuck down, bitch!" said Pistol Pete. He lunged toward the counter, reaiming at Milt's face. As he did so, he called back over his shoulder. "Get the fuck on with it!"

His minions pulled out trash bags. One headed for the liquor aisle. The other went over the counter and started loading up on smokes. As he went, he smacked Milt's forehead with the heel of his palm. Seeing a kid do that to a guy of Milt's age jarred Spencer.

"Cash register, you old faggot!" said Pistol Pete.

Milt hesitated. "I need a sale to open it, man, I can't j—" he stopped when he felt a knife at his throat. The kid who'd been boosting the smokes now had his arm around Milt's neck. The only reason he could reach was because he was standing on the back counter. A frigging twelve-year-old dressed in a black tracksuit and huge Nike Airs.

Suddenly the gun was back on Spencer's face. "How about when I check this guy out? Yeah? That be a sale?"

"I got it," said Milt. He grabbed an air freshener and scanned it. The register bell rang and the cash tray slid open.

The kid with the knife turned back for the last of the smokes. Pistol Pete glanced out the window.

"They your wheels, faggot?" he asked Spencer.

"Yeah but—"

He was cut off by Pistol Pete racking the slide, chambering a round. "Fuck you. You're gonna look good with no—"

A split second before he fired, his gun hand was smacked with a baseball bat. The gun still went off though. Spencer felt a hot rush of air pass by his cheek. He fell back against the shelves and slithered to the floor on a rolling mass of canned corn and hot dogs. As he fought to stand, he saw Milt leaning right over the counter with a baseball bat.

The gun now lay equidistant from its owner and Spencer. They looked at each other, then at the gun. Both dived for it. Spencer tried to lock arms around the guy. As they fought, the gun disappeared under an ocean of Twinkies and Oreos.

17

Thankless Favors

It seemed to Spencer that the guy he was grappling with had fueled up on high-grade octane, maybe even nitro. Spencer was outclassed. He took an elbow to the nose, hard. Blood splashed up his face and in one eye. The guy broke free. Spencer knew he'd lost, knew it was time to run for his life.

He ducked around the corner of the shelf unit and then sprinted down the aisle to the back of the shop, yelling as he went.

"Run, Milt, run!"

Bang! and the glass door of a cooler dissolved in front of him. He skidded on the cascading glass, shoulder charged into the disabled john, slid on the wet floor, and smashed his shin on the edge of the toilet. He threw the lever lock just before the door shuddered in its frame. He guessed that was the liquor kid.

He leaned against the wall, catching his breath and watching the lock dubiously as the door vibrated from multiple impacts.

Time to get some law down here.

He dug in his pocket and found . . . nothing. He'd left his phone in the car, out of sight in the door in case he got jacked again. What a joke. What a shit-forsaken joke.

Suddenly a hole appeared in the door. Instantaneously part of the sink fell to the floor.

"I'm calling the cops, mate," shouted Spencer. He started a fake call but Pistol Pete interrupted the lame charade.

"I'm gonna kill the old guy out here. He your friend? He all wet up now, man. Think he gonna bleed out if you don't give me the key, man. We ain't walkin' home."

Fuck Johnny Boy's forty grand. And Cal. Milt's outside with those three.

Spencer slid his key under the door. He heard muttering and shuffling.

Thirty seconds later he heard a single gunshot.

Then a screech of tires.

Then silence.

Spencer pressed his ear to the tiny gap between door and frame. A knot of helpless anguish was tightening around his guts. He opened the door a hair's breadth and looked out. Tomato juice leaked out of the shot-up cooler. He could just see the convex anti-shoplifting mirror. Nothing moved.

Spencer rushed to the counter and leaned over. Milt lay on his front, motionless in a sea of gum, condoms, and pill packets. His uniform denim shirt was dark crimson, peppered with darker little slits where he'd been stabbed. There was a dime-size hole in his shoulder blade. Blood pooled on the floor around his chest. One of his fingers twitched.

Spencer clambered over the counter. He went down on one knee, put his hand on Milt's shoulder, and gave it a gentle shake. "Milt?"

Milt groaned.

He patted Milt down and found a phone in the front pocket of his pants. It was a real retro model, but at least it wasn't locked. He called 911.

He needed to call Johnny Boy, but he didn't have any numbers. He cursed the strict number-changing etiquette McGrath's crew insisted on, unless it was Spencer. They didn't seem to mind if he didn't change his phone. The thought bothered and distracted him.

Suddenly he remembered the ride home with Johnny Boy the day the dealership died. Johnny Boy had given Spencer a business card.

He dialed the one number he always knew by heart.

A groggy voice answered. "Hi Dad, sorry, I meant to switch it off but Sam's cat's gone missing and—"

"Abby—"

"Chris said I could keep it on in case. Sam's not my boyfriend though."

"Abby! Look, I've got—"

"Problems at work."

"Huh?"

"You've got problems at work."

"Why are you calling this number?"

Spencer gave Johnny Boy a rehash of what had gone down.

Ever so gently, Milt's fingers twitched against Spencer's. Still the same ads played on the TV. A zero gravity chair could be his for two hundred tokens. Loyalty here sure paid off.

"I can't leave him."

"The guy's injured, been shot you say? So tell me, are you some kind of expert on gunshot trauma? You an ER doc when you aren't selling fancy cars and shit?"

"No."

"That's what I thought. And seeing as the guys who are experts in this kind of thing are currently hightailing it to that place, the very place where you're doing diddly-squat, then it would seem like you've done all you can. Am I right?"

"I guess."

"So get your ass out of there." He hung up.

18

Ash in the Night

From the street corner, Spencer watched the medics roll their gurney toward the ambulance. A blanket covered Milt's face. The flashing blues of the ambulance and cop cars seemed washed out by the gas station's dazzling lights. The medics moved through the strobe lights like painted figures in the spinning drum of one of those old zoetrope toys.

"Time to move on, Spencer."

He turned to see a dark-suited Dominic McGrath emerge from the shadows like some spectral mortician. Spencer hadn't even heard Johnny Boy's Merc SUV pull up. Now its engine purred softly in the dark, the Yo-Yo at the wheel. Johnny Boy held the rear door open for Spencer.

A few minutes later they were driving south on Woodward. The atmosphere in the car was weirdly calm, as if this were just something that could happen in their line of work, a little unpleasant, sure, but not unheard of. Spencer could tell that all three of them had had other plans that evening. They'd come together to take care of this "little situation" as McGrath referred to it. He sat in the back with Spencer, asking him about his day. He seemed genuinely concerned about the watch.

"No shit. Up on Gallagher and Davison?"

"Yeah, where you leave the freeway. Big guy in a Tigers cap."

"Sentimental value?"

Spencer was too exhausted to equivocate. "Last thing my wife gave me."

McGrath nodded, knowing when to drop something.

In the front, Johnny Boy peered at a satellite map on his iPad. He muttered instructions to the Yo-Yo, who obeyed in silence.

"You put AtoB in the loop?" asked McGrath.

"Yeah," said Johnny Boy. "Sheila's rearranging for tomorrow, depending on how this pans out."

"You got anything for Spencer's face? Our guy's taken a pounding for us here."

Neither Johnny Boy nor the Yo-Yo even looked around. Johnny Boy opened the glove compartment, took out a pack of tissues, and passed them back, barely taking his eyes off his screen the whole time.

They rolled through the hot city night, past dumpsters and derelict houses, cocooned in air-conditioned, cream-leather luxury. Spencer rubbed at his hands. They felt so dry. Each time the car passed under a streetlight he could see Milt's blood in the creases of his knuckles and palms and fingernails. He just couldn't get rid of it, no matter how hard he tried.

"Tell us about these guys, Spencer," said McGrath.

Spencer gave them a rundown as they homed in ever closer on his phone's tracker.

"The guy with the gun, Dom, he's totally willing to use it, so—"

"These little punks, Spence, they don't want to hold on to a hot float, just want to joyride it a little, be the big *I am*, then dump it somewhere near whatever shithole they crawled out of. It'll be fine. We just need to find it before they carbecue it."

"In there," said Johnny Boy, pointing down an alley.

The Yo-Yo pulled over.

McGrath looked around. Boarded shops, empty offices, no street lighting. Utterly deserted, as if mankind had vacated the planet while they'd been driving. "Take us down there slowly. Lights off."

The Yo-Yo overrode the automatic headlights. They turned into the alley. Their progress was almost silent but for the crunch of tire on trash and rubble. All four men scanned the shadows. Fire escapes, piles of garbage, and the occasional wrecked car loomed and glided silently by.

Johnny Boy signaled the Yo-Yo to stop. He killed the air, dropped his window, listened, then waved the Yo-Yo on again. A few moments later he again signaled a halt. He cocked his head slightly, sensing something. Then Spencer heard it too: the faint boom of heavy bass.

With the subtlest gesture, Johnny Boy signaled the Yo-Yo to proceed.

The bass got louder. It sounded like a hip-hop beat.

With the car's air-conditioning off, Spencer felt sweat gather on his throat and trickle into the collar of his T-shirt. He looked at the others. He was the only one who seemed to be feeling the heat.

The alley narrowed and then ended abruptly at a wall of blackness.

The music was getting louder.

As they passed the last buildings, Spencer realized the blackness was a vast open wasteland. Beyond shimmered the sliding mass of the Detroit River. Lights twinkled far away on the Canadian side of the water.

About a hundred yards in front, Spencer saw a small glow—the interior light of his car. Every now and then whooping and laughter would cut through the aggressive beat of whatever station they'd retuned his radio to. He gave his speakers a one-day life span at the rate they were being pulverized.

McGrath leaned forward between the seats, assessing the situation. Johnny Boy looked at him. "We could back off, wait up for a while?"

"Could wait all night," said McGrath, without taking his eyes off the Infiniti. "Could wait all night and then not have time to do anything if they light it up. And then you got, how many of these little fucks did you say there were, Spence?"

"Three, but two of them were only—"

"Three. So you got three little wannabe Gs running around, making the situation way more difficult to control."

Silent, the Yo-Yo awaited instruction.

"A little closer. Let's see what they're doing." The music was so loud that McGrath could talk normally without fear of betraying their presence.

Spencer felt his guts tighten. He hadn't expected to meet these punks again.

"Dom, these guys—" he started, but McGrath cut him off with a raised hand.

More laughter rippled through the music. It surprised Spencer how young it sounded, like the laughter of a child.

By the time the Yo-Yo stopped, they were barely thirty yards away. The Infiniti's front doors were open. One of the trio sat behind the wheel with his hood down and face exposed. Spencer guessed the kid bouncing in the seat probably wasn't even old enough to drive. Beside him, Pistol Pete yelled down a phone while smoking a joint. The kid in the back leaned forward and passed a joint to his buddy behind the wheel. They were oblivious of being watched.

McGrath sat back in his seat. "Yo-Yo?"

The Yo-Yo's head turned only slightly.

"Happy with this?"

The Yo-Yo looked back at the car. He gave a small nod.

"Johnny Boy?"

Johnny Boy looked around. "They picked a nice place."

"Yeah, they did, didn't they? Yo-Yo, go get my fucking money."

Apparently the Yo-Yo didn't need second tellings. He just got out. Instantly. When he reappeared through the windshield, he was holding a huge caliber, long-barreled pistol. Not having to worry about being quiet, he moved fast toward the Infiniti. He was only ten yards away when its back door suddenly opened. The Yo-Yo stopped, dropped to a half crouch, and raised his gun. Spencer stopped breathing.

But the kid in the back hadn't seen anything. He leaped out and ran to the open front door. He looked even younger than his buddy, no more than twelve or thirteen. Spencer struggled with the fact that these, these *children*, had pulled knives on Milt and him. The kid crouched down by his friend. They put their G faces on and made two-finger gang signs as they selfied up.

As the kid made his way back to the rear of the Infiniti, it seemed he would notice the Yo-Yo for sure, poised just within the pale pool of light encircling the car. But since the kid didn't want to waste a moment to broadcast his badass ways to whatever posse followed his every deed, he kept his head down almost all the way. Almost. Because just before he swung back in the car, something bothered him, jogging his mind's shoulder: a primordial instinct, an imperfection in the blackness that enveloped their little world. Whatever it was, it made him look up, directly at the Yo-Yo.

His eyes widened and his head tilted as he tried to make sense of what he was seeing—a huge white guy pointing a pistol straight at him. And that was the last thing he ever tried to make sense of before the Yo-Yo's gun flashed and boomed, blowing his brains out of the back of his head and over his buddy in the front seat. His buddy yelled in shock and then kept yelling. His high-pitched scream overlaid the staccato urban beat and wafted over to the three men in the SUV.

The Yo-Yo strode to the front of the car. The kid behind the wheel looked up, eyes wide and terrified, face dripping red with the cranial detritus of his friend. He yelled until the Yo-Yo's gun boomed again, throwing him out of his seat and headfirst down into the passenger footwell.

There was a flash from inside the car and a small bang, almost a pop. Pistol Pete had gotten his act together. The Yo-Yo stepped aside and crouched while more flashes lit up the car interior. The rear windshield dissolved. The guy was firing blind. The Yo-Yo leaned against the rear fender. One of his feet was actually on the hand of the first kid's corpse. He took careful aim through the open rear door, through the front passenger seat, and fired again.

Moments later, Pistol Pete appeared in front of the Infiniti clutching his right arm, bug-eyed, hyperventilating. He half crouched, half fell against the front of the car, looked back frantically over both shoulders, and then took off. He hadn't made ten yards before the Yo-Yo's cannon sheered through one of his hips. He went down flailing and proceeded to spin on the ground like an injured fly. One of his Nikes flew off as he kicked at rubble. The Yo-Yo walked up to him and quickly put in a head shot, bringing the deranged movement to an abrupt halt. The Yo-Yo fired one more time. He then returned to the car and fired a carefully aimed shot at each of the kids.

Johnny Boy grunted his approval at this thoroughness. Spencer was transfixed by what he was seeing, and the calm demeanor of his companions freaked him out even more. He'd been thinking the day couldn't get much worse.

Still the music thumped on.

The Yo-Yo returned his gun to his jacket and went to the rear of Spencer's car. He opened the trunk, leaned in and retrieved the money. Moments later he was striding back to Johnny Boy's SUV. Spencer looked for a trace of adrenaline, some vestige of discomfort in the man's face but saw none. It was like watching a cyborg at work. He passed the two bags of money to Johnny Boy and was just about to walk to the rear of their car when McGrath called him back.

"Can you do something about that unholy racket?"

The Yo-Yo walked back to Spencer's car, looked inside, frowned, stepped back, drew his gun again and pumped three rounds into the dash.

The sudden silence broke the spell of horror that was keeping Spencer in his seat. Needing to move, to breathe, he opened his door, slid out of his seat, and leaned against the car. His legs felt leaden as he dragged the warm night air into his lungs. He could smell the mud of the river, fermenting in the heat, could hear a police siren—miles away, though, across the water on the Canadian side. No one was coming for these guys. No one came quickly for anyone these days it seemed. Spencer moved to the front of Johnny Boy's car and slumped against the hood.

Johnny Boy and McGrath watched him through the windshield.

"How do you think your boy's coping there, Dom?"

McGrath thought about it for a moment. "Raising his stress thresholds is all."

Johnny Boy snorted. "Looks close to busting if you ask me."

"We didn't hire him for how chillaxed he could be watching the Yo-Yo go Nagasaki. If it weren't for these little fucks, Spencer could've done what we need him to do with Max Petrovsky and been none the wiser. This," McGrath nodded at the Yo-Yo at work, "this is going to cause him some degree of, uh—"

"Introspection?"

"Exactly. But the guy scared the shit out of me in a car a while back. Left you in the dust as I recall. He has it in him to handle heat."

Johnny Boy watched Spencer walk a few yards and then sit down heavily on a pile of bricks to dry retch. "Well, be that as it may, he sure doesn't know it yet."

They watched the Yo-Yo drag Pistol Pete's body, still wearing one sneaker, back to the Infiniti. He hurled it on the windshield.

"That peewee goodfella, the first one the Yo-Yo smoked?" said McGrath. "He seemed familiar, before his face got wiped."

"Yeah, I thought that," said Johnny Boy. "Been mullin' it. It'll come to me."

"Might be able to use him."

"Clark Park," said Johnny Boy.

"Clark Park. That's it." A pause. Then, "You thinking what I'm thinking?"

"Pucky's crew?"

"Would be a shame if the Clark Park homies over at the Vernor Highway thought one of their little bros was whacked by one of Pucky's guys, wouldn't it? Just when they're getting all tight 'n' all."

"Yeah," said Johnny Boy. "Could feed a little tidbit in on the grapevine. Put in a few facts only the cops or the killers would know. Always good to capitalize on good fortune."

"Like the way you roll on that social media shit." With that, McGrath got out of the car.

The Yo-Yo fetched a jerrican from the SUV's trunk and emptied it over the Infiniti.

"Anything you need from your car, Spence?" asked McGrath, now standing beside him.

Spencer struggled to think about anything other than what he'd just witnessed.

"I, uh, my phone, I guess."

McGrath called out to the Yo-Yo to wait before lighting up the automotive pyre.

The Yo-Yo stepped back to allow Spencer access. He flipped the lid on his Zippo impatiently. The killing had been loud. It was time to be somewhere else.

Spencer delved into the driver's door. He did this carefully to avoid the gore. He grabbed his phone and his hip flask, unaware that the Yo-Yo was watching closely.

Spencer scanned his car's interior. The kid in the footwell's eyes were open and looking in different directions. The Yo-Yo had delivered the extra bullet, the act of thoroughness of which Johnny Boy had so approved, through the temple and it had turned everything inside out on its way through. For a moment, Spencer thought he was going to retch again.

"You wanna make friends with him in there, Spencer, or do you wanna hurry the fuck up?"

Spencer was about to get out when he caught the eye of a dead president poking out of the bag underneath the kid's body. He looked at George Washington's blood-spattered white cravat, wondering how he'd never noticed that the faces on dollar bills seemed to stare right at you, with this look that said, *I know what you did to get your hands on me.*

"Spencer, I swear I'm gonna light you up with them."

Spencer thought about the bag of money, about Milt, who'd filled it barely an hour before, and wondered what to do. Let it burn? Because he felt guilty about Milt? What good would that do? Then it would be just ash in the night.

He lunged into the car and felt a wet crunch under his hand— a fragment of something, something that had been part of one of these guys. With his other hand he pulled at the bag—but it wouldn't move. The kid's body was pinning it to the floor.

"Spencer!"

Spencer had to put his shoulder on the passenger seat in order to free up both hands. It brought his face within inches of the blood-doused fabric. Even through the aroma of gasoline he could smell urine. Pistol Pete had pissed himself when he'd been shot through his seat. Spencer slid his left hand under the kid's shoulder, feeling ragged flaps of skin. His fingers slipped in mush as he tried to lift the corpse a few inches to free the bag.

Sweet Jesus, how did I get here?

Spencer knew he'd see that kid's face with its fucked-up eyes and George with his bloodied cravat judging him for the rest of his days. He was barely out when there was a great *woomph* and the car was engulfed in flames. The heat buffeted his face as he staggered backward, unable to take his eyes off the ungodly tableau.

The Yo-Yo threw the faceless corpse of the first kid in the back. By some macabre fluke, he landed in his original seat, sitting up. Spencer watched his hair smoke and then flare, watched the outline of his body in the crackling flames. A child. Someone's child. What chances had he had?

And then McGrath was beside him. "This'll just look like a case of thieves falling out." He spoke almost soothingly. *Don't worry, this might seem a little hectic but it's actually all that and a bag of Fritos really.*

The burning kid keeled slowly over in his seat. Spencer dragged his eyes away to look at McGrath. He wanted to see what made this man tick, this man he'd thought he could smooth talk into a hare-brained scheme to sell some fancy cars. McGrath had been funny, charming, mischievous. Yeah, there'd been something, something dangerous. But Spencer hadn't thought of anything like this. Maybe some dodgy deals, a little stash of cash, some fun with the wrong women at the right parties, perhaps even a shallow friendship based on mutual business advantage. That's what Spencer thought McGrath would bring to his table.

McGrath took a deep breath through his nose, held it inside for a few seconds, like he was enjoying the smell of burning leaves in his garden, and then exhaled with a content smile. He looked at the vortex of ash and sparks billowing into the night sky. *My, what a goddamn fine evening it's turned out to be.*

McGrath put his hand on Spencer's shoulder. Gave it a friendly squeeze. "Shall we take you home, my man?"

"What shall I do with this?" Spencer held up the bloodied bag.

"Keep it. You earned it." He got back in Johnny Boy's car.

The Yo-Yo, cigarette in mouth and face cast in stone, returned with the jerrican. He walked right up to Spencer.

"Hands."

Spencer looked at him, confused.

"Hold out your hands."

Spencer did so. The Yo-Yo raised the jerrican and sprinkled the dregs on Spencer's hands. He dropped the can on the floor. Then he leaned down and in, bringing his face up close to Spencer's. He sniffed his breath. Spencer felt like Jack hiding from the giant, sniffing out the blood of an Englishman.

The Yo-Yo straightened. He took Spencer's hands, now covered in gasoline, and lifted them up, dangerously close to the lighted cigarette.

"It sure would be a shame, Spencer, if we were all here, those little fucks back there included, just 'cause you needed a drink."

He let Spencer's hands drop, picked up the jerrican, and walked off.

Moments later they were back in Johnny Boy's car, this time with Johnny Boy at the wheel, ready to vacate.

Johnny Boy switched on the radio and flicked it to station-surf mode. Suddenly Taylor Swift was telling them how she knew they were trouble. The car's lush audio system made the glossy vocals more rocking than poppy, a tribute to German sound engineering.

"What are we on here?"

Johnny Boy glanced at the screen. "WDVD."

"Ah yeah, WDVD," said McGrath. "It was better before they fired Allyson."

As they drove back into the alley, the Infiniti's fuel tank exploded.

19

New Beginnings

Spencer tiptoed down the hall. There was a cool bottle of Stoli in the freezer with his name on it. Then maybe the TV would tell him about an earthquake or a plane crash somewhere: something terrible enough to put what he'd seen that night into a more manageable perspective.

He opened the refrigerator.

"Late to be drinking on a school night, Spence?" said a voice in the darkness.

Spencer's nerves were already raggedy. He half spun, half fell into the refrigerator door, causing the contents of its shelves to rattle and clink.

"Why're you sitting here in the dark scaring folk, Chris?"

Spencer threw a vodka and coke together and took a glug.

"Because I fell asleep in here."

He was sitting up in the middle of the couch, looking disheveled in his creased khaki shorts and white T-shirt. His thinning gray hair stuck up in tufts.

"I was here because of these."

There were papers on the floor all around him. Spencer walked into the living room and picked one up. He turned on Chris's desk light.

"A bunch of these guys are filing suits, Spencer. And some of them have been calling my customer support line."

Spencer wasn't looking at the debt collector's aggressive letter. He'd gotten its gist at a glance. A line of dried blood in the skin fold of one of his fingernails had caught his eye.

Spencer dropped the letter on the desk and went back to the kitchen. He needed to wash his hands again. He could have put up with the smell of gasoline a little longer and the dry skin it caused—at least for as long as it took him to finish his first drink—but not Milt's blood.

"They're all for me, Chris. No need to panic."

"Jesus, Spencer, don't be such an imbecile! They've got this address. It's not just my home, it's my business address. If you don't deal with this, it'll affect my reputation, maybe my credit. What if a repo guy comes at night looking for one of your cars and takes Penny by mistake?"

God forbid they kidnap Penny in her sleep.

Chris watched Spencer waste half a quart of detergent on his hands and then pour himself another big drink.

Spencer put his hand up against one of the kitchen cabinets so he could rest his head against it. He felt like he could sleep standing up. He went to check his watch. Still gone.

Spencer knew Chris had a point. It could be a little trying how much of a drama he made of some things though, especially tonight. Spencer had just seen four people die. One would have been a first. When he'd attended the morgue to formally identify Marielle, they'd cleaned her up. He'd touched her cheek and its coldness had shocked him. In that moment he'd known she was gone from this earth. It had been a terrible realization. But at least he didn't have to watch her die.

Chris seemed to see the dried blood on Spencer's face and T-shirt for the first time. It dawned on him that he hadn't imagined the smell of gasoline.

"What happened to you?"

Spencer finished his drink and went to pour another, his hands still shaking. He didn't like what was going on in his head: Marielle, those guys burning in his car. One of his fellow rally competitors had fried in a wreck. Trapped by the steering wheel, he'd melted away while hanging in his harness.

"Were you in a car wreck?"

"Uh, yeah, something like that. Look, I've got to shower. I'll take care of this," he waved vaguely in the direction of Chris's debt-themed floor decor, "tomorrow."

He headed for the bathroom and saw Abby's open door. He needed to be by her side, just for a moment, to make sure she was safe.

He poked his head in. She was sound asleep on her front, face squished on the mattress, hair stuck to her forehead. She'd thrown the comforter aside. She didn't like the noise of the fan at night so when it was hot like this she'd sweat in her sleep.

He crossed to an antique chair in the corner. The chair gave the room a homeyness that made one think of family heirlooms and times gone by. Spencer cleared Abby's stuff off it, moved it to her bedside, and sat down heavily. Abby stirred.

"Dad?"

"Yeah, it's me."

"What happened?"

"Nothing, Abby. Don't worry. Don't wake up. Everything's fine."

"Bruce came home."

"Who?"

"Sam's cat."

Spencer leaned in and moved the strands of hair from her face. "That's good."

Some people won't be coming home tonight though, Spencer, will they?

"Yeah, Sam was crying. But after Bruce came home, he got really mad at me and said he never cried."

"Well, sometimes people say things they don't mean, Abby. Especially guys."

Abby said something unintelligible. It sounded unimpressed. Her hand snaked out from under the pillow toward Spencer, got as far as the edge of the bed, and gave up. She breathed deeply, fast asleep again.

Spencer took her hand and held it gently as he looked at her. Kids were beautiful when they slept. Innocent and peaceful, serene even. He thought about the boys he'd seen die earlier. Had they looked like this when they slept? Had anyone ever noticed? He wondered if the Yo-Yo was right—that he was responsible for all the deaths that had taken place that night. One of them was scum, sure. But there were programs to bring kids back from the brink. Who was Spencer to write them off? And Milt. Spencer would've been long gone from that gas station if he hadn't been drinking in his car. Then would Milt have just been inclined to hand over the money?

The thoughts were exhausting, without end. He closed his eyes to them and let his head fall back.

Chris found him asleep like that: sitting upright, covered in blood, and stinking of gasoline, holding Abby's hand. He looked at peace and it was past four, so Chris left him be and went to try and get some sleep himself.

But Spencer's sleep wasn't peaceful. He dreamed the same dream all night. In it, he sat beside a burning car, holding the hand of a boy in the back. The flames flickered around Spencer, but they didn't burn. The boy asked Spencer if it was hurting him too. Spencer shook his head. The boy asked him why he didn't feel pain. Spencer didn't have an answer. All he could say was that he was sorry. The boy started to scream.

As Spencer sat in Chris's Prius, he wondered how he'd gotten to the address on South Washington. Was it because of Marielle not coming back that day four years ago? It had always been simple to blame. Then he could rant and rail at fate and do another line, light another joint, or refill his glass. But he'd found himself wondering of late whether the rot had started earlier, whether some weakness had actually been smoldering within, and Marielle's death had simply been a fan to the flame. Last week, Abby had been reciting her little-known facts. She read out that kind of stuff all the time, but one fact about the *Titanic* had stuck in Spencer's head. Apparently, there'd been a fire going in one of the ship's coal bunkers for the whole voyage. The crew couldn't put it out.

Doomed from within.

He thought about the coke, the drink, the weed, the antidepressants. He needed them to function, yet he knew he needed to stop. Every time he closed his eyes, he saw a child's body silhouetted in fire, like one of those Tibetan monks that torched themselves. And he saw Milt, or rather the shape of Milt, under the sheet, gliding through the bleached strobe lights of ambulance and cruisers, the gas station looking like some way station to the afterlife.

Spencer had been here several times. But tonight, he could see himself sitting in the car on the dark street. He yelled at himself. He hollered and pounded, but the window was stronger than those used to shield bank cashiers from shotguns or to keep out the sea in the bathyspheres that plumbed the ocean depths. And so the man at the wheel, if he heard anything, then it was just the slightest of thuds, like moths hitting glass.

The Common Ground building looked just like a normal house with its white painted shutters and flower-filled pots. Inside, he'd get support for his drinking, for his drug dependency, and even for his grief. He took another swig from the hip flask.

In the months following Marielle's death, he'd barely functioned. He'd cried at times but not often. He thought it might have been because he was trying to be strong for Abby, but he didn't really know. He did know, however, that he'd loved Marielle with all his heart. There'd always been a plentiful supply of attractive women on the racing circuit and, being a good-looking guy, Spencer had found he could pretty much have any that were available, besides a good many who shouldn't have been. But after Marielle got in his car in that muddy forest back in England, it had all stopped: the partying, the woman juggling, the sexting, even the occasional threesome just stopped. And not only that, but he also felt ashamed about any of it ever having taken place. Marielle had a higher opinion of him, and he wished he'd always been the man she believed he was.

If he got out of his car and walked into the amiable little building opposite, he'd have to leave all the props behind. And if that wave of loneliness he'd felt looming back then was still looming now, a great cresting tsunami frozen in time, then he'd have nothing to stop it. The wave had suddenly, miraculously, been held off one day about two years ago when he'd met up with a friend from his racing days, an engineer whose ability to party was the stuff of legend. They'd hit the coke and, wonder of wonder, for the first time for way too long, Spencer had felt good, like everything might be OK, like *he* was OK.

And that seemed to be the way the props worked. They gave and gave, but one day they stopped giving. Like a beautiful and loyal dog that turns and starts chomping down right on its owner's ass. And there was no breaking loose from those jaws.

Spencer stared through the windshield at the cracked pavement and fire hydrant lit by his headlights, at the dented rear of an old Toyota. He stared at these things but didn't see. Marielle had been uncompromising in what she thought was right or wrong. Sometimes he sensed her presence, as if she were allowed out once in a while from wherever her spirit now resided.

Hey, baby, what's up?

My watch, Marielle—it got stolen. I'm gutted. Everything's just gone to hell since you left.

But Spencer, why would you have your window down at a light in that part of town? Were you smoking again?

And Spencer, not wanting to lie and yet not wanting to fess up, would have said nothing. And nothing would have told all.

That old guy in the gas station, Spencer, Milt did you say his name was? Sounds like a nice man. How come you guys were chatting so long? Didn't you want to get back to Abby?

I needed to stop for a while, needed a drink.

Should have gone home, had a drink with Chris.

I was working.

Working? That late? What kind of work were you doing, Spencer?

Look, go easy on me, OK? I'm only doing all this 'cause you left me, Marielle!

Is that why they all had to die, Spencer? Because of me? Or you? Tell me which you think.

And he didn't even feel the steering wheel dig into his forehead as he cried.

"If you'd come to see me sooner, Mister Burnham, this all would have stopped quicker. My client has been quite, well, agitated."

Chris's lawyer was a corpulent man. Even with a fan at either end of his desk, Jay Rumley's face glistened. He had to push his glasses back up his nose every time he looked down. Spencer wanted to reach over and undo his top button; some of the blood in his head looked like it needed to drain back into his body.

"Chris has a low stress threshold," said Spencer. "But he is getting my calls and letters and they're freaking him out. And a repo guy came yesterday looking for a car that I don't have anymore. It's probably been sold."

"Let them fight it out," Rumley said. "The bank probably took and sold all the stock because they were secured creditors."

Though he may have been corpulent, Rumley was capable. Within an hour he'd handled all the documentation for a Chapter 7 and printed letters to put Spencer's pursuers on to Ron-at-the-Bank's trail.

"Let's just be thorough though."

He made a few calls and tapped away on his keyboard. He made one more call and then sat back in his seat.

"So most of your stock's gone," he said. "Not all though. Some of it was damaged during a break-in. Three cars. They're going to auction next week."

Spencer thanked him and paid him in cash. He got up to leave.

"Chris tells me you were good at selling cars," said Jay suddenly, like he'd remembered something. "Said Winchester's misfortunes were down to, uh, factors beyond your control. Is selling cars something you'd consider doing again?"

Spencer stopped midstride. He'd heard that if you were ready for change then, miraculously, doors would open. He hadn't been to the depot since the night his car had been stolen a few days ago. McGrath had called to check up on him, but Spencer had said he needed a few days to himself.

McGrath's gig was crazy shit. Spencer had made a little pile of money and now it was time to move on, while he was still alive.

"Not for myself," said Spencer.

"That's kind of out of the question for you," chuckled Jay. "No, I have a client who's opening a dealership down in Toledo. Second-generation Pakistani. Did well out of all the Dearborn Muslims who made their money in the restaurant trade. BMW. They like their German cars. He's having trouble finding someone to head the sales. Wants someone a little different. I'm thinking your British-ness, the racing experience, might appeal. That something you'd be interested in?"

"Toledo?"

"Yeah. He's got some swanky location. Was doing a complete teardown, so I don't know where he's at with it. He's quite a, uh, unique character."

Spencer had once delivered a car to a customer in Toledo. It was nice down there. He could commute to begin with, see how things went before switching Abby's school. Spencer was of the mind that it was because of one of Abby's holier-than-thou teachers that he had such an intimate relationship with CPS anyway. On that score, if he did move away, it would mean adios to Lonnie. And suddenly Spencer knew it was the right time for that too. He'd known Lonnie wanted more than he was able to give. And she deserved more too. She'd been a step for him.

After Marielle, he hadn't looked at another woman sexually for a year. He'd hated the fact that his dick didn't want to grieve as long as he did. So he'd started fucking again. Hookers for a while, then casual lays. Angela's predecessor had given excellent head. Lonnie had been the first thing that bordered on any form of regular interaction, although he had to consider the possibility that that had been out of necessity. Spencer wasn't proud of himself. Hadn't been for a long time. It was wearing him out. Perhaps it was time for a change. Isn't that what Milt had said? Most people moved away after something really bad. Maybe that's where Spencer had gone wrong. He'd stayed.

20

The Tough Goodbye

"It's not just our location that makes Fairlane BMW special, Spencer. Excuse me."

Zaid-call-me-Zed took a call. Slick, thick black hair, chubby cheeked with chubby hands and a tweedy brown jacket and white shirt—dazzlingly white next to his dark skin—Zed was every inch the thrusting, successful Americanized Pakistani nailing the New World dream.

Spencer was glad he'd racked a line up in his car before coming in. That was all going to change though with a change of scenery: from the Motor City to the Glass City.

He'd breezed down to Toledo in an hour and a quarter, bouncing along the western edge of Lake Erie and North Maumee Bay. It even felt good to be back in the uniform of a car salesman, slacks and shirt, albeit with the bruised face of a man who'd been leading a different life.

Zed finished his call. "We get a lot of people like that from the country club, Spencer, which is where you come in, my friend. They talk to you and they're going to be thinking European sophistication, precision."

"Precision is what I'm about, Zed. I raced. If you do that without getting the concept of precision, well, let's just say I wouldn't be here talking to you."

"But you knocked the shit out of your face by falling down the stairs?"

"I, uh, yes that's right. But those stairs were . . . still being built. Should have been roped off. Jay offered to sue their asses but I just like to work hard to make my money."

And when he walked out of Fairlane's sliding glass doors, he damn well knew that Zaid-call-me-Zed wanted him.

"I was just thinking about going back into sales is all, Dom." He managed to say it with a little sangfroid, as if this were simply a natural progression. But, in truth, he knew he was in great danger. His heart felt fit to bust its way out and join them both in McGrath's office. There was a comfortable chair ready for it right next to him.

Spencer had wanted McGrath to be busy, like Schwarzkopf's command tent. The hope seemed reasonable now that Spencer knew it was a war out there. But things were quiet.

McGrath went to sit down, hesitated, crossed to the air-conditioner and flipped its switch a couple times. Nothing. He punched its side. The unit whirred to life but with a grating sound. He waited a moment before hitting it again. It ran smoothly. He sat down and lit a cigar.

Spencer's mind drifted back to Toledo. Zed had said he could start as soon as he liked. He'd need an apartment if things went well. And things were going to go well. And he'd walk in the door of the Common Ground down there where some clever guy would tell him how to stop doing what he did. But that couldn't happen if he left here in the trunk of a car.

McGrath eyed him through curling smoke.

"What type of car did you say you'd have bought if I'd given you more money? Four-wheel drive or something?"

Spencer resolved to stay engaged with whatever whim seemed to be preoccupying his old employer. Hell, if he played this right, he might make a sale.

No harm in selling to a guy who watches a few kids get wasted and torched just like he's watching a slow game on ESPN, right?

"All-wheel drive. Less chance of skidding. Something like a Subaru WRX. Powered-up engine, upgraded suspension, rally heritage."

"So for driving the streets real fast but still be able to fit your buddies in and not turn too many heads, that would be your number-one choice?"

Spencer felt sweat trickle down his chest. "Dom, look, the other night, that sort of thing—"

"Doesn't happen often."

"Once was enough. I gave it a few days, like you said, and I just got more certain that I can't do that shit."

He felt McGrath's eyes scanning his thoughts like a pulsar.

"Every job has its tough moments: closing your first sale, and yeah, seeing your first dead guy. People die all the time. In the army we were *paid* to kill people. But at least those towel heads were fightin' for a principle. Two kids, boo-fucking-hoo. All of those punks were happy to stab and shoot up an old guy who saved your ass, right? I mean, come on! And what do you mean by 'do this shit'?"

Spencer said nothing. This was going out of control. He just wanted to shake McGrath's hand and call it a day.

"All you have to do is drive. You pick up, you drop off, you do your rounds." He tapped his cigar into an ashtray made from the base of a mortar shell, put a foot up on the edge of the desk, and used it to creak his seat back. "Tell you what. This Subaru you're talking about, the uh, what was it?"

Spencer held up his hand. "Dom, I don't—"

McGrath held up his own hand right back. "Anyone would think you couldn't wait to see the back of me. You feel like you been treated bad? I believe I can take feedback. Can't be worse than I get from Cal. Well?"

"No, course not. It's been just, uh, fine working here."

"'Fine'? Like when my wife says 'fine'?" McGrath laughed. "Jesus, lighten up. I'm joshing. Maybe you're a little tense."

"Yeah, I guess I am, Dom. I am a little tense. And yeah, I feel bad coming in and saying so, but hey, do you want someone dealing with your shit who's so tense?"

"Spencer, I been here a hundred times. Had guys older than you sitting opposite me, crying their eyes out 'cause they just seen their best buddy's balls blown all over an alley. They couldn't just go: 'Oh this job makes me tense, can I go home?' And you know what?"

Spencer looked hopelessly back at him.

"They get it together, Spencer. 'Most all of them. Hell, some of them, they become machines. Now why don't you wake up and smell that aroma of coffee? What are you running from? It isn't me, don't you know that? You got a kid, debts, responsibilities, and right now you got a gig that's paying hard, hard cash, and the only people who've busted you up are crispy critters now. Thanks to us."

Spencer's shoulders sagged. He had a chance of something new, in a new city. He quested for some inner pool of resolve that might bestow substance on whatever words he found.

"Dom, I haven't ever been to war or been in the army. All I've done, till I met you, is race cars. And when I got married, I became a salesman. I worked for you and, yeah, I guess it was fine. But it isn't for me just because . . . I like selling cars more."

With that, he rose, offering McGrath his hand. "It's been a pleasure. You're on another level. Look me up when you need more car advice." And the chat was back. Spencer felt it.

Nearly through the circle of fire.

McGrath obviously felt it, too, because he took Spencer's hand, looked him in the eye, and smiled. He glanced down at their clasped hands and at Spencer's wrist.

"Sure am sad about that watch of yours."

"It meant a lot to me but, hey, one of those things, I guess."

Fuck the watch.

He could almost hear Marielle yelling it.

McGrath nodded. "I'll walk you to your car."

Spencer sat in Chris's Prius in the loading bay, engine on, window down, elbow resting on the sill. He looked relaxed, but the fingers of his right hand were curled around the shift, applying light pressure, eager to slot Penny into Drive.

"Got something lined up?" asked McGrath.

"Just some promising leads to follow up, that kind of thing."

Spencer noticed Eddie watching from his car.

It's all yours, Eddie.

"Staying local?" asked McGrath.

"Yeah, most likely."

McGrath suddenly slapped the roof, startling Spencer. "Damn! What the hell was I thinking? Hey, Johnny Boy, we nearly forgot Spencer's surprise."

Spencer instinctively looked around for the Yo-Yo.

Johnny Boy appeared at the other window. "Hey, Spencer. Still set on leaving?"

"Yeah but, uh, don't think I don't know where I stand with you guys."

Johnny Boy's hand was heading for his jacket pocket.

"I'm part of what happened the other night, so I'm not going to, you know, say anything, to like *anyone*."

Johnny Boy watched him, with those eyes that had no color, cut nearly in half by sagging lids. Assessing. Emotionless.

Spencer didn't notice McGrath reach into the car and turn off his engine.

"Give it to him, Johnny Boy," said McGrath.

Spencer floored the gas pedal and . . .

Nothing happened. He turned back to Johnny Boy, who was extracting some heavy metal from his pocket.

21

The True Way of Things

The watch landed on the seat next to him with a thump. He stared at it, glanced up at Johnny Boy, around at McGrath, and back at the watch.

Could it be?

He reached out, touched it, turned it over gingerly, ready to discover that it was, in fact, just a similar watch, not *the* watch, not the watch that Marielle had laid next to on their bed, wearing only the shirt she slept in, one of his old shirts but fully unbuttoned.

Time for your real birthday present . . .

But he saw the scratch on the bracelet lock, the inscription on the back. He checked the time—still working. His fingers closed around it. He shut his eyes for a moment. Exhaled.

"The Yo-Yo went and got it for you. From a pawnshop, so don't worry. Like I was saying, it's not often like the other night."

Spencer put the watch on.

"I said it could be like a little family here. Always good to have friends in a city like this."

Spencer felt an enormous surge of gratitude. Almost immediately, this was swamped by a feeling of dire awkwardness. He was leaving. He was going to Toledo, and he was going to sell Zaid-call-me-Zed's cars. He didn't want to work for people who could kill him and set his body on fire without breaking a sweat.

"What did you have to pay the pawnshop? Let me at least cover that?"

"It's not always about the money," said McGrath.

Spencer searched for the words that might allow him to complete his extrication without looking like a douchebag, a taker, and nothing but.

"Then you guys need to let me buy you dinner. Not just food, but a proper night. Beers, shots, hell, strippers too. And then come to me for your cars. I'll undercut whatever you've been quoted."

Spencer pulled away. He felt pretty bad, but that would pass soon enough.

As he waited for the depot barrier to rise, he was already feeling a little euphoric. But the barrier stayed put.

Suddenly McGrath jumped in beside him. Johnny Boy got in the back.

"We just remembered something," said McGrath.

This was like forgetting to say goodbye to a Ouija board.

"Let's go for a drive."

Spencer found the self-assured way in which it was said unsettling.

"Pull over here," said McGrath. "Twenty-Fifth Street. Lived here as a kid. First crew I ran with was the Twenty-Fifth Street Boys. Now look at this place. Beautiful buildings and them demolition boys just knock them down. Soon Detroit's going to be just one big fucking nature reserve. A dead heart surrounded by suburbs."

Johnny Boy sat forward and handed his phone to Spencer. "Hit Play."

Spencer was treated to a video of himself damaging the cars he used to own. Johnny Boy sat back and spoke mildly.

"In case you were interested, what you're looking at is grand larceny: damaging those cars that no longer belonged to you so they'd go for a lower price at auction. And since my guess is you did more than a thousand bucks' worth of damage, that makes it a felony. Oh and the Jaguar we all liked? That went to a specialist auction in Nevada. Out of state makes the crime federal, although with a good lawyer maybe you could argue to keep it in court here in Michigan."

Spencer looked into McGrath's smiling eyes.

What? You thought the ride was over, boy? Nooo, it ain't over till I say it's over, and I say it ain't over for a while yet.

"Why rock the boat? I pay you well? Always in cash just like you wanted."

Johnny Boy took back his phone and placed a large wad of bills in the cupholder. "Thirty thousand."

"Buy that car," said McGrath. "You know the one. All-wheel drive, rally heritage." He laughed. "Come on, it's been a nice trip. Let's get back to the depot."

Although it seemed an age ago, it had been barely six weeks since Spencer's furious attempt to get back at the bank and obtain reduced stock for another start-up. He'd phoned Jay to see if the Subaru was one of the cars still to be auctioned. Turned out it was and when it rolled into the sales hall it looked dirty, damaged, and unloved and Spencer got it for a song. That part of his original plan had worked out at least.

Back at the depot, he sought out Cal to OK the necessary repairs.

Cal paid Spencer's expenses but only after deriding him a little and then sending him to their favored supplier: Action Motorworks on Elmhurst. They didn't bother with invoices. Cal was careful about what he signed.

Batiste and Scott, parked on Noble, watched Spencer's new car drive into the depot.

"It certainly doesn't look like he's leaving," said Scott.

"He wanted to. They have something on him," said Batiste. "McGrath's dead set on keeping him for whatever the hell this thing is he's got coming up."

"Do we know how long yet?"

"No one knows except McGrath and Johnny Boy and they're going to keep it that way until the last possible moment. But I'll tell you something. It's soon. It's plain to see. Two reasons. One. He's focusing resources on this. Closer something is, the more time, effort, and money it takes. Just like a wedding. That car Burnham's driving? He doesn't need that for the standard cleaning run. A little grunt, sure, but not that much. Two, and this is the big one, why bring in someone like Burnham at all? Yeah, sure, no one knows him so he can't be a snitch, I get that. But if you were McGrath you just wouldn't use someone like him. People like him shit their pants when they're exposed to this world. I bet Burnham's pissing off McGrath's crew. I bet he's hard work.

"So why then?"

"McGrath's leaving."

"What do you mean?"

"He's quitting." Batiste laughed, shaking his head as if he'd been stupid to miss it. "He's actually going to quit while he's ahead."

The depot's barrier rose and Spencer's car pulled onto Noble and powered past them.

"The guy's untouchable behind the wheel, Evan. You won't bust him with dirty money."

"Untouchable?" Batiste watched the Subaru take a right on Gibson and disappear from view. "We'll see about that."

22

False Favors

Spencer slipped right back into work. The money kept coming in. Broken parts of town, broken lives, all generating profit. Street, alley, suburb, and city. Seeing without even looking for the different cars that spelled danger: state police, sheriff's department, DPD. Sometimes two hundred miles in a day.

One morning, waiting for a light to change on Martin Luther, he found himself wondering where this man had come from, this auto alchemist who turned tainted money to riches by sleight of hand. Something about it reminded him of his other life.

His watch caught the sun as he gently drummed the wheel, and suddenly he was three miles east, four years back, and it was a bright, cold day in fall. He and Marielle had taken Abby along the Riverwalk, where she'd been entranced by those sidewalk magicians, slickly relieving people of their possessions and then "finding" them in hoods and pockets. It had been the best of days, and Spencer had felt blessed to feel at home so far from home.

Afterward, heading back, they'd been waiting in a long line of traffic when he'd felt Marielle's hand close around his as it rested on the shift. Without looking at her, he'd lifted both their hands and kissed the back of hers.

She'd thanked him. It made him turn to her. She was pulling her scarf off, freeing her dark blonde hair, her smooth skin flushed now by the heat inside the car.

"You don't have to thank me for kissing you," he said.

"That isn't what you were being thanked for."

Abby started making fake vomiting noises.

Marielle unclipped her seat belt and dived into the back, monster growling as she went. Spencer didn't like seat belts being off and had good reason to feel that way, but he knew Marielle would laugh at him if he complained. It seemed none of her family cared. Her dad clipped his behind his back to stop his car from scolding him. He smoked and drank and held staunchly to the view that if it was time for death to find you, he'd find you. Abby seemed to agree because, with Marielle's monster noises having morphed into loud, tickly tummy raspberries, she was laughing uncontrollably and begging her mom to stop.

A little later, when Marielle was beside him again and Spencer had relaxed now that everyone was back where they were supposed to be, he asked her why she'd thanked him.

"For giving my hometown a little of your heart. Not everyone does. And definitely not many who aren't from around here."

"How do you know I'm not from round here?" He said it in a slightly heightened, upper-class English accent.

"Oh, you're definitely not from around here. But don't worry.

I'll protect your English *arse*, unless it means driving a stick, in which case you're on your own."

You're on your own.

He hadn't removed his watch since its return. Now, wanting to rub away some of the grime and sweat from his wrist, he flicked its clasp and pushed the loosened bracelet up his forearm. A sprinkling of tiny dark flakes stuck to his moist wrist. He peered closer, took off the watch, and inspected the gaps between its bracelet links. Some of them were clogged by a dark substance. He flexed and tapped it against his palm. More of the substance dropped out. He smeared a piece of it against his skin. Dark crimson. Dried blood.

He hid the watch at the back of the glove compartment. He'd stop somewhere and buy something to give it a proper clean. He tried not to think about Milt's blood and how difficult that had been to remove.

Spencer cruised west on Martin Luther and changed lanes a few times before moving into the center as if to take a left. Suddenly he shifted down, powered up and ground a ninety-degree turn onto Eighteenth Street like they'd put tram lines down for him to do just that. He kept the gas on for a few seconds, braked hard, and threw a left onto Magnolia. He backed into a space and waited for five minutes to see if anyone followed. When no vehicle went by, he pulled slowly out.

In his mind, a three-dimensional grid descended. On it, a small, car-shaped icon turned north on Humboldt.

Spencer began his rounds.

* * *

Lonnie was no stranger to interaction with the police. It wasn't possible to work for Child Protective Services and not have dealings with them. The two detectives who currently sat facing her were a contrasting duo: a Black guy her own age, all twitching hands and feet, never still, lean in a sharp suit, no wedding ring but not giving out any vibe of being available. The other guy seemed more at ease: dark chinos and open-necked blue shirt, slightly overweight but not so much that it made him unattractive. But the wedding ring made that irrelevant.

"It's not dangerous work he's doing. That's not why I'm asking you to do this," Batiste was saying. "It's just we got an operation going on, and a new face, well, it confuses things."

"So, let me get this straight. You want me to tell him to leave his job?" said Lonnie.

"No, because that'll be too obvious. That'll tell his employer about me. I just need you to somehow put pressure on him to leave."

"It's difficult. Spen—, I mean, Mister Burnham, is no longer an active case."

The stumble didn't go unnoticed by either detective.

The last time Lonnie had seen Spencer had been the occasion of his signing off. She'd gripped the edge of her desk as Spencer pounded the bejesus out of her. And it had been technically great as usual. But, after they'd come, he left, and then the waiting had started, for a message to meet for a drink, maybe a call. And as time went by, her self-esteem had taken its accustomed battering.

"Why was he on your books in the first place?" asked Batiste.

"I couldn't divulge that without a warrant."

"Don't you guys have criteria that have to be satisfied as to how the parent is making his money?" asked Scott. "You know, like, if this guy is making money from crime, then he could have his kid taken off him, that kind of thing?"

"Only if the means of making that money endangers the child's safety. But that would mean telling him I know about his job."

"Look," said Scott after a moment. "We're all the same here really, Miss Estevez. DPD, CPS . . . We're paid by the same people to serve and protect. Maybe you could call the guy in on some bureaucratic pretext, then get through to him it's a real bad idea to be working anything shady."

Lonnie tried to think impartially. She felt more than a little resentful toward Spencer. And yet she hadn't quite given up on him, or on the two of them. Great sex, after all, didn't come without real connection. Maybe this opportunity could bring its own brand of leverage.

Pucky and Scoop and a few hangers-on were shooting the shit in their normal alley. Every so often a minion would run up, hand over some cash, and take a fresh load of merchandise. Business was brisk and it wasn't even noon. And, by the look of things, it was about to pick up even more.

Two hot little twentysomething pieces of mighty fine booty were making a beeline in their direction.

"Well, check this shit out," said Pucky.

"I banged the one on the left yesterday in the lot behind Jango's," said Scoop.

"That a fact? Well, then I'll take the one on the right," said Pucky. He knew Scoop had more than an edge on him in the looks department, but he won out on the pussy fundage and power stakes.

"'Sup, Scoop?" said his recent conquest.

And the four of them were off, into that fast-moving courtship of the hood, greased by money and the heady aphrodisiac garnered by real G status. There'd be some action within the hour, Pucky figured. He felt himself getting a little semi when he saw his target's nipples thrusting through her crop top, right at him.

They were all so distracted that none of them noticed a silver Dodge Dart slow up curbside, its nearside windows dropping as it did so, until the bullets started flying.

Seeing as they were shielding the primary targets, the two girls didn't stand a chance. The impact of the rounds sent them flying into Pucky and Scoop.

Three machine guns continued slamming away. Scoop's neck exploded, and two of Pucky's other guys dropped like sacks of stones, blood spattering the walls of the building they'd been leaning against, watching the foreplay.

Pucky, miraculously, was unscathed. His girl had taken a bullet for him, several in fact. But just as he went to dive out of the way, his left knee joint exploded. He hit the deck and looked helplessly at the multiple muzzle flashes, wondering if they'd run out of ammo before they hit him again. That was the moment he took a couple of slugs in the crotch.

Sweet Jesus, but she was gonna come fast and hard for this guy. Maybe that had something to do with the fact that Lonnie had a plan. And that plan would whisk her up the relationship status elevator from basement booty call to penthouse Pebbles. So after Spencer had given her what he had to give, then she'd give him her news. She'd turn around and, in a hushed conspiratorial voice, swear him to secrecy as she hinted he was in the firing line of an undercover op. They had to meet somewhere secret and safe to talk. Only Lonnie Estevez could help him.

"Go on then," she growled.

Spencer held her from behind, ready to ram her back onto his . . .

He looked down.

What the fuck? What the fucking fuck!

His dick was completely soft.

"Give it to me then," breathed Lonnie again.

Get hard, get hard.

Lonnie really got off on it when guys teased her, made her wait. Spencer had never actually done this before. Usually he was the fast-and-hard type. She looked back, then up at his panicked face.

Abby waited in the CPS reception room, engrossed in her iPad. She didn't look up, because that ran the risk of eye contact with one of the other people waiting to be seen, many of whom looked sick or downright scary.

She had only a vague understanding of why they had to come here. There were things her dad was doing that were bad for her. He'd changed so much since Mom died. Maybe he would change back again if she left him alone, because she certainly didn't make him happy anymore. She used to, when Mom was alive, but not anymore.

Spencer's work phone vibrated on the seat beside her. She wasn't allowed to answer that phone but as it buzzed, it moved around, touching and rattling his car keys. People were looking at her. The situation called for her adult voice.

"Hello, Dad's phone."

"Is Spencer there?"

"He's in a meeting right now. Do you want—"

It took Johnny Boy a moment, and only a moment, to decide whether he should be annoyed at Spencer for not manning his work phone or grateful for being gifted an opportunity.

"Oh, you must be Abby, right? I've been looking forward to talking to you."

"Really? Do you work for my dad?"

"As it happens, I do work for your dad. Did you know he never stops talking about you?"

"Really?"

"You have no idea. Which school did he say you do really well at again?"

"I go to McDade Elementary."

"No way, McDade? My niece might be going to McDade. Say, are you on Facebook?"

Abby hesitated.

"Ah, you're too young, right? My niece is your age, but she has an account. I was thinking she could send you a Friend Request."

Abby knew how bad it could be being the new girl or even just being different. She'd really suffered when word had gotten out that the school was topping off the Burnham tuition fees. "My uncle set me up on it too. I'm only allowed to do it for an hour though."

"Hey, same for my niece! Abby Burnham right?"

"Yeah," said Abby.

"Well, don't tell him I told you this stuff about how amazing he thinks you are or I'll be in trouble. Our secret, OK?"

"OK."

Glowing from the knowledge that her father spoke so highly of her when she wasn't around, Abby was about to say a breathless goodbye but just managed to regain her adult composure. "What's her name?"

"Huh?"

"Your niece's name? So I can look out for her Friend Request."

Johnny Boy was sitting in the corner booth of an all-day bar in the University District. He looked around and saw a waitress cleaning a table nearby. Pretty hot. Tall. He looked at her chest. Nice rack. Well shaped, not too big. He squinted at her name badge.

"Her name's Kelsey."

23

The Worth of an Asset

The hot stickiness of the evening caressed Spencer's skin as he reached out to buzz the gate, but before he could push the button, the barrier rose. In the loading bays, McGrath was talking to Johnny Boy, Eddie, and the Yo-Yo. Bathed in the fluorescent yellow of the loading bay lights, they leaned against the walkway railing, the sheen of sweat on their faces. McGrath's shirtsleeves were uncharacteristically rolled up. Denny stuck his head around from inside the back of his truck, saw it was Spencer, and went back to whatever he was doing.

Johnny Boy signaled him to stay in the car. Seemed they wanted a private little powwow.

Spencer had plenty on his mind to pass the time. He was still in a state of semi-disbelief about what had gone, or stayed, down in Lonnie's office. She'd hustled him out, no longer seeming to care about the forms that had necessitated his return in the first place.

He put the whole sorry tale down to his daughter being in the waiting room. That could get to any man, surely? But somewhere inside a little voice had started whispering uncomfortable truths about how he treated people. He'd known Lonnie had been falling for him, that he was a piece of shit really, and that his recent failure was, just maybe, a reflection of that.

McGrath, Johnny Boy, and Eddie headed over toward him. Eddie showed them his phone as they went, like he was offering to do something with it. It put Spencer on his guard. Eddie got in the front, Johnny Boy and McGrath in the back.

"Evening, Spence."

"Dom. Guys."

"How was today?" asked Johnny Boy.

"Pucky's in the hospital. Drive-by. It was the Clark Park guys."

"Imagine that," said Johnny Boy. "Their new business partners. Told you they could never stay out of trouble."

"So I guess I'll be picking up from over the Vernor Highway any day now?"

"Watch this space."

McGrath dropped his window. "Hey, Denny?"

Denny's head appeared around the truck's tailgate.

"Get moving, Denny, they're waiting. And take precautions. If you think you're being followed, call me."

Spencer backed out of the loading bays and headed toward the barrier.

"Where to?" he asked.

"Left," said McGrath. "See that part of the street where it's really dark? Drive there and park it, facing this way."

Spencer did so. He killed the lights but kept the engine on so he could run the air. They waited in the shadows.

"So today I learned an interesting fact from Johnny Boy, Spencer. Did you know AirDrop leaves no trace? Everything else, calls, GPS, emails, internet searches, can all be checked. Not AirDrop though. I could AirDrop you something and no one could ever prove it."

A phone pinged. The car moved as McGrath extracted his phone from his pants. "OK, Spencer, we're gonna have ourselves a little fun. The AirDrop in Denny's phone's on. We want to see if you can follow him close enough for Eddie to pick up the signal without Denny seeing you."

Spencer thought for a moment about what he had going on in his life. About the six hours of technical or tactical or however you wanted to call it driving he'd already done that day.

"Are you serious?"

"Yep," said Johnny Boy. "And give it your best shot. Dom and I've got money riding on you."

As they waited in silence, Spencer's mind churned. Why were they testing him?

Suddenly the barrier swung up and Denny turned right onto Noble.

Spencer pulled away. He left his headlights off for the time being and kept his distance from the truck as he got a feel for Denny's driving. Denny was certainly being cautious. But a random stop or U-turn didn't really work on a tail that was keeping far enough back. They headed northwest.

By the time they crossed Chicago Boulevard by the sprawling Gothic Revival that was Sacred Heart Major Seminary, Spencer was ready to move in. He worked gears and lights fluidly, switching off his lights on dark, empty streets, switching them on again to mingle with traffic in busier, lit streets. A necromancer of the roads, working dark driving magic.

When the moment was right, Spencer would go really close, so close that the Subaru and truck moved as one: a strange articulated vehicle, its front portion bred for load carrying, its rear for performance. Spencer would always favor the nearside of the truck, to lessen the chance of Denny noticing the glint of lights on the Subaru's body, except when they were making a right, in which case Spencer would move to the offside.

It was classy, subtle work and, with a self-satisfied smirk, Johnny Boy watched McGrath watching Spencer. Eddie watched his phone, but every time it seemed they were as close as it was possible to be without risking a collision, Eddie would shake his head.

"You sure you're not getting it, Eddie? We're almost committing sodomy on the guy," said Johnny Boy.

"Nope."

"You sure your AirDrop works?" asked Spencer.

"New phone, works fine." As usual, Eddie was difficult to read. But then, out of the corner of his eye, Spencer saw him give the quickest of looks back at Johnny Boy. *Told you so.*

Spencer fell back into traffic.

Fuck you, Eddie. Think of something else to do. This is what I do. I drive.

That's all you can do, isn't it, Spencer?

And fuck you too.

He took out his phone, set it to search for other AirDrop devices, and then put it in the crotch of his pants. He knew Eddie saw him do it but he didn't care. Eddie had pissed him off.

He dropped down a gear and the revs climbed; the power was on call again.

At the next opportunity, the Subaru surged forward, attracted as if by magnetic force to the truck's tail. They turned into a backstreet. Spencer concentrated. And for that small window, nothing broke his concentration.

With one hand on the wheel, and keeping the car less than six inches from the truck, Spencer grabbed his phone from between his thighs, refreshed the search, and held it against the wheel. His eyes flicked between it and the windshield.

SEARCHING FOR DEVICES . . .

DEVICES FOUND: Corncat's Phone

Spencer put his phone in front of Eddie's face. "I guess you just didn't know Denny's latest handle? Reckon I could have done this by the time we crossed McGraw, Eddie, but hey, who am I to know?"

Eddie checked his own phone and nodded.

"Praise the Lord," said Johnny Boy.

Spencer pulled up at the curb. Just before he flipped a U, he glanced at Eddie, expecting a look of surly, jealous animosity. What he got surprised him with its enigma. It was either hate—or pity.

Eddie rocked up as Johnny Boy and McGrath watched Spencer drive out of the gate.

"Hey. We done for the night?"

"Yeah," said Johnny Boy.

"So what's goin' on tomorrow?"

"We got work to do with Spencer. You're helping Denny. Keep your phone on."

Eddie didn't manage to hide his disappointment. Helping Denny meant low-level stuff: fencing stolen shit and some arson insurance thing he was getting aroused about.

After he left, Johnny Boy and McGrath walked into the loading bay.

"He's keen," said McGrath.

"Verdict?"

"The Yo-Yo said he was cool when they visited Rosso. Said he thought he was going to ice the cop though. He's going to move on if we don't give him more to do."

They got to McGrath's car.

"He wants Spencer's gig," mused McGrath in a way that said that much was obvious.

"That he does, but he isn't good enough. I strongly advise we accept Spencer's weaknesses; they give us control. But we need to make sure he has no other options."

"You 'strongly advise'?"

"I just got a message. Max Petrovsky wants to talk again."

24

Bait Car

Chris was awake in the small hours, waiting for the sound of an engine. It was past two when he heard it. Other cars purred, whined, or, if they were like Penny, didn't make much noise at all. Spencer's kind of gurgled.

He heard the front door open, then the refrigerator.

When Spencer had first come to stay, Chris sometimes had to go out looking for him in the bars of Highland Park. Spencer didn't go out anymore except to work, whatever that meant, because Chris didn't believe the whole "company driver" hogwash. That evening, Spencer had been back and settled for the night. Three beers down, his work phone had beeped, and he was gone, as if remote-controlled by aliens in one of those old B movies.

Whatever it was, it paid well. Too well perhaps. Jay had reported back that Spencer had settled any debt not zapped by his Chapter 7—in cash. He also said Spencer met with one of his other clients, with a view to working for the guy. Apparently, Spencer had made a biblical impression and then just dropped off the grid. And before Jay there'd been the night of the "car wreck." He hadn't been the same since.

And then there was Abby. Why couldn't Spencer see she wanted her daddy back? Why couldn't Spencer see that everyone was waiting for him to come back?

As of late, Chris had found it easier than ever to hold himself accountable. And he was preparing himself to act appropriately if others couldn't.

Cal got in the back of the Subaru while McGrath rode shotgun with Spencer.

Denny slammed the trunk and banged it with his hand. "Good to go."

He and Eddie watched Spencer's car leave.

"Where they goin'?" asked Eddie.

"Dunno," said Denny.

Denny felt that no one told him much these days. But he did know they'd just put a lot of dough in Spencer's car.

"Get us on the ninety-six. Head north," said McGrath.

Spencer planned on making a few random detours around Core City before they hit the ninety-six but as soon as he threw in his first turn, McGrath told him not to bother, just to take the quickest route.

The Charger's radio hissed. "They're on Gibson, heading north."

Scott acknowledged and signaled Batiste to take a road running parallel to Gibson.

"So just let me confirm: Cal and McGrath? Both of them?" said Scott.

"That's a very definite affirmative," said Batiste.

"That's a very definite amazing. As is that," said Scott, pointing up.

The Detroit Police Department couldn't afford its own chopper. And the last time they'd been authorized air support from Michigan State Police the chopper hadn't even gotten off the ground on account of its fuel gelling due to excessively cold weather. DPD had been unwilling, or unable, to pay the heating bill for the hangar. But this time, Batiste had prevailed.

"What sort of route is he taking?" said Scott into the radio.

They waited for a few minutes.

"Can you clarify?"

"Is he taking detours, doing U-turns, evasive technique?"

"Negative. Direct. North on the ninety-six now."

"OK, we'll shadow."

They were both pretty wired themselves, on tiredness and anticipation. They'd had little time to organize things. Neither had expected such a big mistake from McGrath.

As Spencer drove, Cal and McGrath yakked about which areas in the suburbs were busy and whether the Yo-Yo's rediscovered love of motorcycles would kill him.

"Something has to because no human will," said McGrath before taking Cal into an exchange of manpinions on how badly the Pistons were doing.

It seemed to Spencer that Cal was so wrapped up in being a hard-ass that it adversely affected his conversational ability. Still, he was like a ray of sunshine that morning compared to how he was when McGrath wasn't around. McGrath appeared to recognize it for what it was and then simply wore it out of him with open-ended questions and *bonne humeur*. At times, Spencer thought there was an edge to the way he did it, like he was steamrolling Cal into conversation and ignoring his hard-man persona in a way that almost challenged it.

"How do we know the money they've got is clean?" asked Scott.

They were driving north on the twenty-four now.

"Why would McGrath and Cal risk going out with dirty money? That's Spencer's job. They must be on their way to exchange it. Otherwise, he'd be driving tactically."

"So why would they go with him?"

"Maybe because it's a large sum. Maybe they're keeping an eye on him."

The radio cut through their conversation. "They're heading east on the fifty-nine."

"There you go. Probably got a couple of fat new customers in Pontiac."

But Spencer didn't stop in Pontiac.

Their radio hissed again.

"Four zero minutes flight time remaining."

"Nice out this way," said McGrath, sipping a coffee.

Spencer looked around. They were sitting in a gas station just behind the freeway somewhere in Utica. Cal was still in the car, asleep.

McGrath finished his coffee and looked at his watch. "Let's get back on the road."

* * *

Scott and Batiste held their breath as they waited for the radio to respond.

"Sorry guys, we're gonna be on fumes by the time we get back to Lansing as it is. They're on the ninety-six again, heading back into Detroit." The radio fell silent.

"Jesus fucking Christ," said Batiste.

"We're five minutes behind them," said Scott. "I figure that was a detour. Now they're going where they're going. We'll just have to do this the old-fashioned way. What's the worst that can happen here?"

"We're using risks and favors," said Batiste. "Other peoples' risks and favors."

"No one's going to die if we don't catch him this time, Evan."

They were rolling through Livonia when Spencer felt the hairs on the back of his neck prickle. Several hundred yards back he'd glimpsed a maroon sedan that seemed familiar.

Spencer's days were filled with detail: a homeless person in a bright ski jacket, an I VOTED HILLARY bumper sticker, a truck's gouged and rusty rear underride guard, the bare metal exposed by some inattentive driver. The minutiae of a life on the city roads. As his mind quested for signs of danger, he saw it all. And now he wondered whether there'd been a glut of maroon Chargers of late, or just a lot of one in particular?

He knew that paying heed to his driver's sixth sense could make the difference between champagne bubbles or burning. He faded out Cal's words of wisdom on how the Tigers could do better and feinted a move into the left turn lane while watching his mirrors. And there it was.

"We got a tail."

"Don't worry about it," said McGrath. Its presence actually seemed to make him happy. He was working his phone.

"Stay on the ninety-six. Head for the bridge. I hope you remembered your passport."

Batiste watched the twin towers of the Ambassador Bridge recede in his mirror as they swept west on the seventy-five. Now they knew why it had been easy to keep up with Spencer. They couldn't just follow a suspect vehicle into Canada without warrants. To add insult to injury, they also suspected its monetary cargo had been dirty all along.

What they didn't know was that it had also been easy for a man hanging back on a motorcycle to pick their car out.

25

Playing to Lose

"What's up?" said McGrath without lifting his eyes from his phone.

Their car was sailing high over the Detroit River on the Ambassador Bridge, heading for the Canadian border.

"How come you don't worry the cops are, you know, wise to you, to us?" said Spencer.

"Should we all not go to work because the cops are sniffing our asses?"

Cal laughed to himself. It unnerved Spencer even more.

"But if they are on our case, am I going to get busted for carrying a ton of drug money around?"

"Ah, see that's better. Maybe it's a British thing, but oftentimes you seem to be saying one thing but thinking something completely different."

"I'm glad you approve of the way I'm speaking today."

"Yep, I do." He went back to his phone.

The car fell silent again. Spencer's pulse was racing. He glanced in the mirror, but Cal was gazing out the window, giving him nothing. Paranoia warped his thoughts. Why was McGrath being so blasé? Was that Dodge Charger working for him—or the cops?

Or both? Maybe they're going to sell you out? Pin the three bodies found in your car down in Delray on you someday?

Spencer's mind flashed back to when McGrath suggested he retrieve his shit from the car before the Yo-Yo lit it up.

Oh, sweet Jesus, maybe they filmed you grabbing that bag of cash.

He casually moved his right hand to the top of the wheel, letting his left drop to the door pocket. His fingers curled around his phone. Without appearing to take his eyes off the road, he opened the voice recorder app, hit Record, and gently placed the phone back in the door pocket.

"You never answered the question, Dom."

McGrath looked up. "Sorry, I lost interest somewhere back around when we crossed the river. Come on, say it! Show some balls, man!"

"Fine. Why aren't you even worried about the cops? Especially when, what was it you said, way back? Oh yeah, 'When you're at war, everyone has to do their job. If there's one weak link in a squad, he gets the whole squad killed.' So why am I the only one who seems to give a fuck?"

McGrath had his little smile on his face.

"This is a big joke to you, Dom? I've got a little girl! I go to jail, what happens to her? Why aren't any of you bothered? Maybe because—"

"Because?"

Spencer shook his head. Feigned reluctance. "Whatever."

"Come on, say it for Chrissakes."

McGrath tapped his arm, softened his voice. "Hey, come on. We've been doing this longer than you. Isn't that right, Cal?"

Cal said nothing.

Spencer went for it. "Dom, that was my car those guys were in when the Yo-Yo killed them. Right?"

"Yeah, so? You got a nicer ride now."

"That's not the point. What if the cops think I killed those guys?"

They joined the line at the customs gate.

"Spence, I told you. There's nothing to worry about on that score."

Now Spencer didn't need to feign difficulty reining himself in. "Don't fucking 'Spence' me, Dom! You had those guys killed, and you're holding that over me, a bigger gun to my head than a few busted cars!"

McGrath looked incredulously at him for a moment, then around at Cal, then back at Spencer, and burst out laughing.

Cal snorted derisively and shook his head. He fished his passport out of his jacket and handed it to McGrath.

"Oh that's really funny, is it?" said Spencer. He dropped his window and handed over their passports.

"Fingers crossed, gentlemen," said McGrath quietly.

The customs official asked them the nature of their trip.

"Business," said McGrath without hesitation.

"How much money are you taking into Canada today?"

McGrath got out his wallet and leafed through the notes. "I got . . . about a hundred and fifty bucks. Guys?"

"About one twenty," said Cal.

"Maybe ninety," said Spencer.

The customs officer leaned out of his booth. He gave the three of them and the car a once-over, deliberating whether they deserved additional scrutiny. Spencer was glad he'd chosen to bring his US passport. It made their party more nondescript.

"Enjoy your trip to Canada, gentlemen."

Soon they were cruising up the Canadian side of the Detroit River.

"Caesars is closest," said Cal

"Sounds good. Could get lunch at Neros," said McGrath. "Stay on Riverside, Spence."

Spencer was still recording but had no idea how much space there was on the phone's memory card. He wondered if it would start beeping. Caesars was the closest casino and he suspected McGrath's mind would be on other things the moment they walked through its doors.

"'The supreme art of war is to subdue the enemy without fighting,'" McGrath said. "You know who said that, Spence?"

"Can't say I do."

"Sun Tzu. He was some Chink general. From two thousand years back. You ever wondered why it is our customers don't take care of their own shit?"

"They certainly talk about it often enough."

"Exactly. They talk about it. They even get together and make a start. Things go well, then someone gets a puck in their face and *boom*, they're having a major beef."

Spencer had noticed it.

"So you see, Spence," continued McGrath, "we're kinda like the puck. You feel me?"

Spencer thought about the phone. "Not fully."

"You remember the Vernor Highway homies were getting all cozy with their bros at Nately Place?"

"Pucky's crew you mean?"

"Yeah, Pucky's crew. Well, we were the puck that fucked Pucky's crew. You can't say that after five bourbons I tell ya. And soon I figure we'll fuck the Vernor Highway crew too. We've fucked most of those boys one time or another. Except none of them knows it. Kept them fighting, biting, and fragging each other like rats in a sack. Turn right here."

"But what's that got to do with those three guys the Yo-Yo whacked?"

"One of those kids, the one that lost his face and then got flame grilled in the back seat, he was related to the head honcho over at Vernor Highway. So a certain someone you know whose aging appearance kind of belies an expertise in the world of social networking, he dropped into the grapevine a few little scene-of-crime facts that only the cops or killers would know and might have laid a little trail of bread crumbs back to Pucky's crew, which is why—"

"Fuck *me*," said Spencer.

"Ahh, our boy's caught up, Cal."

"Took him long enough."

"That's right, Spencer. Pucky's gonna need to find another two right-hand guys. But that's probably gonna take some balls on his part, and rumor has it he don't have any of those no more. And as for the cops, well, they're just clutching at straws, trying to find out how we operate, what we're planning, but they got no clue because they have no accurate intel. They'd need a guy working with us for that."

They pulled up in front of Neros Steakhouse, Caesars' in-house eatery. A valet with military-style epaulettes and gloves approached. The three of them went to get out. McGrath grabbed Spencer's arm and looked him dead in the eye, still smiling, still likable.

"One thing, Spence. Why would you think I'd be thinking about pinning something like that night in Delray on you? That's just stupidity on your part. Why, you're here for just the same reason as the rest of us. You've just been slow to realize is all. And I don't know why, boy. Making money, laughing. What's not to like?"

"People dying?"

"People like your old guy in the gas station? Or people like the crack stacks who wasted him and wanted to waste you?"

Spencer said nothing.

McGrath nodded. "Let's go to work. You should be good at this too."

Spencer hit Stop on his phone as he got out of the car. Cal went for the trunk.

Spencer believed his rib eye béarnaise was the best steak he'd ever had.

Cal tapped his knee under the table. "Take it."

Spencer looked down. Cal was offering him a thick wad of notes.

"There's four grand there, Spencer. Take it for Chrissakes."

Spencer took it. He had to straighten out in his seat in order to work it into his pocket.

"Soon as you've lost around two hundred bucks then stop whatever the fuck you're doing and come find me. Got that?"

Cal said to forget the blackjack and go for the faster games. Whether losing or winning, he needed to do it fast. As soon as the check was paid they went and changed their cash into gaming chips.

Of late, Spencer had managed to cut back on his gambling. There'd been the occasional binge at the MGM Grand and Greektown Casinos, but they'd been punishing. He'd gone online on Chris's laptop a few times—until he forgot to delete his search history one night. Chris had gone batshit and put all sorts of blocks in place. Now Spencer couldn't even google any gambling-related word without sending a flare up over Highland Park. He suspected Chris had recruited Abby as an informant too.

Spencer did pretty well to start with but the same old fail streak came back soon enough. He tracked Cal down to the craps table.

"I'm down two fifty," he whispered.

"I thought I told you around two hundred?"

"Sorry. Got carried away."

"Well don't get carried away. We got a lot to get through today. I'm just wrapping up here."

"How you doing?" said Spencer. He asked automatically rather than out of interest. He'd given up making small talk with Cal.

"Thought I was done but I just won three hundred bucks."

Spencer nodded. "Nice."

Cal shook his head. "Find Dom and tell him we're done. Then go cash your chips in."

"We're going already?"

"You got a problem with that?"

"I just don't see the point of changing four grand and then changing it back after we all lost a couple hundred bucks."

"Really? It ain't a tough one to get your head around."

The penny dropped for Spencer.

For the rest of the afternoon the three of them hit the tables of Windsor, Ontario. Craps, roulette, baccarat, even the wheel of fortune. They'd drive between casinos, sometimes pulling over to let Cal retrieve or stash cash in the trunk. Before they went into each place, he'd share it out like a big candy stash. One time Spencer was five hundred bucks up. Cal told him to change it back and just to keep it. He was the only person Spencer had known to be irritated by a winning streak. Even McGrath seemed to enjoy a big win every so often.

On a mojito break, Spencer asked McGrath what the point of trying to lose was. Surely it didn't matter, so long as their cash was getting cleaned.

"We come here quite a lot. It's not our only method as you know, not even our biggest, but the casinos are less likely to take notice if they're winning. It's a small price to pay."

Spencer knocked back his third mojito. He was starting to wonder whether he needed to reevaluate things. He'd won another three hundred in front of McGrath. McGrath had slapped him on the back and asked him why he looked so unexcited. On hearing what Cal had said, McGrath just smiled.

"That's his job, to take care of numbers. It's why I hired him. What? You thought I hired him for his ray-of-sunshine personality?"

Spencer had laughed at that. He'd then gone on and lost the money anyway and McGrath had laughed at him in turn.

Maybe this whole gig wasn't so bad. He hadn't realized there'd been a bigger picture, that they weren't out to get him. Maybe they hired him, and kept him on so persuasively, because they knew him better than he did. Maybe he goddamn well could cope with this, and not just cope with it—maybe he could ride this wave like a boss.

He needed a piss. He'd downed just enough mojitos to get that little buzz—and the dulling of his wits.

He left his phone on the bar.

26

Melvin and Caitlyn

Melvin sat down on the bench beside Johnny Boy. He stayed upright, rather than sitting back. Hands drumming the tops of his knees, he looked around at Johnny Boy, smiled, then laughed. He made out he was laughing at Johnny Boy's choice of meeting place, but Johnny Boy knew better. Lots of things made Melvin nervous, including changes in routine. Melvin liked routine. Needed it.

"How come you didn't just come to the shop like normal, Mister Pace?"

Johnny Boy had known Melvin was an unstable quantity from the moment he met him when he was working at a small computer repair shop near Chandler Park. And just as quickly, Johnny Boy had worked out that this skinny nineteen-year-old in his massive combat pants and *Star Wars* T-shirt was an IT genius and a budding hacker. The fact that Melvin wasn't especially cautious about who he enlightened as to his talents made Johnny Boy cautious, hence the alias.

"What's wrong with a park bench on a nice day like this, Melvin?"

Melvin sniggered, then shook his lank black hair out of his face. "I guess."

"How's things?"

"Yeah, good man, real good. Looks like I've got an all-area pass to Comic-Con."

"Wow, that's great. How much did that set you back?"

"Nothing." Melvin said it in a who's-the-man kind of way. He didn't really do the modesty thing. Johnny Boy knew what was expected of him and fell in with it. He didn't have all day.

"You're kidding me? A VIP pass to Comic-Con for free?"

"Uh-huh." Putting his hands behind his head, Melvin sat back finally. He held the new pose for all of thirty seconds before needing to sit forward and tap his knees again. The fidgeting irritated Johnny Boy, but he kept a handle on that. Getting what he needed from Melvin was like getting what he needed from a puppy. Be sweet, be interested. Stroke the ego of a teenager who was different from other teenagers.

"So come on then, Melvin. Or are you going to keep me hanging here? How'd you pull a stunt like that?"

"My mom's seeing a guy who makes all the Marvel figures, man. It's a frigging dope job."

"What? He designs them, or he actually makes them?"

"Makes them."

"Every single one?"

Melvin laughed. "No, man! Jeez! Do you have any idea how many that would be?"

"Well, they're goddamn popular, so it would be a lot."

"Exactly."

"Like a real lot!" Johnny Boy left it at that. Stopped himself from clarifying that the guy in question probably pressed a button on a mold machine. No point in taking the wind out of the kid's sails. He suspected Melvin's mom and her new guy would be counting the days until Melvin trotted off to Comic-Con for a week. Money well spent.

Johnny Boy took his jacket off and laid it on his lap. He rolled up his sleeves. It was too hot to be outside, but this meeting needed to take place away from prying eyes, both human and electronic.

"How's the hacking? Any great successes?"

"My mom's really come down on me for it. But—"

"Ah, I knew it! Don't leave me hanging, partner. Spill!"

"Well, put it this way: if Mister Pace wanted to take Mrs. Pace on a swanky little spa vacation with—"

"You're kidding me."

"With!"

"Oh, sorry. Carry on."

"With some free car hire thrown in, then Melvin here may just be able to help you."

"Melvin, you are one clever dude."

Melvin sat back again, readopting his "yeah bitches" pose.

They both looked at the trees. An attractive woman jogged by. Johnny Boy watched Melvin out of the corner of his eye, to see if the kid perked up, checked out her ass. He didn't. A small dog ran up to them, wagging its tail, wanting a stroke and some fuss. Melvin leaned forward, letting the dog sniff his hand. He patted its head.

Johnny Boy mused about how differently he and Melvin saw what was in front of them. Johnny Boy saw normal kids playing, kids who reminded him of his grandkids. He saw the sunlight shining through the trees, dappling grass and path. He saw retirement. Comfortable retirement. Wheels had been set in motion that would make this possible. He looked at Melvin and couldn't figure out for the life of him what the kid was thinking.

"So what about, let's see," said Johnny Boy as if thinking aloud, "if I was to set you a challenge like, say . . ." Johnny Boy delved into the pockets of his jacket, found a piece of paper. "I got a license plate here. Unmarked cop car, probably DPD. If you could tell me who it's allocated to, man, I would be so impressed."

"But why? I mean, is he, y'know, with your wife?"

"My, uh, y'know, Melvin, you're right. And all I've got is a license plate."

"Maybe, I guess."

"I'd be so goddamned impressed, Melvin. Tell you what. What was that model thing you liked?"

"Death Trooper Specialist? Dude, it's like two feet tall. It's fucking sex ninja."

"How much?"

Melvin laughed. "Like, six hundred bucks."

"OK, Melvin, you up to it?"

"I guess. If I can't do it by myself, I've got a buddy who can help."

"OK, well, that's between you and him. I don't like to meet lots of people, Melvin. You know that. You're the best. That's why I only meet you."

He sensed Melvin swell with pride.

"Do we have a deal?"

"Sure, Mister Pace. Shall I message you like normal?"

"Nah, use my Facebook. One other thing. Can you do some research into the best suicide sites?"

"Huh?"

"Those sites people go on before they throw themselves under a train, play the Blue Whale Challenge, that type of thing."

"That's kinda sick shit, man."

"Sure is. It's really dark, right?" said Johnny Boy.

"Dark."

"Yeah. My daughter is, well, she's a teacher. She wants to give parents a rundown of the sites to look out for. It'd be worthwhile work, Melvin. You could save some poor kid's life."

Johnny Boy watched his words work their magic. He nailed it home. "I was sure you'd want to help her out. I told her I knew a guy who did superhero shit for a frigging living."

Melvin nodded. That was him, alright.

Caitlyn Dunn hadn't been popular at the Delray CPS. Not because she had a name that screamed WASP. Not because she didn't much engage in office banter, although neither of those helped. It was because she seemed to have no idea how tight resources were. Every time she escalated a case or recommended an intervention or petition to the court, the finance controller would catch her breath and take another antacid.

So when she applied for a position as one of Oakland CPS's senior case officers, Delray was only too glad to say goodbye. To boost her chances, they gave her a reference that could have been written by God, which was kind of helpful, since a normal reference from even the highest in Detroit civil service wasn't worth a great deal these days.

The transfer took Caitlyn north, out of Detroit's industrial dumping ground and into the suburbs. But it wasn't an escape.

It was part of her plan. She needed a promotion. Not because she craved validation or money but because she needed influence. Caitlyn Dunn was one of those rare breeds working in state government who wanted to change the world or, to be precise, the world of any child in need. If she got high enough in CPS, she'd be able to change policy. In the meantime, between promotions, she'd concentrate on each case that hit her desk.

At Delray they'd called her the 3-2-1 Girl behind her back. The name had followed her to Oakland; she knew that much. She was sure someone in Delray had been happy to pass on warnings after the transfer became official because by that time it was too late; Oakland was getting what it was getting. The office manager and finance controllers could only sit tight and hope that the less eventful surroundings of the suburbs might tame the 3-2-1 Girl.

On this particular morning, she sat at her desk looking at a strange file. A foreign father. Local business owner. Reports from a teacher who suspected an alcohol problem. He'd been one of Lonnie's cases and according to her notes he'd seemed fully cooperative on the alcohol issue and had agreed to attend meetings at Common Ground.

From the get-go, the case had barely made it into Category Four—some evidence of neglect but not enough to substantiate. CPS allocated thirty days to assess whether a case merited a full-blown investigation and for this one the thirty days seemed to have passed without incident. He'd turned up for meetings. Physical examinations of his eleven-year-old daughter had thrown up no signs of abuse or malnourishment. Lonnie had signed the guy off.

Then another call came in. Source wished to remain anonymous. Nothing unusual there. Teachers and family members often took that route. Unfortunately for the guy in question, Caitlyn was new in her job at Oakland and her workload hadn't stacked up yet. So she had time to make more inquiries after the anonymous call had come in. She dialed Lonnie's extension.

Lonnie answered and Caitlyn got straight to the point. The two of them didn't have a warm relationship. Caitlyn put it all down to Lonnie seeing her as competition. She wished she could have just said to her that she had no intention of encroaching on Lonnie's hunting grounds.

"We just had an anonymous call through on one of yours, Lonnie."

"Really? Which one?"

"Abby Burnham."

There was a pause. Caitlyn sensed something. Was Lonnie bristling?

"OK," said Lonnie hesitantly. "What's the scoop?"

"You want me to send you the caller details and what they said?"

There was another pause before Lonnie spoke. This time it was with an uncharacteristic warmth.

"Look, Caitlyn, can I ask you to take this one on?"

"Take your case on?"

"Uh, yeah, I guess. You won't have to do much. Spencer, I mean the father, he's not . . . You should just leave it at Cat Five."

"Why so certain?"

Again, Lonnie paused before responding. "He's mixed up in some shady stuff or something. I had a visit from a couple of detectives about the guy. They were trying to get me to put pressure on him to stop working for some sketchy people, that's all."

"'Sketchy'? As in?"

"Criminal, I guess."

"OK. And did you?"

"I, uh, tried, but, well, it's hard to know if it goes in."

If the conversation had taken place face-to-face, Caitlyn would have seen Lonnie wince at her choice of words.

"From what our caller was saying, it would seem he hasn't listened to you on anything, Lonnie."

"You might have more luck with him. I was probably too soft on the guy."

Spencer returned from the casino restroom to see McGrath talking on the phone. When Spencer realized it was his phone, his heart rate redlined in a nanosecond. He tried to walk fast without looking like he was walking fast.

"He's right here now. I'll hand you over," said McGrath. He handed Spencer the phone.

"Hello?"

"Mister Spencer Burnham?"

"Speaking."

McGrath tapped Spencer on the shoulder. They were leaving. Spencer fell in behind them as they walked past the one-armed bandits and roulette tables.

"This is Oakland Child Protective Services. Mister Burnham, we need you to come in and see us again—"

"Hang on, my case is closed. I was signed off."

"Yes, but your case has been reopened."

"By Lonnie Estevez?"

His question was ignored. The caller was obviously following a crib sheet.

"Could you come in and see us today, please?"

Spencer looked at his newly cleaned watch. They were at the valet station, waiting for their car.

"Today? No, it's gone four, and I'm in Windsor. Why has my case been reopened?"

"I'm not at liberty to say. I'm going to have to insist that you come in today, please."

"Did you not hear me say I'm in Canada?"

Their car rolled up.

"OK, Mister Burnham, would you mind holding for a moment?"

"Sure," said Spencer as they all got in the Subaru.

A few minutes later, as they were rejoining Riverside Drive, the CPS woman came back on the line. "OK, I've checked with your case officer and she says tomorrow morning will be fine."

"Tomorrow morning?"

"That is correct, sir. Eight thirty."

"Eight thirty?"

Seriously, Lonnie, what the fuck is your problem?

"Yes, sir. Have a nice day."

Spencer was stunned. Then he remembered where he was.

McGrath was looking at him. "Trouble?"

"I, well, I'm not really sure what it is."

"Sorry I answered your phone, but it was ringing off the hook 'most as soon as you hit the john."

Spencer relaxed, remembering how he'd been feeling back in the bar about work, about money, and about McGrath. "Sorry, Dom, these people, they're really busting my balls over nothing."

"Who are they?"

"CPS."

27

Max

Max Petrovsky thought he should already know what unconditional love was, seeing as he had two kids. But sitting on the bench in Palmer Park watching his nine-year-old grandson play soccer, laughing, skidding, and rolling in dust kicked up from sun-scorched grass, Max had something like an epiphany. It dawned on him that he loved someone so hard it caused his heart to ache. He wondered why this should be the first time he'd felt love so strongly, so unquestionably, seeing as he was a father nearly sixty-five years of age.

He hugged and fussed over that boy. He'd sweep him up in his arms as soon as he arrived to look after him, while his son was getting ready to go to work. He'd bury his face in the boy's soft neck, tickle him with his stubble, and say things like: "Boy, are we gonna have an adventure today!" And sometimes, out of the corner of his eye, he'd catch his son, frozen in the kitchen doorway, lunch pack and thermos in hand, looking at them both. And Max knew he'd be wondering why Max had never been like that with him when he was growing up. Max knew it probably hurt his son, but he was no more able to stop himself hugging his grandson like that than he was able to piss in a continuous stream these days.

Max would lay down his life for the boy. Cheap, clichéd sentiments and yet for him, so very real. The thought of the boy suffering in any way, if there were a chance Max could have taken on that suffering himself, would make living unbearable. What should have been purely the reflections of a hardworking man approaching retirement, sentiments mulled but not put to the test, had become strangely topical. Max was starting to think it was a fated thing.

Because the boy was about to suffer—a lot. There was a chance he was going to die. And if he were to die, it would leave Max behind on this earth still, wondering if there were anything he might have done or given up to prevent it.

One month ago, Max and his son had found out the boy, their boy, had leukemia. First there'd been the bruising, which they'd put down to the rough-and-tumble of childhood. But the bruises had been slow to go. And quick on their heels had come the tiredness. Not the tiredness of a boy who'd run and played and stayed up late for a whole weekend but a deep tiredness, a tiredness that seemed to infuse his very spirit, making it an effort to pack his bag and get in the car to go to school. Then the tests had started.

For some unfathomable reason, Max had started to get an awfully bad feeling. He'd asked his son whether he had decent health coverage. His son had said they had the basics, but times were a little tough. Their house, like many houses in Detroit, had been a stretch to buy but was now foundering in the doldrums of negative equity. The Petrovskys were a family of hardworking souls but not of wealth. Blue-collar immigrants who had settled in Detroit in the boom years and taken pride in their tiny but tangible contribution to their adopted homeland's economy.

Getting sick in America costs. Even if there are no guarantees and the patient—the name, the number—doesn't make it, the doctors and hospitals still have to be paid. If the healthcare provider deems the prognosis—the prognosis of the name, the number, not the beautiful boy running and falling in the grass—bad, then they can suddenly become . . . unforthcoming.

What Max was going to do next could well cost him the pension and comfortable retirement he'd worked hard for.

In a couple of hours his son's wife was going to be home. Max would drop his grandson off and say his goodbyes. But he wasn't going home to get ready for his shift. He was going to drive a half dozen blocks west into the University District, a quiet and respectable neighborhood but not so well-to-do that its residents have to know what all their neighbors do for a living. A man lived in the University District who wanted to pay Max a lot of money for a favor. He was charismatic and persuasive, to be sure. It would amount to no more than ten minutes' work. Max had been wavering, but now he'd made up his mind. Ten minutes' work and forty thousand dollars. The man didn't know that Max would sell his soul for all eternity for a lot less these days. How times change.

28

Three, Two, One

Spencer felt everything about Child Protective Services up in Madison Heights was unimaginative. The building looked like a city architect had phoned in some specs and they'd got to work. Where the hell were the windows? He'd asked the receptionist if she could turn up the air-conditioning. She'd said the levels were preset.

Not for a heat wave.

He needed a smoke and coffee. His head ached more than usual.

He still didn't know what had made Lonnie go all hard-ass. This was bullshit! He was done with CPS. Nothing ends well. Just accept it was fun while it lasted and move on. Did she want to take her perpetual singledom out on the guy who'd been using her as a booty call by laughing at his floppy dick? If that was the case, then she was going to be sorely disappointed. The Viagra he'd taken before he and Abby left Chris's was going to make sure of that.

His crotch ached, as it had done for the entire journey to CPS that morning. He felt his dick pulsing as they waited at the light on Conant and 8 Mile. So hard, like it had been cast in stone. It had been awkward getting out of the car.

Back in the game.

He felt his dick unfurling again. He had never taken Viagra before. What if he'd taken it too early? The thought gave him an unpleasant jolt. His dick stopped getting hard too. He didn't think to put the two together. Instead he wondered whether he should take a second one.

He messaged his query to Vincent the dealer, hoping for an immediate response. None came. What was the worst that could happen? He'd fuck Lonnie too hard? Would that even be possible?

He dry swallowed a second Viagra and tried to herd his thoughts back to times when he and Lonnie were going at it over her desk. Apparently, this double strategy was effective, because soon he was *very* hard again.

Abby was reading something on her iPad. She'd barely spoken on the car ride up there.

Spencer didn't need these guys to tell him what needed to stop, but he'd play it cool and polite, maybe crisp up the accent a little and be that guy that leaves them wondering just why he was there in the first place. It had certainly worked on Lonnie and it would work on her again—well, that and the pulsing truncheon of love currently tent poling the crotch of his chinos.

The receptionist called him back over.

"Mister Burnham, could you take your daughter to the clinical therapist and then return to the waiting room?"

Abby's time with the therapist was just a routine part of the whole box-ticking brouhaha. Abby said she had to answer lots of questions about school, home, parents, friends.

Spencer's phone pinged as he returned to the waiting room. It was Vincent. *"Call me asap!"*

"Mister Burnham, could you go to Room E please. That's upstairs."

Upstairs? This is new.

There was a knock at Caitlyn Dunn's door. It opened before she had a chance to respond. She looked up to see a slim white guy in his thirties closing the door behind him. Slightly too slim in fact. He seemed surprised to see her. In fact, he stopped closing the door and reopened it to check the letter on its other side.

"Mister Burnham?" asked Caitlyn.

"Uh, yeah, that's me."

"Would you care to sit down?" She pointed at a seat. Spencer looked at it, then at the woman pointing at it. The room was identical in terms of layout to Lonnie's office. But Lonnie's room was on the floor below.

"Look, uh . . ."

"Caitlyn Dunn."

"OK, I think there's been some confusion here, Caitlyn. I was one of Lonnie Estevez's cases. And I was signed off like ages ago."

Caitlyn noticed the accent. British. She checked her notes. "Yes, three weeks ago almost exactly."

"Like I said, quite a while ago, so, frankly, I don't know why I'm here."

She couldn't work out whether he was slightly agitated or just in a hurry. She'd heard from the receptionist the guy could be quite the charmer but that today he was in a pretty tetchy mood. What she saw now was a face that was just managing to hide that. And she couldn't work out whether or not he was attractive because of it. His collar was open several buttons and sweat glistened below his Adam's apple. He stood strangely, too, with his hands clasped in front of his pants. Maybe that was a European thing.

He sat quickly, almost gratefully, in the proffered seat.

She went back to finishing her notes.

Spencer looked at her. He wondered why he hadn't seen her before. He reckoned he'd seen most of the people who worked at the Oakland CPS, even if it was just a glimpse. Her long, unstyled dark hair was tied back, but worn loose it might have worked pretty well for her. As far as he was aware, Lonnie had been the most attractive chick there and he'd thanked his lucky stars he hadn't had to bang some old dragon in order to pass the time and lubricate the bureaucratic process. But this woman, Caitlyn she'd said her name was, she was kind of easy on the eye. As soon as Spencer had the thought, he knew he was kidding himself. She was right up there, except for one thing. Her vibe was cold, asexual even. Her loose blouse hid everything, and she wore almost no makeup.

He wondered if this was some sort of formality and soon he'd find himself back with Lonnie. He was certainly ready for her. His dick was actually hurting now. He looked down in his lap trying to figure out how obvious his arousal was.

He decided to speed things along. "If you don't mind my saying, I might be able to save us some time here."

Caitlyn glanced up but went back to reading as she replied. "How's that, Mister Burnham?"

"Spencer, please. Well, as we both know, I've been signed off and nothing's changed and today I am kind of pressed for time."

Caitlyn detected a tinge of impatience, not yet exasperation although she felt that might be in the cards. She glanced up again. "Well hopefully this isn't going to hold you back too much. I'll be right with you."

She decided she didn't like the way the guy spoke, like he was turning up the Englishness. It reminded her of that stuttering English actor, the guy who did nothing but chick flicks but in real life was apparently cantankerous. She hated chick flicks, but she'd watch sci-fi quite happily.

"What I mean is . . ." He petered out as he saw she wasn't going to stop reading. Obviously, she hadn't even looked at his file until five minutes ago.

She looked up at him, giving her polite, no teeth, no-effort-required smile that said, *Go on.*

"Well, what I mean is, nothing's changed in my situation since Lonnie closed my case. Work's picking up. Abby's doing fine. Your nurse has probably finished with her and could confirm that."

Caitlyn nodded. Spencer felt his anger simmer. When Caitlyn was sure he'd finished, she spoke as if he hadn't.

"OK, Mister Burnham. Do you mind if I ask you some questions?"

His mask of patience was slipping. "No, let's go for it."

"Three meetings ago your case officer suggested you attend counseling and support meetings at Common Ground on Washington for drinking, which you agreed to. How's that going?"

"It's great. Not that I have a drinking issue. Whoever phoned that one in, she smelled alcohol on my breath when I came to pick up Abby after a working lunch. They can be quite boozy."

"Which evening support group was it?"

Spencer sighed. "Thursday night. Alcoholics."

"Right. That's what it has here," she said, pointing at his file.
Dear Lord above.

"You're pretty sure it's that night you've been attending?"

"Hundred percent."

"Common Ground over in Royal Oak?"

"Yes. Are we going to go through everything this carefully today?"

"That depends I guess on how forthright and cooperative you intend to be with me, Mister Burnham."

There was something not right here. The sun was beating through the window, hitting the entire left side of Spencer's body. His crotch and inner thighs felt moist with sweat, his dick hurt, the back of his shirt was sticking to the seat, and he found the way this woman spoke to him, and looked at him, disconcerting.

"And you haven't been attending those meetings."

"I . . . what?"

"The last two Thursday nights, I've been there. The first time because I was curious to check it out as I'm newly transferred to this office. Second time to accompany a vulnerable client. You weren't there."

This was so left of field that for a moment Spencer had nothing. Caitlyn waited. He rallied.

"Look, I've come up here whenever you guys have called me. There is no reason for you to suspect I have a drinking problem. I can see in your line of work why you'd think any mention of alcohol is bad news but in the real world sometimes—"

"OK, we can come back to the alcohol. I have another question, possibly more sensitive, but it is relevant to Abby, so I have to ask."

Spencer made a throwaway gesture and sat back.

"Is there a reason you didn't take up our recommendation for bereavement counseling in regards to your wife's death?"

Spencer's game plan of cool politeness went up like the New Mexico desert during one of those underground nuke tests.

"What the . . . seriously, I've got to ask here, what the fuck has that got to do with you guys?"

She noticed the accent was losing a little of its shine.

"As I said, Mister Burnham, we're talking about Abby this morning and it's relevant—"

"It's got fuck all to do with Abby, Miss . . . whatever the hell your name was. I'll tell you what concerns Abby. One thing. And that's me keeping a roof over our heads. You have nothing, fucking *nothing*, other than some teacher overreacting. I came here out of politeness. Do you understand? Came here and answered all your questions till you had no questions left. You guys are a waste of my taxes if we're gonna be honest and if I wanted to, I could just take my daughter and tell you all where to go."

He went to get up but his erection became trapped in the fold of his pants, forcing him to abandon the attempt.

Caitlyn waited to be sure he was done. "We do have a lot to get through today. Would you like to take a moment outside before we continue, Mister Burnham?"

He noticed that she'd said "today," not "this morning," as if this wasn't going to be the usual thirty-minute meeting.

Her eyes seemed to look right through him, seemed to say, *I know your type and I know what your game is.* Her calm, professional demeanor unnerved him. He remembered the security guard he'd passed when he entered the second-floor corridor. A big Black guy. Armed. Looked like he could handle himself.

There was something about the girl, no, woman—she was at least twenty-nine or thirty—facing him that said she'd faced scarier guys in her office.

There was a quiet knock at the door. It opened without waiting. Sure enough, the security guard looked in.

"Everything OK here, Caitlyn?"

Caitlyn looked at Spencer. He sighed. He'd finally begun to realize he had no control in the situation. His phone vibrated. That would be Johnny Boy or Sheila.

"We're fine, Ray, thanks."

The exchange was relaxed. All in a day's work.

"Could I ask if you wouldn't mind switching your phone off while we're here, Mister Burnham? I think it might be a distraction."

Spencer obeyed.

"So, Mister Burnham, here's the situation. For the four weeks of it being open, your case was scored out as a Category Five."

"I have no idea what that means. Some kind of hurricane classification?"

"Category Five means there is no evidence of abuse or neglect."

Spencer gestured as if to say, *Exactly.* Caitlyn ignored it.

"I've been doing this job nearly ten years, and I've probably only seen that happen a half dozen times. We recently received information from an anonymous source saying your daughter is in some danger—"

"Anonymous source? So anyone can phone up, dish some dirt, and, big surprise, here we are?"

"You mean a malicious referral? That isn't the case in this regard because my investigations have shown it to have more than a basis in truth, to be entirely true, in fact."

"Who called you up? It was Abby's school, right? Well just let me say—"

"If I did know the source, Mister Burnham, it would contravene all rules for me to divulge it." She held up a thick sheaf of papers. "So I have here a breakdown from your doctor of your medications, urine tests—"

"Excuse me? You're not allowed access to my medical records."

"You gave us this access, Mister Burnham."

"What are you even talking about? I would not do that. Ever."

Caitlyn hesitated. She flicked through his file. "You're mistaken. You've ticked the boxes granting us all these permissions. And signed the form. You've filled in these forms that way every time you've seen your case officer. No, wait, I stand corrected—from the third time onwards."

Christ, Lonnie! So much for trust and professionalism.

He looked to Caitlyn as if he was about to speak. She gave him a moment to do so before continuing.

"So, the results showed high levels of alcohol, cocaine, and marijuana, besides antidepressants and sleep medication. This brand of antidepressant shouldn't be mixed with alcohol and is known to raise the body's tolerance to drugs like cocaine. You've said to Lonnie on several occasions that you often have your daughter in the car. Despite requests from your previous case officer, you never supplied any negative drug test results or consented to ongoing drug screening. It was a serious procedural infringement on her part to overlook this. I work differently. Now, on to your bank statements and financial status. You recently filed for bankruptcy. You mentioned earlier that you have rent to pay, however you no longer rent private accommodation. You left the address this office had for you without leaving a forwarding address and owing two months' rent. This is the answer your daughter gave when she was asked to describe her father's bedroom."

Caitlyn removed a page from the file and held it up for Spencer to see. It was a drawing of a couch. "You're with me so far on this, Mister Burnham?"

Spencer looked at this woman and couldn't work out which he hated more. Her or the fact that he was being so comprehensively busted by her.

"Now, coming back to our categories. For your information, we have five. Five says nothing's wrong. You're no longer in that category. Nor Four. You would have been a Category Three, which says there is evidence of neglect and a ninety-day investigation is to be opened and support services offered to parents. However, since I've confirmed you haven't cooperated on the support offered, it means you're now a Category Two."

Spencer waited, breath shallow, hangover concentrated into a small point of pain just above his brow. He hadn't noticed his dick had finally gone soft.

"Category Two means there *is* evidence of neglect and danger. The case is open for another thirty days so there'll be further investigations. Your name is going on a list called Central Registry. This means you can't be a teacher or nurse or do any job working with the public. But I have to further advise you, Mister Burnham, that in view of the immediate danger to Abby from your drug and alcohol abuse and inability to provide a roof over her head, it's my intention to move this up to a Category One, where the children are taken out of the home, or wherever home might be."

And *boom*—the 3-2-1 Girl was back.

29

Pushing the Button

"I just want to make sure I heard Johnny Boy right. We're talking forty grand of clean money," said Cal, putting his feet up on the empty chair beside him. To McGrath, that was a pretty bald-faced affront; those chairs retailed at a grand apiece. They were stolen but still. More to the point, by putting his feet up like that, just after he'd questioned McGrath's judgment, it was as if he were saying, *Oh this should be good. Let's hear it.*

Cal was becoming a source of vexation. The underlying reason was clear: he felt McGrath was making poor decisions. Cal thought highly of himself.

"Cal, do you remember when Max Petrovsky came in here last?"

"Sure. He was wavering."

"Exactly. Wavering," agreed McGrath. "How many times had he been in?"

"No idea. I lost interest after the first two visits."

"Now that's the difference between you and me, Cal. I manufacture opportunities. Most times, that takes longer than folks expect. But you? Well, you work the numbers. But you wouldn't have any numbers to work if it wasn't for me. Or Johnny Boy. I know you're struggling with the Max Petrovsky thing but being as I'm a patient sonofabitch I'm going to walk you through it one more time. After one thing. Either you slide those hooves offa my seat or I'm gonna put mine right up on that suede dash next time you take me out in your sparkly little Porsche."

Cal obliged with a shrug.

"So, Max Petrovsky. He's worked for that company for thirty-five years. Spotless record. No one thinks him remotely capable of doing anything that involves tech shit. So he's an essential part of what could be a fucking perfect crime. But he's scared shitless he might lose his pension or give himself away by getting all shaky and nervous, that kind of shit. So he'll only do it on his last day. That's one shot, Cal. That day is coming. Every time he came by here he was like: 'Oh, I dunno, Mister McGrath.' And of late he even asked us to stop asking him. It wasn't looking good."

"Should have just threatened him."

"Excuse me?"

"Should have just found something that mattered to him and—"

"Oh wow, you really like to go straight for your guns, don't you, Cal?"

"Hey, you always say you want an honest opinion."

"Always value an honest opinion, just not one that's more likely to get us a lifetime pass to prisneyland. Tell me, honestly, which is the best scenario. I say to a guy who's been an honest working man his whole life: 'Hey, Max, either you play ball with us or I'm going to arrange for your daughter-in-law to have a life-changing encounter with a train.' Or: 'Max, I know you're in deep shit so I'm going to help you take care of a loved one, but I need something in return and no one else need ever know.' Tell me, Cal, which option do you think is more desirable if you were this guy?"

The two looked at each other. Cal took a certain pride in not caring whether anyone liked him. McGrath, on the other hand, was brilliant at winning people over. Cal mistook that talent for need.

"Johnny Boy says the kid's probably not even going to make it anyway," he said.

"Not my problem, Cal. Just make sure his bills are paid. All of them. If he's going to buy the farm, then he can have a nice funeral on me."

Johnny Boy entered as Cal left. He stood passively, hands in pockets, until they heard the reception door swing shut.

"We're a go," said McGrath.

"As of when?"

"As of when I got back from Canada last night and Max was standing on my porch."

Johnny Boy nodded, mulling what this meant, what needed to happen. "How long?"

"Waiting for his last shift schedule but he figures his last day will be end of next month."

"You want me to move it up a gear with Spencer?"

"Yep. And your little freakster, he come through for us?"

"I'm going to put my money on Asperger's. But put it this way: I have a goddamn two-foot doll in my car."

* * *

Spencer felt numb as they headed south down the flat open road that was Dequindre Street.

Caitlyn Dunn had said he had no support base "to compensate for the difficulties he was facing." He actually had a sister, back in the UK. They weren't close, never had been. Old streaks of childhood resentment. Their dad had found it much more to his taste going along to his son's karting meets than watching her play clarinet. She'd reached out though, after "it," the game changer up on I-75. Spencer hadn't been interested. Why would he care about the past when his whole future had just died?

He'd heard people say, wives whose husbands had been blown to shit on a road in Fallujah, heard them say that after a time most folks didn't understand how long the pain went on for. Was that why these widows and widowers still went to support groups? He wasn't ever going to do that. He'd never been a team player. Drivers weren't team players.

The sun glinted on his watch as they drove past Hazel Park Raceway.

But you're losing our daughter.

Marielle, it's not like that.

Tell me how it is.

They don't understand. No one does. I need those things.

You call them things, but you know what they are.

I was going to stop it all. When I made that new start for us in Toledo.

She is what we made, Spencer. Abby came from our love. You're all she has. And she's all you have of me.

I know! I'm fucking on this, Marielle!

Abby watched her father drive. They cut southwest. Spencer avoided the freeways today. They all seemed to be slow, sticky with the heat. Their car barely stopped. Abby was used to that.

They drove past mansions, abandoned and overgrown, that must have been beautiful in Detroit's heyday. To Abby they were still beautiful, just in a different way. Like the crumbling ruins of a lost empire. Paris of the West, Mom had called it. Dad used to care about that stuff. She felt the burn of imminent tears. Not good, not just because she didn't cry about Mom anymore but also because school was five minutes away. She was going to arrive in time for break and people would know she'd been crying.

He glanced at her, saw her staring straight ahead, somewhere else.

How long have you been losing her?
Since I lost you, Marielle.
Since you lost yourself, Spencer.

Later that day, when he knew Abby would be back from school, Spencer took a break from his rounds and headed home. He wanted to talk to her, to see if she understood what was going down and to see if there was some way he could reestablish their connection. At least then, when the next CPS meeting happened, she might make them reconsider, even if he couldn't.

He waited over an hour before Chris had cause to go out. Then he went and found her on the fire escape. She was on her back on the couch playing a driving game on her iPad, legs up against the wall, bare feet scrunching up and down the cool brickwork.

Spencer took a beer from the fridge and sat on the armrest.

"Mind if I join you?"

Why do you need to ask? She's eleven and it's not even her bedroom.

She ignored him. She was wearing earphones. He tapped her shoulder. She took one of the earphones out, holding it as if to ask whether this would take long.

"You could take a faster line on those corners," he said.

"I get more points for drifting." She went to put the earphone back in.

"I need to talk to you, Abby."

"Uh-huh?"

"Can you take the other earphone out?"

She did so, crossed her arms over her iPad, and waited. Spencer couldn't decide whether or not the attitude was petulant.

His phone pinged. It was Vincent, wanting to know if he was the greatest stud in Oakland. He put it on silent.

"So I just wondered if, uh, someone were to ask you, would you say you're happy here?"

She eyed him, trying to figure out why he'd ask such a thing, but then remembered he missed a lot sometimes. In fact, he could be a bit of a doobhead these days. "Sure," she said. "It's the coolest part of the apartment."

"I mean with Chris and me?"

Abby struggled to verbalize what she was thinking.

Her dad never got on board with anything. It was like nothing excited him. Chris always said he had problems at work. Time and time again he made her sad or upset. Made her feel guilty and stupid for missing Mom. And that upset her as much as thinking about Mom. She liked Uncle Chris, liked her room there, but didn't like the way her dad was like an unhappy visitor passing through.

"Things aren't the same." It was the best she could come up with.

"You mean, they're not the same as when Mom was with us?"

Abby nodded. Spencer swigged his beer, tasting nothing. He watched a squirrel work its way up one of the pine trees. "Things are going to be fine, Abby. OK, I'm not saying they'll be the same as when Mom was alive, but I promise they're—" He saw a tear roll sideways off her cheek. It splashed onto the fabric of the sofa, leaving a small dark stain.

Great. We've barely said anything.

"Abby, listen, whatever those people up in Oakland try to sell you, they're not going to bring Mom back or make things just like they were. You need to know it's bull—, nonsense, I mean. OK?"

Abby said nothing.

"Abby. Speak to me."

But Abby was already off the sofa and doing that angry fast walk-run thing that girls learn to do when they're oh so young. Her iPad slipped slowly off the edge of the seat and landed unhappily on the metal floor, earphones slithering after it.

Spencer hung his head. He let the pattern of metallic diamonds on the fire escape floor go out of focus.

Talk to me, Marielle.

Nothing.

Caitlyn Dunn was thinking about the guy whose life she suspected she'd ruined, although he'd been doing a pretty good job of that himself. She liked to think of herself as a fair person but he'd been given too many chances by Lonnie.

Even though she was new to Oakland, Caitlyn already had her doubts about Lonnie. She wondered whether her colleague had been swayed by the whole charm offensive the Burnham guy was apparently capable of pulling. It was hard to miss how desperate she was to bag a guy. Ray told anyone who'd listen that she'd given him herpes.

Whatever had gone on, or not gone on, between Lonnie and Burnham, Caitlyn realized that he'd really annoyed her, to the point that she hadn't gotten around to raising the matter of his employment with him. How had he gotten under her skin so? The sarcastic British thing?

The hurricane comment had pissed her off. But she shouldn't have shown him Abby's drawing. With a degree of shame, she realized she'd wanted to punish him, a man who'd lost his wife in a car wreck only four years before. He'd been a normal father until then it seemed.

And that was when it dawned on her. Abby Burnham's parenting hadn't been normal. Even if her father had been normal, then her late mother couldn't have been. Because Abby was an extraordinary kid. Some of her grades were off the scale. She hadn't even been asked to draw a picture of the couch. Sally-Ann, the clinical therapist, had laughed herself stupid over it, hadn't been able to help herself. Then apparently Abby had joined in. She could converse like a fourteen-year-old. That would be partly down to necessity; when parents were absent, figuratively or literally, kids had to grow up fast.

Caitlyn was going to save that girl from a father who'd obviously decided she should go down on his sinking ship. He wasn't Caitlyn Dunn's worry, but Abby Burnham? She deserved better.

Normally there would be a tide of procedural hearings and meetings to follow if a case were to be escalated. But less than a month had elapsed since Spencer Burnham was last the subject of an investigation, an investigation in which there'd been serious oversights. And he was now a confirmed Category Two.

She knew she'd neglected to raise the issue of his employment but did that really matter? The detectives who visited Lonnie had confirmed Burnham worked for criminals.

And Caitlyn was now a senior supervisor.

All this meant a great deal of that bureaucracy could be by-passed or sped up. It was time to get things rolling.

30

Blowing Chances

The nature of Spencer's work changed after Canada. The pickups and drop-offs became less frequent. When he wasn't doing the normal laundry runs, he had to go out west to Warrendale and River Rouge Park.

If no one was available to go with him, he'd have to call Johnny Boy to say he'd gotten to whichever start point they'd given him. Sometimes Johnny Boy would ask for a picture of what he was looking at. Then the stopwatch would click and he'd go, fast, by different routes but always to the same general destination: Downtown and its Financial District.

Denny would sometimes follow in his truck, but he was allowed to take a direct route. If he beat Spencer the drive was considered a failure, and Spencer got a pay cut.

He suspected some of the other guys were taking up the slack. He was only partly right. When the Yo-Yo blasted out of the gates on his Ducati and disappeared for hours on end, he was doing something entirely different.

The Yo-Yo had been given an assignment of his own, the sole purpose of which was the gathering of information. The time was coming when the Yo-Yo would be put to work again, doing what he did best.

"I'm no longer his case officer," said Lonnie. She quickly went to close the door of her office.

"That won't wash, Miss Estevez," said Batiste on the other end of the line. "I need more. First time we all got together, everything was real polite. I wasn't so pressed for time."

Lonnie was glad she'd no longer have to see Spencer. Often of late she'd caught herself loathing him for making her feel so worthless. But she had no means of exacting any revenge and seeking it wasn't good for a person anyway. That's what all the self-help gurus said on her Instagram feed anyway.

"He treated you badly, didn't he?" said Batiste suddenly.

"Excuse me?"

"Miss Estevez, Lonnie, I know you and Burnham were . . ."

He left it hanging, letting Lonnie fill in the blanks. Her heart was pounding. She hadn't expected her career to go the same way as her self-respect because of Spencer.

"You see I called your mobile, not your office line?" said Batiste. "I don't want this recorded. I don't want to get you in trouble here."

"What do you want, Detective?" she asked quietly.

"I need to do my part, Lonnie, so that other people can do their part. I'm just a cog in a machine. And what our machine needs is a way of getting Spencer out of the works."

"Oh," said Lonnie. And it was as if Detective Batiste, not a friend as such, but the enemy of her enemy, had drawn aside a drape and shown her the way.

"He has a DUI," she said. "His daughter's school reported him for driving her while under the influence."

"That's not going to cut it."

"A DUI with a child on board, Detective, is deemed 'Child Endangerment.' A first child endangerment offense is only a misdemeanor, a second within seven years is a felony. It carries a jail term of one to five years. I'm a little surprised you don't know this, but then I can tell you're not a father."

"But I wouldn't know when—"

"Detective, I'm going to give you the name and number of someone who'll be able to let you know where and when."

Spencer might have wondered more about the driving "missions" he was being sent on if he hadn't been distracted. Letters had started coming from CPS. Most were standard templates confirming things he already knew, like the reopening of Abby's case. But they came fast, an unstoppable torrent, sent his way by Caitlyn Dunn. Spencer had a really bad feeling they were the harbinger of something worse. He couldn't believe he'd lost control of the CPS situation so spectacularly. He'd crashed cars more slowly.

Chris actually seemed to be handling things better. One day, Spencer came back to news there'd been a home inspection by CPS. Zero warning. Chris maintained he'd handled that well too. Someone had to keep things together after all.

"I showed them she had her own bedroom," he said. "The refrigerator was full, I work here all the time, all that stuff."

"You told them how good her grades were?"

"Of course."

"So, how did they react?"

Chris pondered for a moment. "Well I, now that you mention it, they didn't seem too bothered, I guess."

"Like they might just be going through the motions?"

"Which is good, right?"

Spencer looked at the CPS building through his windshield.

Marielle, talk to me.

Why?

I need to stop this happening.

There's no point asking me anymore, Spencer.

What do you mean?

You don't listen to me. You don't listen to anyone.

I'm asking you now. They want to take her from us.

What do you do well, Spencer?

All I could ever do was drive.

You raced.

So what good is that now?

You said a race could be like a fight.

So what?

So then fight. Fight for our daughter.

"Ms. Dunn has no available appointments today, Mister Burnham." The receptionist's voice was gaining an edge.

Spencer became conscious of the people in line behind him: shuffling, an impatient exhalation of breath. He was sweating.

He leaned over her desk. "I am not going anywhere till I get five minutes with my case officer, the one who's decided I'm not able to keep my daughter. How hard is that for you to understand?"

"I'll see what I can do, Mister Burnham."

Her finger slid under the desk and pressed a panic button.

"Thank you." Spencer sat down. He felt the eyes of everyone in the room on him.

A few minutes later a door opened and Ray the security guard appeared. His eyes fell on Spencer, then flicked to the receptionist who confirmed *target acquired* with a discreet nod.

"I'm going to have to ask you to leave, sir."

If the reception had been quiet before, silence attained new meaning now. That poorly air-conditioned and windowless room seemed to pulse with the anticipation of something fairly dramatic on the bill.

Spencer looked at Ray. The guy was big. Looked like he could have been a varsity football player in his youth and like he still lifted big weights. Spencer couldn't remember the last time he'd engaged in exercise for exercise's sake. He'd gotten into a few fights when he used to go out to drink, but on all of those occasions he'd been too drunk to remember what he was fighting about and who'd won. The same had gone for most of his opponents.

Ray held the door with one hand and rested the other lightly on his utility belt. Spencer looked at the belt. Not just a gun but mace, a nightstick, cuffs.

Spencer sat back in his seat.

I'm not going anywhere.

Ray advanced, flipping open the pouch containing the mace while extracting his nightstick. The technique was one that often worked well. Most people needed time to psyche themselves up. He chose not to give them that time.

Spencer rose, getting ready to land just one hit before the mace or the nightstick got him.

"Mister Burnham?"

The female voice penetrated the arena, freezing both men in their tracks. They turned to the doorway where Caitlyn Dunn stood holding a folder.

Once again, Spencer found himself in Caitlyn Dunn's office. Again the sun beat down on him. He thought about asking whether he could adjust the blinds but decided against it. Clearly, she was unimpressed by his entrance as it was.

"You realize your behavior merely confirms we're doing the right thing with regard to Abby, Mister Burnham?"

"What, you think me being prepared to raise a little hell to keep my daughter is a bad thing?"

"I think the methods you use and the decisions you make work against you."

"Look, I'm here now. I'm listening. Tell me what I have to do."

"What do you mean?"

"Tell me what I have to do to keep her. Tell me how I change your mind."

"OK, firstly, this conversation should have happened months ago, with your original case officer. She assures me you were given all necessary support and advice. You told us repeatedly that you were complying with what she asked of you. Secondly, it's not just my mind you have to change. My superiors get the final say on whether to petition the court and commence adoption proceedings. I can only recommend it to them."

"So, if they take your recommendations, then you could recommend holding things back?"

With Lonnie, Spencer had known he had the situation under control by the end of their first meeting. But if the woman sitting opposite shot him down, he was fresh out of moves. It felt like drifting on an unfamiliar road, where the slightest twitch, omission, or overload could end things badly. Super-tuned senses scanned for signs of indecision. It didn't help that there was something about her making him want to be a little more impressive than he suspected he was.

Caitlyn wondered how gently or firmly she should shoot him down. She was no longer swimming in time but she did have some residual guilt for not giving a damn about the guy's past. And sometimes, when there was the possibility of an impending loss of custody, parents could get their act together.

She looked down at her paperwork. Formality was a shield for her. It stopped her from investing emotion in her work. She didn't realize this was what stopped her from being a great case officer, as opposed to just a conscientious one.

"Mister Burnham, I appreciate—"

Spencer detected a hint of reluctance. So she was going to let him down gently.

"Look, Caitlyn. Do you mind if I call you Caitlyn?" He waited for her to acquiesce with a shrug. "Thank you. Caitlyn, I know you get all types in here. I know I was rude and disrespectful on our first meeting. My bad. But no one comes through these doors without shit going on in their lives. And I love my daughter—"

"Would you give consent for drug screening?"

"Would I . . . Sorry?"

"Would you leave a hair sample here, knowing I'm going to send it to the lab?"

Spencer's mind was blank. Why hadn't he planned this better? He thought about the new start in Toledo that had never happened and all the good intentions that had gone with it.

"I've been working on all that. These issues only became issues when my wife died. And I've got good money coming in."

"On that, do you have bank statements, a tax return, bearing in mind we have you in our system as filed for bankruptcy?"

Caitlyn waited a beat to be sure. "OK, medical and financials aside, I have to ask you, is your daughter currently exposed to any other risk that you haven't mentioned?"

"Risk, as in?"

"Is there anything else concerning Abby's well-being that I should be aware of? Your work, for example. Does it involve criminal activity or close contact with criminals?"

Spencer didn't even think before responding. "Absolutely not."

No sooner had he spoken than it seemed the meeting was over and Caitlyn was holding the door for him. Ray appeared, all pumped up and ready for trouble. Behind him, a scrawny, backward-baseball-cap-wearing guy in his twenties with hollow eyes and cheeks, Dunn's next appointment, bounced impatiently from one foot to another. Spencer's time was up, and it wasn't really clear how the knife-edge scenario had played out, whether his ride was on its roof or back on track and still a contender.

He hesitated at the door, wanting to test the water to see whether he'd won her over, or at least bought himself a stay of execution. She saw it coming, though.

"Thank you for making the effort to see me, Mister Burnham."

"No problem. Thank you for your time. Sorry about . . ." he glanced at Ray, before nodding and indecisively ambling off.

While Caitlyn's next appointment made himself comfortable, she clicked an option on her screen to file a petition with the court. This would request an order for the removal of Abby Burnham from her home.

Spencer's stint as Abby's father had been doomed by a meeting between two detectives and Lonnie Estevez. Caitlyn Dunn knew Spencer Burnham was involved with some bad people. She didn't know whether that meant he couldn't be a good father, but then that was his fault. He'd had his chance to tell her and he'd blown it.

By the time Spencer hit 9 Mile he'd convinced himself he'd clawed it back from the edge. He was so convinced, in fact, that he attended his first meeting at Common Ground that very night. He stood up in front of a bunch of people and confessed his life had gone to hell not because of the death of his wife but because he drank, smoked, and sniffed too much.

He then managed forty-eight hours without a drink or a joint but was awake for pretty much the entire time, even with sleeping pills. Sometimes he'd have to grip the wheel just to stop his hands from shaking. He got confused on two driving missions and rode the lightning from Johnny Boy and McGrath on it, and took a pay cut.

That night he looked down at himself and wondered whether he'd end up alone in every sense of the word. No wife, no daughter, no future. Maybe he was the stumbling block here. Maybe his best-before date as a father had expired and he'd just been slow to realize it. Would Abby be better off with someone else? And if that came to pass, would her new parents talk sometimes about her real dad? They'd do this out of Abby's earshot, of course. Perhaps they'd wonder why he hadn't been able to get himself together since his wife died. And when those thoughts came, he would have to get up and find his friend, the friend who was on call at all hours in all places—the forty-proof friend.

31

The Limiting of Options

One of the perks of owning an internet-based company is that home can be anywhere. Why, if things are set up right, a guy could be sitting above the snow line in the Himalayas seeing his garden supply company sell a leaf blower to some dude in Vermont. He doesn't have to lift a finger other than the one working his smartphone. Even the delivery is handled automatically, probably by another online company started up by another clever guy or gal sipping mai tais on a beach somewhere.

Chris didn't start internet selling so that he could climb in the Himalayas or live by a beach. He'd taken redundancy before they simply took away his role. For a lot of folks, redundancy means the chance to travel, to get a little spiritual in a yoga retreat, or to learn a language, before moving on to the next job. But at Chris's age, the word "redundancy" can be dangerously synonymous with early retirement.

He'd always had a little dream of working for himself and selling something real. Although he didn't have a great deal of interest in living a healthy lifestyle, he'd liked the look of a certain health and fitness supplement franchise and their support had been good. Now he was starting to do well. His mentor said Chris could be quite a success. Not so long ago, growth in any business meant hiring people. Not so much now. Chris's company could grow a whole lot more before another human was needed.

If Chris had had a family, then things would have been just peachy. But life hadn't worked out that way. The first woman he'd married had wanted kids when he felt he hadn't been able to afford them. His second wife left when Chris left his dependable salary behind. Abby was the closest thing he would ever have to a child of his own. And it was because of that he found himself, on what should have been just another working morning in his sun-drenched apartment, wondering which countries didn't have an extradition treaty with the United States.

He'd heard Costa Rica didn't have an extradition treaty with anyone. He wondered if Abby would take to it. It sounded hot, remote, and a little backward. There had to be more than just one place without a treaty with Uncle Sam. Hell, just think of all the countries they'd pissed off. The entire Middle East for starters. Still, not an ideal choice. What about Russia? If the CIA couldn't get that guy Snowden back, then they sure as hell wouldn't throw out too many legal grappling hooks for Chris Wilcox and his gang of desperados.

He knew in his heart, though, that Abby would suffer in a country where English wasn't the first language. Chris would be fine. People would still buy Thermo Booster Burn wherever he was.

And Spencer? Well, fuck Spencer, because as far as Chris was concerned, it was down to Spencer that he was now standing in his quiet hallway, his overly quiet hallway, holding a letter that caused his heart to pound so hard he could swear it was making the paper shake.

In the maelstrom that was a typical day in the life of an overworked DPD detective, things often went from bad to worse—and stayed there. Staffing issues had decreed Batiste spend the entire morning running base. Then a rejection email from his latest Michigan State Police application had come through. But just when it seemed the day was a goner, he'd received an urgent call from a teacher at McDade Elementary. She and Batiste had spoken several times, and Batiste was of the mind that she was extremely upstanding, highly efficient, and not someone to cross.

Now, through branches gently waving over cut lawns, Batiste and Scott watched the road outside McDade Elementary, where an endless stream of parents jockeyed for parking. Some had commandeered spaces in good time, and sat waiting in their cars. Spencer Burnham was one of them. Their new confidential informant had spotted a hip flask in use.

"Nearest school building's got to be a hundred yards away," said Scott. "Did she used to be a SEAL?"

A bell rang out.

Any moment now.

Spencer watched the horde spill out from the school gates. His phone started ringing again. It hadn't stopped for the last hour.

Johnny Boy would want to know why he hadn't made any drops since his last AtoB pickup. But Chris had called right afterward and, since then, Spencer couldn't care less about money, because Spencer had just started to grasp how far he'd fallen.

Chris had found out about CPS's petition to the court. Had found out before Spencer, in fact. That was the downside of a mailman not asking whether the guy signing for the official-looking document was its designated recipient.

Spencer had stopped his rounds and driven straight to Abby's school, arriving nearly an hour early. He wanted to be with her. He wanted to make things right. Perhaps he could do that if he took her away somewhere, before Caitlyn Dunn took her away.

The door opened and Abby jumped in.

As he watched her don her seat belt, he longed to make her know he loved her, and to ask if she still loved him. But he couldn't seem to express these things. It was like a spell shut his brain down when he even tried to think them through. He was getting desperate.

"Abby, listen, I want to—"

He was cut off by the short blip of a police siren right next to them.

About the same time in McGrath's office, dissent was showing itself from unexpected quarters.

"He ain't one of us. He's from another country and he's a drunk," said Eddie out of the blue. It was uncharacteristic of him to be so forthright, and for some reason it bothered Johnny Boy.

"Foreign is good," said McGrath.

"Why is foreign good?" persisted Eddie. "Rosso's gone! I don't even drink. And I came here from miles away too."

"Fucking Nebraska," agreed Cal. "At least they drive on the

right there. I found Eddie. Eddie helped the Yo-Yo take care of things with Rosso."

"I could do it," added Eddie.

"With all due respect, you can't even work your phone," said Johnny Boy.

Eddie knew he had to make a stand. This is where the action was going to be and he needed to be close to it. "You tell me where you want me, where to meet Dom. I'll get it to you guys."

"We aren't going to know where it happens until the last minute, Eddie," said Johnny Boy. "That's the whole point of Spencer. And when it comes to meeting Dom, Dom decides where closer to the time. Why is that? Ask Rosso."

"You guys need to get a little real," said McGrath. "Spencer comes from nowhere, so he'll go back there real easy."

It was rare for both McGrath and Johnny Boy to miss things. But they were distracted by the annoyance that was Cal and by the sound of Sheila's phones blowing a gasket, which was all too common these days. AtoB was in meltdown.

"Max's last run is the end of next month. No one else'll be ready. You guys got that? No one. If this doesn't happen with Spencer, it doesn't happen. Now someone get him here."

Then McGrath told them to leave his office.

But the croupier should never turn his back to the table.

"Officer, could we do this somewhere else?"

Kids and parents were swirling around, gawping. It didn't help that the Charger had a flashing red light on its dashboard.

"Right here is good," said Batiste, leaning in close to Spencer. "Driver's license and insurance, please, sir."

Batiste straightened up, made eye contact with Scott across the roof of Spencer's car, and waved his hand over his nostrils. Spencer reeked of booze.

Spencer handed his license over and then leaned across Abby to get his registration out of the glove compartment.

"Mister Burnham, if you don't mind me pointing it out, I think I can smell alcohol on your breath."

"I can assure you I haven't been drinking."

"In that case, it'd probably be best if you let my partner here run a few quick sobriety tests. That way we can clear this whole thing up and you can be on your way."

Spencer didn't move.

"Sir? You want to step out onto the sidewalk here, please? And while my partner helps you out, would you have any objection to me searching your car?" said Batiste. He was enjoying this moment and being especially polite made it all the more exquisite. His phone pinged. He ignored it.

"Sir?"

Spencer opened his door and joined Batiste on the pavement.

"Pop the trunk for me please," said Batiste.

In a kind of daze, Spencer obeyed and then watched Batiste dive in.

"Over here, sir," said Scott.

Batiste went straight for the speaker casings.

Spencer was trying to walk in a straight line and watch Batiste at the same time.

"Keep your eyes on me, please, sir," said Scott. Burnham had already failed to touch his nose. The walk test was really just a case of buying his partner time.

Batiste's phone pinged again. He caught his partner's eye and signaled him to start the charging process. Then he looked at his phone and couldn't believe what he was seeing.

Batiste moved behind Spencer's back and drew his hand across his neck, telling Scott to drop it. Scott looked at him incredulously. Batiste waved his hands across each other: *Drop it all!*

"I, uh, we're gonna have to leave it there, sir," said Scott. "My partner and I have had an urgent call. Be a little more careful with your driving."

Back in their car, he turned to Batiste. "What the fuck?"

Batiste started up. "We'd better make it look like we do have somewhere to get to."

They pulled away, leaving Spencer on the sidewalk, dumb-founded, but not so much that he didn't clock what they were driving.

Abby was squinting at his registration certificate. "Your registration is expired, Dad."

Once out of Spencer's line of sight, Scott killed and stowed their emergency light.

"Seriously, Evan, the guy was wasted. You had him."

"I know," said Batiste. "And I found a big stash too."

"Then why—"

"We didn't want him to drive but now . . ." He showed Scott his phone.

The secret Batiste, Scott, and Captain Schaeffer shared had to be obeyed immediately and without question, even if it could not explain its reasons at the time. And the secret had ruled that, for things to go their way in the end, Spencer needed to be in this *until* the end.

Spencer took off his shades as he drove across the depot lot. It was getting overcast, like a storm was coming. It needed to come but it would probably be another false alarm.

He parked up and was barely out of his car when Denny called out to him.

"They want you upstairs."

Spencer nodded.

Johnny Boy emerged from the stairwell, and Spencer debated whether to mention he'd just pulled the heat down.

You're in the front line, with the cash. It's you they're going to target.

"Johnny Boy. I, uh, got pulled by the cops just now. Maroon Charger. Black guy. I was with Abby. I think it was the same car that tried to follow us the day we went to Canada."

Johnny Boy looked thoughtful. "You haven't done your drops. So you still had the AtoB cash. Did the cop see it?"

He was strolling around the car.

Spencer hesitated.

Johnny Boy looked at him as he popped the trunk and Spencer felt those searching eyes of his, like ocular polygraphs seeking to penetrate his memories.

"Yeah, I guess he might have."

"Might?"

"Probably he did."

Johnny Boy nodded again. He removed the money. "I'll deal with this tomorrow."

He shut the trunk and headed for the stairwell but stopped as he passed Spencer. "I've had my doubts about you. Sometimes I doubt your nerve, your resolve to see things through. But loyalty? Well, a snitch you aren't. You're not that stupid, right?"

"Sure."

"It's Dom they're after. Always Dom. They tried by getting to a guy working here. But that didn't pan out well for them. Let's go."

As they headed for the stairs, Johnny Boy called out for Denny to join them.

It seemed everyone else had been waiting for them in McGrath's office. Eddie and the Yo-Yo leaned against the wall. Sheila had brought in her own seat. McGrath was at his desk. Johnny Boy sat down in one of the comfortable seats facing him. Cal was already in the other.

Heat exhaustion had apparently done in the air-conditioner. The windows were open and two fans pointlessly shoved the hot air around. The room was full of warm bodies, all of them perspiring. But it wasn't just the heat that hit Spencer. There was something else: a grim tenseness. It was like walking into a foundering peace negotiation.

"Been waiting for you, Spence," said McGrath mildly, as if he'd been wanting to chat about the Lions' chances. Then he addressed everyone in the room. "Our driver here wanted to leave our little family. Wanted to go into respectable business. That right, Spence?"

Spencer wondered where this was going since he was pretty sure the whole room knew that McGrath had him on a chain anyway. "Yeah, well, it wasn't personal. CPS was busting my balls over how I was paying my bills. They still are."

McGrath said nothing but kept looking at Spencer, as if assessing whether he cut the mustard. Suddenly, he held his hand out to the Yo-Yo.

"Phone."

The Yo-Yo handed McGrath his phone. McGrath checked the screen, then held it out to Spencer. "That little video you're so worried about? That's the original, right there. Wanna delete it?"

Trying to read the eyes that laughed at him but with him at the same time, Spencer walked over and took the phone.

"Go on. Johnny Boy will do the same with his copy."

Deleting the video didn't give Spencer much relief and not just because they'd probably kept a copy anyway. McGrath never gave anything for free and always took more than he offered.

"You like the Windy City, Spencer?"

"Only been there once but sure."

He and Marielle had had an epic St. Patrick's Day weekend in Chicago. Marielle's parents had taken Abby away and Spencer and Marielle had made hay while the Chicago River ran green. They'd made love, talked about having another baby, got wasted, fucked. Spencer had held her hair while she threw up. Laughing, both of them. Yeah, Chicago wasn't so bad, as a memory.

"I could see you running a dealership out there. Johnny Boy has contacts, could help you set up," said McGrath.

Spencer was aware of how quiet the room was. "That would be pretty cool, Dom."

McGrath nodded. "Everything I've said I'd do for you, have I done it?"

Spencer nodded. He had to. It was true.

"That's right. And in return, everything we've asked you to do, you've done. You've done real well. All the figures tallied, right Cal?"

Cal gave what was probably the closest approximation of a grunt of assent he could muster.

"One last job, Spence. You might not even realize it, but you're pretty much ready to roll on it. Then you're out, on your way. Respectable car man again, new start, new city. How's that sounding?"

Spencer knew how it was sounding. It was sounding like it always did with McGrath.

You think you been on a ride, boy? Oh no, that was nothing. I'll show you a ride. We're just getting started.

"Pretty interesting, Dom."

McGrath nodded. "Over in Dearborn Heights, just west of Rouge River Park, there's an armored delivery company. Every morning, they roll out of them gates and some of them head to one of the big banks in Downtown."

Already, Spencer wanted to be out of that room so badly it was making his stomach burn.

"So I don't know if you know this, but most armored truck crimes, they're inside jobs. This company takes heavy-duty precautions. Only when their trucks are on the road do they get radioed which bank they have to get to. At the same time, they get an access code which authorizes them to pick up the money. And they get told to take different routes, to keep everyone guessing. So end of next month is going to be the last day of an unblemished employment record for crewman Max Petrovsky.

"You remember those demolition companies we were talking about? Well, Max is going to be riding shotgun in the truck that supplies a bunch of sites. They got CCTV in the cabs of these trucks, so Max has learned to work his phone by feel, and as soon as they get the bank name and access code, he's going to AirDrop the info for ten minutes. When his other hand's against the window that means he's sending. When you—"

Spencer sighed and shook his head.

"What?"

Spencer's tone was resigned. "I'll be following him, real close. Then, just like before, Eddie picks it up on his phone and I drive fast to the bank and Johnny Boy'll use the code to collect before your guy Max's truck gets there."

Johnny Boy smiled. For a drunk cokehead, Spencer could be pretty sharp.

"Close," said McGrath.

"The Yo-Yo'll be with you," said Johnny Boy. "Not me and Eddie."

"It should be two of us," said Eddie all of a sudden, like he'd been chewing on the matter.

"What do you mean? You go as well?" asked Johnny Boy.

"Yeah. We were talking about it." Eddie waved at Cal. "What if the Yo-Yo's phone doesn't work? We got one shot."

Johnny Boy looked at McGrath questioningly.

"Fine," said McGrath. Then he turned back to Spencer. "The big thing, though, I mean what really matters, is that all of this has to be done without getting interest from the cops. If they knew something like this was going down and they got aerial support, then . . . well, it's not like in the movies. You can't get away once they've tagged your ass with a chopper. Not even you, Spencer."

McGrath slouched back in his seat, resting his chin on his hand, waiting. For Spencer, everything in the room was magnified. The fan blades spun in slow motion, like big heavy-lift helicopters taking off—*thwump, thwump, thwump*. A fly trapped between the window glass and the blinds buzzed angrily. Spencer just needed to get out of there somehow. Even Sheila watched him with scorn in her eyes, eyes that said he was too soft, in the wrong place.

Well, you are in the wrong place.

"Dom," he said eventually. "You, uh, you didn't tell me I was signing up for this."

Cal snorted and shook his head with a tight-lipped smile.

"Show some cojones," said McGrath. "I've given you opportunities to prove your worth and you've come through. There's no difference between this and life for a junior exec at Coca-Cola."

"There's a big difference, Dom. 'Life' means something totally different here. I have a little girl! If I go to jail, she has no one."

As he said it, he realized how much he wanted to be there for Abby, for her not to be brought up by some sweet family while her no-good dad rotted away in a cell.

"We're all playing those stakes, Spence. 'Most all of us here got family. But you seen the way we operate. We aren't normal. We aren't some bunch of lame-assed street trash with YouTube attention spans. This is planned, paid for. Cost me a lot already. You ask me or Johnny Boy a question about anything and we'll answer it."

Spencer felt like he'd be struggling for breath if the heat in that room got any more oppressive. The fan *thwumped* away but even slower, like time was grinding to a halt and they were all falling into a black hole. He looked from face to face. Seemed like he was the only one who realized they'd reached event horizon. Seemed they were all cold cooling. Then Spencer realized that they'd all passed their event horizons long ago. He looked again at the Yo-Yo, at Eddie—guys who knew where they were headed when they were kids, who knew they'd only get if they took. And now they were waiting to see if Spencer would catch up and see that he, too, was a man whose only hope was to learn to take, really take.

"I'm in."

32

Escape Velocity

Johnny Boy stood on the john. He had to stand on the john in order to see out the little window and down onto the depot lot. He half watched, half just listened. McGrath leaned against the sink. He watched Johnny Boy watching, while taking the occasional puff on his cigar.

"How's he seeming?" McGrath asked.

Johnny Boy looked out the window again.

"I can't see him yet," he said. "But I can hear him talking to Denny."

"What's he talking about?" asked McGrath.

"Matters pertaining to cars."

"How's he sound?"

Johnny Boy listened some more, then turned back to McGrath. "Relaxed."

McGrath nodded. They heard a car door slam and then an engine start.

Johnny Boy looked out the window again. He saw Spencer's car cruise slowly over to the barrier. Spencer's arm came out of the window and pressed the button, then dangled, limply. No finger tapping or hand slapping on the door while he waited for the barrier to raise. When it did raise, Spencer's car rolled slowly forward, stopped at the road, and waited for a while before cautiously pulling out onto Noble.

"Yep, pretty relaxed," said Johnny Boy.

"Would you say he was peachy keen to tell you about the little narco nigger stopping him?" asked McGrath.

"He definitely hesitated. But I think that might be because he thinks we're as nervous about the cops as he is."

McGrath nodded.

Johnny Boy watched the barrier clang down and then stepped down from the toilet.

McGrath took a final puff on the stump of his cigar before running it under the tap and tossing it in the trash. He faced Johnny Boy. Their relationship would always be simple. Johnny Boy would provide McGrath with information and opinion. And then McGrath would decide. The two men looked at each other while this process took place. Two men who could rock a well-cut suit and order up sudden death without qualm.

"Do it," said McGrath.

Spencer waited until he was out of sight of the depot before putting the hammer down. The Subaru's tires smoked and spat gravel as he carved a tight turn onto the Lodge Service Drive. A stop sign loomed, but he merely checked his blind spots before blasting through. As he powered over the freeway, he was doing all sorts of things at once. Brain cogs spun crazily as he tried to come up with a plan. And a lie. Sometimes the cogs intermeshed smoothly, and an idea fused into being, one with potential. Sometimes they ground and sparked, blowing gaskets and sending rods through cerebral camshafts.

He maxed and matched his car's speed to the distance remaining before the next light, turn, or intersection. He wondered whether his show of nonchalance, his controlled excitement at the prospect of being involved in McGrath's great opportunity, had been convincing enough to buy him some time. All the while he fearfully checked his mirrors. He dreaded seeing the outline of a big man on a motorcycle. Another mental cog whirred stressfully into life.

What the fuck will you do if you see him on your tail?

Drive faster. You could lose him.

Lose a Ducati? Really?

Knock him off? Yes! Knock that big bad killing machine off his damn bike.

He knows where you're going anyway.

So Spencer drove even faster, careening from gap to gap, lane to lane. Sweat ran down his body in rivulets, soaking his stinking T-shirt. He didn't notice. He drove as if fleeing a phantom.

He fished his phone out of his pocket, flicked through the numbers, and looked up just in time to slam on the anchors to avoid smashing into the back of another car. Phone in hand, he shifted down and sliced around the offending vehicle, ignoring the pale face of shock worn by its driver.

He hit Dial. The ringtone reverberated in the car.

Come on, Chris, come on . . .

Chris's voice filled the car. "Where the hell have you been?"

"Chris, listen—"

"You drop off the grid after—"

"Chris, shut up and listen to me. We don't have much time."

"You just realized that?"

"No, you don't understand. We really don't have much time."

Car horns rebuked him for slashing across the freeway from carpool lane to exit on a forty-five-degree trajectory.

Follow that, Yo-Yo.

"What are you talking about?" asked Chris.

"The court petition's been granted."

Silence.

"Chris? Did you hear what I said? CPS is—"

"I heard. What do you mean? They can't. They only just told us!"

Spencer tried to lie as fast as he was driving. "Well, that CPS officer is just, she's like, some psycho child-stealing terminator bitch."

"They can't. I mean, how can they? Abby's safe. She's—"

"Chris! I been doing a lot of thinking."

"That'll be a goddamn first."

"That's right, Chris. You're so right, but hey at least I've started to realize . . ."

More car horns.

"That you were right."

"How so?"

"I needed a new start. We needed a new start, I mean. All of us. I can still keep, we can still keep Abby, but we have to act now. You just need to trust me. We can make this all turn out OK. But Chris?"

Tire squeal. Engine roar.

"What?"

"You need to start packing. You need to start packing right now!"

The silver Volvo was a legit rental, but its plates were stolen from a Nissan. It would have been better if they'd been stolen from another silver Volvo, but Denny hadn't been given a lot of notice so he'd done the best he could. The automotive alias wouldn't stand up to a police check but it was enough to fool CCTV. And it wouldn't be needed for long. Denny expected to return it to the rental company that same day, with its original plates.

Cal drove. McGrath sat next to him. They waited for the barrier to rise.

"Which way?" asked Cal.

"Head west."

"Where's he at now?" asked Cal as he turned onto Noble.

"The Yo-Yo says he'll be leaving soon."

"We know which way he goes?" asked Cal.

"The Yo-Yo's been on it."

Chris's apartment was not a relaxing place to be.

"Can we fit my desktop in?" asked Chris.

Spencer was looking out the window. He replied without taking his eyes off the apartment lot and McLean.

"Anything that can fit in Penny and that you need to sell Thermo Booster Burn, you should take."

"I could transfer everything onto my laptop."

"OK, fine, do that."

"Your packing looks like it needs work," said Chris.

Spencer absentmindedly glanced at the couch, where his suit-case lay open. The few clothes he'd thrown in covered his stash of cash and the money from the gas station robbery, now in a different bag but kept separate. It just didn't feel like it should be his.

Because your money you made in such an ethical way, right?

Give me a break. It should go to Milt's daughter.

She's lost, like you need to be.

"How's Abby doing?" he said.

"I don't think it's really clear to her what's going on. I told her we had to go away and it was an emergency. But she still thinks she's seeing her friends tomorrow."

Spencer nodded. "Have you told her where we're headed?"

"No. I don't see why—"

Spencer sighed impatiently and went back to packing, throwing in some work clothes and a toiletry bag.

"Chris, just . . . trust me on this. I'll explain to Abby when . . ."

When you think of another lie, Spencer?

In a few months, there'd be no need for lies. They'd have made a new start, somewhere safe.

"You know it's nearly six?" said Chris.

"Yeah, so?"

"Well, if CPS were coming today, surely they'd have come by now?"

"You want to take that risk?"

"No, but why not just go to a hotel tonight and one of us comes back tomorrow, without Abby, to pack our shit up properly?"

Spencer's brain was overheating with the sheer scale of fabrication being asked of it.

"You have to trust me on this. We'll come back but not for a while."

"I'm not a damn kid, Spence. And you're a bonehead at times, so excuse me if I don't feel like blindly following you to my doom. Why do we have to take so much?"

Spencer zipped his case shut. "Because the job is between me and another guy. And the other guy has offered to start tomorrow. And as for all of us having to go, well, Common Ground said I have to take myself away from the, uh, the environment where I've been drinking, and y'know, all that other stuff but keep my support base around me. And . . ."

Spencer's mind recalled something Marielle had said when he was trying to give up smoking.

"It takes like, a couple of months to form a new habit. So we have to pack for a couple of months. And when I'm working, who's going to look after Abby, until we find her a new school?"

"A new school?" Neither of them had noticed Abby standing in the doorway.

While he waited for the barrier to open, Johnny Boy looked at the picture on the large box belted securely in his passenger seat. It showed a space-age warrior dressed in high-tech black body armor and a Darth-Vader–like helmet. So that was how a bringer of death should look? Interesting. The Yo-Yo did wear a helmet these days.

He drove out of the depot and headed for Chandler Park.

Batiste followed the winding, empty road that was his back way to the gym at Sterling Heights. He needed a workout. If the day's unexpected development in the McGrath investigation had come through a few minutes later than it had, which was just as they were about to bust the Burnham guy, then everything might really have gone south.

He dropped the windows and switched off the air, allowing his left hand to ride the warm breeze.

The car behind pulled over to allow a motorcycle by. The guy was flying. Made Batiste thankful he didn't work in the traffic division. Imagine chasing down guys like him. Now that would be dangerous.

"Is this where you do all your work, Melvin?" asked Johnny Boy.

"It is, Mister Pace. This is the center of the empire," said Melvin, making a grand gesture that encompassed his room, a room that contained a single bed and walls lined with action figures and spaceships. No pictures of women, no football team paraphernalia, no posters of bands beloved by rebellious teens.

Johnny Boy nodded. Melvin was a happy soul, in his own world.

Melvin pointed at the box on the floor by Johnny Boy's feet. "Can I see the goods?"

"Sure," said Johnny Boy. "Let's see what all the fuss is about, right?"

"Oh, you'll see."

Johnny Boy started opening the box. "That was great work you did finding the name of my wife's, uh, friend." He extracted the space warrior figure and handed it to Melvin.

"D-u-u-u-de," said Melvin.

Johnny Boy nodded at the state-of-the-art computer on the desk in front of them. "So, is this the one you do all your work on?"

"The Beast? Yep."

"You erased the history, right?"

Melvin gave him a sideways look of mock pity. "Mister Pace, really? I mean whaddya think it is here? The peewee league?"

He started taking some shots of the Death Trooper Specialist with his phone. Then, as an afterthought: "Anyhow, I don't just delete history. I shred that mother. Not even the FBI could get the Beast to give up her secrets."

Ah, so at least there's one woman in your life, Melvin.

"Good to know."

Johnny Boy waited a moment before trying to bring things back on track. "Tell me about the Blue Whale Challenge, Melvin."

"Sure." As Melvin lovingly placed the big figurine aside and fired up the Beast, Johnny Boy listened to the silence of the house. He listened for anything that might hint they weren't really alone. He'd made it very clear to Melvin that Mr. Pace required privacy and discretion, and Melvin liked that cloak-and-dagger, secret mission kind of bullshit. As for Johnny Boy, he liked to be careful and thorough.

Abby was upset about not going to school the next day, Chris was upset about Abby being upset, and Spencer was scared shitless about still being at the apartment. He contemplated telling them the stakes but held back; this chapter of his life was about to close and then everything would be alright. He was going to be that father, that successful salesman, that more appreciative friend, but not here. Anywhere but here. Milt had been so right; people need to move away after a tragedy. Not even far. Just down the road could be far enough.

"Why does it all have to go in Chris's car?" asked Abby.

"I told you, we have to take my car back. My car was a company car."

Eventually the wagon train was ready to roll. Abby wasn't happy squished in the back with a ton of stuff. She didn't understand why she couldn't ride shotgun with Chris, at least until her dad jumped in. She didn't know that was because Spencer would be doing precisely that—jumping in. Because the moment they ditched the Subaru, they really were going to be on the run.

33

Sweeping the Trail

The Yo-Yo felt the Ducati lighten on its suspension as it crested a gentle summit. He'd dropped the throttle right off because there was a sharp bend coming up. He'd gotten to know this piece of road in this quiet part of Detroit real well.

Suddenly he stopped, right in the middle of the road. His prey was heading this way. He needed to be ready.

"So here's the deal on the Blue Whale Challenge, Mister Pace. You got some kid who doesn't feel loved or valued, blah blah. They go online and see shit that kind of depresses them and—"

"Show me," interrupted Johnny Boy.

"Huh?"

"Show me the kind of thing they'd look at."

He watched patiently as Melvin whizzed around the darker places of the web: sites set up in Russia and Ukraine and copied by twisted cyberpredators around the world. Windows popped up bearing images of death, loss, and longing. Then there were other themes, more ambiguous in their darkness. These were the cults: The Slenderman and his haunting peers.

"So you've got your super-sad schoolgirl, Mister Pace, and—"

"Keep those tabs open. I might want to check them out again."

"Sure. So you've got some loser who has no buddies or their buddies are mean, whatever, I dunno, and they find this online thing called the Blue Whale Challenge. They get set challenges, like waking up early, watching a horror movie, then the challenges get more, like, hard-core, and 'cause they're super tired and all depressed, their thinking goes nutzoid and so they go along with it."

"What kind of thing would the harder challenges be?"

"Self-harming, that kinda shit."

"OK and then?"

"Well, then they get told to kill themselves. And they do 'cause they've been, like, conditioned. So the last thing they do is post a picture of a blue whale and then sayonara dude."

Johnny Boy was nodding. "And it's as simple as that."

Batiste dialed Captain Schaeffer's number while he drove. As the ringtone sounded and just as he came out of a sharp curve, Batiste saw a motorcycle lying on its side in the middle of his lane. Its rider, unconscious or dead, lay sprawled beside it. Batiste had to react fast to avoid driving right over them. He slammed on his brakes and veered off the road into a dirt turnout, stopping in a cloud of dust.

Batiste looked over at the bike wreck, muttering to himself about how people needed to take greater care. A loud *bleep* filled the car. He'd forgotten about his call. Seemed like the captain's voice mail had kicked in anyway. Batiste cut the line. He decided to check on the rider before calling out an ambulance. If the guy was dead, he'd tell them not to rush.

He glanced over again at where the bike lay and was surprised to see its rider was now missing. Suddenly his passenger door opened. A bulky figure wearing a motorcycle helmet got in beside him. He had a colder-than-ice stare and a gun pointing right at Batiste's guts.

"You move, you sleep."

As Batiste tried to make sense of the situation, he heard a voice in his ear.

"How's it going, Evan?"

Batiste spun around in his seat. Inches away was the face of a man he'd only dreamed about meeting in person—to read him his Miranda.

"You don't seem so happy to see me," said McGrath. "Now that don't make a whole lotta sense, 'cause I know you been following me, following folks who work for me. Why, frankly, some might say you been goddamn obsessing about me."

Batiste tried to think quickly. He couldn't get far past his stupidity, his arrogance, at failing to even consider the possibility that his quarry might double back on the trail.

Another face appeared at his open passenger door. Buzz cut, slightly overtight shirt. McGrath's accountant. Seemed like the gang was all here except for the lawyer.

Batiste felt McGrath's hand slip inside his jacket.

"Where is it?" asked McGrath.

"In the glove compartment. Too hot for a shoulder holster," said Batiste.

The Yo-Yo switched hands with his gun, opened the glove box, and extracted Batiste's service weapon.

"What's your beef with me, Evan?" asked McGrath, taking Batiste's gun from the Yo-Yo.

"I ran the crime stats. They didn't add up. Knew someone was running a cleaning op like a boss. Might not be so easy anywhere else. But here? In a bankrupt city?"

Batiste was working hard to come across as in control. No one would be relaxed in his current situation, unless they were stupid. He'd just been expertly jumped. But if he at least came across as in control, then there was a fair chance they would think he had a good reason to be so. He decided it might also be prudent to look like he was really listening to whatever horseshit they were going to threaten him with. It was a tough job though. Every one of his senses seemed to hum. His mouth felt dry. He felt it showed in his voice, like those first-time TV interviewees with their parched clicking throats. He heard birds singing, the hum and throb of distant traffic.

Why are no cars coming by? Because this is the back route to the gym, Evan, the one that dodges the crowds, remember?

He smelled the motorcycle leathers of the big guy next to him. He knew who he was, too, knew he'd killed, but only lowlives and maybe a witness once. He felt his hands in his lap on the fabric of his suit trousers. Gray. His second-favorite suit. Slightly thinner than his favorite. Better for the heat.

There was other stuff Batiste knew. And he was confident that McGrath didn't know he knew. So he found himself wondering why the ambush.

He heard a small *click*. Sounded like a safety catch.

There was no time for his brain to ponder it any further. Or anything any further. The round from his own weapon punched up through his chin, through the roof of his mouth, his brain, and out the top of his skull, embedding itself in the car's roof, thereby turning the Charger from departmental ride to suicide scene in a microsecond.

McGrath turned away as the detective's blood sprayed his face. Batiste's head lolled forward, in its crown a craterlike aperture from which a dark, shiny river of blood flowed continuously.

"Jesus," said Cal.

"What's wrong?" said McGrath, without looking up. "You never seen a guy kill himself before?" McGrath had seen two suicide scenes, both during his Gulf War days. Both guys had chosen the same method: bullet through the chin, forty-five degrees through the software and out of the dome. Lights out and a big ole mess.

McGrath was wearing white latex gloves. Being careful not to interfere with the blood spray patterns, he closed Batiste's fingers around the handle of his own gun. He leaned back to take in the scene. The car looked like some sort of gory cave. Dark, jagged fragments, unidentifiable, clung to the roof fabric. Batiste's white shirt was almost entirely red.

"Cal?" said McGrath, peeling off his gloves and shoving them in his jacket pocket. He'd burn his entire outfit later; the disposal of evidence linked to this wasn't something to delegate.

Cal jogged back to the Volvo, opened its tailgate, and took out a yard brush, one of the birch-branch types favored by photographers in their Maine and New Hampshire–style home decor shoots: ineffectual for proper yard clearance but perfect for eradicating footprints left in dry dirt. With Johnny Boy's guidance, the Yo-Yo had researched this place well for them.

"People coming," called out the Yo-Yo as he hauled his bike up.

Cal was sweeping his way back to the road. "Fuck, Jesus," he said to himself at the added pressure. He stepped onto the asphalt and threw the broom to McGrath.

McGrath laughed as he caught it. "Now bring the car up, fast." He knew his attitude spooked Cal and that that could only be a good thing, but he actually was enjoying himself. He'd gotten the same thrill in his army days, when there'd been something dangerous going down. It was a thrill he'd enjoyed since he was a kid, the thrill of knowing he was, most likely, just going to get away with something.

The Yo-Yo yelled out that whoever was coming was just around the curve. He gunned the Ducati and took off.

McGrath threw the broom in the back of the Volvo and climbed in. "Go, Cal!"

Cal didn't even check his mirrors. He just floored the gas and they hightailed it after the Yo-Yo.

Neither spoke for a while. McGrath was waiting. He didn't have to wait long.

"What the fuck, Dom?"

"What?"

Cal looked at him askance.

McGrath said nothing.

"You said you were just gonna get a make on the guy, get a feel for whether he worked alone or whatever."

"I already know he works alone. He has a rep for it. He was trying to get out of the DPD. Trying but failing. He must have got depressed about it."

"This is all for your Max Petrovsky thing? Whacking a cop?"

"Our Petrovsky thing, Cal. I don't see you turning down any checks. And we whacked a cop. He was on our case. You think DPD has the buck power to have more like him on our quiet little op?"

Cal was silent. Mouth agape, he wore the face of a man just trying to keep up.

"Sorry, Cal, I'm confused. Seems like only yesterday you were reprimanding my ass for not being as raring to go for my guns as you."

Johnny Boy saved the image of the blue whale to Melvin's desktop. He, too, was wearing white latex gloves. They came from the same box as McGrath's. He returned to the internet. Multiple tabs were open. He shut some down, left others running. He opened Melvin's Facebook, went to Friends and deleted about half, including Mr. Pace. Then he uploaded the image of the whale to Melvin's feed. He typed "Goodbye," hesitated before hitting Post, deleted "Goodbye," and typed "May the Force be with you all." Better. Random and quirky, like Melvin was. He glanced around.

There hadn't been space for Melvin to fall completely on the floor. When the gun had gone off, he'd toppled backward in his chair and landed awkwardly against the foot of his bed, with what was left of his head pushed forward onto his chest. Whatever T-shirt he'd been wearing was now entirely dark crimson, making its geekster motif indiscernible.

Guess they'll have to check his dog tags to see which star trooper squad he belonged to.

Johnny Boy went to go but sensed something looking at him. The Death Trooper Specialist.

Five hundred bucks.

He checked carefully around the figure to see if its removal would disturb anything, thereby turning the bedroom from suicide scene to crime scene. Johnny Boy plucked the figure from the desk and replaced it in its box. He'd wipe it for prints thoroughly later. Time to go.

He wanted to find out how things had gone with Detective Batiste, but that would have to wait until he'd driven his obligatory five miles before turning his phone back on.

Spencer parked the Subaru a block down from the depot. It was just past eight and still sunny. He would have preferred it to have been dark. He knew that the paranoia would really kick in when he did what he was about to do. If someone had been watching him the entire time from when he'd left the depot and been giving him the benefit of the doubt, then this would be the moment there'd be none. He could just about explain away Abby and Chris going on a road trip. But leaving the car?

He walked a short distance away and stood in the shade of a hickory tree. He pretended to check his phone while scanning the immediate vicinity. Nothing moved. No other cars or motorcycles had followed him into the street. He forced himself to wait another full minute before walking back to the car and placing the key on the rear tire.

He walked back up the street and around the corner. Chris and Abby were waiting in the Prius. Spencer jumped in. He scribbled the address of where he'd left the Subaru on a piece of paper and mailed it to the depot before they hit the freeway. All three were hungry but they wouldn't stop until they reached Toledo.

34
AWOL

"Another?" said Zed.

"Another two," said Spencer.

Zed had stopped being incredulous. There was something about the British element of the Fairlane experience that was really working. Spencer's figures were going to be out of sight if it kept up. It was weird when he'd strode back into the dealership, having dropped off the grid since their first meeting. But Spencer said he'd work for free until his first sale. That kind of thing resonated with Zed's own zany brand of moxie. "Take the floor, my friend," he'd said. An hour later a couple put their card down for a fully loaded BMW 5 Series. That had been two weeks ago.

Three days ago, he'd given notice to the rest of his sales guys. Then Zed had employed his eldest niece as receptionist. Her sole duty was keeping people sweet with drinks and small talk while taking their details until Spencer was free to take their money.

Zed still knew little about his latest employee. Spencer turned up, chatted amiably about cars and the weather, and left at five. He politely declined offers to socialize outside of work hours and any form of social networking was a definite no-no. He wouldn't even let his picture be taken for fear of being tagged somewhere.

Zed knew from his lawyer that Spencer had a seriously bad credit history. When the matter of pay and Social Security numbers came up, Spencer mumbled something about seeing how things were going after a few more weeks. The guy was obviously the type who'd sailed too close to the wind: a man after Zed's own heart. Besides that, he was apparently more preoccupied with working than with worrying about how or when he was going to get paid for it. And that made him catch of the century.

One afternoon, Zed watched Spencer wave off a customer.

"You think Mister Indecisive is going to buy something?" he asked.

"Definitely. He loves the car but doubts his judgment," said Spencer. "Been married three times so I guess he wants to choose the right car at least." He lit a cigarette.

"You want to quit that, Spencer. You have way too bright a future ahead."

"Working up to it."

"About your money," said Zed after a few moments.

Spencer looked on edge.

"Cool those jets, my friend. I'm not pushing for your life history, I just want to pay you. It gives me pleasure to reward you. I mean you're not here for your health, right?"

Spencer smiled.

"I get the impression you need to be like the tires on this M3 here," continued Zed. Spencer looked at him quizzically.

"Low profile," explained Zed. "So, we can do that. My wife's cousin, Youssef, he is, how can I put this nicely? I can't. He's a goddamned oxygen thief. He is the most useless motherfucker I know. He will never hold a job. So, here is my idea, my friend. I pay your money to Youssef. You let him keep, say ten percent and . . ."

He trailed off. "Ah, I see you follow me. Tell me how this is sounding to a man who wishes not to be found?"

Spencer smiled.

Take the right steps and things fall into place.

Chris wasn't a fool, so Spencer came clean, sort of: the people Spencer had been working for, they weren't to be messed with. The night Spencer had come home covered in blood and smelling of gas? They'd done that. Just because he'd made a stupid little mistake on a delivery. If Chris went back, they'd probably have some kid watching his place and next thing there'd be a knock at the door of the apartment they were renting down here in Toledo. All Chris had to do was forget Detroit for a while and help them all get settled. And that meant keeping Abby together. Spencer reluctantly agreed to thirty minutes a day on Facebook, but supervised. No Snapchat or Instagram. Abby didn't like that. Facebook was for old people after all but it was clearly the best she was going to get.

Spencer phoned Abby's school to tell them they'd moved out of state, just to stop any missing child alarms going off. He did the same with CPS. That hadn't gone quite so smoothly. Without asking to be, he was put through to Lonnie, who was still down as his case officer. She refused to speak to him, promptly transferring him to Caitlyn. When Caitlyn started asking questions Spencer couldn't field, he hung up and blocked the number.

He and Chris set a plan in motion for getting CPS off their asses. Spencer would change their name back in the UK by deed poll. They'd have to visit a British embassy somewhere for passports once the change was finalized. When that day came, Spencer decided, he'd book them a vacation.

They paid the family next door to piggyback their Wi-Fi and they changed their phones to prepaid plans that didn't need billing addresses.

Chris had long mastered the art of VPNs so they had Netflix and the sports and movie channels. And Chris seemed to have more time to enjoy them. Even before they'd left Detroit, he'd become preoccupied with automating his business. And all the while, sales of Thermo Booster Burn climbed. With that, and with what Spencer had saved, money wasn't a problem.

Abby had two excellent tutors. They cost a lot, but they made her laugh and enjoy learning, so they spent most of the day with her. They were the only other adults with whom she had regular contact besides the apartment complex manager.

The manager was a single mom to a boy near Abby's age. Ethan was a shy kid who hadn't made friends easily at school. He and Abby took a real shine to each other, and they'd hang out most evenings, either playing XBox or messing around by a muddy little lake a couple hundred yards from the complex. Ethan had been bullied in both the real and virtual worlds, so he had no interest in social networking, making him ideal buddy material.

Spencer smoked more cigarettes but less weed, which he'd smoke in his room before bed with his arm hanging out the window, thinking no one knew. As his supply of prescription meds dwindled—and not wanting to risk registering with a doctor in Toledo—he found an alternative supplier. Youssef may have been good-for-nothing workwise, but he had a source for Ambien and Prozac who could probably deliver in an apocalypse. And Spencer no longer drank to oblivion every night. But regardless of how much he drank, smoked, or self-medicated, when he closed his eyes, he would still see a boy burning in his car.

He was determined to change. He didn't have the whole picture of what he was aiming for, just bits of the canvas. He wanted to take care of Abby, he knew that much, wanted to address her growing moodiness and distance, unaware that the disconnect was largely down to his distance. And, although it felt like a betrayal, he wanted to think about Marielle less or at least with less pain. Occasionally on summer evenings, he'd notice new thoughts sneaking up on him; maybe it might be nice to find someone special, someone who wouldn't put up with his shit, just like Marielle hadn't, just like Lonnie had.

One blazing Saturday afternoon, Spencer was taking his turn at sitting with Abby for her Facebook session. He needed a cigarette. Smoking was a big no in the apartment, and Abby didn't want to go outside with the laptop because of the heat. She had about five conversations going on Messenger and didn't look like she'd be finishing them anytime soon. Spencer was getting fidgety. It was a day to be out. He thought they'd agreed they should all hit Wildwood park.

"Hey, Abby, you don't have any Friend Requests pending do you?"

"No, Dad. You and Chris deleted them."

"So you're just talking with friends you know, right?"

"Do you want a list of who they are and how long I've known them for?"

Spencer took a deep breath. He reminded himself that she didn't know what the stakes were. He decided to take Chris's advice and talk to her as an adult.

"Look, Abby, I get that this is all a pain in the ass for you and I'm sorry. I'm working things out here and—"

"Your problems at work."

"Excuse me?"

"You're working out your problems at work. Then everything will be fine." When he said nothing, she looked at him demurely. "Caitlyn didn't want to give you and Chris time to work things out. I got it."

"You guys were on first-name terms?"

"Yeah. She was cool." Abby looked at her father. She knew he needed to have a smoke. She decided to accelerate the process. "I don't accept Friend Requests. I don't talk to adults I don't know. If any of my friends' parents or my teachers get in touch, I ignore them. Basically, I ignore adults unless you say I can speak to them, Dad."

Spencer heard Chris stifle a laugh somewhere behind him. Abby was now staring intently at the screen, not even waiting to see how her response had landed. Her comebacks were getting sharper. Her mother had been pretty much untouchable, unless Spencer had been on form.

"OK, Abby, so do you mind if I—"

"Please go have a fag outside, Dad."

"I don't call them fags, Abby."

"British people call them fags."

"You're half-British, Abby, just saying."

"No, Dad. I'm just AWOL Abby."

AWOL Abby was what she'd become known as back at school. She'd challenged the moniker hard, saying she was, in fact, on a surprise extended family vacation.

At least her dad had changed a little since they'd come to Toledo. More than a little, in fact. Chris said he was doing well at work. He did seem happier here. The only problem was, he was the only one who did.

Hammering the rumors down was never-ending, like bashing moles in that carnival game. But in spite of her best efforts, the AWOL thing stuck, and its persistence seemed to signal the start of a slide for her from being one of the crowd to, well, she wasn't sure exactly where it was headed. Anything that had made her even slightly different before, her British roots, her sky-high intelligence, things that hadn't mattered when she was hanging out daily with her friends, became possible reasons for her disappearance. It hurt. And her dad and Chris had no clue. They must have no clue, because they were happy to make things even more difficult by limiting her fighting time.

She looked to her side. Her dad was no longer there. That was a first. With his absence she felt the pressure lessen. Normally, she'd be tapping furiously at the keyboard right to the end of her time allowance. She looked back at the screen and found herself wondering. If her popularity was so badly on the slide, then why were so many people trying to be her friend? Nearly every day there was a new Friend Request. She didn't get to see who it was from before it was deleted.

She wondered if there was a way to retrieve deleted Friend Requests. She minimized her ongoing conversations and changed the display on Chris's laptop from mobile to desktop, then went back into Messenger and hit Settings. There was nothing about Friend Requests, but there was an option entitled Message Requests. Interesting. She clicked on it. Instantly a stream of messages came up. She looked at the name and drew a blank. Kelsey? Then it dawned on her. That phone call she'd taken on her father's phone from the guy who worked for him. His niece was named Kelsey.

She opened the message stream. Coincidentally, Kelsey had been sending messages since they'd left Detroit. Because they weren't friends, they'd gone into this hard-to-find folder.

"All good, Abby?" said Chris suddenly.

"Yeah," said Abby, without taking her eyes off the screen.

Suddenly Chris was by her. "You're just messaging people you know, right?" he said.

"Yes, Chris." She said it in her long-suffering tone. It was a lie but only a white one. She kind of knew Kelsey. And Kelsey was probably having as rough a time as Abby; being the new girl wasn't fun. And, although she didn't like to admit it to herself, Abby had already had the idea that if she helped Kelsey out, then maybe Kelsey would fight in Abby's corner.

She opened the first message.

"hi abby kelsey here my uncle said 2 look u up b4 I went 2 mc-dade. I keep sending friend requests but u don't answer?"

Abby skimmed through more messages. She had a growing anxiety that she'd missed the boat.

"hi again probably ill give up soon. guessing u probably don't wanna b friends. I was just scared cuz im gonna b in a new place + it's pretty scary if u don't know anyone"

Abby felt a response was imperative if she was to salvage this opportunity to gain an ally. She glanced around. Her father was still nowhere to be seen and Chris was crashing pots together in the kitchen. She typed fast.

"hiiii kelsey sorree but didnt get ur requests. sending u request now then we can message like normal r u at mcdade now how is it?"

She hit Send Friend Request and then sat back with a little sigh of relief. She watched the screen.

Too late, Abby. She's been at your school, like, forever. Probably knows all the stuff they're saying anyway.

She heard the apartment door open, heard her dad's voice.

"Come on, guys. It's beautiful out there! Let's go!" He started peeing with the bathroom door open. It sounded like he'd just had another of his weird mood changes.

Abby didn't want to go out. She wanted to watch this message box. She wanted to watch it all day if necessary. Suddenly:

"abby woo hoo thought u didn't wanna b buddeees" A healthy dose of happy emojis rounded it off.

Abby leapt forward and was about to start typing when another message appeared.

"my dad doesn't allow me on fb often. same w u right?"

"yep same."

"ok we better b quick then right ha so u wanna hear some news?"

"sure."

"we got a puppy"

"omg what type + name?"

"not named yet. he is super cute. but that's not the only news. something bigger 4 u"

"?"

"not going 2 mcdade."

"no way."

"yes way."

"why not?"

"dad doesn't wanna stay in detroit. new job. says he can work anywhere now + guess what"

Abby heard the bathroom flush. Something told her her session was about to be ended. Thankfully Kelsey seemed to be facing the same urgency wherever she was. She sent another message before Abby had had the chance to reply.

"top secret rite?"

Abby felt her heart pounding for some reason as she typed back. "understood pcb!"

"pcb?"

"parent coming back!"

There was a face palm emoji then: "so dad says my bro + me choose where we want 2 live"

"no way!"

"yes way!"

"where u gona choose?"

"need a buddy?" A winking face and puppy emoji followed.

Abby thought about her one friend here in Toledo, thought about how often her dad said it was safer here than Detroit. Much safer. Surely she could . . .

"abby i gotta go"

. . . share her secret with just one person . . .

"not sure when ill get online again"

. . . one person she'd known about before they moved. So, strictly speaking, Kelsey wasn't someone trying to be her friend since they left Detroit.

"let u kno where we end up." Sad emoji.

Abby reached for the keyboard just as her dad entered the living room. She'd better be fast.

The hand of Mr. Indecisive was poised above the dotted line. He looked around at Spencer.

"I think this will be the most I've ever spent on a car," he said.

Spencer nodded. "Well, I'd say that's a reason to be cheerful."

"Cheerful?"

"Why sure. You're focusing on the wrong thing here."

"I am?"

"You should be happy that you're successful enough to afford that car, not whether or not you're doing something bad here. It'll serve you faithfully every time you get in it."

"I never thought of it like that."

As he leaned down to sign, Spencer made eye contact with Zed over his shoulder. They smiled.

Spencer's phone vibrated. He ignored it. He moved another set of papers in front of his buyer. "And next, these two. Just right there . . . and there."

His phone vibrated again. Spencer slid it out of his pocket just enough to see the screen. Chris. Spencer felt that taking a family call might help Mr. Indecisive stay calm. The guy still had to actually hand over that cashier's check after all.

"Spencer Burnham," he said without taking his eyes off the pen skipping along one dotted line after another.

Chris's voice screamed in Spencer's ear. "Spencer!"

"Chris, how's it go—"

"Abby's gone!"

"She's probably playing with Ethan."

"She isn't. After her lessons she said she was going out with him. But he hasn't seen her since last night."

"I'm on my way."

"I'm calling the cops right now!"

"Don't call the cops. I'm coming back right now!"

Mr. Indecisive looked up. Zed looked over. Zed's niece stopped chatting with a couple about their toddler, and they all looked across the showroom.

"Why the hell not?" said Chris.

Spencer was running for the door. "Chris, listen to me. Don't call the cops! I'm on my way."

35
Lost and Found

Spencer's phone lay on the table in a patch of sunlight. He and Chris sat on either side, waiting. A séance for technologically inclined spirits.

An hour passed, each tick of the wall clock a geological age.

The phone rang. Both got hands on it. Chris snatched it away. But it was Zed. Chris passed it back to Spencer. The ensuing conversation was short and stilted.

"No, no, everything's fine," said Spencer. He killed the call and put the phone back on the table.

Chris gave a grunt of exasperation and started pacing.

They waited. Another hour passed.

The phone pinged. Spencer opened the message.

Go to the lake.

He rose from the table.

Go to the lake?

Was she at the lake? Or was she in it?

Marielle screamed in his head.

Our daughter, Spencer! What have you done?

"What have you done?" asked Chris.

If they wanted revenge, then why bother kidnapping Abby? Why not just wait at the apartment. No, it was him they wanted. And they knew he wouldn't care about anything if they killed Abby. He surprised himself with his certainty.

Why then, Spencer?

Can't you see, Marielle? I took your advice, everyone's advice. I got out. I got a job. We ran. And now they've found us. Why? Because the Game is still in play—whether we like it or not.

Chris followed Spencer down the overgrown path behind the apartment complex. The early evening sun was losing its warmth faster now, but it would be a while before it was too chilly for the midges and mosquitoes that flitted and danced around them. They passed through the line of trees that ringed the lake.

Johnny Boy stood on the lakeside, hands clasped in front of him and a face that said he was disappointed but not surprised. He looked to his side, along the shore, where McGrath, jacket slung over shoulder, was skimming stones across the water. Beyond him the trunk of a fallen birch lay across the shingle, its branches, still leafy, held by the muddy water like a harvestman in a web.

The Yo-Yo was sitting on the trunk. Abby cowered beside him. She saw Spencer, but fear held her still.

"Stay here, Chris," said Spencer.

And Chris knew to stay. He knew that whatever had come back to haunt them lived in lands unknown to him, lands he had never wanted to know.

He watched Spencer walk through the ferns to the lakeside and head toward the stone-skimming man in the white shirt. The bearded man with the glasses who looked like a lawyer or an undertaker fell in behind Spencer. No words were passed.

Chris became conscious of how unwell he felt, like someone had squeezed him into a box that had no give in its sides. He couldn't decide which he needed most: his inhaler or a bourbon.

Spencer went as if to go past McGrath to get to Abby, but McGrath held up his hand.

"I don't think you want her to hear what we have to talk about, but it's your call."

Spencer hesitated. He called out to Abby.

"Don't worry, Abby. I'll sort this out, and we can all go home. OK?"

Abby looked at him, aghast that she would have to stay put a moment longer.

"I promise, it's going to be fine. Chris and I are here. We're not going anywhere without you. You hear?"

She nodded. Spencer couldn't hear her crying, but he could see the shine on her cheeks. He looked at McGrath. McGrath turned back to the lake.

"I knew you might do this, Spence. Hoped I was wrong, but you got to consider all the angles, right?" He threw the stone he'd been holding. It skipped fast and straight, almost to the far bank, leaving a myriad of expanding circular ripples on the still surface. He searched among the pebbles on the ground for the next contender.

"Like I said, Dom, I have a little girl. You were asking me to help you rob a bank. I'm a car salesman. That's what I do. I don't like it much, but it's all I got."

McGrath straightened up, throwing down the stone he'd just selected. "What the fuck is it with you? That your go-to? Your standard little bleat?" He put on a whiney voice. "'Oh, my name's Spencer and all I can do is sell cars. Don't give me any other shit to do or I'll just run the fuck away.'"

Spencer said nothing.

"Why didn't you just trust that I had your best interests at heart? I see potential in people. Potential. I put hard bank into this, into you. You knew that. You could have done this."

Spencer was trying to work out the likelihood of all three of them being killed on the lakeshore. There were no witnesses. Still, there was nothing to be gained from lying as to why he'd run. He'd made his play. And they'd found him. Furthermore, it was thanks to McGrath that he'd figured out something that had long eluded him.

"I did everything you asked of me, Dom. Stuff I haven't ever done. I saw stuff I haven't seen and quite frankly wish I'd never seen. Why did I turn down your offer?" He pointed at Abby. "Because of her? Yeah, partly. CPS is looking to take her off me. You knew that. Why? Because of the choices I've been making. But she isn't the only reason. Fact is I don't have the balls, Dom. I don't have the cojones, the backbone, however you want to label it in the world you live in, the places you been, whatever. But I don't have it. That's why I gave up racing. Not because of Marielle's job, I just grabbed that as an excuse. If you really knew people, you'd know that self-belief is where it's at. Why couldn't you just let Eddie drive? He wants to do it. He *believes* he can do it."

McGrath gave a derisive snort. "There's self-belief and there's delusion."

He saw a flat piece of shale by the water's edge and went to pick it up. Before throwing it, he looked back over his shoulder.

"You guys need to pack." He threw the shale hard. It slid, rather than bounced, over the water's surface and didn't stop until it smashed into a rock on the far side, sending splinters showering into the undergrowth. McGrath walked past Spencer, back toward the path.

"Johnny Boy, show Spencer what's been happening back home while he's been away, just so he's up to speed."

Out came Johnny Boy's phone. He worked the screen and went to pass it to Spencer but suddenly brought it back and turned the phone on its side.

"There, that's going to be easier for you," he said considerately.

Spencer started reading a *Detroit Free Press* article from a few days before.

OAKLAND CHILD PROTECTIVE SERVICES EMPLOYEE KILLED IN HIT AND RUN ran the headline.

> Lonnie Estevez, 36, was hit by a dark pickup truck outside her apartment on Grobbel and Martin. She was pronounced dead at the scene. Police are appealing for witnesses. The suspect vehicle was later found burned out near Belanger Park. Melissa Kaplun, office manager of the Oakland CPS said that Estevez was a valued employee who will be greatly missed. Anyone with information should call Detective Bryant at the DPD where investigations are said to be ongoing.

Johnny Boy gently took the phone from Spencer's hand. "Terrible how that kind of thing can happen, don't you think? But hey, good things come out of bad sometimes. At least that should take the pressure off you from CPS, right?"

36

Ghosts from the Past

Spencer opened Abby's door a crack and looked down the hall. He could see Johnny Boy's legs stretched out on the coffee table and his hand with the TV remote dangling off the arm of the couch. The channel changed and cheering was replaced by the voice of CNN.

Spencer closed the door. He crossed to the window and peeked through the blinds. McGrath's Mercedes sedan was parked in the apartment lot next to Penny. He could see the Yo-Yo's hand on the wheel.

"Are you going to call the cops, Dad?"

"What do you think the cops would do for us? Put us in that witness protection program you hear about in movies? Away from all your friends? The cops only help people who have something to give them."

Abby feared that if she spoke the tears would come, and she wouldn't be able to finish whatever she started.

"That guy watching TV, those people out there, Abby, they'll kill us all in a heartbeat. That's why I brought us here. That's why I told you to be careful who you spoke to."

Abby started to weep.

Spencer stared at her, confused. He wanted to punch through a wall. They'd used his daughter as a warning.

And he needed her to stop crying, to stop crying like . . . like *that*. The last time he'd heard her cry like that had been . . .

Don't say it.

Had been . . .

Don't even think it!

It had been the day they'd heard. A normal day to start with. They'd all said their goodbyes but not a warm goodbye. Marielle and he had squabbled the previous night about something stupid.

And he hadn't actually seen his daughter crying and sobbing like she was right now. He heard her being comforted while he'd lain on his bed, the bed that his wife would never join him on again. He'd been unable to move, unable, almost, to even breathe. It was as if high-voltage cables enveloped him, making his head buzz and hum.

And the guilt he'd felt for not being there for his daughter had been hidden away in some cerebral safe, not the cruddy type that hotels use but the kind made from drill-killing hard plate and antijack bolts. And that safe was set in the floor of a tiny closet, guarded by roaches and spiders, never to be opened, forgotten in a forgotten house.

But now his daughter's racking sobs raced through that old house, swept away the cobwebs, smashed the safe asunder with a clang and—

"Abby, stop!"

He went to her, flying across the room. "Abby, please stop!"

She couldn't though. She didn't think she could ever stop now that she'd started. He held her tight and turned her head against his chest.

"It's OK." The words were choked and broken as he began to cry with her.

"I thought I'd lost you, and I love you, Abby. I'm so sorry. I went off the rails, and I just couldn't seem to get back."

Spencer promised he would never leave her again, either in heart or actuality. It was a promise made with the best will in the world.

And one that wouldn't be kept.

Spencer lifted Abby's sleeping head and slid a pillow underneath it.

He went into the hallway. Chris's door was closed. He cracked it and peeked in. Chris lay on the bed, down for the count. His face looked gray and unwell. Guilt burned Spencer's gut. He went to the bathroom.

He looked in the mirror and saw himself looking back but not as he usually did, as in how rough or tired he looked or how much coffee, coke, or showering he'd need to get himself ready to walk out and face his fellow humans. Rather he saw his real self, in all its unimpressive, damaged glory. And he could hear himself, too, the self that had been screaming at him through the impenetrable glass up on Royal Oak.

His face disappeared as he opened the mirrored door. He looked at his "legit" meds: the antidepressants, the Vicodin and diazepam, the nicotine patches and the beta-blockers.

He took out the nicotine patches, trying to work out if he'd ever used more than two consecutively. They went in the trash. He popped antidepressants one by one into the toilet. He did the same with all the other stuff and then, calmly, he pulled the flush.

Next he started packing for all three of them. Johnny Boy watched with mild interest as he went back and forth, loading Penny. Eventually the only things left to go in the car were Chris and Abby. Spencer stood in front of Johnny Boy.

"I need to go and pay the rent and get our deposit back."

"It's done."

Spencer nodded. "OK, we're ready."

Johnny Boy clicked off the TV and looked at Spencer coldly. "Those two go in the Prius. You follow with us. Bring their phones. And yours."

Chris drove as slow as ever up the seventy-five, and it was dark by the time they got back to Detroit. Sitting in the back seat of McGrath's car as they rolled into the lot of Chris's apartment block, Spencer felt sick. The Yo-Yo parked behind Penny. Spencer went to get out.

"Hold your horses," said McGrath. "Next Friday. Means you got a week to get ready. Anything you need, you ask. And we better make sure you focus and, you know, don't go off on any tangents again. How many rooms he got up there?"

"Two. Why?"

"You guys are going to have a houseguest."

Moments later, Spencer was standing by the apartment block entrance, watching McGrath's Mercedes leave. In the corner of the lot, the Subaru was back. The car sneered at him, like a friend he'd left for dead now returned, a friend no longer.

He sent Abby upstairs with Chris and started unloading Penny. He was worried about Chris. The stress of the day had taken its toll.

Abby held the apartment door open so he could at least walk straight in with each load.

"Last one," he said as he headed for the stairs.

This time, when he arrived back at the apartment, the Yo-Yo was waiting for him.

"We need to look at your car," he said as Spencer dropped an armful of stuff in the hallway.

He followed Spencer down the stairs. Just as Spencer went to open the communal door of the block, he was yanked backward. The Yo-Yo spun him around and threw him against the mailboxes. It was as if he weighed nothing. Suddenly he was off the floor and flying backward until impact. The sharp little handles cut deeply into his back.

The Yo-Yo grabbed him by the throat and gave his face and stomach several hard slugs in quick succession. Spencer couldn't breathe. His vision started to cloud.

Suddenly the beating stopped. The Yo-Yo leaned in close, showering Spencer's face with spittle, whispering harshly.

"Dom's the chief, Spencer. He works in his own way. My way would be different. There's three of you. I only need to let you live. I really wanna go up there and kill one of them just so you do what you're told. You know I ain't got no problem wasting a kid. If you go out for something, remember I'll be here with them. You bring anyone back, any cops, I can work real fast. Understand me?"

Spencer nodded. The Yo-Yo let go and he slithered to the floor. As he lay there gasping, he heard the Yo-Yo's footsteps ascend the stairs. Chris's front door opened and slammed.

* * *

Spencer didn't want his daughter to see the state he was in, but Chris said she needed him, so he cleaned off the worst of the damage and went to join her in Chris's room.

"Abby, listen to me," he said to her. "All this stuff that's happening to us? It isn't your fault. It's mine. And I'm sorry, to you and to Chris. Those men today, they were going to find us wherever we went. And because they know how much I care about you, they were always going to threaten to hurt you, to make me do what they want me to do."

"What do they want you to do?"

Spencer looked at her. She'd be twelve in less than a month. He tried to figure out what she could be expected to understand.

"They want me to do something bad . . ."

He trailed off when he saw her face. That wasn't going to cut it. She was her mother's daughter.

There was something uniquely humiliating about sharing living space with someone who'd just beaten the crap out of you. Spencer looked at the Yo-Yo kicking out on their couch, TV remote in one hand and Spencer's beer in the other.

He limped out onto the fire escape, grabbed a bag of ice from the fridge, and collapsed into the couch. As he stared at the chalk outline on the floor, Spencer's mind flicked back to McGrath's office, back to when he thought he was getting ahead of the game with his big ideas and oh-so-cleverly damaged cars. But McGrath had been ahead of him. Always. Spencer hadn't decided to get back in touch with McGrath. Dominic McGrath had brought Spencer back, back to his lair. And when he'd suggested they not call each other on their own phones and paid Spencer in cash, he wasn't doing Spencer any favors. He was making sure there was no record Spencer ever worked for them, because Spencer was always going to be just one of the costs of his Max Petrovsky thing.

Chris appeared. "He said he's sleeping on the couch, so he can watch the exits I guess. How long's he staying?"

"A week."

Just then there was a knock at the front door. Chris moved as if to go answer it, but before he was off the balcony they heard the door open. He frowned.

"Who is it?" asked Spencer.

"Pizza delivery guy for our new friend," said Chris. "He's not interested in my cooking." He pointed at Spencer's swollen face. "If I'd seen this, I wouldn't have been so hospitable."

"You offered him dinner?"

"I thought it might help get him on our side."

Spencer shook his head. He squished the ice pack against his eye socket. "That man in there, he'll never be on our side. He's the most dangerous thing you've ever met."

Chris pondered for a moment. "I'm not sure about that."

37

Outrun by Fate

Spencer didn't like the fact that Chris's apartment was open plan.

The Yo-Yo watched him as he went from fridge to freezer to liquor cabinet. Vodka, beer, brandy, and bourbon. All of it went down the sink. At the same time, he put together a sandwich he didn't really want. As he sliced some cheese, the TV was suddenly muted.

"I counted the knives," said the Yo-Yo. "And I sleep light."

Spencer said nothing. He took his sandwich out onto the fire escape. As the TV volume went back up, Spencer opened the fire escape fridge. He'd known for some time that Chris would probably have listened to his doctor by now and stopped drinking if it weren't for him. He wanted to trash all the alcohol and not just for their benefit; he didn't want the guy on the couch drinking any more of their beer even if they didn't want it anymore. At the same time, he knew he couldn't afford to provoke him. He left a six-pack. One by one, he emptied the others over the fire escape. As he watched the tentacles of foamy liquid twist down into the darkness, he was struck by a newfound ease with which he considered others. And the novelty of it shamed him.

He took the cushions from the fire escape couch through to Abby's room where he made himself a bed on the floor. Abby was fast asleep. Spencer looked at her. Tomorrow he'd have to think hard. He knew he was finished. He was going to have to do the job for McGrath. And then McGrath would surely kill him. The real question now was how to ensure Chris and Abby survived. He didn't believe for one moment that McGrath wanted anyone left to tell tales.

He'd just laid down when Chris's face appeared around the door.

"Our friend is asleep."

"I'm happy for him."

"Come through to my room." He left without waiting for a reply.

Spencer flopped back with a great sigh. He gave himself a moment before getting back on his feet and padding into the hallway. He glanced into the living room. The TV was still on. The Yo-Yo was stretched out on the couch, eyes shut, fully clothed but for his white-socked feet. Spencer would have liked to at least hear a snore, something to convince him the man really was asleep and no longer monitoring his surroundings. Even asleep, Spencer was scared of him. He didn't have any trouble admitting it to himself.

He entered Chris's room and closed the door quietly. Chris was sitting on his bed. His room was dark but for a small reading light. A slight breeze wafted in the open window, ruffling the drapes.

"What's up?"

"'What's up'?" said Chris, stiffening. "What the fuck do you mean, 'What's up'?"

"Chris, I know this is really bad right now but—"

"Whoa! Just let me stop you there before you say what I think you're gonna say."

Spencer stopped.

"For a second there, it seemed like you were going to come out with one of your 'oh-I-got-this-under-control-so-don't-worry' bullshittisms. You're worse than Fox fucking News."

"Chris, calm down, I'll tell—"

Chris spoke in a furious whisper. "Don't give me the 'calm down'! I don't know if you noticed, but your daughter was kidnapped today, and now there's a two hundred and forty pound psychopath on my couch. And he has all our phones. You mother-*fucker*, Spence."

They began to talk over each other.

"Chris, we need to keep it together here. If we don't—"

"Oh, rich coming from you." Chris was shaking his head. "People said I was being suckered by you."

"What's that supposed to mean?"

"Hey, I never kept a tab, but everyone else gave up on you."

"And we fitted in with your life."

"Fuck you, Spencer. Fuck you! This shit's been going on for a long time, from way before the Rock's crazy cousin came to stay. That Spencer-shaped line out there on the fire escape? That was just another night for you. But when I dragged your sorry-for-itself ass to bed it meant five trips to the chiropractor for me."

"Come on, Chris, you'd have paid a lot more than that to keep Abby around. Did you ever want me to get it together?"

Chris leaped off his bed. He jabbed his finger at Spencer. "Jesus, I . . . just fuck you! You think I never thought about you? I tried to get you all the help I could. I got wasted with you here, so you wouldn't wake up in the drunk tank or worse. I cooked and I cleaned. I watched my neighbors cut me off, one by one. And I took it all for Team Spencer. Why the hell do you think I—"

He broke off.

"What?" said Spencer.

"Forget it."

"No, what?"

All of a sudden, Chris's anger visibly drained away. He sat back down on his bed looking guilty, terribly guilty. The light dawned on Spencer.

"You made the call."

Chris sighed. He got up, walked heavily to the window, and leaned on the sill. He stared out over the trees and rooftops of Buena Vista and Tyler, far away to the headlights twinkling through the smoggy haze above the Lodge Freeway.

"You're the one who called CPS. Just when I was going to be signed off."

"I thought they would help you. I knew you weren't . . . weren't alright. Even if they signed you off. Their website said they offered support to parents. I'd tried everything with you. But then they just, it was like they wrote you off. And me. That Dunn witch . . ." His voice trailed off. The two men looked at each other.

"Chris, it doesn't matter anymore. None of it. I lied about the work I'd been doing. I knew you'd have given me a hard time. And you'd have been right. But now you've seen what these people can do. Abby, you, even the Dunn witch as you call her, you're all prices I'll have to pay if I don't do what they want. They killed my last case officer while we were away."

Chris looked at him aghast. Then he, too, seemed to accept the reality.

They talked late into the night. Facts, options, ideas. At some point, Abby crept in and crawled into Chris's bed. Still they brainstormed, and yet there seemed no viable way out. Spencer, it appeared, would have to do as he was told. And if that were so, there were things that needed to be done to increase the chances of success. Even if he were expendable, he still had a service to provide.

Spencer spent much of the rest of that night awake as he'd expected. And the day would bring the cravings. But now they came with the sound of his daughter sobbing, the same as he'd heard when Marielle died. Marielle, the woman he loved and who loved him and yet with whom he'd never made his peace because he'd been too weak.

It occurred to Caitlyn, as she waited for the phone to be answered, that the last person who'd held the scrap of paper she was looking at was Lonnie—a woman she hadn't been especially fond of and one who wouldn't have thought of Caitlyn as a friend. And yet still Caitlyn found it sad. Lonnie had been a decent soul who didn't deserve to be robbed of all her hopes and dreams by some nineball in a pickup.

Her handwriting was atrocious, though, and it had taken Caitlyn several passes to decipher.

Detective Batiste + Scott DPD. Undercover op
Spencer = obstacle. Make him stop working but don't tell him why.
Threaten him re: Abby

And then, in a different pen:

Dinner?!

Did that mean what she thought it meant? Or was Lonnie just desperate to help them?

"This is Detective Scott. Who am I speaking to, please?"

"Caitlyn Dunn. I'm with Oakland CPS. Would I be right in thinking you're Detective Batiste's partner?"

Her question was ignored. "What can I help you with?"

"You came and spoke to a colleague about one of her cases. Lonnie Estevez and Spencer Burnham?"

"I remember."

She waited for a moment, expecting more for some reason. Nothing else came. "I had taken his case over from my colleague, Lonnie, but that's only been official since she, uh, you know Lonnie was killed?"

Scott paused before answering. "I am aware." Another pause. "My condolences."

Again Caitlyn thought he might say just a little more and again she was mistaken. The hell with it. This wasn't her first rodeo when it came to dealing with people of few words. She shifted gear.

"Do you have a current address for Spencer Burnham?"

"Not at this time."

"He left town shortly before Lonnie was killed. I know that you and your partner asked her to encourage Spencer to leave the job he had in Detroit. Can you tell me anything about his line of work?"

"I'm not at liberty to say."

"Why?"

Silence.

"Is that because it's an ongoing investigation, Detective?"

Another pause. "I have nothing for you on the guy, Miss Dunn. Anything else I can help you with?"

"Officially, Lonnie Estevez was still his case officer when she was killed. And that happened a short time after he left town. I think he went on the run. I assumed it was from us."

"From CPS?"

"We filed a petition with the court to gain custody of his daughter. Do you think his leaving and Lonnie's death are connected?"

Yet another hesitation. "Not to our knowledge."

"OK, Detective, thank you so much for your time. One more thing, before I let you go. The safety of Abby Burnham is our responsibility. And when I say 'our,' I include you; we serve and protect the same people. If you become aware that she might be in further danger, it's your duty to ensure her safety or help us to ensure it."

Scott didn't respond, but she'd seen that coming. "I'm going to need to hear an affirmative from you on that, Detective."

"Yes, Miss Dunn, we fully understand each other."

"Have a nice day, Detective."

38

Life Insurance

I've always believed that you should never, ever give up and you should always keep fighting even when there's only a slightest chance.

—Michael Schumacher

"Rev it," said Chris.

Abby obliged.

A cable ran from Chris's laptop over her legs, under the steering column, and into the car's diagnostic box.

"Little more," called out Spencer from under the hood.

"Let's lock and load this bitch and set her to kill," said Abby to herself.

Chris made a mental note to check the age recommendation on whatever driving game she was hammering these days. He tried to finalize the engine remap, but the sinking sun was in his eyes. He flipped down the visor. The expired insurance certificate fell out.

Spencer felt a tap on the shoulder. He looked around to see Chris holding the certificate. "I think I've figured it out," said Chris. "Insurance. We need so much insurance it's coming out our asses."

As they worked, Chris made Spencer run through everything he knew about McGrath's operation, from day one when Spencer had made such an impression on everyone, especially Cal, to how the robbery was supposed to work. The brainstorming led to a plan, not the best of plans as there were way too many variables to inspire confidence, but a plan nevertheless.

That night Chris was careful to finish cooking before the Yo-Yo's pizza arrived. The aroma from his buttermilk chicken was sublime and he knew it.

"There's some left. If you want it, you better call it because this has been known to get my neighbors knocking on the door hunting for leftovers."

And thus the Yo-Yo ate from the table of those he would kill.

As soon as the AtoB courier entered the Taco Bell, Spencer double-parked by his truck, got out, and grabbed the digital signing box off the dash. Then he was gone. The courier didn't realize it was missing until his next delivery. He was dead certain he'd either left it at his last drop or it had fallen out of the cab. After all, who would want to steal it?

Later, with online assistance from a geek buddy in Kansas, Chris would learn how to master the box's software without leaving a digital footprint. To anyone watching, though, as the Yo-Yo often was, it would seem he was just selling Thermo Booster Burn.

"Steak?" said the Yo-Yo.

"Yeah, big day tomorrow, right?" said Chris, clutching his Whole Foods bag.

"I want her in here with me."

Neither Chris nor Spencer liked the thought of leaving Abby alone with the Yo-Yo, but there was no way he would allow all of them out of the apartment at one time. However, the situation had been anticipated. Spencer had taken her aside the previous night.

"I know it's asking a lot," he'd said. "I'm sorry, baby."

She wiped a tear away but said nothing. She was trying valiantly not to cry. Her father spoke differently to her these days, and it made her want to be strong.

So Abby came when Chris called. She sat down at the opposite end of the couch from the Yo-Yo. Chris couldn't look back as he closed the front door.

"Who's playing?" asked Abby.

"You watch basketball?"

"Sure," said Abby.

"Then you don't need me to tell you who's playin'."

Abby felt her mouth go dry. She looked over at the wall clock and wished she could time warp the little hand into moving as fast as the big one.

"Hey, man, I was starting to take things personal. Been like, missing my British bro. You closed up shop. What's been happening?"

Vincent placed his Bose headphones on the table, sat back, and fluffed his dreadlocks over the back of the Starbucks couch. He could be found there most days, working on his Mac, perfecting the post-production on his latest track while taking orders on one of three phones.

One or more of those phones vibrated intermittently as Spencer gave him an update based on what the guy needed to know.

Vincent tried to figure out where Spencer's buddy came in: older guy, didn't look so well, or like a potential customer, but hell, you never could tell.

"We need your acting skills, Vincent," said Spencer.

"And lest we forget," added Chris, "I need to buy a wrap."

Just never can tell, thought Vincent.

39

Fooled by the Fool?

When Spencer got out of his throatier-sounding Subaru in the loading bay early Thursday afternoon, the guys were of the mind that they were looking at a dead man walking, but one too stupid to realize it.

McGrath looked up from his desk to see him in the doorway, sporting a fine black eye, some serious bruising, and a missing tooth.

"I didn't tell him to do that," McGrath said, waving him to a seat. "Neither did Johnny Boy. The Yo-Yo, he's—"

"Someone you wouldn't want to meet in a dark alley, yeah, I know, Dom. I guess Lonnie found that out too."

Experiencing this type of situation with a clear head for the first time, Spencer saw what a fool he'd been to think he could ever have played this man before getting clean.

McGrath got up, walked around, and sat on the corner of the desk. He leaned in to talk to Spencer as he would to a young grunt with potential who'd screwed up. "Spencer, last week? A misunder-standing. Lonnie? A favor. There's no reason you couldn't go back to doing the rounds for us."

The two of them looked at each other, both wondering who was fooling who.

"You know it costs a couple hundred grand to set up a dealer-ship in Chicago?"

"Serious green."

"I'm going to do this gig for you tomorrow, so I was hoping your offer still stood. I mean, everything you've said you'd do you've done, right?

"You've got to earn it first."

"None of us might be around after tomorrow. But my daughter will still be around. Forget the dealership. Give me a little up front. Fifty grand. If you're confident about tomorrow, that saves you a lot of money."

McGrath's face had never looked so hard, so dangerous, and yet not out of its depth. It was Spencer who'd moved up a level in the art of dealmaking.

McGrath took the piece of paper Spencer offered him.

"In that account, by today. And there's one other thing. It might seem a little strange, but it's been bugging me. Cal."

"Don't worry about him, you'll get the money."

"Maybe, but I want to make peace with the guy. Can you get him up here? And while we're waiting, I need a piss." He didn't, but he knew McGrath would need a moment to tell Cal to play nice.

In the bathroom, Spencer tipped the wrap Chris had bought onto the shelf underneath the mirror. He messed it around, a line done in haste, and tipped the rest in the sink where it glistened enticingly: a quality product, as Vincent's always was. He turned on the tap and watched the water swirl the coke away. He left the distinctively folded paper on top of the trash.

Cal was already in McGrath's office by the time he got back.

"Hey, Cal." Spencer played it as if he'd been psyching up to eat this humble pie for a while. He hesitated. The silence in the room became awkward.

"Let's all take a seat," said McGrath.

"Listen, Cal, what I did with your car, it was wrong. I just needed a job and—"

"What's done is done. Forget about it."

"Cal," said McGrath. "Let the guy speak for Chrissakes."

Cal shrugged. Spencer plowed on.

"So I've organized a little something for you, to, uh, make amends."

Cal eyed him suspiciously. Spencer pretended to read it as curiosity. "Yeah, it's not a big thing. I ordered you four new Pirellis. Guy's going to deliver them today."

"You're saying four tires are gonna turn up here? You could have just paid Action."

"Yeah, well, since I'm buying, I figured you wouldn't mind if I went through my own sources."

Cal looked at Spencer as if he were the most slack-jawed dumbass that ever drew breath if he thought they could be friends or that he'd have any days after the next day. But Cal seemed more willing to follow orders these days, so when Spencer offered his hand, Cal took it.

"We're good?" asked Spencer sincerely, almost desperately.

"Sure, we're good."

Cal left them.

"That Buick down in the loading bay, Dom, covered in dust. Whose is it?"

"A guy called Rosso's, before he moved up in the world. Why?"

"Can I have it? I want to do some recces, and I don't want the CCTV getting used to my car over in Dearborn."

McGrath thought about it. "Sure, good idea. Get Denny to give it a jump. When you're done with it, get rid of it, though."

Later, as McGrath watched Spencer leave in the Buick, Eddie appeared at his side.

"Why'd he want that car?"

"Wants to do some recces."

Not long after Spencer left and McGrath was dusting tiny remnants of coke from the shelf in the restroom, an unmemorable truck pulled up at the depot barrier.

Cal signed the digital signing box offered four times. One for each tire. How fucking stupid was that? About as stupid as those dreadlocks that delivery driver was sporting.

Cal's reluctance to forgive a slight was, it seemed, even greater than his reluctance to sign anything.

40

The Shadow of War

Spencer headed east in the Buick. He laid the hammer down. There was a lot to get through. Clouds rolled in from the eastern lakes. Headlights went on, spooked by the bloated, dark gray sky. He didn't know that Eddie tried, and failed, to keep up with him.

He came off the ninety-four on Van Dyke, stopped at a Home Depot to buy two thick planks of timber, and then headed north for the industrial area he'd discovered the day he'd been mugged. By the time he drove up the dusty road to the derelict factory, the weather had finally broken.

Chris was waiting for him in the factory entranceway. He looked tired and sallow.

Spencer had to yell over the sound of the rain. "Sure you're up to this?"

"Yeah, don't worry, Spence. We all managed to function somehow before you joined us back in the real world."

Thunder and lightning were the backdrop as they scoped out the building's dank bowels.

They left in Chris's car, seeing as the Buick was now in its own special place. Chris dropped Spencer on Noble and headed home via the Glory Supermarket on Woodward where he would buy whatever steak they had. But he would say he'd traveled far and wide to find the best cuts in town.

By the time Spencer was parked up on West Lincoln watching the Oakland CPS, the sun was shining again. The door swung open and this time Caitlyn Dunn emerged. She walked smartly across the lot through tendrils of rising steam, talking on her phone as she went. She wore a dark blue knee-length dress, not too tight but not so loose either. She disappeared from sight and Spencer heard a car door shut, followed by an engine starting.

Moments later, a blue Mini pulled out of the lot and headed west. Spencer followed at a distance.

Caitlyn Dunn hadn't halted the CPS petition to court just because the Burnhams fled town. Why would she? There had been something very dangerous about Spencer Burnham. And why would the court not grant a petition if the parent whose worth it called into question didn't even turn up to the hearing. A letter giving CPS custody of his daughter had been amid the pile of mail and fast-food offers they'd come back to from Toledo.

In the leafy crescents of Lathrup Village, Caitlyn pulled into the drive of a tidy little one-story house. Spencer continued past, noting the address. He just had time to make out that she was still talking. And something told him it was all about her work.

Caitlyn Dunn, he had to admit, was conscientious. And un-compromising, like Marielle had been. Abby needed people like that in her life.

Seven o'clock. Chris dropped a basket of uncooked fries into a pot of boiling oil. As it sizzled loudly, the thought struck him how such a thing, hurled well, could be an effective weapon. He glanced through the smoke toward the couch, only to find himself locking eyes with the Yo-Yo. The center of the couch afforded the best view not only of the TV but also of the kitchen area, front door, and part of the fire escape balcony, although not the fire escape stairs. His eyes wore a TV glaze but would flick toward the source of any sound or movement. When they did, the glaze was gone.

"Shouldn't be long!" said Chris quickly. He said it with the dumb enthusiasm of his "character": the man he had gradually but convincingly become over the last few days.

He called out for Abby to come and open the fire escape door before the steaks sent the smoke detector loco. Abby did as she was told but clumsily, causing the door to hit the railing with a clang that must have reverberated up the fire escape.

In the bathroom, Spencer snipped a lock of his hair, folded it in a letter and stuffed both in his pocket. He came out of the bathroom and yelled down the hallway as he crossed to Abby's room.

"Abby, stop taking the bathroom towel into your room."

Abby answered without taking her eyes off the steaks sizzling in the skillet. She really wasn't hungry. "Sorry, Dad."

In Abby's bedroom, Spencer snatched her bag from the closet. He rummaged inside. The money from the gas station register was hidden under her stuff. His eyes met President Jackson's disapproving frown.

You're not mine anymore, Andrew.

Before he zipped up, he did a quick 360. Something wasn't right. Then he realized. The framed photograph of the three of them in Termessos. It was lying facedown. Surely Abby would want that? Spencer grabbed it and saw that it was now an empty frame. She'd packed light, just like he'd asked. He dropped the bag out of her window into the boxwood that lined the parking lot.

He had a sense he'd been in her room too long already. The Yo-Yo was like an automaton programmed to zero in on any aberration from the norm. Spencer grabbed a towel off Abby's bed and nearly walked straight into him.

"What the fuck is going on, Spencer?"

"I, what do you mean?"

"Why's there a fuckin' party going on?"

Spencer heard voices and laughter coming from the living room.

"Ah, shit. That's Rick and Denise, Chris's neighbors from upstairs. They must've smelled Chris's steaks and come down. They do that quite a lot."

"I don't give a shit what they do. You know what's happening tomorrow. I don't wanna meet them. Tell Chris to get rid of them."

"Look, Yo-Yo, I hear you, but listen. We can't suddenly start acting weird, can we? This time tomorrow, the cops are going to be looking for witnesses. Chris has never sent his neighbors away.

If he starts now, they're most likely going to guess something isn't right."

The Yo-Yo stared at him with eyes colder than the grave.

"Dom would want us to play this clever," continued Spencer. "Tell you what. I'll get them out on the fire escape with me and Abby. I'll keep them out there."

The Yo-Yo considered it for a moment. He didn't want them to see his face. Besides which, he was goddamn hungry and the thought of no one ear hustling him was attractive.

"How about this, Spencer. They eat out there, away from me. But when I'm finished with my chow, they're fucking gone, 'cause if they ain't, I'm gonna go to work on someone."

"Leave it to me, I said."

Denise turned to Abby and asked if she'd enjoyed her little vacation. Denise, like her husband, was only a few years from retirement and the first time Spencer had met her he'd thought this woman had the air of a straitlaced Sunday school teacher. Now he wondered where he'd gotten that from. She was warm, and she was up for helping a neighbor out without even needing to know why. Spencer suspected he'd been wrong about a lot of people.

He and Abby let the others do most of the talking while forcing Chris's beautiful cuisine down their dry throats. They sat at the end of the fire escape nearest the stairs. Out of the corner of his eye, Spencer could just see the Yo-Yo's feet on the coffee table. He reckoned the Yo-Yo would be about a quarter of the way through his food. He glanced around at Abby, eyes asking if she was ready. She nodded.

They were just putting their plates quietly on the floor when Spencer saw Abby's eyeline change to the doorway behind him. He knew the Yo-Yo was there. He carried on putting his plate down but then held his hand out to Rick, who was next to the refrigerator.

"Hey, throw me a beer, will you?"

Rick obliged, and by the time the cold Coors landed in Spencer's palm, the Yo-Yo had gone back to his food.

Spencer and Abby looked at each other. *What now?* her eyes asked. Spencer cracked open his beer. "We'll try again in a while," he breathed.

Ten minutes later Spencer zoned out of the small talk and into the TV commentary. The game was hitting some kind of crescendo. He heard the clink of the Yo-Yo's cutlery. The guy could certainly eat.

Well, let him. Let him eat so much he doesn't feel like moving his ass from that couch for hours.

Spencer tapped Abby's leg. Quietly and unceremoniously, they both got up and started down the fire escape stairs.

As if on cue, Denise turned to Rick and started an argument about whether Chris had mixed the Amarillo chili mayonnaise from scratch or used a paste. The argument would last for as long as it took them to finish eating and then yell out to Chris they were taking their disagreement up to the privacy of their apartment.

41

Borrowed Time

Spencer took the right onto the 696 late, cutting across the shoulder so he could pass a bunch of cars. There was some horn blare and light flashing as they swept up and around to the west.

"How long before you have to be back?" asked Abby.

Spencer didn't answer. The truth was he didn't know. A basketball game lasted at least fifty minutes, not counting penalties and time-outs. He'd hoped to hit the road as the game started. That had been a fail. Now they were flying on a wing and prayer, and Spencer's prayer was that the Yo-Yo found something else to watch as soon as the game ended.

Spencer glanced at her. A tear rolled down her cheek. He took his hand off the wheel for a moment to touch the side of her face.

"Abby, I'm not going to lie to you. I'm scared that man is going to hurt Chris, but for some reason Chris has promised me he can handle it. Do you know why that might be?"

Abby shook her head.

"There's a lot I want to tell you, but we don't have time. I want you to know I've always loved you. I'm sorry I was so . . . different, the last couple years. I'm sorry I was so bad-tempered and I drank. When Mom left us, well, it kind of broke me. You understand?"

She sniffed and nodded.

"If I get through this, Abby, I promise I'll never leave like that again. I won't take stupid pills to stop me thinking. Because I have plenty good to think about. I think about all the things I want us to do together, before you become a teenager and start thinking how uncool it is to have your dad around." He tried to laugh but he could hear his own voice breaking. "I'll take us both to that place we went to with Mom. You hear me, Abby?"

But Abby was crying. She no longer cared about keeping it together. She knew that just when her father had finally come back, he was about to leave.

Ten minutes later they were racing through Lathrup Village. Spencer tried not to think what they would do if their quarry was out. It struck him as unlikely on a weekday. Caitlyn Dunn seemed dedicated to her work, maybe a little too dedicated for her own good. And what if she had company? A boyfriend? And then, out of nowhere, while desperately looking for a house he'd seen only once in daylight, the thought hit him of how lucky that guy was, whoever he might be.

He saw Caitlyn's Mini and pulled up. He killed the engine.

"We need to make this work," he said quietly. He looked at her. "Are you with me, baby?"

She took his hand. Neither wanted to let go. With his other hand, Spencer fished the letter from his pocket and placed it in Abby's. "Go."

She grabbed the bag and got out, crossed the lawn, and rang Caitlyn's bell. Moths and bugs buzzed around the porch light above as she waited. The frosted-glass window atop the door was suddenly illuminated from within.

Her eyes met Spencer's and then he was gone.

Scott waded into a Hungry-Man Frozen Dinner while he talked shop on his work phone. This dinner ritual was an accurate reflection of how far his marriage had deteriorated of late, since his partner had done a Hemingway to be precise. It was as if Batiste had bequeathed not only sole responsibility for the McGrath investigation but also the overriding obsession that had gone with it.

If proof were needed that obsession bore results, he'd just been given plenty. At a quarter to nine he'd finally gotten a call telling him the Michigan State Police chopper would be available to him the following day. He'd laid it on with a trowel to get it a second time, and for as long as he needed it; this case was all the work of his late partner, Evan Batiste, one of Precinct Thirteen's finest.

I got us the chopper, Evan. We're gonna ride Burnham's tail right to McGrath. We'll send them all to the federal hotel.

The successful conclusion of this case would be a fitting tribute to his partner. It would also, Scott had decided, be his own swan song with the Detroit Police Department. And the moral code that applied to his present employment would soon be irrelevant, a thing of the past. His mind was streamlining and reediting it already, without him being aware. Take Abby Burnham for instance: the child of a junkie drunk. As if her life were worth as much or more to the good folks of Detroit than the benefit of getting McGrath off their streets. What a ridiculous thought. He wished he'd had the balls to tell Caitlyn Dunn exactly that.

42

Fallout

My biggest mistake is something yet to happen.

—Ayrton Senna

Spencer stood in the front doorway. He could hear TV sports commentary, but it sounded strangely muffled. He walked down the hallway.

"I'm back. You hear me, Yo-Yo? I've been out with Abby. And I've come back alone."

The living room was a scene of devastation, like a tornado had passed through. The TV was facedown on the carpet, still on the sports channel. Nascar now, though.

The Yo-Yo stood by the upturned couch. At his feet, amid the wreckage of the coffee table, Chris lay battered and bleeding, too scared even to move, like prey gone limp in a predator's claws.

"You keep making mistakes, Spencer, but other people suffer for them. You noticed that?"

"A while back."

"You see the way he's looking at me? I seen that look a hundred times. You don't know it though, 'cause you ain't from around here. No, that sounds like I got it in for ya 'cause you're English."

"I said I realized. All this is my fault, not his."

"It's 'cause you ain't from my world. You don't get the rules: you do what you're fuckin' told. So your buddy here, he's lookin' at me with that look that says he knows he's gonna die. It's just a matter of how much pain."

"Yo-Yo, I had to take Abby. We both know you were going to kill her. I had no choice."

"I love this look, Spencer. Animals have it, too, when you first start killing. 'Oh please, Mister Yo-Yo, I *know* you're gonna take my life offa me now, but is there anything I can say to make it quick?'"

Desperate now, Spencer looked around the apartment for any viable weapon.

The Yo-Yo grasped Chris's ankle.

Spencer looked at the stove. The burner was still on, heating the pot of oil.

The Yo-Yo dragged Chris through broken glass and furniture toward the fire escape.

"Yo-Yo, I'm begging you. It's my fault. I see that now. *Please!*"

"Too late."

Chris tried to get a handhold on the doorframe, but his fingers pinged off like Wile E. Coyote letting go of the cliff edge. The Yo-Yo swung him up like a rag doll over the railing, dangling him over nothingness.

"Yo-Yo!"

The Yo-Yo looked back to see Spencer standing with his left hand curled in a fist over the pot of boiling oil.

"Watch this, you sick fuck!"

He plunged his fist in. The initial shock froze his brain, because he only started screaming after he'd yanked it out. When he could speak, it was in gasping sobs. He held it aloft, scarlet and dripping oil, even though he longed to cradle or, better yet, plunge it under the cold faucet.

"You see that, Yo-Yo! Sweet Jesus." He struggled to stay upright. "That's my steering hand, just my steering hand."

Now he brought his right hand to within inches of the bubbling, roiling yellow liquid. As he felt his knuckles blister, he thought of Milt, whom he hadn't been able to save, shot, in fact, while Spencer cowered in a restroom, and of Lonnie, a decent woman who had meant nothing to him. But he wouldn't lose Chris.

"My right hand, Yo-Yo!" Lungs tightened by shock made his breathing shallow. He spoke in high-pitched, broken tones. "My right! I shift with this. You understand me, you fucker? If this goes in, I can't change gears. That means I can't drive. How are you going to explain that to Dom? That was your job, looking after me till tomorrow. I swear to God if he dies, tomorrow won't happen!"

The Yo-Yo looked at Spencer from the fire escape. His outstretched arm lurched and trembled as Chris front crawled in the dark void below. Spencer, eyes wet with pain, met his gaze. But the Yo-Yo saw in them the resolve of someone who no longer cared about living or dying, so long as they went out fighting. And that was one of the few sentiments with which he empathized. He jerked his arm up.

Chris crashed headfirst in a heap on the metal fire escape floor, right on top of the chalk outline he'd drawn around Spencer what seemed like a lifetime ago.

If Spencer held on to the railing of Chris's bed, he could take the weight off the cable tie and stop it from cutting into his wrist. His palm had come through surprisingly fine because he'd kept his fist so tightly clenched in the oil. He hadn't thought it through at the time so this was pure luck. Even so, the rest of his hand was a marbled mix of white, red, and yellow, pulse beaming its agony to his brain.

Chris lay beside him, also cable tied to the bed. It was going to be the longest night with nothing to look forward to.

"What am I missing here, Chris? He doesn't like witnesses. Soon as I go out the door with him, he's going to come back and kill you."

"Spencer, you have to trust me on this. Tomorrow, that man in there and I are going to come to an understanding."

"Even if he lets you live, he's not going to set you free."

Chris said nothing.

"They can't get her now," said Spencer.

"No." Chris's eyes were closed. He seemed almost Zen-like.

"Back there," said Spencer, "in the living room. I thought he was going to kill you. Made me realize something."

"Yeah? What was that?"

"All this time, all my life, I've never been a team player. I've taken stupid pride in that. Maybe it's a driver thing. I only realized how much I'd been relying on Marielle when she didn't come home that day. And I only just realized you're the best friend I ever had."

Chris smiled to himself. "Tell me, Spence, how's your core strength these days?"

"Huh?"

"'Cause if you're done sentimentalizing, there's a ton of high-quality pain management in the bedside drawer next to you, along with some nail scissors I might have need of tomorrow."

*   *   *

The next morning started hard and fast.

Wordlessly, the Yo-Yo strode in and cut Spencer loose. He marched him downstairs to his car and half threw him into the driver's seat. He cable tied him to the steering wheel and went to shut the door but stopped. He leaned in.

"You better think about what you gotta do today, friend. I'd have listened to Cal and eighty-sixed you and used Eddie. Long time back. How's that doin'?"

He gave Spencer's burned hand a couple of firm slaps. Spencer yelled in pain as the Yo-Yo slammed the door.

Spencer watched him through the windshield as he headed back to the apartment block. Never had he felt more helpless. He was sure Chris had misjudged terribly.

Chris lay on his bed, waiting. He could feel his heart pounding. Really pounding, like he'd taken a bottle of Thermo Booster Burn and then some. Couldn't be good for him. He laughed inside at the way such commonsense thoughts still popped up even when disaster loomed.

The Yo-Yo's massive bulk filled his doorway. His gun was already out. Later, it would be in pieces on the bed of the Detroit River. Seeing no reason to stand on ceremony, he walked around the bed to Chris's side.

"Before you use that, Yo-Yo, let me ask you something."

"Make it quick."

"Are you used to people being scared of you?"

"They have reason to be."

"Some things can be scarier, I tell ya."

The Yo-Yo said nothing. He flicked off the safety, searched for that look in Chris's eyes, and, for the first time in his career, couldn't see it. He cocked his head.

"Ah, I see you're in new territory. Well, that makes two of us," said Chris.

"You got somethin' to say, say it. I might even pass it on to your deadbeat friend. Before I waste him. But I'm already runnin' behind."

"You don't want to risk being late, do you?" said Chris.

The Yo-Yo raised his gun and aimed it at Chris's forehead.

"OK, OK, let's talk about risk-taking, Yo-Yo, and how it applies to you, right now."

Spencer wondered what time it was. He'd taken his watch off after burning his hand. He guessed it was past eight. They were late.

Suddenly the Yo-Yo opened the passenger door and got in. He pulled a knife from his boot, reached over and cut Spencer's cable tie. Instantly, Spencer pulled his injured hand back to his body.

The hand with the knife remained on the steering wheel. Quietly, and without looking around, the Yo-Yo said one word.

"Drive."

43

Showtime

And so you touch this limit, something happens and suddenly you can go a little faster. With the power of your mind, your determination, your instinct, and the experience as well, you can fly very high.
—Ayrton Senna

Johnny Boy's SUV was rolling into Dearborn Heights. Eddie sat beside him. The car was silent, tense, both men feeling the stakes. They pulled up close by the armored truck depot: a windowless, concrete slab–sided building with a tunnel in its center.

They didn't have to wait long before they heard the sound of multiple diesel units echoing from the building's passageway like bears in a cave. The barrier juddered and rose and the white, snub-nosed front of the first cash-in-transit truck emerged. It clanked to a halt at the curb. Sunlight glinted off the truck's turquoise-blue bulletproof windshield as it pulled onto the street and headed west.

Eddie and Johnny Boy watched it go by. They looked around for Spencer. By the time the next few trucks had steamed out of the hole, they were finding it tough to keep their cool. Eddie leaned forward, elbows on knees, watching the disastrous scenario taking shape through steepled hands.

Johnny Boy found himself willing Spencer to appear, refusing to believe his judgment could fail him so badly. The next truck that jerked to a halt curbside threatened to put the mother of all wrecking balls in that conviction. The white, swept-back hair of Max Petrovsky was clearly visible in the shotgun side of the cab. The truck pulled out and turned left. Engine rumbling, it slowly picked up speed, coughing up through its gears.

"Jesus," said Johnny Boy.

"I told you," said Eddie. "I fucking told you we were fucking up."

"He'll be here," said Johnny Boy. He tensed, racked with doubt, on the edge of making a decision. Then: "Get out." Eddie didn't move. "Get out! Now! Wait for that clown. I'll follow Max and call you to say where we've got to."

Moments later he was gone, leaving Eddie standing on the sidewalk with a big empty duffel bag.

Johnny Boy wasn't the only one having a bad start to his day.

"What the hell do you mean, 'revoked'?" said Scott.

The civilian flight scheduler at the other end of the line peered at his screen in the MSP's Aviation Unit office at Lansing.

"Yeah, you had clearance last night. Not this morning, though. Happens automatically now. DPD's often late paying fuel bills, sometimes by weeks."

Scott pulled over onto the shoulder of the seventy-five. "This is a high-priority op."

"I want to help, but, fact is, someone in DPD accounts will have been notified, it—"

"Happens automatically, yeah I get it. What can I do?"

"Depends on whether your precinct needs an emergency extra allocation of funds."

"The mayor," said Scott. The irony was painful.

"Yeah, or the City Council, but . . ." the flight scheduler hesitated. "Truth is, we've got heavy demand today. If you lose your place on the list . . ."

Scott ended the call. Panic burned his insides.

Eddie sat on a bench with the duffel bag in his lap.

Suddenly Spencer's car roared past him, skidded to a stop, and backed up.

Eddie leapt up from the bench, yanked open the rear door of the Subaru, and piled in.

"Head north, hit Warren, and head east," he said to Spencer. "They've got a thirteen-minute head start."

Spencer was jerked sideways as the Yo-Yo gave his seat an almighty punch.

"Go!"

Spencer flipped a U into a nonexistent gap and lit the fires.

He worked through the sludgy morning traffic, milking every gap, every underused lane. His moves were so quick, so judged that not one car sounded its horn or had to take evasive action. The Subaru was simply there, in their view for an instant, and then not there.

The Yo-Yo made a call on his phone. "Yeah, Denny? You at McLean yet?"

The mention of Chris's street caught Spencer's attention. He glanced around and found himself eye locking the Yo-Yo, who'd obviously been expecting him to do just that. Spencer turned back to the road, but he could feel the other man's eyes on him during the ensuing conversation.

"Go home, Denny. It's taken care of." The Yo-Yo killed the call.

Spencer couldn't figure out whether Chris was dead or the Yo-Yo was just mind fucking him. Chris had sounded so sure.

"Hey, watch the fuck out!" said Eddie.

They screeched to a halt. Spencer had nearly hit a stroller on a crossing as they ran a red.

The Yo-Yo snorted disdainfully.

They pulled away. Spencer tilted his seat back a little, cracked his fingers, trying to find the zone, downshifted, and got crack-a-lacking.

They blasted up a freeway on-ramp, engine roaring on a high rev, third gear giving and giving and ready to give more, Spencer's vision blocked by a high-sided semi, but it didn't matter since he'd seen that coming and memorized the traffic pattern in all five lanes. He floored it and moved across the mental snapshot right into the carpool lane.

Eddie was speaking to Johnny Boy on his phone, on speakerphone since he was swaying around so much it was difficult to keep it pressed against his ear and stay upright. "We're tryin' the freeway. We're four blocks west and I don't know how many north: five, maybe six."

About eight blocks south, on Rotunda Drive, Johnny Boy was managing to keep pace with the truck. He cut into the inside lane, getting honked to hell as he did so, and pulled up a little closer. He looked across just in time to see the back of a hand press itself against the thick glass.

Johnny Boy cut Eddie off. "His hand's up! His goddamn hand's up, he's sending! You tell Spencer to pull his finger out of his ass, you hear me?"

Even over the sound of the Subaru's engine, Eddie didn't have to relay the message. Or its sentiment. The Yo-Yo turned in his seat, talked calmly, reasonably, his control merely enhancing the threat. "If you don't catch him in ten minutes, we can't get the access code or find out which bank he's goin' to."

"Four blocks east, six south, ten minutes. Easy," said Spencer, just as the traffic ground to a standstill. They had a heart attack moment when they heard sirens, but the cruisers raced by, up the shoulder.

Fucking freeways, what were you thinking?

Spencer's mind churned. He looked around.

The Yo-Yo faced forward. "So help me, you better do something."

Spencer jerked the wheel right. The BMW to their offside had no intention of letting him in, until their fenders touched. BMW guy clocked three men in the car forcing its way in front of him. One of them was huge. He decided he'd save his battles for the boardroom. They worked their way across to the shoulder like that and took off, just in front of an ambulance and behind a sheriff's cruiser.

They saw the cop looking up in his mirror. Could sense his disbelief. He pulled up, forcing them to do likewise.

"You motherfucker," said the Yo-Yo.

"Desperate times," said Spencer. "Work with me."

The deputy was out in an instant and furious. Spencer dropped his window.

"What the hell are you doing?" the deputy said.

Spencer crisped up his accent and concocted something as random as possible to break up the guy's train of thought and take advantage of the fact he had better things to do.

"Sorry, Officer, but I had to get your attention. I'm getting the tour of your city with my cousin and his boyfriend," Spencer jerked his head back at Eddie, "but he's got a weak bladder and we're lost. Trying to get to the Ford Model T plant but I think we're going to have an emergency soon if—"

The sheriff's deputy stared at the three of them, open-mouthed. "You're from . . . England?" he managed.

"Yes, but I have relatives here in Detroit. Never visited before. Amazing place."

Shaking his head, the deputy pointed at the off-ramp two hundred yards ahead. He was walking backward toward his cruiser as he replied. "Take that, head east, there'll be a restroom in a gas station."

They took off.

English privilege . . .

"Jesus," said Eddie. "He's been sending for seven minutes." Suddenly he had a thought. "Yo-Yo, why'd you cancel Denny?"

The Yo-Yo kept his eyes on Spencer as he answered. "Denny was on cleanup. Supposed to wipe the whole place. Would you wanna rely on him not to miss anything, Eddie? Plus, the two neighbor fucks upstairs saw me there. Now get this: turns out cooking ain't the only thing Spencer's friend's good at. Told me about taking risks for nothin'. That shit got me in Carson City pen first time around. So, you know what, Spencer? I didn't whack your buddy."

Spencer looked at the Yo-Yo.

"Yeah, that's right. Left him tied up. Hardly what you'd call a crime scene. You know why?"

Spencer's stomach tightened. He waited.

"He's dyin' anyway." He glanced around at Eddie. "Can you believe that shit? Guy's got cancer. In his pancreas. He's gonna be dead within two weeks. Now that ain't gonna be too credible a witness, right, Spence?"

The Yo-Yo cracked up.

"Cancer," he gasped, like it was the funniest turn of events anyone could imagine.

It was the first time Spencer had ever heard him laugh.

Meanwhile Southern Avenue was about to become John Kronk Street for Johnny Boy and Max. Johnny Boy was frantically working his phone as he drove.

"How fucking difficult can it be?"

He'd managed to get his AirDrop to search for devices, nearly sideswiping a pickup in the process.

The armored truck seemed to be accelerating on the straight. Johnny Boy kept pace, then worked his way closer, checking his phone all the time. The wing on the Merc was less than a foot from the truck's heavy steel bumper, the closest Johnny Boy had ever gotten to another moving vehicle. He didn't like it. They were going fifty now. What the hell was the guy thinking? He thought they'd drive those babies like a goddamn school bus, not a Saturn Five.

Just then his phone screen stopped beach balling.

Devices found: MAX.

"Well, I'll be damned."

He looked up just in time to see but not avoid the high edge of a sidewalk. With a bone-jarring crunch, the Merc was thrown four feet in the air as its speed dropped from fifty to five. Its wheel disintegrated and the axle fractured. Johnny Boy yelled as he got a face full of airbag.

The Subaru was scorching the surface streets, the devil himself on its tail. Still no tire screech, no slide. All-wheel drive on hot, sticky Pirellis just holding on.

"Next intersection maybe," said Eddie, as they passed Johnny Boy's SUV. Inside, Johnny Boy, dazed and disorientated, nose bleeding onto his shirt, tried to find his phone.

"Got about one minute left," said the Yo-Yo.

They saw the back of the truck ahead, waiting at a light to go left. The light was changing to yellow. The truck would just get through. Left turn lane still full. Spencer grimaced, decided to go for it, shifted down, pedaled down, barreled down the straight-ahead lane.

A guy in a Porsche in his own sweet hurry was waiting to cross the intersection, nosing forward, watching Spencer's light change. He decided to go, though, while his own light was still red.

Spencer had seen it but was committed to the move. Too fast now to abort, he touched his horn, tried to make the left turn even sharper just as the Porsche stopped. It was too tight, though, and understeer came in. He was turning the wheel and nothing much was happening. Seconds, seconds, everything going into a slow-motion heartbeat that would take up pages of a witness report. He touched the brake with his left foot, felt the front end bite again. Their bumpers kissed and Spencer lost his. Under his wheel with a crunch. And then they were around and through and they'd actually passed the truck as Spencer was trying to get things back in shape.

They slowed and waited for Max's truck to catch up. The Yo-Yo and Eddie peered at their phones.

"Get us close," said the Yo-Yo. Unfazed, totally unfazed by how close they'd been to getting cut out of a pile of twisted Japanese and German metal by a fireman's oxy torch.

The truck rumbled past them, and Spencer fell into its wake, matching its speed and drawing up close.

"Not getting anything," said Eddie.

"Work your phone better then."

"I'm not either," said the Yo-Yo. "Must be the armor. Get closer."

"Do you see how close I am? I'm nearly riding the guy's tail."

"Closer!"

Spencer figured the rear doors of the truck might be strengthened. He changed to an inside lane, on Max's side of the truck, pissing off a couple of other cars in the process, and moved forward. Max's hand pressed against the glass but surely only for seconds now. Spencer moved in, touched his fender gently against the truck's running board, trying to keep the contact super light, predicting the slightest movement, so nothing, no sense of their presence was transmitted to the truck, up through its steering wheel and into the hands of its driver.

When it went to turn left and head north on Grand, Spencer saw it coming just in time. They went around like they were glued, the weirdest sight, so weird other drivers did a double take and then discounted it. A gray sedan stalking an armored truck like a sub stalking its Soviet counterpart during the Cold War.

"Motherfucker. Got it. First Union Bank of Detroit on Lafayette Boulevard. Big one."

"You got the access code too?" asked Spencer, finger on the afterburner.

"Yep. Go!"

The truck took a left on Grand, heading north, up toward Michigan Avenue. Spencer knew Michigan would be slow. He threw a right on Toledo, started blasting through the backstreets, heading down to the Vernor Highway. He planned to come into the financial district from the southwest. He knew all the backstreets and alleys if Vernor was bad and he'd work the hell out of them, just as he was working the hell out of the car.

As they closed on Lafayette, Eddie and the Yo-Yo took off their jackets, exposing blue uniform shirts underneath.

Spencer pulled up almost in front of the bank, a grand old neoclassical building with a fountain outside. The Yo-Yo and Eddie got out and marched across the busy sidewalk toward the revolving glass doors.

The seconds ticked by. Spencer squirmed in his seat. He had no idea how much time he'd bought them. Max's truck was behind him somewhere, heading for right where they were, ready to send two guys in with the same access code. It was like waiting for the *Enola Gay* to turn up.

"Gonna have to give you a ticket if you don't move on, sir."

Spencer looked up at a female parking enforcement officer.

"I'm waiting for my mother. She can't walk far."

"There are disabled spaces around on Eighth, sir."

Spencer looked at her blankly. This was passing the time.

"Are you gonna move it along, sir?"

"I don't think I am, ma'am."

As she started writing a ticket, his rearview mirror filled with the letters MACK. Max and co had arrived. He watched Max and a colleague walk toward the bank entrance.

Inside, the Yo-Yo and Eddie were heading for the same doors carrying a large metal case. The doors were smoked glass. They could see out, but people couldn't see in—a fortunate state of affairs, since they saw Max and his colleague coming toward them but not vice versa. They veered over to the farthest set of doors.

Moments later they were in the back of Spencer's car. Spencer scrunched up the ticket as they moved off.

"Head east," said the Yo-Yo. "And you can take it easy."

"I'm going to head around the top of Downtown," said Spencer.

"Whatever," said the Yo-Yo, removing his blue shirt and putting his own back on. Eddie did the same.

The Yo-Yo keyed in a code on the case and opened it. He whistled. Spencer looked over. A whole case of green looked back. Even in his distracted state, the sight gave him a thrill. Pity none of it was for him. The Yo-Yo shut the case and passed it back to Eddie. Eddie started unloading it into the duffel bag.

"We're on Gratiot," said Eddie a quarter of an hour later.

"Yeah," said Spencer.

"What the fuck for? We're goin' northeast. We're supposed to be heading southwest."

"That's right. And we will, in a while."

"What do ya mean, 'in a while'?" asked the Yo-Yo.

"Haven't you noticed how quiet it is? For all we know they're on us with a chopper."

And they were.

44

Collateral Contingency

*The same moment that you are seen as the best, the fastest and some-
body that cannot be touched, you are enormously fragile.*

—Ayrton Senna

Scott had wanted to pull the plug on the whole op when MSP held
their chopper back, but the horses were out of the gates. He was
pretty certain he was going to lose his job and rightly so, because
one or two people would likely die as a result of this clusterfuck.

But the thought of what he might do when he was no longer
a detective made him think of his buddy who worked for the coast
guard. And now an orange coast guard MH-65, known affectionately
as a Dolphin, was heading northeast from Brest Bay. One hell of a
favor traveling at 160 knots.

On Gratiot Avenue, the Yo-Yo was wary of the change in plan.

"You fucking with us, Spencer? You know it would be a seriously bad idea to do that?"

"I'm not fucking with you. I'm being thorough. That's what
you're paying me for. Just run with me on it. I've got us this far,
right?"

"Get on with it then."

"No, fuck that," said Eddie. "Dom doesn't wanna be waiting around for us. Stick to the plan."

"He won't care," said the Yo-Yo. "Long as we get there clear. I can message him we're gonna be late."

The coast guard chopper ID'd their car at about the same time things really kicked off inside it.

Eddie pulled his gun as Spencer turned north on Van Dyke.

"Y'know, Spencer, I'm fucking tired of your shit. Like you think you're just the kick-ass champ of all things with wheels. Drive to the fucking meet!"

The cop car waiting at the light they were passing through was treated to the somewhat surreal sight of a man putting a gun to the head of his driver.

By the time the Yo-Yo clocked them it was too late. The cruiser pushed a left through a red, and followed.

The Yo-Yo watched their new tail in his side-view mirror. "So help me, Eddie, what the fuck?"

Spencer watched the cruiser draw closer, checking them out.

"Just drive normal," said Eddie, sitting back. "They'll think we were dickin' around."

The cruiser lit them up and gave a blip on its siren.

Spencer, shaking his head hopelessly, ignored it and shifted down. "We could have done this, Eddie."

The cop car moved up close. Spencer threw a left, slipping like a phantom through three lanes of traffic.

The cops had to work their way through with sirens and lights. They sent the 10-35 call out as they put the hammer down. More cops answered. The chopper answered, dropped down, and closed.

They continued northeast, the roads becoming emptier, the city ghostlike. Spencer used all three lanes to smooth corners. Engine wail echoed among abandoned buildings.

Spencer didn't even know about the chopper, but he knew *something* was converging units on them. However hard he worked, he seemed to lose one just as another found them.

Sweat stung his eyes and soaked his back. He dropped off the power a little. A cruiser came right up behind, looking for its chance to flick them into a spin.

"He's comin' up, he's comin' up close," yelled Eddie, holding on to the seat and the duffel bag.

"You keep up that driving shit, Spencer," said the Yo-Yo. "Either till they take us down or we get loose."

"Shut up, I'm trying to . . ."

They skimmed a wall as they skidded onto a track running between derelict factories and warehouses.

"To concentrate. This guy's good, so I want him close. Be ready to bail."

"We're not running, Spencer. Get us loose." The Yo-Yo racked the slide back on his gun and checked the chamber.

Spencer tried to shut out the sound. Last week he'd been selling cars. Just yesterday, he'd had an amazing daughter and the best friend a man could hope for, even if he'd only just realized it at the time.

Stick to the plan.

He glanced around at the Yo-Yo. "We're going to have to make them think we're running, OK?"

The Yo-Yo looked unsure. Spencer had no time to explain. The lead pursuit was bumping their tail, looking for its chance. "Just be ready, you two."

He slowed down some more, made it look like he was deciding on his next move. He wasn't. He just wanted to make sure the cops stayed tight.

They turned almost as one into the drive of the derelict factory. Spencer accelerated. The cops did the same. With several cars in support and the pack behind them, plus air support, they sensed the kill was imminent.

Except they didn't have air support. The chopper was in a hold a mile back. They couldn't just fly into Coleman International's airspace without permission. They were awaiting clearance from the tower.

Spencer headed for the trench in front of the dark entranceway. He rode the Subaru onto the planks he'd laid across the gap and yanked the hand brake just as his rear wheels got to the other side, pulling the planks with him. They fell in the gap. The lead pursuit had no hope of braking, and they followed the planks right into the trench. Forty to zero in a big crunch of metal and forgotten concrete.

Spencer drove across the dark hall, not caring about the bricks and bottles biting at his tires. He drove the Subaru's passenger-side fender right into the doorway and floored the gas pedal. All four wheels belched out thick smoke. The smoke billowed around the car, and they were lost to view.

"Follow me," said Spencer as he bailed. Then all three of them were out and clambering over the hood and through the doorway. The Yo-Yo turned and fired a few shots in the general direction of the cops to keep them cautious, buying time. The Yo-Yo, ice-cold in an emergency and especially so when he had no choices. He'd already dodged twenty years once in his life. That sort of luck doesn't come twice.

They thundered down the stairs, Spencer leading the way, Eddie clutching the bag, the Yo-Yo catching up.

They hit the basement. When the factory was alive, stock had been loaded or unloaded here from the railway yards. Now the Buick waited for them.

Spencer opened the trunk. "Throw it in here, Eddie, and get the hell in, both of you."

Neither needed a second telling. Spencer watched them dive into the Buick. He slammed the trunk shut, keeping his finger on the release button as he did so. The trunk stayed slightly ajar.

He crouched, looked beneath the car, and saw a pair of feet. He grabbed the ankles and pulled out a very frightened Chris. Frightened and unwell. Spencer wondered how he'd missed the pallid skin and dark circles under the watery eyes. Chris's arms were crossed protectively over his chest, as if he'd been laid to rest already. There was no time for words, but when their eyes met, Chris saw that Spencer knew.

A police bullhorn echoed down the staircase, advising everyone to give up.

As Spencer jumped in and started the Buick, he acted flustered and panicked, keeping the ignition key turned, even though the engine had fired, causing the starter motor to grate loudly in the confined space. He glanced in the rearview and saw the trunk lid lift up. He revved the engine, seemed to struggle with the shift, grinding the gears, giving Chris more time. When he saw the trunk lid go down, he gave it another beat and then chugged slowly out of the building. Soon they were driving among the hills of gravel and salt that supplied Detroit's Department of Public Works. Just working men doing their rounds.

Chris lay on the ground for a moment, eyes closed, the duffel bag heavy on his chest, still praying, praying that the Buick didn't stop, praying he didn't feel a gun against his head. When neither happened, his brain told him to get moving. He sprang from the ground and ran through a doorway, along passageways, and up and down stairs. The route had been preplanned, committed to memory and replayed time and again in his head since he and Spencer had left the Buick there and scoped out the area in the rain and thunder.

His heart pounded, its capacity falsely bettered by a near overdose of Thermo Booster Burn. His lungs struggled to keep up. He dropped the bag and leaned against the dirty, graffiti-laden wall, gasping. He couldn't believe he'd been fearful of a life too quiet.

The chopper had gotten clearance. Being coast guard and not so familiar with the airspace, they'd wanted to be sure. The cops on the ground had reported it was now a foot pursuit anyway. All they had to do was make sure no suspects ran out of the building while it was being locked down. Shots fired had been reported, so the air asset had to stay high. They swept over the derelict factory but didn't pay any mind to a nondescript sedan going about its business half a mile to the north, making for McNichols, where it would head west and then south on Livernois.

And they didn't even notice a Prius, bumbling eastward.

Spencer hadn't expected any gratitude, so he wasn't disappointed when none came.

The Yo-Yo gave curt directions, and they worked their way south and west, down toward River Rouge and Ecorse. When they hit Delray, he made Spencer pull over several times. He'd get out, check the sky, wait in case they'd picked up a tail, and then they'd be on their way again. Eddie was quiet, as if concentrating. Spencer detested him for his stupid, hidden competitive streak, his crazy little edge thing he had going on. They'd nearly been busted because of it. Prick.

"Take a right, down that road, between those two empty buildings."

Spencer did as he was told. On their left he could see glimpses of the water. He knew they were getting near the final destination. His heart was hammering. He felt like checking his rearview, just to see what the grim reaper drove these days.

"In there."

Spencer turned into a huge, rusty, iron-sided warehouse. Graffiti and filth covered its walls and doors. Puddles of oily water glinted amid rubble and garbage. A large portion of one wall was open to a quayside and yet the building was still gloomy. Spencer picked his way through fallen concrete pillars, their steel reinforcement rods twisted and exposed like veins yanked from a cadaver.

"Over near the water."

Spencer guessed the water was where the Buick was destined to end up, probably with him in the trunk. Soon now.

They sat in the car, waiting.

Ten minutes later, McGrath's silver Merc appeared at the far end of the warehouse.

"Flash your lights twice, Spencer."

The Merc flashed back and started moving toward them.

Spencer felt light-headed his heart was thudding so hard. Although virtually nothing had been said to suggest it, he had felt himself being cut off by the other two men. Segregated, marked, already a dead man. He wondered whether it would come from Eddie or the Yo-Yo. He kind of needed to see it coming. Every rustle of fabric and creak of a seat spring was a harbinger. Would it be his throat slit or a bullet?

The Yo-Yo took out his gun.

45

Rolling with It

McGrath knew that the moment he flashed his lights a countdown started. Spencer's countdown.

He worked the Merc through the trash and potholes on the warehouse floor while keeping an eye on the Buick. He was waiting for the flash of gunshot. Probably wouldn't hear the noise; the Merc's sound insulation was really good.

He'd quite liked Spencer. Played him from the start. But it was always easier to play someone you liked. He was always going to be from the other side of the tracks, the other side of the world.

Right about now. McGrath sensed it.

He braked, watching the Buick. Suddenly one of the Buick's back doors opened and Eddie got out. He stomped to the rear of the car, opened the trunk, and stood there with a dumb-as-fuck expression.

McGrath focused on getting over there. He pulled up nearly at right angles to the Buick, facing the quayside, got out, and walked around Spencer's car.

Inside, the Yo-Yo stared straight ahead. "I'm gonna ask you once only, Spencer. Then I'm gonna start blowin' body parts away." He grasped Spencer's burned hand in a viselike grip, then twisted the blistered fingers savagely. "Where. Is. It?"

Spencer screamed and screamed until the grip relaxed. "I told you. I put it somewhere safe! I don't want to keep it. Sweet Jesus, I just want to be left alone. You think I didn't see this coming?"

The Yo-Yo knew he would struggle to keep the pace slow when he got to work on Spencer. He jammed his gun hard into Spencer's cheek.

"First one'll go right through. You'll leak like a watering can. Now, where the fuck is—"

And those were the last words the Yo-Yo ever said, as suddenly the windshield shattered and his shirt puffed open like a ragged flower, a thick fountain of blood at its center. The back of his seat erupted. He slumped forward, pistol clutched loosely in his hand, its muzzle smoking.

Spencer looked down at his right thigh, where blood welled, soaking the singed fabric. "No, fuck!"

A bullhorn rended the gloom. "This is the police! Lay down your weapons. Put your hands out of the windows! Do it now!"

McGrath had hit the deck the moment the Yo-Yo got his ballistic therapy. He crawled around the back of the Buick. Spencer half fell out, clutching his leg, trying to staunch the bleeding.

Again the bullhorn hollered. "You're covered by a marksman. Stand up!"

Eddie joined them. He didn't look too keen on going out in a blaze of glory. McGrath didn't miss that. He took out his gun: a Glock 22.

"Get your gun out, Eddie."

Spencer groaned, only vaguely aware of what was happening now.

"This is fucked, Dom," said Eddie.

"Get your gun out, Eddie."

"Dom—"

"Eddie, what did you say back in my office? We're all looking at serious time here. Now you see what they got out there? Just a few shooters. This is Detroit. Spencer?"

Spencer was staring at the blood surging up through his fingers.

"Spencer!"

Spencer looked at him, wide-eyed and ashen.

"The money, Spencer. You sure it's safe?"

Spencer nodded.

"Eddie," said McGrath. "Put some covering fire down on them."

Eddie looked at McGrath blankly. McGrath raised his gun over the hood of the Merc. "Like this. *Do it!*" McGrath started firing.

Eddie shook his head, raised his gun, and started firing blindly.

The cops returned fire. Windows on both cars collapsed. A tire went down. Rounds pinged off bodywork.

Spencer watched them, aghast. Suddenly, McGrath turned and fired once into Eddie's face. One moment, Eddie was there in front of Spencer, alive and firing, the next he was flat out and still. A pool of blood ballooned from his faceless head on the filthy ground. After a moment, Spencer had to shuffle away from it.

McGrath shook Spencer's shoulder. "Listen to me." But Spencer couldn't take his eyes off Eddie's faceless body.

McGrath threw his gun and phone out into the water, the movement masked by the darkness and chaotic shooting. He grabbed an old rag and washed his hands of gunfire residue in an oily puddle. "Spencer, look at me. Whatever happens, you keep your mouth shut. This didn't happen. Eddie took a cop's bullet. Got that? *Got that?* You don't know me, Spencer, and you don't know where those two put their money. Nothing else. Make the rest up."

McGrath took off his jacket and waved it above the car, yelling out surrender. The firing stopped. McGrath stood with his hands raised. Spencer heard the shuffle of fast-moving feet and shouting as the cops closed in.

"I don't know what this is about," McGrath was saying. "You hear? They asked me to meet them here." His voice sounded anxious but when his eyes found Spencer's again, they were cold and calm and so very clear in purpose. They were the last thing Spencer saw before his own closed.

46

Team Draft

Blackness.

Time. Time to work things out.

Was I good enough? To get to the nice place? Or is this it? Just . . . blackness?

A big pool of blackness. Swimming in it. Lost.

Pools of blackness.

"That's it, Spencer, wakey wakey. We don't have ourselves a whole lot of time."

"Johnny Boy?"

"Well, strictly speaking, you don't know that. And I don't know you either. In fact, we just met, you and I."

Spencer looked around. Hospital room. IV drip. Bleeping. He looked back at Johnny Boy.

"My leg? My leg, is it OK?" He tried to sit up. Couldn't. So tired.

"Still there, Spencer. Chipped femur. Missed the femoral artery or you'd be talking to a guy with wings right now. You lost a lot of blood, hence the drip. You've been through the wars, Spencer, but it's not over yet. And we don't have a whole lot of time before the cop outside gets word that I'm not a practicing lawyer anymore. So, you need to reassure me that you're going take in what we're going to discuss."

"Dom killed Eddie. Why did he do that?"

"I'll take that as a yes then. Didn't you know? The cops killed Eddie? They'll dig out a bullet that could have come from any police-issue handgun."

"I don't get it."

"Come on, catch up with me here. Dom's who they really want, so they'd offer Eddie a sweet deal. Now with Eddie and the Yo-Yo dead and no money, there's nothing to link Dom, or you, to this job. Sometimes things just turn out well. Could have gone very south, because somehow the cops found the drop-off point."

"You were going to kill me."

"And so you took the money. It was a good move. You were bright enough to plan all that, so it won't be too hard for you to see that if you do time it'll be, at most, two years. You most likely won't, because you can say you were forced at gunpoint to drive. Two cops saw that, and cops make great witnesses."

"I can't go to jail."

Face tilted, Johnny Boy looked at Spencer, assessing him. "Listen carefully. You think we're spending our last years in Club Fed just because Spencer couldn't keep it together? You'll hold on to that money until we see how this is going to pan out for you. You'll get a bigger cut. There's more of it to go around now. We'll send a lawyer your way. They have nothing on you. When it's done, we'll take what's ours. Stay quiet and keep cool. I hope you're buying what I'm selling, because if you're not, I will personally see to it that everyone you love dies. I am a careful and thorough man, Spencer. I've faced bigger challenges than hacking a CPS computer."

He eyeballed Spencer. Johnny Boy had seen the look before, the look of someone who would never quite grasp the way of the world he'd strayed into, who thought he might yet walk out and just leave it behind. Spencer might need more convincing that that couldn't be so.

Chris sat on the metal floor of the fire escape. In one hand he held his inhaler, in the other a whisky. His hands were cuffed. He had to raise both to his lips, so he could make his choice at the last moment. He was on the floor because his trusty sofa was being shredded by a tech from an Evidence Response Team. They'd turned up in a white Ford minivan with mirrored windows about an hour after Chris had gotten home. He'd opened the door and in they'd come with their big yellow boxes that looked like cool boxes you'd take on a picnic.

Chris had resigned himself to the destruction of his apartment and the trashing or temporary confiscation of all his worldly possessions. He'd backed up his business and banking records to the cloud, all except one bank account that they wouldn't find even with a team of detectives. And anyway, these guys didn't yet think Chris had anything to do with it. They hadn't even read him his rights. So he waited, not just for them to go, but rather he saw this as the last bit of excitement in what he'd started to think of as his time in this world. He was feeling pretty damn tired these days; pain could be so wearing. He'd been dreading a lonely life. No danger of that anymore. Funny how the things that worried folks the most almost never came to pass.

Spencer thought about the way the guy sitting opposite had entered his room, the way he was impatiently going through his papers, messaging on his phone. He hadn't even acknowledged Spencer.

His phone rang. He looked at the screen and then left the room again. Ten minutes later he was back. He walked to the window and looked out at the darkening sky.

"My name is Detective Scott. And what I want to know is whether Spencer Burnham is a teammate or an inmate." He turned to Spencer. "That's what I want to know."

Spencer was pretty damn certain whose team he was on. The coach had already visited.

"I'll help you wherever I can, Detective."

Scott nodded. After a pause, "What did they do with the money?"

"I have no idea. I wasn't driving by choice."

"Uh-huh, forced to drive at gunpoint. Really unlucky."

Scott's manner was discomforting in its dismissiveness.

"I've had a shitty day, Burnham. I'm hoping you're going to make it better for me. Things you should know: One, I play hardball better than most, but I do give-and-take very well. Two, I know lots about you—when you started working for Dominic McGrath, who you replaced. He was tortured to death, by the way."

Spencer kept quiet.

"This may hurt, Burnham, but you could have driven up Gratiot like Dale Earnhardt. No one would have stopped you. You see there isn't a recorder here, Burnham?"

"What am I being charged with?"

"We'll get to that. Answer's going to depend on you. McGrath planned the robbery, paid off Max Petrovsky, and met you at a pre-arranged location to collect, right?"

"I don't know the guy who turned up."

"McGrath killed Eddie, right?"

"I didn't see anything. I'd been shot."

"OK, thank you, Burnham. I just wanted to see how you intended to roll. I've been trying to figure out whether you're just an opportunist, taking a chance to keep a hold on your daughter, that kind of thing, or a real player. I hear you already had a visitor? Probably told you to just keep quiet and you're going to be fine, right?"

Nothing.

"So, back to your question, here's what I'm going to be charging you with. Laundering the proceeds of crime and accessory to murder. The second is the one I'd be worrying about if I were you."

"How do you get to that?"

"This is how I get to that, you motherfucking piece of shit."

Scott rummaged in his file, removed a photograph, and slapped it on Spencer's chest. Then he leaned against the wall, watching.

Spencer lifted the photograph.

47

Playoff

Eddie smiled back at him—in full police uniform with the Stars and Stripes behind. There was no sign of that off-the-wall stare.

Spencer's insides lurched and the bleep rate on his ECG rose. His hand dropped back on his chest.

"My late partner was his best man," said Scott. "They met at recruit training. Eddie was navy intel for four years before DPD. He got tasked out to state police for an undercover op, the op got pulled, so we had this pristine identity all backstopped: fake driver's license, Social Security, even a couple of warrants out for him in Nebraska. We decided to use it for McGrath. Eddie hung out with one of his accountant's buddies in Pontiac on the weekends, looking for work. You have any idea how much time and effort that was? You got any idea what kind of a guy it takes to do that shit? It's not just having balls of steel. It's about seeing things, sometimes having to do things. It affected him. He said he could only cope by going kind of blank. We called it his switch-off stare."

Scott walked over to Spencer's bed and looked down on him.

"That time his phone didn't get the AirDrop when you were doing your fancy driving? He was trying to get your ass out, to make an opening, to make McGrath use him today. And when we stopped you with that dirty cash? We just upped and left you without so much as a DUI? That was because Eddie messaged us from McGrath's john. Told us McGrath wouldn't roll on this without you. All Eddie had to do today was lead us to the meet. That was all, so we could get McGrath for armed robbery. You had a tracker on your car. It would have been fine. Chopper was backup. Just to keep Eddie safe. Then you had to throw in your clever swap shit. Eddie had to message us all the way from Hamtramck, to where your ass got saved. Now you're alive and he's dead. That's how I get to accessory."

Spencer turned in his seat to stretch out his injured leg. His court-appointed attorney moved obligingly. He was a nice enough guy and honest; Spencer had virtually no chance.

Occasionally, the bald, bespectacled judge glanced Spencer's way from his wood-paneled pulpit, framed on one side by the Stars and Stripes, on the other by the state flag. Spencer could see in the man's eyes how he appeared: a bruised, shot felon with his state-funded attorney on one side and a cop on the other. The judge had been droning on for fifteen minutes, but now it seemed the final score was coming in.

"In view of all this information provided by CPS and the authorities, the court sees fit to decree full and immediate termination of parental rights. Abby Burnham is to be placed in protective custody until a suitable home can be found. Mister Burnham's access and visitation rights I'm setting at zero. Mister Burnham, you will be entitled to appeal before this . . ."

Johnny Boy had been watching the proceedings from a back-row seat. He got up quietly and left.

Spencer leaned forward and looked across the courtroom to where Caitlyn sat with her colleagues. As far as he was aware, she hadn't looked his way since his identity had been confirmed at the start of the hearing. She looked tired.

Spencer's counsel made an attempt at commiseration and talked about appealing. Spencer ignored him. He worked his way along the row of seats, an awkward process on crutches with a burned hand. Caitlyn reached the aisle first. Their eyes met. Spencer deferred to her and her colleagues.

Scott stood waiting at the rear of the court. His eyes also met Caitlyn's, but they failed to hold her gaze. And then Caitlyn was gone.

Scott walked beside Spencer as he limped down the corridor.

"So we're going to follow you but stay out of sight," he was saying. "I got two cars on call if you get in trouble. All I need is McGrath admitting he planned the robbery or talking about why he killed Eddie or both. And I want to know where the Yo-Yo hid the money. We've been over your route with a fine-tooth comb. Figure he dropped it and one of Cal's boys picked it up. You sure you didn't see him do anything with it?"

"I didn't see anything except the road. They were on my case, making me work pretty damn hard, you know? And then your boys were making me work harder."

"You know if you're dicking with me, I will bury you in the worst possible way, right?"

Spencer stopped and turned to him. "Why don't you wake up? You saw where I figured in the plan. I was collateral. So all they told me was what I needed to know. Just like you did with Caitlyn Dunn."

They looked at each other, neither with any respect. People swirled around them. "So let's just do this thing, Detective."

They emerged from the artificially cooled building into the baking heat of the lot. As Scott led him over to an ops truck, Spencer saw Chris leaning against his Prius. Chris gave him a discreet nod.

Inside the truck, Spencer sat down to take the weight off his leg. He was sweating already, and his stomach was kicking up from the antibiotics. The doc had wanted to keep him on an antibiotic IV for another week.

A police surveillance technician proceeded to wire Spencer up.

"Where are you going to be if I get out, so I can find you?" asked Spencer.

"Lincoln and Grand River. And I've got an unmarked watching the depot right now. And McGrath's there, so we need to roll."

When the wire setup was done, Spencer got in the rental car that the DPD had provided for him. It was a stick shift. He started up and drove across the lot. The ops truck followed.

In spite of the pain, Spencer was managing the driving and the gear changes. But when he got to the exit, he suddenly turned the wheel sharply, taking the car against the sharp curb corner. The tire blew. He stopped.

In no time, Scott was at his window. "What the fuck are you doing?"

"You try driving a stick with one leg for Chrissakes."

Chris suddenly appeared behind Scott. "Spence, use Penny. She's an auto. You've got to get this done."

They both looked questioningly at Scott. "Whatever," he said. "I don't give a shit. Let's be green." He turned back to the ops truck.

"I'll just get my bag," said Chris, handing Spencer his keys.

Spencer yelled out to Scott. "Lincoln and Grand River, right?"

"That's right," said Scott without stopping. Chris wheezed past him, seemingly oblivious.

Moments later, Chris threw his bag in the DPD's rental. He watched Spencer leave in the Prius, the ops truck following. Then he got down to fixing the busted tire.

Spencer hit the seventy-five and headed south. He checked his rearview and saw the surveillance truck staying up close. He thought about the deal Scott had offered: get Dom to incriminate himself and Spencer's gunpoint alibi would stand. No offer of protection for him, Chris, or Abby. Scott said they didn't really have the budget but "the DPD would take measures" and Abby would take the name of her new parents and that would be kept secret. It was a shit deal.

He turned south on Gibson. The cops stayed on Martin Luther.

Spencer drove around and into the depot gateway. He pressed the buzzer.

"Yeah?" It was Denny.

"Spencer to see Dom."

Silence.

Bit of a bombshell for you, Denny?

The barrier rose.

Spencer backed into the loading bay next to Cal's Porsche. He backed in so the rear of his car would be in shadow and hidden from the cops watching the depot. No one was around. Denny had probably rushed upstairs to announce Spencer's arrival, so he was on borrowed time.

He opened the trunk of Chris's Prius to find the large duffel bag that Eddie had stuffed with cash. Spencer hobbled with it to Cal's car. He popped the front trunk and threw it in. He got his crutches from the Prius and headed for the stairs.

The reception area was empty. He heard voices coming from McGrath's office.

The room fell silent when he entered. Sheila was leaning against the filing cabinet. Cal and Johnny Boy sat facing McGrath's desk. Denny stood by its side. McGrath looked at Spencer. Gone was the twinkle. Spencer knew he was tainted. No one in the room was stupid enough not to realize a deal must have been made for him to be out of cuffs.

Spencer put his fingers to his lips and lifted his shirt to expose the wire. He indicated "just you and me" to McGrath. McGrath pondered it for a moment, then motioned everyone to leave. Spencer stopped Sheila as she passed by, pulled her close, and put his mouth against her ear. She flinched at the unexpected intimacy. He whispered something and then spoke aloud.

"Hi Sheila, I need to talk to Dom."

"You'll have to wait. He's on a call. It may take a while."

"OK, then I guess I'll wait."

Denny left. Cal hovered. He wasn't going anywhere with this sonofabitch wearing a wire and wanting intimate time with his boss.

Spencer started removing the wire, an awkward task with crutches. McGrath stepped in to help. He handed it to Sheila to take out with her and signaled Cal to leave them to it. Cal grudgingly obeyed. McGrath closed the door of his office.

"What now?" he said.

"I'm going to disappear, Dom. I have nothing here now. No daughter, no friends, no one for you to use to get back at me."

McGrath nodded, thoughtful. "Who'd have thought it, huh? Eddie."

Spencer said nothing.

"Where is it?"

"In Cal's trunk. He said he wanted to count it. Cops think you had it all along. Now you do."

"You taken any of it?"

"No."

A pause.

"Where you gonna go? Cops'll be watching for you."

"America's a big place."

"I could help you get to Mexico."

"FedEx me in pieces?"

McGrath had the grace to smile.

My ride's always runnin', boy.

But Spencer wasn't falling for it anymore. "Buy me some time," he said, "and a way out of here onto Gibson that's not in sight of Noble. That's where they watch from. And Dom, if ever I so much as think you've put someone on my case I will come back and sell my soul to the DPD. There's a man there who wants you more than he wants to breathe. If I'm going to die, I'll do it in jail knowing I put your ass there too. And that fucker from Chicago."

McGrath led Spencer into the reception. The wire lay on Sheila's desk. He spoke for its benefit.

"Sorry, Mister Burnham, really busy here. Property deal going through. Be with you as soon as I can."

Then he carried the wire into the restroom as if it were a rattler playing possum.

He came back out. "There's a corridor at the far end of the loading bay. Take it."

He watched Spencer lurch off on his crutches. "Sheila, get Johnny Boy."

Spencer moved down the corridor so fast on his crutches that his feet were nearly coming up too far, like an overswung pendulum. It didn't matter. The clock was ticking and the cops were waiting. His window was closing. The emergency exit was ten yards away. He went at full speed. Right into a fist that came from nowhere.

His body turned in the air. He landed on his back, crutches clattering around him, face numb, leg firing pain bolts through his nervous system.

Cal stepped out of a storage room, looked down at him and smiled.

48

On or Off the Train

In the loading bay, McGrath opened the trunk of Cal's Porsche, took out the duffel bag, and carried it upstairs to his office, where he tipped its contents onto the desk. He and Sheila started to count.

The ops truck waited in an alley off Lincoln. Nothing had come through since McGrath had mentioned a property deal.

"Something's not right," said Scott.

"Why'd you say that?" asked the tech.

"Burnham didn't give a reason why he was there. McGrath knows we've had him in custody. It'd be the first thing Burnham would cover so McGrath wouldn't think he was being set up. And if he didn't think he was being set up, he wouldn't have been all 'Mister Burnham this, Mister Burnham that.' He would have been like 'What the fuck are you doing here, Spencer?'"

Chris drove the rental down Martin Luther, searching.

* * *

Spencer crashed backward through the door into the loading bay. Before he could get up, he took a kick in the ribs, ribs that hadn't healed since the last beating. Blood began to pool in his liver. He rolled protectively onto his front. He could only exhale if he forced the air out with a loud moan.

"Hey now," said Cal, grabbing his shoulders and flipping him onto his back again. "What's that? Not like you not to have some wiseass shit ready?"

Spencer struggled to speak. "For fuck's sake, Cal, it wasn't me who brought the cops to the drop-off."

Cal scrunched Spencer's shirt up in his fists and pulled him up close. "Since you got here, everything's gone to rat shit."

"I just brought back all the money—"

"I hated your face from day one, the way you talk, the way you drive."

Cal wasn't going to let up. Spencer reached up, embraced him tightly, and then used his weight to pull back. Unbalanced, Cal fell forward and went mad. But at least they were on the same level.

As they rolled on the floor, Cal's phone fell out of his pocket and went skittering across the ground into a corner. Neither man noticed.

Cal was strong and madder than a wrongly shot hog. Soon he was punching the hell out of Spencer's face and Spencer had no moves left.

Inside the ops truck, Scott was facing a small rebellion.

"You do this with backup," the tech was saying. "Or a SWAT team on call. These guys, they've killed a cop."

"We've got two unmarked close by, that's another three guns," said Scott.

"Wow! This isn't my op so just excuse me if I'm saying something you don't want to hear. But why did your Burnham guy want to know where we'd be? 'Cause he's gonna make a deal with them. CPS has taken his kid for Chrissakes! The guy's got nothing!"

There was a knock at the back of the truck. They looked at each other.

"Oh, sweet Jesus, I hate being right," said the tech.

Both cleared leather.

Johnny Boy looked down at Spencer and Cal.

"What the hell is it with you two? The cops are waiting for him, Cal. If you kill him, I think they may suspect foul play."

Reluctantly, Cal stopped pummeling.

They watched as Spencer, wheezing and bleeding, rolled over and crawled away on all fours. He shoved through the door at the end of the bays and disappeared.

Cal noticed a crutch on the ground. He picked it up and headed after him.

"Cal," said Johnny Boy. But Cal was gone.

In the corridor, Cal saw Spencer struggling with the fire escape door. He ran up and Babe Ruthed the gunshot wound on Spencer's thigh with the crutch.

Spencer heard someone scream. He didn't realize it was him. He felt himself get lifted and then his head used like a battering ram. Dazzling sunlight blinded him. He flew through the air to the sound of Cal's delighted laughter and lost consciousness.

* * *

Scott looked at the back doors. Bullets would have no trouble penetrating them. Whoever was outside would know that too.

There was another knock. "I know you're in there, Detective."

Spencer crawled across the trash- and rubble-strewn vacant lot. His head was swimming in the heat and when he coughed, blood speckled the ground. He reached a chain-link fence and used it to pull himself upright. Working his way along, he found a hole. He lay back down in the filth and slithered through. His right leg felt numb and virtually useless, but he had to keep moving.

"What am I looking at?" asked Scott, holding the plastic sandwich bag in front of his face.

"That's a digital signature machine in there," said Chris. "Those things that couriers use. But this is a very special one."

"Enlighten me."

"It's an AtoB signature box. We both know that's the courier company McGrath's outfit uses to launder. This thing has got four signatures on it from McGrath's accountant guy, Cal, with his prints. And those four numbers he's signed against, their total matches the amount stolen."

"What does this do for me?"

Chris shrugged. "If McGrath knew you had this, he'd kill Cal for sure. That's leverage, Detective."

"Where's Burnham?"

"Forget Burnham. Did you really think a drunk, certified hopeless dad would get them to incriminate themselves on tape so you

360

could swoop in and clean up? The big crime show spectacular thing? This is about you getting McGrath."

"What about the money they stole? I'm supposed to just write that off?"

"Detroit writes off other people's money all the time. The place is known for it. Anyway, move fast and then it'll be McGrath wanting to make a deal to spend the last few years of his life out of jail. And what'll he have to bargain with?"

"I, uh, you realize they killed a cop? And you're giving me . . . What the fuck are you giving me?"

"We're sorry about your guy, for what that's worth. That's why I'm here. McGrath knows Spencer has no motive or means to give you that evidence you're holding. It belongs to AtoB. McGrath will think Cal's selling him out to you guys. And Cal will think AtoB is selling *him* out. They're all jumpy because of Eddie. They'll be wondering which of them is going to get scared, jump ship, and cut a deal. Their house of cards is ready to come down. So why don't you offer Cal a deal? Here's his number."

Chris took a Post-it note from his pants and offered it to Scott. Scott took it robotically, with a face that said he was still playing catch-up.

Chris started back for the rental car. "I'll give this back tomorrow."

"Burnham won't get far," said Scott.

Chris dropped his window. "You need to be calling that number, Detective. Check he's alone and don't be afraid to lay it on him hard."

*   *   *

Spencer sat on an empty crate with his back against the wall. He'd moved the crate to the shady side of the alley. He wanted to go back to the hospital. He heard the sound of a car crunching its way slowly down the alley. He cracked his swollen eyes open.

Chris killed the engine and got out.

"Sweet Jesus, Spencer."

"You should see the other guy."

"Take those pants off, Spence." Chris started taking his own off. He took his T-shirt off too. He threw them both at Spencer. "Put them on. Stuff your T-shirt down where it's bleeding. It'll soak it up. Might give you enough time to get through. Take my sunglasses. Come on, time to haul."

Spencer pushed himself to his feet, groaned, and lurched back against the wall.

"Come *on*, Spence. I've bought us a gap, but it won't stay open long."

Spencer struggled into Chris's jeans and then fell into the driver's seat.

Chris took his bag out of the rental's trunk and opened it in front of Spencer. It was full of money.

"I thought you told me I gave it all back?" said Spencer.

"I knew I'd be too scared to lie."

"Oh Christ, they're going to think I fucked them."

"If they think anyone fucked them, they'll think it's Cal. And anytime now he's going to know that, too, so he'll be cutting himself a deal."

Chris put his sunglasses on Spencer. "Wipe some of that blood off your face, Spence, before you try to go through."

Then Chris needed to sit down too. He leaned against Penny. The two men looked at each other.

"Why didn't you tell us, Chris?"

"I don't know. First, I was in denial, I guess. But I knew I didn't want you guys behaving all weird around me."

"But—"

"But what? You'd have cleaned yourself up sooner? You did the best you could, Spence. You were always in there somewhere, trying. But here's the thing: Marielle died four years ago. That's when this train started rolling. It's time to get off it. Your mourning's done."

A great claw clutched at Spencer's heart. He started his engine. Before he took off, he said, "Chris, thank you."

"Same. You both kept my life interesting."

In the rearview he looked at Chris, standing in a shitty Detroit alley in his boxers, watching him go. He wiped his eyes roughly with his sleeve to stop the tears from blurring his vision.

Johnny Boy strode down the loading bay walkway. He was on his way upstairs.

On his way . . .

It was time to count money. He thought about the rich people he'd known. Admittedly, most of them had been happy to handle the heat of operating on the wrong side of the law. But even those who'd made their money legit, they all seemed to have one thing in common: some jittery times. Little bankruptcy here, little court action there, some close-but-no-cigar moments. Hell, he'd had them himself. He'd been making bank working for the guys in Chicago. Thought he'd been on his way then, about to jump aboard that gravy locomotive, but then, *boom*. Had to consider himself lucky just getting his ass disbarred. But after the small-balled ones had had enough and dropped out of the Game, the guys who stuck at it, they claimed the prize: comfortable retirement, electric gates, no missing your grandkids' birthdays. Dom had been right about going for a big payoff. Risky, yeah, but so was staying in the Game with its snitches and wiretaps.

He heard a phone ring and it wasn't his. He looked around and saw Cal's phone on the floor. Cal had gone to clean himself up. Christ on a pony but the guy could be a jerk sometimes. He would have killed Burnham if Johnny Boy hadn't turned up. If anything, if he'd been Cal, he'd have been keeping a lower profile. After all, Eddie had only gotten in because of Cal's buddies up in Pontiac. That didn't make Cal look good.

Johnny Boy picked up the phone. He looked at the screen: number withheld. He looked around before pressing Answer.

"Hello."

"Hey. You alone?" asked Scott.

Johnny Boy only hesitated for a second. "Yes."

"Do you know who I am?" asked Scott.

"No. Do you know who I am?"

"Sure. You're the guy stupid enough to sign AtoB receipts for what your boss stole. I'm looking at them. Either that or you've been real clever and made sure you had something to offer me if it all went to shit."

Johnny Boy started walking up the stairs.

"You want to meet so you can tell me which it is?" continued Scott.

Johnny Boy approached McGrath's office. "OK, but you must appreciate it's dangerous for me now so from now on let me call you, Mister . . . ?"

Johnny Boy entered the office. He sat down opposite McGrath and Sheila, who'd just finished counting. He was happy for McGrath to hear the rest of the conversation.

"OK, Detective Scott, thank you, I'll be in touch. Don't call my number again."

Johnny Boy deleted the call from the phone's log. Soon afterward, Cal entered the office. Johnny Boy handed him his phone. "You dropped it downstairs."

Cal was in high old spirits. And now he'd come upstairs to find out how much money they had. He was on his way too. But if he'd noticed the look that passed between his colleagues he might have wondered if they were all boarding the same train.

About the same time, Spencer was driving over the Ambassador Bridge, the busiest international land crossing on the North American continent. Just a nondescript little car among the hundreds of other nondescript cars, rigs, and bikes. He felt the numbers would work in his favor, because even with sunglasses, his face was a three-ring circus. The customs officer on the other side didn't seem to notice or care. Spencer handed her his British passport, left in the swag bag by Chris. The guy had thought of everything. The Wilcox selling arm of Thermo Booster Burn had been destined for great things.

Five minutes later, Spencer was in Canada.

*　*　*

By the time Detective Scott got home, he was feeling more philosophical about things. That guy Chris had been right. This had always been about getting McGrath.

As he slid the key in his front door, he steeled himself for what was ahead. But he was in for a pleasant surprise. The house was quiet. For the first time for as long as he could remember, he couldn't hear the sound of a TV blaring. Maybe she was out with the kids. Thank Christ. Now he could crack open a beer or three and have himself a little celebration. Sooner rather than later McGrath's accountant was going to be calling him. There was a deal to be made.

He closed the front door. When he turned back to the hallway, he was confused to find a tall man standing in front of him pointing a gun at his face.

Denny pulled the trigger.

Detective Scott flew backward against his front door and then crumpled to the floor in a heap.

Denny waited to see any movement. He was pretty confident the guy was gone seeing as he'd just had a face full of forty caliber. Denny was pretty stoked. For years, he'd been kept on the sidelines. Then he'd been given the Chris cleanup mission. That had been his baby. He'd been all revved up to clean that apartment so good it would be like no one had ever lived there. But it had been taken away from him at the last moment.

Then this had come up. He had a name and address and it needed to happen quick. And then he had to trash the place, so it looked like a B and E gone wrong. And trashing a place was so much easier than wiping one clean.

The wife of the guy he'd just whacked was in the living room. Two holes in her tits. One dead kid upstairs. The other was out. Kids could be conscience kickers, but this job was worth fifty grand.

On his way . . .

As McGrath pulled out of the parking structure and joined the flow of traffic on Lafayette, he felt like he'd dodged a bullet. And the way things were looking, it would be the last he'd have to dodge. So it seemed kind of appropriate that he'd taken the necessary actions himself rather than delegating.

A national guard truck passed by in the opposite direction and he thought back to his decision to turn down an army commission. That was always his litmus test on how well things were going. Right now, it felt like the decision had been a mighty good call. For one thing, he was now retired, as of about ten minutes ago. Not many could do that before sixty. Not in style anyway.

Back in the parking structure, one of several lesser-used facilities in southeast Detroit, down in the bottom levels where the lighting wasn't maintained so well, a Porsche sat in darkness. It wouldn't see the roads anytime soon. Cars that were crime scenes tended to be impounded for a while. And this girl would need work before anyone ponied up the payola for her. The interior was splashed to hell with blood that used to belong to the guy now taking a dirt nap at the wheel. He certainly wouldn't be cutting a deal anytime soon. A thorough job done by a thorough man. Loose ends all tied up.

49

Cities of the Dead

Three thousand feet up in the Taurus Mountains of Southern Turkey, a man sat in an ancient amphitheater. The theater was set in a natural bowl formed by the mountaintop and offered mesmerizing views of the Mediterranean coastline.

The man had been sitting there every evening for nearly a week. Only the more adventurous travelers visited this place. And at this time of day, even they were heading back to their homes and hotels miles away down in the bustling city of Antalya. Foolish really, as this was when the ruins of Termessos were especially magical, when the sun was falling toward the pine-clad mountains behind the theater. Its orange glow drybrushed the finely cut stone of wall and archway or was dappled by overhanging branch and creeping vine. Street, temple, house, and marketplace prepared for another night without their townsfolk, gone now for two thousand years. The light captivated the man and made him sad at the same time. The last time he'd seen this beauty, he'd been a family man.

The phone in his pocket bleeped, the modernity of the sound made ridiculous by the setting. After checking it, he got up and started to work his way down the tiers of seating, moving fast but awkwardly, as if stiff from sitting on the hard stone.

He picked his way through fallen and overgrown masonry and then joined a path that led through the pines to a mountain track. On the track, he approached a small motor home, took a key from the wheel arch, and went inside.

"Hello?" he said to the empty interior.

Silence. On the table, a small, padded envelope was ready for posting. Destination: Detroit.

Beside it a laptop was on standby. Learning how to manage a successful online business had been a welcome distraction over the last week, both from the pain and the waiting. He looked out the side window, where the ground dropped steeply away from the road, but saw no one. He made his way to the front of the motor home and looked through the windshield. About a hundred yards up the track, he saw two figures, an adult and a child, except Abby didn't seem quite so childlike anymore. She was looking out over the mountains, pointing something out to Caitlyn.

He clambered over the passenger seat, opened the door, and dropped down onto the dusty track. He called out as he broke into a limping run. Abby turned at the sound of his voice. She didn't run toward him, though, didn't know whether he would be the same father who left her on a porch in Lathrup Village. But Spencer knew he'd make that right. He'd make her feel so loved she wouldn't think about the last four years during which she'd had to shut her need for love away.

Caitlyn Dunn had most surely gone out on a limb for him. She'd learned to play the system. Willing relatives took precedence over adopters. However Caitlyn had spoken to his sister, she'd done it well. Now his sister was Abby's official guardian but with tacit agreement that her brother was getting a chance. His sister had insisted on meeting him again, to see if he'd really turned the corner. And that meeting would happen in the next few days. Either way, the rest of Abby's childhood would happen a long way from Detroit.

And as for the woman who'd made it happen, well it was a crazy thought but maybe she'd give him a chance too. She'd devoted her vacation to giving Abby this closure. Time enough for him to make a good impression perhaps. He was glad he'd healed a little, glad he'd let a dentist in Antalya fix his broken teeth.

Six months later . . .

Captain Schaeffer looked through the internal office window at his department, wondering who'd hit the jackpot by predicting the date accurately. He'd kept the whole precinct guessing as to how long he'd hang on. They thought he was just being stubborn, but the truth was he was scared of retirement. He was more scared of it than of anything he'd faced in his life. Since his daughter had passed, he'd hated being at home. His wife refused to move to a new house and went around all day in a kind of half-there state. He'd been a police officer for over thirty-five years. He had no idea what he was going to do with himself after today.

There was a large box of personal effects on his desk. Gifts, certificates, paperweights. Stuff accumulated over a fairly illustrious career. All of it just seemed like clutter now. He looked at the police Medal of Valor poking out and gave a quiet sniff of derision. Valor. He was scared to go home.

His team, who were no longer his team, were getting back to work. They'd had the speeches and the toasts, the handshaking and the "So, how are you gonna spend your long vacation, Captain?" banter. A GOOD LUCK banner stretched across the wall. He'd smiled and chatted through it all. And it had been as hard as he'd expected. He rose from his desk.

Just one more walk of the farewell gauntlet . . .

A couple of the guys carried the box downstairs and put it in his trunk. More painful small talk.

Schaeffer got in his car and started up. He drove out of the precinct lot onto Second Avenue for the last time. But he didn't go home. He headed west for a rough part of town. He still had one last piece of business to take care of.

Twenty minutes later he was cruising around Nately Place, looking for a familiar face, as in familiar from an investigation file. When he saw one, a tattooed-up dealer in a wifebeater and a black Nike beanie, he pulled up and got out of his car. Instantly, the dealer wasn't alone. His cronies and homies materialized out of the shadows. Apparently, Schaeffer's car had seemed out of place.

"Hey, old man, you lose your way to the golf club?"

Schaeffer ignored them. He walked up to the dealer in the beanie.

"Mack Daddy Scrilla, I presume?"

Scrilla looked taken aback for a moment. "Who the fuck are you?"

"Captain Jonathan Schaeffer of the Detroit Police Department."

Now Mack Scrilla really had nothing. He and his homies looked around to see if this strange guy in slacks, shirt, and sweater had backup.

"Nope, just me, I'm afraid. I want to speak to Pucky. You know where I can find him?"

"You know why we should give a fuck?"

"Yeah. I have something he wants very badly. And, if you're lucky enough to be the guy who takes me to him, he'll want to give you the motherfucker of all thank yous."

Ten minutes later, Schaeffer was being lead down a dingy corridor. Scrilla knocked on the last door. Rap music thumped from within.

"Yeah?" came a voice.

"Niggas, it's Mack Scrilla. Got someone here wants to see ya. He's got something for ya."

The door opened a few inches and a hand holding a forty-five emerged. The barrel touched Mack's cheek.

"Who is he?"

Schaeffer decided to speed things along a little.

"He's Jonathan Schaeffer. Until an hour ago I was captain at Precinct Thirteen of the Detroit Police Department. I'm now retired. I'm here alone and I'm unarmed."

Moments later, Schaeffer faced half a dozen men, all of whom had rap sheets longer than his service record. He placed a USB stick on a messy coffee table. Pucky and his associates stared at it.

Pucky had to speak loudly over the music. "What is it?"

"Play it," said Schaeffer.

Someone changed the source on the big TV, thereby cutting the music. The USB was plugged in and voices filled the room. The quality was poor, due to the recording having been made in a car, but the words could be heard plainly enough.

*Well, we were the puck that fucked Pucky's crew. You can't
say that after five bourbons I tell ya. And soon I figure we'll
fuck the Vernor Highway crew too. We've fucked most of
those boys one time or another. Except none of them knows
it. Kept them fighting, biting, and fragging each other like
rats in a sack. Turn right here. That's right, Spencer. Pucky's
gonna need to find another two right-hand guys. But that's
probably gonna take some balls on his part, and rumor has
it he don't have any of those no more.*

The recording stopped. Silence reigned. Pucky stared at the
screen.

"That recording," said Schaeffer, "is inadmissible as evidence.
And you and I both know you wouldn't want to help any investigation into that hit on you anyways."

"So why'd you bring it?" said Pucky. The fury sizzled in his
voice.

"I'm not a cop anymore. I don't have to follow the rules. And
that piece of shit you're hearing there? I hate him as much as you
do. Why don't I just give you a couple of names and we forget we
ever met?"

Five minutes later, Schaeffer was escorted to his car. He got
in, started up, and drove off without a backward glance.

When he got home, he went to his study and sat down at his
desk. He looked at his daughter's picture for a long time. Then he
opened a drawer and took out his first service revolver. He put it in
his mouth and, still looking at her smiling face, pulled the trigger.

The End

Acknowledgments

There were a number of reasons why this story had to take place in Detroit and hence why I needed to speak at length with the Detroit Police. In spite of my assurances that this was a work of fiction, the Detroit Police Department rebuffed my requests to talk with their investigators for eight months. Quite understandable. For all they knew, I might have been seeking to "do a number" on them. Eventually they said they had someone who'd speak to me and who I can now thank. Ellis Stafford retired from Michigan State Police as Inspector and Assistant Division Commander and continues fighting crime as Deputy Director of the Detroit Crime Commission, a nonprofit organization that works collaboratively with residents and community leaders to create safe communities for all of Detroit's citizens. Ellis's assistance was invaluable in making this book as feasible and accurate as it could be.

I should also thank my friend and fellow TV presenter, Alexandra Legouix, for facilitating meetings with the next person I want to thank: David Llewellin, two-time winner of the British Rally Championship. On one occasion, while surrounded by eavesdropping racing enthusiasts at Goodwood, he earnestly explained to me how to build the perfect getaway car. I wonder what they made of that.

One could not hope for a better agent than mine. Thank you, Clem, for being your passionate, meticulous, and beyond capable self.

Grove Atlantic hardly needs its praises sung. I'm honored to be a small part of their classy operation. And I will always be grateful to the man who gave me my first shot—Morgan Entrekin.

I also have a talented and perceptive editor at Grove—thank you Sara Vitale.

There were a number of employees of Child Protective Services who gave me insight and detail into the challenging nature of their work. Our conversations were off the record so I cannot mention them by name but thank you.

A good number of people, some of them personal friends, spoke with great candor to me about their battles with substance addiction. I am extremely honored to have been so entrusted.

Alistair Gilchrist, former law enforcement and always on call to fact-check—thank you.

To my diligent and helpful beta readers and especially Susan Opie and Rebecca Wade, thank you.

I wish to thank the others who have encouraged or supported me along the way, even if it was just out of fear of what I'd get up to if I didn't write: Michael, Sue, Garry, Marcus, Keith, Michelle, Hayley, Mike, Kristin, Howard, Kat, Jase, Steve, and Rebecca. Jesus, I didn't realize I had so many good friends.

Lastly, I'd like to thank my partner, Louisa, not just for the support, unwavering even when I work during our vacations, but also for the informed opinion of one who investigates for a living. If I thanked you for everything you should be thanked for, some annoying fool would start the play-off music.